A Rust of the Heart

Jane Barrie

'But what a gnawing worm of the soul is it, what a plague-spot of our thoughts, what a rust of the heart, to be jealous of another,'

Cyprian of Carthage

1974

The grown-ups decide to take me home in one of the police cars and, as we drive through the village, I can see more officers standing by Christine's bungalow and by Maureen's house. There are many more cars parked than usual and strangers in clusters. The stocky detective who broke the news, is taking me back to The Castle with a uniformed officer. Mrs Berman is sitting in the back with her arm around me. It's a bit odd as I only met her a few hours ago. I have been given a large white handkerchief for my tears which, unfortunately, have stopped. Maybe I can get them going again.

We solemnly process up the path to the heavy front door and I let DCI McGlinchey ring on the doorbell rather than go in myself as I easily could. Dad comes to the door and the detective and Mrs Berman explain in a bit of a muddle what's happened. I rush to Dad when they get to the bit about Christine and cuddle into him so they can't see that I am smiling a little bit because this is just like the telly. From the way Dad is reacting, he's not surprised.

Dad herds everyone along the long dark corridor to the kitchen where Mum, Mrs Stoddart and her daughter, Gillian are sitting at the table clutching mugs of tea. Mrs Stoddart and Gillian have lately been roped in by my lazy mother to do the work she has undertaken, namely, to get this hovel of a house ready for paying guests. Mrs Stoddart's face is smudged and her eyes fill with puddling tears at the sight of the police officers. She stands up quick sharp and goes to the detective.

'Dan. What the hell is going on? What do you think's happened? Has anyone any idea?'

'I don't know Jean. Its early days. We're doing house to house and starting a search party in the next hour. I've called in extra officers from Carlisle and the Lakes. It's a top priority.'

'That's a news conference Dan,' Mrs Stoddart spits, angry. 'What's really happening?'

'There's no one in the frame, Jean. If that's what you're asking? Christ, it's only just twelve hours since it was reported. Give us a chance eh? Let me talk to this lass and I can get on with the job of bringing young Christine home.'

He turns to Mum and Dad. 'Now Mr and Mrs Wentworth, I have a few questions for Jenny. Would that be okay?'

Mrs Berman steps forward, 'Gideon and I didn't want the police asking any questions without you there. She didn't take the news well, poor lamb.'

Tillie Berman and I had been hooting around in her bedroom when Mrs Berman had called us down. We'd just eaten a whole bar of chocolate between us. I thought Tillie had snaffled it and we were in trouble but no, it was about Christine, someone Tillie didn't even know really because, even though she lives in the village, Tillie goes to a boarding school in Yorkshire. I've never been to Yorkshire. Christine was missing. She had Failed To Return Home after having tea at Maureen's last night. It was tremendously exciting. When I announced to the assembled adults that Christine was my Best Friend they had made a great fuss of me, bringing sweet tea and fretting over what to do for the best.

'No, I don't suppose she did,' Mum isn't looking at me but I can hear the accusation in her voice, 'Thank you, it was very kind of you to bring her home.'

'I'd better get back to my girls if that's alright with you?' Mrs Berman asks Detective Dan. Her lovely girls, all six of them will need their beautiful, blonde mother who even in this terrible crisis manages to look as waxy pale and delicately perfect as a flower from an exotic bouquet. My mother looks untidy, all blotchy mascara and birds' nest hair.

'Naturally,' Detective Dan says dismissing her and turning back to me. 'Now Mr Wentworth, are we okay to ask Jenny some questions?'

'Of course,' Dad says, 'If it's okay with you, Jennifer.'

I nod, silently, making my eyes as big as I can, aware that every adult in the room is looking just at me.

We sit down at the kitchen table. The detective seems too big for the chair, his lips too wet. He is Expecting A Lot.

'Now, Jenny,' he says, in what I suppose he thinks is a kind voice, ' I want you to think back to leaving school yesterday. Can you do that for me?' Of course I can, I'm not an idiot. 'Was there anything unusual that you noticed or, more importantly, anyone that you haven't seen before, hanging around?'

I sigh and try to look like I'm thinking. 'It was raining,' I start.

'Yes. Good. Very good.'

'I had the hood of my Mac up. So did Judy, my sister, we walked home together. We walked up to our road at the top of the green. I had said goodbye to Maureen and Christine in school.' I sniff when I say her name the better to show my distress, 'We were all in a good mood because of breaking up for half-term but they came out behind me. We didn't see anyone all the way home. There's only The Castle up this lane.' The Castle sounds grand, but it isn't. It's practically falling down and freezing cold and I hate it.

Detective Dan is making copious notes all the time I am speaking and everyone is quiet and expectant. I know none of it is any good. There is collective sagging disappointment when I am finished. I can feel it.

'Are you sure there were nothing else, pet?' The detective sounds desperate. Desperate Dan.

I pretend to think harder.

'Wait!' I exclaim. That's how it will be written in the book. And I have everyone's pert attention again. They all needed me to give them a little nugget of hope that Christine would or could be found so that's what I would do.

'I think I saw a red car parked at the bottom of the green which I haven't seen before.' They strain forward. Could this be a clue? I look at my hands. 'We haven't lived here that long so I don't know everyone's cars but I definitely didn't recognise it.' The village is tiny. A tufty, bumpy green, sliced up the middle by a road, a stupidly small school house plonked in a triangle of tarmac at the top and a hotchpotch of houses running round the outside skirted with a mud track. It's entirely believable that I could know every villagers' car in six weeks of living here. I am a very clever girl.

'Good lass!' says Detective Dan, baring his plump white teeth, teeth too big for his mouth, 'That's brilliant.' He turns to the other officer, 'Radio it in,' who turns and leaves the kitchen.

'You're doing so well. Now just think if there's any part of the number plate you can remember?'

Now wouldn't that be a miracle? I look straight at him, adopting a sorrowful face, perhaps on the brink of tears. 'I'm so sorry. It was so far away. And it was raining.'

'Ok. Ok. Do you think you might recognise what type of car it was?'

'Maybe?' I speculate.

Detective Dan stands up, full of purpose. 'Mr and Mrs Wentworth, I'd like to take Jenny down to the station in Penrith to see if we can get a bit more on this vehicle. It could be crucial. And, I'd like to speak to your younger daughter, Judy.'

'She probably won't have seen anything. She's only seven,' I say quickly and Mum catches my eye. I look away.

This is working out better than I'd planned. I'm going to a police station. I'm a witness to maybe a murder. Dad goes to get his coat, Mum says she'll fetch Judy from Sally Turner's.

I lie and seethe in bed that night. Mum arrives at the station later with Judy who, of course, cannot remember a red car but can remember a white van, as can several Other Witnesses. I have been shown through a mucky folder of plastic pictures of current cars and I go through it several times before I pick the one I think is most likely to be, a) driven by a child murderer and, b) parked in a tiny Cumberland village on a Friday afternoon in February. A round faced lady police officer called Wendy brings me a can of cola and everyone speaks more quietly and smiles weakly as I walk past them. I try to look shaken and suitably important.

When they come and tell us about the white van, I realise my red car is going to take a back seat. 'Perhaps you got confused, pet,' Detective Dan says, kindly, 'but your sister has given us a very clear description which matches several others. No one else has said anything about a red car.'

As we all leave the station together, Judy is the conquering hero, having remembered part of the number plate, which no other adult has, and offered up a drawing of a logo from the side of the van. All eyes are on her and now she sweetly sleeps, curled like a cat, in the bed next to me and I want to take my pillow and smother her. Yet again, she has stolen my thunder.

When I wake up, the bare windows are frozen at the bottom, again, and Judy is already out of bed. I can see the sky so it must be quite late. It is iron grey, full and dark. Looks like snow. Christine won't last long outside in this weather. I remember my bad mood. I lie for a moment glowering at the room. The ceiling is high and corniced but there are chunks missing like someone has taken a few mouthfuls from the icing on a wedding cake. There is finely flaking paint on the chimney breast and, in the tar-stained grate, there is a punched lemonade can and a balled up piece of grubby paper instead of a cheery blaze. The walls are yellowish white, a colour not helped by the dreary light struggling in through the dirty glass. It is horrible. And it is freezing cold.

I put on a jumper over my nightie, tugging it angrily over my head and catching the tender hair at the nape of my neck on the button at the back. I don't know where my slippers are so I shove my blue white feet into my shoes with no socks. The backs nip at my heels as I trot to the bathroom for a wee. I can see my own breath as I sit on the loo, it is so cold. I almost announce to the world my disgust that I have to live in this ramshackle slum in the middle of nowhere. I am perpetually forced to suffer because of my parents' ridiculous idea to turn this crumbling ruin into a Bed and Breakfast. It's cruel, like the little princess locked in the attic or the little matchgirl freezing to death and now, I discover, they've brought me to a place populated by child killers; real life baby snatchers. However the thought of all the new people and the police in this dull little village is quite exciting.

I stalk along the landing muttering at the horrible crimson carpet which is curling and brown at the edges, and tramp down the broad stairs. There's another set of stairs through the back of the kitchen. They are dark and narrow and twisty like the servants' stairs from _Upstairs Downstairs_. They smell funny though, like too ripe apples. I avoid them.

I reach the stone cold floor of the entrance hall. I can feel the flags through the thin soles of my shoes. Why would someone put paving stones indoors? I march towards the kitchen, down another long windowless corridor. Judy is at the table and a gummy smile breaks out. I see the pap of toast she's chewing.

'Morning!' she pipes up.

I say nothing.

My mother is grappling with the squat range. There is the smell of fresh coal under the whiff of singed bread. 'Toast?' she says, in a non-committal tone, her back to me. Mum does not usually prepare breakfast. Dad does. In Buckinghamshire, which I consider Home, Granny made it. Cooked breakfast for Grandad who had to go up to London on the train, bacon and eggs and one single slice of bread and marmalade. Granny buttered the loaf before she cut the piece, hugging the bread to her apron as if it may make a run for it. The slice was always cut in four square quarters. When Grandad bit into it, the pale homemade marmalade squelched up between his sharp white teeth. He finished each piece in two mouthfuls. Judy and I had surprise bread or boiled eggs and soldiers and sometimes fluffy omelettes. Mum and Dad weren't usually there for breakfast, or weren't there until Grandad had gone for his train.

I slump into a chair. 'Do you want toast?' my mother asks again, tetchily.

'Okay,' I sulkily reply, hoping to communicate my misery.

'There's no butter. We've run out.'

'Great,' I huff.

'It's actually quite nice with just jam,' my loathsome sister chirrups.

'Where's Dad?' I bitterly enquire. Mum's still got her back to me. Why won't she turn and look at me? The woman always has her face in a book or a newspaper or is on the phone to a friend. She never actually looks at either of us. Let's hope we're never abducted and she has to give a description to the police.

'He's having a look through the outbuildings, just in case.'

I raise my eyebrows. So Christine's disappearance has caused a Lazarus-like resurrection of Mother from her bed and she will do her part and feed her children this morning. I hope Dad doesn't find anything too grisly out here, though it would be a good story to tell.

Mum delivers the plate. The toast is pale and limp on one side and charred black on the other.

'Sorry,' Mum says, though she is not.

I viciously and deliberately incompetently smear jam on the damply white side and tear it in half. I quite like burnt toast; it tastes like the smell of bonfires.

Mum eventually sits down, a grubby cup of dark tea in her pink hand. She hasn't brushed her hair and her mouth is a hard tight line. Her eyes flicker over me and then out of the window. 'What are you going to do today?' she asks.

'I'm going to help everyone look for my Best Friend,' and I tear into my toast. She rolls her eyes.

Later Dad and I drive into the village to see if there's any news. In the car Dad is quiet, as usual. He is concentrating but he doesn't seem as sad as he is sometimes so that's a change.

'So did you find anything unusual in the sheds?' I ask, keen to make some use of the time on our own.

'No. I don't really know what I was looking for. Don't know what was in them to begin with actually. Found an old box of *Giles* annuals though.' He looks at the road, both hands relaxed on the steering wheel, cigarette cocked in his right hand, occasionally flicking ash out of the crack in the corner of the window. My father has beautiful hands, broad palms, long tapering fingers, smooth brown skin.

'Oh,' I quite like *Giles* annuals. They were in the loo at Home. I liked the wide-faced grandma with the bird umbrella that all the men hated.

'I'll help you unpack those into your study if you like,' I say.

'Good girl.' He isn't really listening. We have driven down the dirt track, full of deep, muddy puddles and pocked with sturdy rocks and are now in the village. There are lots of police cars, still more, I think, than yesterday. A wider search, further onto the fells, is going to start and a crowd of people with grey, set faces are milling around near the bottom of the green. There are police dogs straining to get going, panting and staring, big-toothed and purple-gummed. I think of Christine's vivid scarlet gums and wonder if I'll ever see her again.

We park down at the bottom of the green towards the church and walk back up. Mr Stoddart comes over to Dad. He is often in The Lamb and Packet when Dad has a Swift Half. Dad says he likes the horses, but I haven't seen many since we've been here. They nod cautiously at each other.

'Heard your little 'un did good yesterday.' Mr Stoddart starts. I tut.

'Yes, I just hope it helps.' Dad doesn't sound like he thinks it will.

'Grim business,' Mr Stoddart shakes his head.

'Yes terrible,' Dad agrees. Both men are now looking over towards the search party.

'I think they should be talking to that writer myself,' Mr Stoddart leans into Dad as he says this. The way he says writer suggests a sneer in his voice.

'Writer? You mean Berman?' Dad sounds a little surprised.

'Yes, that's him. They don't have much to do with the village and,' he pauses and lowers his voice, 'he's a kike.' The sneer is there again.

He straightens up. 'You can't trust them is what I say. They need to get down there and find out where he was Friday night.'

'You may be right, John. You may be right. Hard to think it's someone in the village though.'

'Well he's not from the village, is he? He's an outsider. German or Dutch or something. A foreigner anyways.' Mr Stoddart clearly thinks he's proved his point but Dad's reaction makes him realise who he's talking to. Dad gives him a half-smile.

'We'd best be getting back. See how Judy is.' I tut again.

'Right. Yes. Maybe see you in the pub later.'

'Yes. Hopefully, there'll be better news.'

We turn and walk back to the car. Dad stops to light a cigarette, turning away from the wind and shielding the fragile flame with his cupped hands.

'What's a kike, Dad?' I say.

'A Jew,' he answers and strides on ahead of me.

'Do you think Mr Berman murdered Christine?' I say as I trot to catch up with him.

He doesn't stop. 'No I do not,' he sounds cross.

I am getting a bit out of breath, 'Why did you agree with Mr Stoddart then?'

He stops and turns, irritated, 'What?'

I stop too. 'Why did you say he might be right? About Mr Berman?'

He looks cross, 'It's just one of those things you say, Jen. I'm not going to disagree with the man, am I? His wife works for us and does a bloody good job as does his daughter – don't know what we'd do without her or Gillian come to that. Everyone's entitled to their opinion.'

'But it's not your opinion. You don't *not* like him because he's a kike or German?'

Dad winces, 'No Jennifer, I hardly know the man, seems like a nice enough chap. And don't say that word. Kike. It's not a nice word. Don't you start repeating it.'

'But you said Mr Stoddart was right. Twice.'

'Oh for God's sake Jennifer. It was just talk.'

'But he thinks you think the same as him now. That Mr Berman murdered Christine.'

He's getting exasperated with me. We've had conversations like this before where I can't quite let things go. 'Look,' he says, 'we don't know what's happened to that poor little girl yet. She's not dead until they find a body. And will you stop talking about her being murdered with such relish, Jennifer. This is a terrible thing. A terrible, terrible thing. It could have been Judy. Or you. God, it doesn't bear thinking about. What those poor people must be going through. Let's hope she's home by supper time and everything goes back to normal,' and he marches ahead so I can't keep up with him and so I walk deliberately slowly and he gets further and further away and I hope The Murderer will come and grab me and that'll serve him right for being cross. Then he might think about me first for a change. He just sits and waits for me in the car though and doesn't say a word on the way back to The Castle. He shuts himself in his study for most of the rest of the day. I can hear Françoise Hardy playing on his record player when I listen at the door.

When we sit down for supper, Christine is still not home.

On Monday I wake up early even though there's no school and eventually, out of boredom, walk back down to Tillie Berman's and her five sisters' hoping for a break from the Christine saga. It is now on the national news and in all the papers. The village green, the school, Christine's and Maureen's houses are regularly flashed up on the telly as well as last year's school photo. Christine's on the telly with her abundant black hair and tiny, thick lashed piercing blue eyes.

She is smiling her noticeably gummy smile. I ponder her tiny white teeth. They're almost like baby teeth. Her white skin and black hair is the same as her brothers. And her blue eyes. But only her older brother Bryan is gorgeous. It would be much nicer to be seeing a photo of him every news bulletin. Kevin her other brother, who's thirteen I think, has spots. I wonder if Christine was going to get them too. Now we'll never know.

Sometimes on The News there is a map and I can see how far away Cumberland is from London which is near to where Home is. Sometimes there's a chart with times on. Sometimes Bryan and Kevin pushing through the cameras outside the house or Mr Bell with a newspaper shielding his face. But there is little new news despite it being called The News. Christine has vanished. Vanished into thin air.

When I get to Tillie's, the house is blank and looks empty. No car. I push through the gate and go to the door and knock anyway. There's no one home. I notice a window has been broken upstairs and a board hammered over to keep the weather out from inside the house.

I sit on the front step for a while. I am deeply disappointed. I only met Tillie on Saturday and she's the only girl I want to be friends with in the village and now she's not here. Tillie goes to Harrogate Ladies College and, though she was quite annoying she was friendly enough. I was enjoying their central heating when Mrs Berman called us down to break the Bad News. They had been skiing at Christmas Tillie said. Some of them still had a bit of a tan. Perhaps, they've gone skiing again. Half-term will be very dismal without Tillie or Christine.

I decide I'll go and see Maureen Kirby as a last resort. At least she can tell me what's been happening and there's nothing else to do. Mum has told me I mustn't speak to any reporters but she doesn't seem to care that much about where I am, though, admittedly, at the moment, they think I'm still in bed. They were both asleep when I left. Mum said she was in the mood for gin last night so they were dancing slowly to the record which jumps on the final track in the sitting room when we went to bed.

When I get to Maureen's, there are policemen having fags and drinking tea in her front garden. I smile at them as I knock on the door. Her mum answers with a large plate of parkin in one hand. She has the same pink face as Maureen and is very fat. A little while ago, she said to me 'We big girls need to stick together, don't we Jennifer' and I wanted to smash her face into the pan of eggs she was scrambling. Christine and Maureen giggled and I blushed, which I hate to do, and I couldn't think of anything to say. The only things we ever do at Maureen's are hang around in the Pets' Room or look through her Mum's Littlewoods catalogue. Maureen is the eldest Kirby and there are several much younger wet mouthed, pink splotched cheeked versions of her in various states of grubby undress; they all have Pets. The Pets are kept in a gloomy room off the kitchen in a range of cages, hutches and tanks. There are guinea pigs, rabbits, gerbils, mice, snakes, salamanders and fish. There isn't much natural lighting and the room is unpleasantly hot and sweet smelling. Maureen clicks open the cages and the creatures scrabble away from her pudgy fingers but she always catches them and then she holds them and we pet them. Christine loved the guinea pigs and always went on and on about how they were Not Like Pigs At All in a delighted squeaky voice. I was always asked for my favourite. I said a different one each time. I hate them all, especially the mice. They're so pinkly white, they're practically see-through. After Mrs Kirby said I was fat, I left a catch off the mice cage as we left the Pets' Room and I hoped they would escape and, at least, frighten her or, at best, cause her to fall down the stairs as they scuttled unexpectedly in her path. Maureen never said anything about it though, worse luck.

Maureen's mum is smiling warmly at me, 'Morning Jennifer. You're early today. I'm just taking these for the lads. Maureen is in the kitchen. Just go in, love,' and she breathes and rolls her way noisily past me.

Maureen is sitting at the table colouring with one of the younger Kirbys who is filthy and smells of rusks. When she sees me, her lip begins to tremble and her little cocoa brown eyes get shiny. 'Oh Jen. Poor Christine,' she manages before she starts wetly sobbing. I sit next to her and wait for her to calm down looking at the terrible pictures on the kitchen walls while she does.

'What happened Maureen? What do you think's gone on?' I ask, trying not to sound too eager.

'I don't know,' she sounds like she is in pain. 'She just left here like normal. I didn't even go to the gate with her. Just said goodbye at the door and I came in to watch the end of *Captain Pugwash*. It wasn't until I'd had my bath we knew something was wrong. Mrs Bell came round. Said she was calling for Christine as it was getting so late. Well, it was past nine by then and Mam said she'd left at six and, oh Jen, you should've seen her face, she couldn't believe it. 'Well where has she gone then?' she said and Mam said she didn't know and then they both began asking me what had gone on, and then Mam said she'd better come in, and she shouted me dad, and before we knew it the police were called, and they've been here ever since.'

'Bloody hell,' I say.

'I know. They went round Andrea's first but she wasn't there and then her brothers appeared and they were just knocking on all the doors, and more and more people were coming out. It were awful.'

'And how was Mrs Bell?' Mrs Bell is the most glamorous person in the village.

'Well, at first she kept saying Christine must've gone somewhere with another friend and she was saying she'd give her a hiding when she got her home and it was like she was saying cross words but she was really worried not angry with her. Then it got dead late and this detective arrived, and he'd been here first, and he said, 'I'm sorry Mr and Mrs Bell but it looks like Christine's been abducted,' and Mrs Bell got real hysterical and her hands were all shaking and Mam made her drink brandy, and they had to get the doctor to her dad because he began to have chest pains, he were crying that much, and saying her name over and over, and her brothers just stood there looking at the floor. It were awful.'

'Oh Maureen,' I try to sound sympathetic.

'I've been too scared to leave the house. I mean what if he's watching me? What if he thinks I saw anything? Oh, it's not fair. Why won't she come back? Christine. Christine,' she descends into full-scale wailing and the smaller Kirby begins a duet with her. I noticed they've been colouring in the house of sweets from Hansel and Gretel; they are making a nice job of it. The noise gets a bit tedious.

'Now come on you two,' I'm saved by Mrs Kirby, 'What have we said, eh? Christine wouldn't want all these tears. We have to be brave and try not to think about it all.' She looks at me, 'Are you okay, Jennifer love?'

'Yes thank you, Mrs Kirby,' I sniff and turn away so she can't see I'm not crying. She places a hot, plump hand heavily on my shoulder, 'Good girl. You see how brave Jenny is being. You need to be brave like her. For Christine,' she says to her girls.

After that we're allowed up to Maureen's room and play *Kerplunk* and *Frustration* until I get irritated with her soggy panting and tongue lolling. I try to persuade her to go out to talk to the policemen but she won't. Eventually I say I'd better go home and I head back looking across the green to Mrs Bell's. The first time I went over to Christine's for tea, Mrs Bell made me a wonderful cup of coffee. I'd like to go over for a cup of coffee now but I suppose she has other things on her mind.

It is past lunchtime when I get back and Mum and Dad are standing in the kitchen looking crossly at each other, as if one of them is about to strike the other. This is unusual as mostly they can't be bothered with such activities.

'There she is!' Mum points an accusing finger at me, 'Where the hell have you been?' She starts towards me and launches into a tirade before I have a chance to speak. 'A child is missing and we wake up to find you gone! What the hell were you thinking? It's not safe out there, Jen. When are you going to think about others before yourself?'

'I was letting you sleep off your gin.' I say, standing my ground.

'What?' Mum is shocked. I wonder if I've gone too far.

'I thought I'd let you lie in, like you always do. Dad said the murderer is probably long gone and the village is crawling with police and it was Broad Daylight so I thought I'd let you both sleep as usual and get on with looking after myself.'

'I... What?... You...' Mum stammers but I turn and leave the kitchen.

'What the hell has she been reading? Are you sure she's only ten?' Dad says quietly, 'The nerve of that child! She's old beyond her years.'

'I would never have spoken to my mother like that!' Mum shouts after me.

I nip back in. 'Yes you bloody would!' I say and run as fast as I can up the stairs and into my room.

I can hear Dad laugh.

On Wednesday, there is a Reconstruction of Christine's disappearance, designed to jog people's memories. This seems really stupid as the village is tiny and no one comes to visit. It is all anyone has talked about since it happened and every detail has been picked over and over like the dry turkey bones on Boxing Day. They have brought in child actors to play Christine and Maureen. One of them has reportedly been in *Crossroads*. 'Christine' is much prettier than in real life. I really would want to be her best friend. 'Maureen' has to have extra rosy cheeks painted on with make-up. There is a TV crew with the director and they set up by the school with a camera on a trolley which tracks the girls as they walk together down to Maureen's house. The girls link arms and chat in a way they do in old-fashioned films. It doesn't look like real life. They flutter their eyelashes and throw huge smiles at each other, every so often 'Christine' throws back her head and laughs loudly, shaking her thick black hair like an indulged pony.

The director has a word with them.

They try again. This time they walk together, quickly, quietly, no laughing, no chatting. It's much more realistic.

The whole village is watching from behind police tape.

They show it on The News that night and I watch carefully to see if I'm on it. The cameras pan around the village several times and the reporter voice-over recounts that the village is still 'reeling after the disappearance of this much loved little girl.' There is a general muddy coloured shot of groups of onlookers but only one lingering close-up of a forlorn and angelic Judy, golden haired, red scarf snuggled around her easily snappable, little neck, big blue eyes in despair at the events before her.

'Oh look, it's Judy!' Mum says in excitement, leaning forward on the sofa, and seconds later the phone rings. It's Granny. She was watching The News and saw Darling Judy and didn't she look beautiful but wasn't it So Awful what happened and was Mum sure

Judy was safe because she is Just So Little.

'The murderer wanted a ten-year-old!' I pipe up.

I am sent to my room for several reasons.

By the weekend they're searching the scattering of abandoned buildings in an ever increasing radius and going through people's houses, if they agree. Mum says they'll be knocking at our door soon enough. It's been a week and the police have nothing but half a number plate on a white van. All the men in the village are being questioned one way or another and I've overheard that some have been places they shouldn't have been, including Mr Bell, but nothing has come up connected to Christine's disappearance. It's slipping down the stories on The News though it's still top on the local *Border News and Look Around* – there's not much for the poor old reporters to report though.

We're just having sandwiches and finishing a cake that Dad and Judy baked at the start of the holiday, when there is a confident knocking on the front door. It's not Mrs Stoddart, she and Gillian work on Saturdays but they don't bother knocking, they just shout as they come in. We never have visitors, not like we used to at Home. Dad gets up to see who's there and Mum begins to clear the table.

You can tell they're police officers even though they're not in uniform. They take up too much room.

'Afternoon Mrs Wentworth, sorry to interrupt, we're just tidying up some loose ends around the current investigation. Just needed to talk to Mr Wentworth here.' The detective is probably the same age as Dad with very neat, mousy hair and thick, shining glasses. He doesn't seem that sorry to be interrupting.

'Of course, it's no problem, whatever we can do to help,' my mother is all smiles and charm. Dad is lurking behind the officers. 'You might be better chatting in here, I'm afraid we haven't lit the fire in the sitting room yet.'

'Right you are.' The officer takes out a notebook as does the second man. He is softer looking, pinker and more twinkly somehow. I notice Judy smiling at him. He winks at her. I wish I was close enough to pinch her.

Dad moves past them and sits back down at the table, 'Would you like a seat, officers?' he asks.

'Yes, do sit down,' says Mum, 'and can I make you a cup of tea?'

Officer Twinkle looks quite pleased at the thought of this but Officer Frosty Four Eyes frowns and shakes his head. 'No thanks. We're fine, aren't we Willis?'

'Very kind, Mrs Wentworth but please don't trouble yourself,' Willis twinkles at Mum.

'Now then Mr Wentworth, we just need to ascertain your movements on the evening of Friday 15th February between five o' clock and midnight.' Frosty Four Eyes is very serious and Dad looks across at Judy. I sense he would rather we weren't there but the rest of the house is cold so it's a tough choice.

'Yes, of course, well Vivian and I spent the evening together as we do for the majority of time. I think I went down to The Lamb for a swift half just after six, there or thereabouts, and I was there for half an hour at the most, I would say and then it was supper and a night in front of the television as far as I can remember.' He looks across at Mum who nods as confirmation.

Officer Twinkle takes a halting step forward, a little smile of recognition on his face. 'Hang on,' he says, ' Are you that fella from the telly?' Dad smiles apologetically and Officer Twinkle grins wetly, licking his lips.

Dad used to be an actor. He was on the TV in some sitcoms. Dad played minor characters who were a lot older than he was in real life. He featured in one fairly regularly, *Diamonds in the Rough*. It was about a poor London family who win some money on the pools and move into a posh neighbourhood. Dad played their annoying neighbour, busily clipping his hedge or washing his car. He didn't like the Diamonds and was always getting the wrong end of the stick about what they were up to. It did quite well for a while and is sometimes shown on telly at funny times. Dad still gets cheques for it – royalties. He also narrated a few wildlife programs. These were terrible. Poor little creatures who we are just getting to like who are then suddenly eaten by another bigger or faster creature. It always ended badly. We had to stop watching them as both gormless Judy and Dad would cry.

Anyway his career never got very far which is why he's sitting in a draughty kitchen in Cumberland being interviewed by Officer Dribble and an increasingly grumpy Frosty Four Eyes.

'I knew it! Top Hole! Eh? Top Hole!' he sprays a bit of spit on Dad's jumper which Dad politely ignores. 'Top Hole' was Dad's character's catchphrase. Dad smiles weakly.

'Yes, yes, you're absolutely right. That's the one,' Dad resists saying the phrase himself. Frosty Four Eyes lets out a huff.

'Can we get back to the matter in hand Sergeant Willis?' he is abrupt and licks the end of his pencil when really I think he'd rather jab Willis in the eye with it.

'Of course, Sir, sorry Sir.' He is sorry, but then, 'It's just I can't believe you're here. My mam loved that show. Dad did the pools every week. She thought we were going to be the Diamonds. Bloody hell and here you are. Top hole! It really bloody is ..'

'Willis!' Four Eyes barks and Willis jumps a little, 'Christ, we've got a child missing. Can I have your attention please?!'

Willis looks appalled, 'Sorry sir, not another word.' And he steps back away from Dad who gives him a little apologetic nod for getting him into trouble with his crabby boss.

'So, Mr Wentworth, did you walk down to the pub?' Four Eyes' voice is hard, demanding focus from the room.

'Er no, I took the car. It was too cold as I remember,' Dad speaks quietly like he's talking to a teacher.

'I see. So you won't mind if we have a look in the car?' Four Eyes is all business now.

'No, no, I don't see why not,' but Dad sounds like he's trying to think of a reason.

'It's a big place you have here.' Four Eyes gives the kitchen a dismissive sweep with his massive specs.

'Yes it is, I suppose,' Dad sounds wary. .

'Do you have a cellar or attics?'

Dad just looks into the man's hard face.

Mum answers. 'No cellar but there are attic rooms. They were the servants' rooms. We're not using them at the moment.' Her voice is a little breathless but chirpy.

Four Eyes drags his glare to Mum. 'So do you plan to have servants in the future?' he asks as if this a despicable idea.

Mum laughs lightly, 'No, no, I just mean, we're trying to get the house in order and we haven't opened up all the rooms yet, that's all. We're turning it into a B and B,' she finishes as brightly as she can muster.

Four Eyes stays fixed on her for a moment then goes back to Dad. 'I think it would be a good idea for us to have a thorough look over the property Mr Wentworth. I'll get Willis to organise a few officers.' He is peering down at Dad suspiciously.

Dad stands up. He thrusts his hands into his pockets. He's quite a lot taller than Four Eyes. 'That's fine with us. We have nothing to hide,' he speaks in his Best Actor Voice, rich and clear and effortless. 'Sergeant Willis, let me know how I can assist the search. I'm sure it will be Top Hole.' He turns to Four Eyes, 'I'm sorry, I didn't catch your name, but unless there's anything else, we have other matters we need to attend to,' and he strides to the door and both officers follow him down the corridor.

Judy and I are made to stay in our bedroom during the search the following afternoon. We open the window, which is practically impossible because it probably hasn't been opened for about a hundred years, and lever ourselves out onto the cold stone ledge to try to see the police trailing in and out of the stables and the potting sheds. We barely catch a glimpse of anything. We open our door a crack and tie a little mirror on the end of a pogo stick to see if we can see what's going on up and down the corridor but the mirror keeps falling off or tilting as we haven't got any *Sellotape* only socks and bits of ribbon and hair bobbles and a set of clackers. We try listening at the wall and the floor with an empty glass like they do in films. Neither of us can hear a thing.

There is a musty built-in cupboard in our room with shelves, painted doors on the outside but dark wooden varnish edged with paralyzed drips on the inside. The varnish is the toffee-apple brown of my recorder. I like my recorder. It smelt fresh and strong when it was new, like you didn't need a lesson to play it, just the warm aroma and the rich colour was enough promise to make a tune; the cupboard has always been a little frightening though. I have a brilliant idea and pull and tug out the tumble of toys I have shoved in at the bottom - an Etch-a-Sketch, a box of stickle bricks, a few grubby Pippa and Sindy dolls and a picnic basket of dollies' clothes. There's quite a lot of room so I persuade chirpy Judy to climb in so I can shut the doors on her. First, I get a black jumper and cover up her butter blonde hair. I arrange her arms and legs like a rag doll. It's very funny. I tell her she has to be completely still and silent.

And so we wait.

It's quite a young policeman who comes in to search. He smiles in a friendly way. 'I don't suppose I really need to look in here do I?' he says, barely stepping into the room.

'Well you don't want to get into trouble,' I say, 'and I can't get my toy cupboard door open anymore. I think there's something stuck in there.' He looks a bit worried and then takes a step in. He has a quick look under the bed first but there's no monster hiding. Then he grips onto the cupboard door firmly, breathes in and yanks hard. There's nothing wrong with the door so the force he uses makes him stagger back across the room. He is, however, treated to a beautifully clear view of a little girl squashed into a cupboard.

'Oh my god,' he manages, breathless with shock, and he is about to yell when Judy lifts her head, pushes back the jumper and says, 'Surprise!' just like I told her to.

I'm a bit annoyed that more of them don't find all of this funny.

Judy cries and cries and everyone believes that she is too young to understand the Gravity Of Her Actions. Dad gives the young policeman a brandy in his study and Mum makes Judy a Hot Drink.

I have to stay in my room.

Eventually Mum comes to say the police are leaving and they've found nothing. Whilst this is no surprise I'm a bit disappointed; we could do with a bit of fuel to add to the fire and it would have been great if it had been at my house.

On the local news on Sunday night Mr Bell and Christine's brothers have been filmed going to church that morning and I curse my heathen parents again as I miss out on this event. I don't see Christine or Maureen or Andrea on Sundays because they all Go To Church. Everyone seems to Go To Church. Our teacher, Mrs Platt, has repeatedly asked when I will be Going To Church. Judy is desperate to go but Mum and Dad like to stay in bed on Sunday mornings and read the paper so I can't see that happening unless we go ourselves. So on Sundays, Judy and I do our main bickering and I do as much complaining as I can.

On the telly Bryan, the eldest brother, is wearing a dark suit and looks really dishy, a bit like Donny Osmond. I wonder if he already had the suit or if he bought it specially. I wonder if he'll wear it to the funeral. Mind you, we'll need a body for a funeral. From the looks of it the church is packed and the vicar, thin and chilly looking, is full of vigour as he delivers special prayers for Christine's return. And before we know it half term is over and we are preparing to go back to school again. My bedroom, or should I say, our bedroom, is very untidy, Mum and Dad have drunk a lot of gin and neither Christine nor Tillie have come back.

There are television and newspaper reporters outside school in the morning but not that many as it's freezing cold and gloomy. Mrs Platt is standing at the door to greet us all which is a surprise, and the few parents that there are have walked their children to school or stood at their front gates to see they get there safely. Dad has given us a lift in the car for once. Judy has sat in the front. I am still in trouble over the cupboard incident. I pick viciously at a hole in the back seat.

I again wonder whether I attend the smallest school in the country with only sixteen pupils in total.

The porch, where we hang our coats and Mrs Stoddart serves us our dinners, opens onto a large rectangular room with a vaulted ceiling and high leaded windows, too high to look out of, which reminds me of a church. In the centre of the right-hand wall there is a fat stove, just like in *Anne of Green Gables*, with a chimney that goes right up through the roof. Evidently, few believe in central heating in Cumberland.

Mrs Platt, a grey-haired pudding of a woman, sits behind a sturdy wooden desk next to the stove and the rest of the room is divided into two halves, smaller children at little wooden tables with stools, the infants, and larger children in groups of four, at old-fashioned wooden desks and straight-backed chairs, the juniors. The only sign that we are in the 1970s is the television which is in the front of the infant area.

I slide onto my chair, my fingers feeling the worn smoothness of the desktop. I think of the bright modern plastic of my old school.

Christopher and Robert, the twins who own the biggest farm in the village and who sit opposite me, look up from their flattened reading books. They are identical. They have got dull brown, vacant eyes and slack, crusted mouths. Their hair is poker straight and cut with a rough fringe. Their skin is sallow and their thin necks, above matching scarlet polo necks, are grubby. Neither of them blink. 'Hello,' I say rather formally and add a nod after a slight pause. They continue to stare and then both nod slowly, at the same time then return to their books. No development in their social graces over the holidays then. I still can't tell them apart. They are both Christopher Robert to me.

Christine's place is glaringly empty, the chair tucked neatly under the desk. I wonder how long I can leave it before I can ask to move there and sit with Maureen and Andrea and her brother, Timothy. Mrs Platt does a long assembly and we say endless prayers asking for her safe return through which quite a lot of the children cry, particularly Maureen and Andrea. I try to summon tears but they won't come. Mrs Platt says school will finish early to make sure everyone is home before dark. She looks out over her half-moon glasses, then breathes in deeply for a heady announcement.

'In order to keep the search for Christine fresh in people's minds, this afternoon, I have agreed to allow a television crew into the school to report on Christine's daily routine. We must do everything we can to help. All you need to do is to go about your lessons as you normally would and only speak when you are spoken to.'

I consider what the camera crew are to make of this little Cumberland gem of a school.

As we funnel out of the porch for morning playtime the weather is similar to the first bleak playtime I experienced in January. We had stood dismally huddled against the easterly wind in the triangular playground in front of the school house. Christopher Robert had kicked a dirty football with the hopeless Timothy Gallagher without much enthusiasm. When he missed the ball I feared their joint stare of disapproval might vaporise him.

A cluster of girls had come up to me. They were, I supposed, potential friends. 'I'm Christine,' the first girl said. She was smiling, and I'd noticed her plump scarlet gums above teeny white teeth, her glinting blue eyes and sooty lashes. Her Snow White colouring and tiny, intense features didn't translate well into the blurred newspaper print that was to come. That day she was wearing a complicated coat with a buckled belt, buttons and a hood lined with pretend fur.

'Maureen,' the second in line said. Her lips were chapped and her cheeks were hot pink. She looked startled with liquid brown eyes and was hopping like she needed a wee, tugging at the hem of a chunky home knitted jumper. 'Why aren't you wearing a coat?' I said, 'You must be freezing.'

'Forgot it,' she said quickly, as if even speaking would make her colder.

'How?' I said. How could she have left the house without it I thought?

'She only lives there.' Christine pointed to the closest house to the school, a double fronted white cottage, solid looking.

'Just ran over on the bell.' I could hardly hear her.

'Why don't you go home and get it?' I asked.

'Can't. Mam'll clap me one.' She looked at the sky in despair.

The third girl was just smiling. I turned my attention to her. She was much smaller than the other two. 'This is Andrea,' Christine said. 'She's in J2 but Viper let's her sit with us.'

'Viper?'

'Mrs Platt. She's called that because she's had three husbands and killed them all and her first initial is V. V for Veenie.'

This had seemed unlikely on all counts.

'Well why do I have to sit with the Bill and Ben? I'm the oldest.' I was put out to put it mildly.

'Dunno,' Christine shrugged. 'She was here first. Was born here. Do you want to play something?'

I had an elastic in my pocket. I took it out. 'We could play this or have you got one? '

They looked at me like I had produced a potted plant.

'What's that?'

'It's for French skipping. Don't you do it? It's really good. There's songs.'

They exchanged looks. I'd seen those looks before. My stomach turned over.

'Okay then,' Christine said brightly. By the end of break, they'd all had a turn up to kneesies and everyone had stood and watched and Maureen wasn't quite so cold.

This morning, Maureen and Andrea and I just sit on the doorstep, close together. Andrea's hair smells of baby shampoo. I quite like it. Her bare knees are tucked up to her chin and bone white with cold. She drops her chin onto them. She looks tired, purply green smears under her pale blue eyes.

'Didn't want to get out of bed this morning,' she yawns a mighty yawn.

'Me neither,' Maureen mutters into her hands. She's pulled the slack cuffs of her jumper down to keep the biting wind off them.

'Are you having bad dreams?' Andrea says, turning to me.

'Not really,' I say, 'I don't remember many of my dreams. Judy does though. She insists on telling us all the details every bloody morning.' I roll my eyes.

'I keep having the same one.' I wish Andrea would speak up but I suppose it would be rude to tell her this.

'Is it scary?' Maureen sounds like there are enough creepy things in her life at the moment without hearing Andrea's dream, thank you very much.

'A bit. I suppose so. Yes.' Andrea decides.

'Well tell us then,' I say irritably. Normally Andrea has to be coaxed and cajoled to join in with everything but I can't be bothered with that this morning.

'Ok. It all starts quite happily but sometimes in different places, like once I was in Carlisle Castle and once I was at Appleby Horse Fair and once I was in the Lakes but I'm not sure where. And I'm with different people at the start and in my sleep I think it's ok, it's not going to be the dream but then I always end up in the same place. I always end up having a picnic with Christine and Brian Connolly from *Sweet.*'

'*Sweet*, the pop group?' says Maureen. She sounds like this is the most ridiculous thing she's ever heard.

'Yes, *Sweet*. I've got a poster of Brian on my wall. But I've had to take it down. I think it's a bit scary now.'

'Ok so you're having a picnic with Christine and Brian Connolly. I bet they've got a lot to talk about,' I say wanting to get back to the dream.

'Yes. It's a very nice picnic with one of those big posh hampers and a lovely rug and Christine's wearing a pretty orange dress and I've got new shoes but they don't talk to me they just talk about their hair.'

Brian Connolly, though blonde, has very similar hair to Christine, thick and long and straight, cut in more or less the same shape.

'Well what do they say?' Maureen says. She is looking at Andrea as if she is a total numbskull.

'I don't know, just stuff about brushing it and keeping it tangle free and then things change and Brian says to Christine, 'Now I've spoken to you about my hair, you have to come with me,' and he opens up the hamper and he jumps in it up to his armpits and he pulls Christine towards him and she doesn't want to go and I peek over the top of the hamper and it's all just black and she starts crying and reaching out to me but my arms won't move to help her and he very slowly drags her in and then closes the hamper shut on them both and I'm there on my own and I crawl over really slowly and open the lid of the hamper even though I'm dead scared and there's just a big glass bowl of red jelly with lots of mandarin segments trapped in it. Then I wake up and I can't get back to sleep.'

This is the most I've ever heard Andrea speak.

'Ooh Andrea that's creepy,' says Maureen.

Andrea is looking really worried and a bit tearful.

'It's unlikely Brian Connelly is the murderer,' I say, though you never know I suppose.

'Do you think you know something though?' says Maureen, 'Do you think you've seen something and you can't quite remember it?' Andrea looks even more worried.

'Where did Christine get her hair cut?' I ask, aware that I am clutching at straws but quite keen to keep this line of enquiry going now.

'Her mam did it,' Maureen says.

We are silent.

'Eh Andrea, perhaps you're a psychic! Perhaps there's a message in the dream. I saw an episode of *Kojak* with someone who could solve crimes with their psychic powers.' Maureen is getting very excited at this thought.

'Perhaps Christine is talking to you,' I say and Maureen and Andrea huddle together in terror and shriek as Mrs Platt opens the door we are leaning against to ring the bell for the end of playtime.

It's no real surprise a camera crew are visiting; Viper loves the telly. She does very little actual teaching. Every day is dull and the room is stifling hot as she Feels The Cold. There is no blackboard and she rarely moves from her desk, apart from for assemblies and for dinner. Instead, in this teeny school in the middle of nowhere, there is no art or geography or Mr Smith's impromptu lessons on wildlife. I loved my last teacher Mr Smith. He would read us stories at the end of every day turning a stick of chalk over and over between his dusty finger and thumb on the desk as he read. It made you sleepy to watch it. Sleepy and calm. No, here in this miniature school, there are many, many telly and radio programs; we are constantly carouseling around the screen in front of them. Sometimes, Viper puts a whistle round her neck and we are all taken outside for Games. She decides this will be a good idea today for half an hour after playtime. Christopher Robert push out a cage on wheels full of odd balls, rope circles, beanbags and suchlike and Mrs Platt instructs us in various half-hearted competitive activities. I am now to be paired with Timothy, Andrea's older brother, as we no longer have Christine. He is half my size and he stammers. We are supposed to throw and catch a ball. It is tedious and I am bored. He just grins and drops the ball frequently.

'S s s so sorry.'

'Mum m mm muma ma my fault.'

I say nothing to him. I can't believe I have to be in a pair with a boy. Quite often, I look over and Viper is playing catch with Judy. Mrs Platt adores Judy. Most grown-ups do.

Today Viper is wearing a smart lilac twinset and, just before lunch Mrs Irving, the village mobile hairdresser, arrives and spends a good half hour on her thin, mousey hair. I think of some of the naughty boys at my last school and what they would've got up to while their teacher was having a Shampoo and Set during class but we are all Good As Gold, not that she actually has a shampoo.

After dinner is cleared away, the television crew arrive. The director is young and good-looking with longish dark hair and looks a bit like David Cassidy. There's a woman reporter too who is blonde and very skinny, with a tan dress and knee-high boots. She looks like one of *Pan's People*. It's very exciting but we're all supposed to be sad so we can't show it. First of all the girl does an interview with Viper standing up next to Christine's empty desk.

For some reason Viper keeps closing her eyes for long periods of time while she's talking. It's very odd. Then I notice her hands are together too and I realise she's answering the questions in prayer form. She's also smiling a lot, which she is not very good at as she usually doesn't do it much, so quite a lot of the time it looks like she's just baring her teeth or parting her lips. I see the reporter and the director exchange looks.

They move onto Maureen and Andrea but they just resort to hiccupping sobs and wails so that's not much use.

At last they arrive at mine and Christopher Robert's desks. Christopher Robert give them the same hostile stare. I smile with encouragement as if I am a normal human being. They ask for names and are a little unnerved by the Christopher Robert monotones.

'And how have you been affected by Christine's disappearance?' The beautiful blonde woman, Jan asks. At last, the question I've been waiting for over a week to answer!

'We...'

'Haven't.' say Christopher Robert and clamp their mouths shut.

She turns to me, a little sharply. 'She was such a dear friend,' I begin warmly, 'I mean she *is* such a dear friend. I only arrived here in January and, straightaway, Christine accepted me and we had such fun together.' I smile, but not too much, there is a bittersweet sadness moving across my face.

'Go on,' Jan encourages, brightening up a bit.

'Well, I do remember the first time she came to my house. You see, my mum is an artist. Quite talented, actually. And we have some of her sketches in the kitchen and Christine was immediately drawn to them. I don't know if she ever went to an art gallery but she had such...' I pretend to search for the word, 'sensitivity. She was old beyond her years,' and then I put my hand to my forehead like I've seen the posh ladies do on *Upstairs Downstairs* after the Titanic sank drowning some of the Bellamys – I can't remember who. I keep my head down as if I am too upset to speak and count slowly up to ten. Then I look up, 'I don't understand who would want to hurt her. She was so kind and brave and clever.'

'There, there Jennifer.' I feel Viper's grip on my shoulders, I notice she's painted her brown fingernails pearly white for the cameras, like gnarled seashells. 'Let's have a break and get you a glass of water,' and she bustles me out of the room and into the little kitchen in the porch. She shuts the door behind us.

'You need to calm down, my girl. What on earth are you playing at, telling such stories?'

'I'm just letting the viewers hear about the Christine I know,' I say sweetly but I am livid. I have so much more to say. I had rehearsed it all in front of the bathroom mirror, ready for just such an occasion, and this ugly old woman has snatched it away from me. She breathes in close to me. I can see the powder crusted in the deep lines on her brow and her lipstick caked in the cracks on her dry, thin lips. She smells of bitter coffee and lavender talcum powder and a little bit of vomit.

'No more of your uppity nonsense, miss, do you hear me?'

I meet her eye, 'Yes Mrs Platt.'

'No more of it I say,' and she squeezes my arm, 'Christine was a good girl. An ordinary little girl.'

'Don't you mean *is* a good girl,' I tilt my head insolently.

I think she might slap me but instead she opens the door and pushes me back into the classroom. The camera crew are interviewing Judy and Sally. Sally looks a bit bemused but Judy is straight backed and attentive. Jan adores her.

We watch The News, which we now do as a matter of course. Everything is timed around the bulletins. Meals, bath times, washing up; all planning is 'We'll get that done before The News' or 'You can do it when The News has finished'. We watch the whole programme in case there are any news flashes; there never are. My general knowledge is improving a lot as a result. Another girl, Patty Hearst had been kidnapped in America, a few weeks before Christine. This seems to be a different case as they are a very wealthy family. I don't think Mr Bell has much to offer in terms of a ransom. Before this I only really knew about kidnapping from *Scooby Doo* but sometimes I think about where Christine might be and when people say 'the body', I picture her dark, dark hair but I see her as stone cold and her skin lard white, like a leg of lamb before it's cooked on a Sunday; solid, unmoving. I see her lying by a rock on the fells, or in the back of the van under a scratchy blanket, or by a rubbish dump. I don't ever see her face though. Mostly I just see her hair and her long skinny legs and her thin, little feet. Still. A body. Dead. Then I have to stop thinking about it.

I am finally on The News telling my story about the sketches. I am after Viper and after Judy – the van, the beauty et cetera et cetera – and after Maureen/Andrea sobbing but I am still there, at last, and I think I look quite nice and believable. Mum tuts. Dad says 'I didn't know she liked your paintings Viv?'

'Yes, she did comment on them.'

'She loved them,' I confirm.

'Sensitivity,' Mum throws in, 'that's a big word for a ten-year-old to use.'

'Is it wrong?' I say, innocently.

'No,' she knows we are playing a game.

'I do read a lot of books,' I say haughtily. 'I pride myself on my vocabulary.'

'I'm sure you do,' and she opens the Sunday paper, dismissing me.

I can't quite believe she hasn't finished reading it yet. She's done little else since its arrival yesterday morning.

The first time Christine came to The Castle, she was horribly excited and I was annoyed before we even arrived as I knew she was going to be disappointed. We cut across the spongy, soggy lawn and I heaved the heavy rough door open, shouting 'We're here,' as loudly as I could, hoping against hope that my mother would have rallied and at least brushed her hair for our arrival. Christine was automatically slipping off her shoes, 'Leave them on, it's freezing here,' I said. I am cruel, but not that cruel. Christine looked a little alarmed. We trudged down the dark corridor to the kitchen. Alas, no smell of home baking to lure us in, no motherly hum above a reassuring pop tune tripping along to a homely domestic chore being deftly completed by a well turned out warm soul. No, nothing. As I opened the door, the *Rayburn* was on but the kitchen was empty. Mum and Dad's lunchtime dishes were shipwrecked in greasy washing up water in the grimy sink. Countless coffee cup rings, like old potato print pictures, decorated the table topped with a scattering of breakfast breadcrumbs.
I cursed them.
Granny would have made rock buns with cherries in and probably bought strawberry *Nesquik*.
I cursed them. And I hated them.
I quickly got the grey dish cloth and ran it under the freezing tap and attempted to wipe the table, slopping water clumsily onto the floor in my haste. I began to chat to Christine. 'I don't know where Mum and Dad are. Probably busy organising for the guests.' There were no guests. 'I mean, there's still loads to do to make sure everything is Top Hole.' I sounded like an idiot. Christine had subconsciously made her way to the *Rayburn* and was standing with her back against it. Amazingly she was not looking at the piles of flattened newspapers in the corner by the door, or the crowd of opaque milk bottles patiently waiting to be put out on the doorstep, or the flowers that should have gone in the bin two weeks ago and were now a bouquet of slimy stems and naked stamen, brown petals

curling at the base of the grimy vase, dark with pond water. All of this I could now see with one sweep of the room. How did I not take it in this morning? All that Christine was looking at were my mother's sketches flimsily pinned to the wall by Gillian Stoddart.

Gillian had found the pictures in the unpacking and had made a tremendous fuss over Mother's talent. Mum was, of course, tremendously flattered and, after lots of cajoling, agreed to the pictures being 'temporarily' displayed in the kitchen. Gillian said she should get them framed. Gillian said she should have an exhibition. Dad said Gillian should calm down.

My mother is not really a proper mum. Not like the ones you see in the ads with pinnies on and gleaming kitchens who really want to know what's best for their kids and their husbands. Most of the previous day she had been tucked up in a chair with a book as per usual. No, Mum was supposed to be an artist so that means she sits around and reads most of the time or, if the sun is shining, she lies in the garden with the radio on, or, sometimes, she has one or two friends round and they talk, sometimes quite crossly and sometimes quite sadly.

Because of Mum's art, Granny did most of the cooking and the looking after back at Home in lovely centrally heated Buckinghamshire, and Mum spent some time in her studio which was a little converted shed which she filled with lots of stuff she had done at Art College, and we weren't allowed to go in there or touch anything or ask about anything, especially not the bare lady sculptures, who were also a bit cross or a bit sad. I didn't see her actually making anything, not like we did in our Art Room at school. We did lovely bright poster paint pictures and it smelt chalky and fresh and once we used dye and hot wax and made little batik pictures from old pieces of cloth. We had to be very careful and we had an extra teacher, Miss Tolhurst, standing next to the wax, all the time. We did printmaking with rollers and thick glossy paint and glass. I loved it in there. I don't know what Mum did in her studio.

I followed Christine's gaze to the sketches. One of them is a nude woman tipping a jug of water over her long hair. It is graceful. Her arm is balletic. Her leg is long. There is a curve of breast and buttock and a dark tip of the nipple. It is done in sepia charcoal. Then there is a dark-haired child cross-legged, thoughtful, sad, looking into the distance, a chair suggested, not really defined. It's not clear if it's a girl or boy. There is something very wrong with him/her though. The third is an old woman. A grim, shadowed, lined face, small-eyed and furious. She's lived a life that has enraged her. She wears a scarf, tight around her head, protecting her or keeping something in, containing her.

Christine could not take her eyes off them. I was wary. I stopped my mopping up. 'What do you think of them?'

'Is that a naked lady?' Her voice was hushed.

'Yes.' I was resigned.

'In your kitchen?'

'Yes.'

'Where did you get it?'

'My mother drew it.' No point lying.

She looked at me.

'Bloody hell!' Then she slapped her hand over her mouth. 'She drew it?' Her voice squeaked.

'Yes,' I nodded, serious and wise.

'What did your dad say?'

I paused.

'He liked it.'

Christine took in an enormous breath and held it. She had no idea what to do with this information. Eventually she let her breath out and looked at me. 'My dad has dirty pictures too,' she said slowly, 'but we don't hang them on our kitchen walls and,' she paused, 'my mam did not draw them.'

For a moment we looked at each other, then burst into breathless, shrieking giggling. We clutched at each other, helpless and kept pointing at the picture. It was wonderful. Eventually we calmed down and this made me a little sad; I wanted to laugh like this all the time. I had a rummage through the cupboard. There was only a tin of tomato purée, a tin of anchovies and half a packet of *Ritz* biscuits. We chomped through the salty crackers and drank some milk. I can't make coffee and there was nothing else. Christine genuinely didn't seem to care and it surprised me when she was used to central heating and proper care and attention. It was dark outside when Mum put in an appearance. She'd obviously been asleep, her red hair messy and her eye make-up smudged. She'd got Dad's dressing gown on and it puddled behind her, the sleeves too long, so she looked like a little girl playing dress up.

'Oh hello darling. Who are you?' she said, stretching lazily, fingertips slowly uncurling like slow motion flowers.

'This is Christine, Mum. I told you she was coming for tea.'

'Did you?' She was staring at Christine.

'Pleased to meet you, Mrs Wentworth.'

'Oh darling, call me Vivian please. Mrs Wentworth is my mother-in-law,' and she smiled into Christine's eyes. Christine was thrilled. My mother is gorgeous and charming and lovely, just like bloody Judy. I wanted to vomit.

'I like your pictures,' the idiot Christine blurted out. Mum turned her head slowly to her sketches and took a step towards them. She gently touched all three, her tiny, creamy-blue wrist slipping out from the large brocade cuff of Dad's dressing gown. Her slender finger traced the line of the crone's jaw, the child's mouth, the woman's buttock. She turned back.

'I did those years ago. Didn't spend much time on them. Dashed them off really. Don't really know why they're up here.'

'Neither do I,' I said, crossly.

'I think they're lovely. You're very talented. Vivian.' She added 'Vivian' with such pride I wanted to kick her under the table. Hard.

'What's for tea?' I asked, knowing it was going to be a disaster.

'Dad's gone for fish and chips,' she turned to Christine, 'That okay darling? Isn't your hair fantastic? So black and thick!' She touched it.

'Thank you, Vivian.' I half expected Christine to start purring.

'Right Christine, let's go to my room.' and I stormed out though I was very pleased about the fish and chips, as was Christine.

In school, Christine told everyone Mum was an artist in slightly hushed tones and I was both a little bit proud at how impressed they were, catching Christine's obvious adoration for Mum's scrappy work, and also a little bit annoyed that I could not reveal the truth that she is a slattern of the highest order who lounges around, often on her unmade bed, often not suitably clothed, smoking cigarettes and reading, rather than cooking and cleaning and caring for her children like mums are supposed to do.

When Judy and I open the door to go to school in the morning, there is a huddle of reporters at the door.

'Morning. Any chance we could have a look at the sketches girls?'

'Any more stories about Christine, Jenny?'

'Give us a smile, Judy. You're a pretty one, aren't you?'

I blink, genuinely surprised.

Judy turns. 'Mum!' she yells.

Mum appears sluttishly in Dad's dressing gown and hangs in the door frame, knotty hair, sleepy eyes, pouting over a cigarette which crackles as she draws on it. The dressing gown reveals her creamy freckled skin and a hint of smooth thigh. The reporters are thrilled. Why did she have to come to the door?

'Morning lads,' she talks softly which quiets them too, 'what are you doing here so early?' She makes it sound like they're being very naughty.

'Just wanting a look at your lovely pictures, Vivian, if that's okay?' one of them says. His accent is southern. Must be from one of the big papers.

'They're not worth looking at,' she murmurs, dragging another puff, tilting her chin up and blowing the smoke away.

'Christine thought so,' piped up another.

'Christine's a kid,' she bats away.

'Come on Vivian. Just show us one. Let the nation decide if they're any good,' they wheedle and whine.

She yawns and stretches like a cat, the dressing gown slips down revealing her skinny arm. It's clear she's naked underneath it. I can see her nipple through the silky fabric. I feel hot and embarrassed.

'Oh, if you insist,' she sounds bored 'Wait here,' and she slopes off.

'Where's she been hiding?' one of the reporters mutters quietly.

'She spends a lot of time in bed,' I say. It's meant as a criticism.

'Best place for her,' says another and they all laugh hard and I don't like it and Judy edges closer to me.

Mother returns holding the sketch of the child and that silences the men. She stands like a girl in assembly with the paper against her chest and they snap their cameras. They pass some comments, 'Very good love,' 'You've got some talent there,' but I can tell they're disappointed the atmosphere has changed. I'm glad Mum didn't bring the bare lady.

'Right,' she says, 'show's over. Off you go. Nothing more for you here today,' and they turn and troupe off down the path, throwing some 'Cheerios' over their shoulders as they go whilst trying to get a last look at Mum.

After a bit Judy and I set off to school. It's now eleven days since Christine disappeared.

The village falls into a bit of a routine. There are fewer police or rather, the activity in the village is tidal. At various times, mainly at weekends there seems to be a rush of people puddling around the green. Dad says a lot of them are Mawkish or Rubberneckers; some just drive slowly round the green and then leave. Some park up and go to The Lamb and sit quietly with a drink, hoping to hear titbits not divulged on the telly or in the papers. Some bring things for Mrs Bell; food, flowers, prayers written down, teddy bears for when Christine comes home.

We've had more search parties. Names have been put forward and rejected. There have been sightings that have proved to be False Hopes. There has been Nothing Concrete. Whenever I walk I scour the hedges and paths and I would love to be the person who found the shoe lost in the struggle to bundle her into the van, or the knife used to... I don't think in too much detail but it would be like finding the golden ticket. They'd definitely want to interview me again.

Most of the children have been being kept indoors or have been accompanied by parents to each other's houses. Mum and Dad did this a bit at first but they can't keep up that level of commitment and, as long as it's light, I'm able to wander about pretty much as before. February has given way to March and Mum's sketch has appeared in the papers. There was a flurry of interest. Some people speculating Christine foresaw her own demise (this was a new word for me) in the sketch and, thus, was so drawn to it. Mum had read this out and Dad had said, 'Bloody ridiculous,' in a cross voice and that they print 'Utter tripe' but they keep printing the picture and Mum had a phone call from an agent and now she's getting money every time anyone wants to use The Lost Child, as it's been titled.

Easter is on its way and, surprise, surprise, advanced bookings are looking good. Neither Mum nor Dad seem particularly happy about this. Dad wants to stay in his study and smoke and listen to his sad French women sing and read PG Wodehouse and Mum still loves her bed and is working her way through the books left by the previous owners in the guest lounge. However, Mrs Stoddart and Gillian are lugging rugs out into the garden and beating them with old wooden tennis rackets; they are polishing the floors and furniture and blacking the fireplaces. The Castle is coming back to some sort of life though it is a chilly and gloomy one.

I steal 2p from Dad's trouser pocket while he's sleeping and head down to the village shop turning the coin in my pocket as I go. I had contemplated snaffling a couple of cigarettes too - I've never tried smoking – but I have no one to try it with so didn't bother. I push open the metal gate of Mrs Stewart's shop and walk through the front garden which is currently sleeping. At Home there is a neat row of shops; a newsagent's, a butcher's, a greengrocer's, a hairdresser's all in a tidy row with big windows so you know they're shops. Here it's just a small house window with half a heavy lace curtain. It has two shelves in it. On one there is a dusty packet of Dreft. On the other there is a box of Brillo pads. They are keen on cleaning in the village I think.

On our first visit to the shop my hope was it would be how I imagined the shop in Little House on the Prairie; stocked to the rafters with crisp bolts of fabric and glass jars of wholesome oats, flours and dried fruit, everything popped into brown paper and sold to you by a kindly chirpy Mr Olsen.

I was disappointed. The shop smells of aniseed and bleach. It is very murky. There is a long dark counter and there are stocked shelves behind it but it is all a muddle. Big, scratched plastic jars of battered sweets are pushed up against rusting tins of peas and potatoes and double packs of loo roll. There is a stack of faded Mills *and Boon* romances next to a teetering pile of mouse traps. Everything is a bit dusty and greasy.

Mrs Stewart is dealing with a couple of reporters. Since Christine's disappearance she's taken to stocking made-up rolls and lots of newspapers. It's busy in here first thing and she wheezes her way up and down the counter, never cracking a smile, begrudgingly taking every penny she can from the passing trade.

I hang about, reading the noticeboard, waiting for my turn. Sunday School is at ten – someone has drawn a flower on the postcard, all the more reason to attend. Mrs Platt is selling an Ercol suite. POA. There is a Pie and Pea Supper in the Church Hall in September to celebrate Harvest Festival. All Welcome. That one looks grubby so is probably not an example of forward planning. Mrs Turner is offering piano lessons. Davey Thompson's dog has had puppies – free to a good home.

It's not particularly fascinating and there aren't any dates so they could all have been there a long time. I wonder whether we'll get a dog now we are country folk. Tanya Butler had a puppy at Home and I thought it was lovely but it nipped me and wee'd on my sock and it got very excitable and kept barking and her house smelt a bit horrid once she had it. I expect Judy would love a puppy.

I get my *Black Jacks*, a lot for 2p, and shudder at Mrs Stewart's bony, thin-skinned hands as she twists and nips the paper bag shut.

I cut down past the church and the Bermans' house and begin to wander along aimlessly. There are now some young cows in the field who are minutely more interesting than sheep but they're all going to end up as mince so what's the point in getting attached.

Around the corner, I see a dark hunched figure sitting on the five bar gate at the next field. It's Kevin Bell. As I get closer, I see he's been crying. His red rimmed eyes match his acne marked skin. He is not an attractive sight. He sees me and slides down from the gate, wiping his nose on the back of his anorak sleeve.

'Hiya,' he says, grimly, a crack in his voice.

'Hi,' I say.

I stand and look at him. He's thirteen but not much taller than me. He is looking over my shoulder.

'How's your mum?' I try.

He shrugs, 'Crying. A lot.'

He is silent again. Kicking at the ground.

'How's school?'

'Not been in.'

'Why not?'

'Because my fuckin' sister got fuckin' murdered!' He stares at me, furious.

'You don't know she's dead,' I say, in what I hope is a calm and reasonable voice. I am a bit shocked at his language but also a bit exhilarated.

'Well where is she then? She's not here is she? He's not brought her back? No one's found her or seen her? Of course she is...'

He's quiet again.

I bite my lip. We wait.

'What does Bryan say?' I try again.

'Not much. He's got some older mates. He's been going out drinking in Appleby. Can get served there alright.'

'Oh. Right.'

For some reason, despite his horrible skin, I want to give him a cuddle and make him feel better.

'I'm sorry Kevin,' I manage.

'I'm sorry too,' he mutters to the ground.

We stand sighing and looking about. I don't know whether to carry on walking. It all seems a bit hopeless.

Then he says, 'Do you want to come back and see Mam for a bit?'

'Yeah. Okay. If you think that'll be alright.'

'We've had all sorts in but no kids, like. I think she'd like it. See Christine's friend. If you're not busy.'

'No. No. I'm just having a bit of a walk. Nothing else to do.'

'Okay then,' and he sets off back to the village, walking quickly. I keep having to skip a bit to keep up. I can't think of anything else to say so we say nothing. I'm thrilled and have to stop myself from smiling.

At the house, Kevin pushes through the gate. There are no police or reporters. It's a quiet day; no new News. He slips off his shoes in the porch, and I follow suit, then we hang up our coats. I am hit by a wall of heat in the hall and I see Kevin is in a T-shirt.

41

'Mam feels the cold since Christine,' he says quietly. He walks through to the lounge and Mrs Bell is sitting tucked into a corner of the sofa, under a thick, crocheted pink blanket. Her hair is done but there is no make-up. She looks older. She is watching telly.

'Mam. Look who I've brought to see you. It's...' He turns to me.

'Jennifer,' I say.

'Jennifer,' he repeats slowly to her.

She looks at me for a long moment and her face crumples and she chokes out tears but beckons me over at the same time. She has a cotton hanky and she's dabbing and wiping with it as she gulps away her feelings.

'Oh Jenny pet, how are you? Have you heard about my Christine? They can't find her. It's terrible. You haven't seen her, have you?'

'No Mrs Bell I haven't sorry. Yes I have heard. I think everyone has.'

'I don't know why she won't come home. Why won't she come home? Kevin? Kevin?'

'I'm here Mam,' Kevin moves to his mother.

'Why won't she come home, Kevin?'

'I don't know Mam. Listen, we'll go and make you a nice strong coffee, okay?'

'Okay Kevin. You're such a good boy. Not like Christine. Running off like that.'

'Okay Mam, just you be quiet now and I'll get you some coffee.'

He signals for me to follow him to the kitchen where he angrily flicks the kettle on and it roars into action. He heaps coffee into a mug and fetches a bottle of milk from the fridge.

'What does she mean 'running off',' I say.

'She can't accept it. Can't take it in.' He is pouring in the milk and adding loads of sugar, stirring vigorously. 'We can't get her to understand she's been, you know, taken. She won't have it. She just starts wailing, going crazy if anyone says anything near the truth. Dad's going nuts with it. Like she can't cope with what might've happened to her, you know, what he could have...' and then Kevin squeezes his eyes tight shirt and suppresses a sob. He takes a huge breath.

'Sorry,' he says.

The kettle boils. He fills the mug most of the way, then gets a flat bottle of brandy from the cupboard and pours a glug in.

'It's the only way she can get through the days now,' he says, his voice full of shame. He carries it back through and I follow, amazed at everything. There is dust on all the ornaments and it needs a good hoover. There is a general air of disorder, like the house has a fissure or fracture. It hasn't split apart completely but something has changed. There's been an earthquake and everything has shifted place, nothing is right anymore.

Kevin encourages his mother to drink down the coffee and it soothes her. He tucks the blanket round her like she's an old woman and turns the telly up louder to drown out her thoughts.

It's hard to believe I am in the same place I visited for the first time with such anticipation just a few weeks before. I'd persuaded Christine to invite me round for tea though she clearly wasn't used to such formal arrangements. Walking back from school with Christine had felt a little strange and she was talking very quickly so I thought she was nervous. It was near the end of January. Practically dark. I had a plastic bag with me. Dad had bought me a lovely soft cream jumper and clear nail varnish and little pads of remover ready soaked in a round red box. I had showed them to Christine at break. We'd been careful to exclude Maureen and Andrea from seeing what I had.

There were many reasons for my excitement; I was finally doing something after school, other than trudging up that claggy lane to the gloomy Castle, even if it was only going to Christine's. Plus there was the thrill of Christine's two older brothers, both at the grammar school in Appleby, who I had only caught glimpses of as they tipped off the school bus at the bottom of the green. Also I hadn't been in Christine's house. Her mum was House Proud so she wouldn't let us come in on a Saturday when we met up to play. We had to go into Maureen's or Andrea's when we got too cold. Christine's house was at the bottom of the village; it was a big, modern bungalow with a neat garden and a robust clipped hedge. We went to the side of the house to go in and Christine took off her shoes in the porch. I copied her. The house was warm with a busy flowery carpet that I wanted to stare at, and many ornaments that I wanted to touch, and it smelt of polish and a funny perfume. It was very clean and tidy. Christine's voice dropped to a more hushed tone as soon as we entered the house and I followed her in silence into the roomy fresh apple green and lemon yellow kitchen. Lovely Mrs Bell was at the sink, busy with a mound of glistening bubbles, an orderly row of freshly washed glasses on the drainer next to her. She turned and smiled. Her hair was immaculate, backcombed and lacquered and very old-fashioned. She had coral lipstick, false eyelashes and a floral house coat on over a snuggly fitted dress of heavy polyester. She had slippers with pink marabou feathers on.

Mrs Bell was the most splendid person I had seen since our terrible move to Cumberland in January. Full make-up just to do the washing up. I don't think my mother had put on lipstick since we had arrived. 'Hello girls. Go and wash your hands and I'll get you a drink. Would you like a coffee Jennifer?'

I startled. A coffee? 'Er?'

'Don't you drink coffee? Tea then?'

'No, coffee will be fine.' Why not? I thought.

Christine grinned gummily and we went to her bedroom. It was very pink and toothpaste white with all her toys neatly arranged like in a shop but without the wrapping. There weren't any books but she had her own dressing table with a stool covered in shiny pink velvet. She immediately sat down and started brushing her abundant black hair. I sprawled on the bed that seemed to slip and slide beneath me as if it was alive. It wasn't unpleasant so I tried to get comfortable. 'We'll get changed in a minute.' announced Christine in quite a bossy tone. She was a bit older than me and her room was nicely decorated but I wasn't sure I was going to put up with that.

'Okay. Maybe.' I said, trying to sound noncommittal.

'Christine!' Her mother called, sweetly.

'That didn't take long.' I was impressed by such focus and attention paid to any child but Christine clattered down her brush and headed for the door. I slip slid from the bed and followed her.

The coffee was delicious, silky and sweet, quite unlike the bitter liquid tyre concoction Mum and Dad drink. There were *Jammie Dodgers* on a dish and we had plates too, and Mrs Bell wanted to talk to us, though she didn't sit down, but busied herself around the kitchen as she chatted, opening and closing the enormous fridge, deftly drying the glasses, setting the table around us, 'Excuse me, pet.'

'So, your mam and dad bought The Castle?'

'Yes they did.'

'Must need a lot of work. How are they getting on?'

'Well, it's a big old house.' I repeated what I'd heard my father say. Mrs Bell stopped and looked at me. Then laughed.

'It certainly is,' she said. I got the feeling I'd said the wrong thing. I tried to make up for it.

'They're hoping to have it ready for Easter.'

'And what is happening at Easter?'

'It's the start of the season.'

'The season?'

'For tourists. The Castle is going to be a Bed and Breakfast.' I had tried to sound proud but I was not. My parents plan to transform the ugly, and frankly, scary, old castle into a Lovely Bed-and-Breakfast had been a constant source of fury for me. There were eleven bedrooms and I still had to share with my moron sister Judy.

Christine took a loud bite of her biscuit then looked strangely ashamed.

'Yes. I'd heard as much. Though we are, of course, an established guesthouse.' Mrs Bell tugged at the neck of her house coat and worked her mouth as if she was sucking a hard mint.

'Oh really? How lovely,' I said brightly.

'Do your parents have experience in the hospitality and catering business?' She was now attacking a stain on the worktop with a dull *Brillo* pad.

'Um. Well. I don't know. My dad had a part as a restaurant manager in *The Customer's Always Right*.' I realised this was feeble but I was hoping this might distract her. People sometimes like talking about Dad being an actor.

Mrs Bell arched her beautifully plucked eyebrow in reply.

I took another gulp of the coffee. 'The coffee is delicious, Mrs Bell.'

'If you look in our many visitors' books, my morning coffee is often remarked upon.' Her head twitched a little then settled.

'Perhaps Dad will have to get the recipe,' I joked. Or not as it

45

turned out, as Mrs Bell's mouth set into an off-kilter coral line of fury and she marched out of the kitchen as quickly as her marabou slippers would allow.

'Why did you have to say that?' whined Christine, sipping at her coffee timidly.

'I was only joking. What's the big deal anyway?' I snapped.

'Mam thinks your place will take all our business, is the big deal. I should've told you not to say anything. Come on, let's get changed.' She slid quietly from her chair and motioned we had to be as quiet as quiet as we progressed back to her hectic room.

She had a wardrobe packed with clothes and I wanted to push her headfirst into them as she stood and idly rifled through them choosing what to put on. It looked like the family business could stand some competition to me. Christine said nothing about my new jumper but I could tell she thought I was a bit fat from the way she looked at me then smoothed her hands over her tummy and bottom. I asked her what she got in her spelling test. I know she did really badly. I got 100%.

We painted each other's nails with my new nail polish and then took it off because we smudged it and put it on all over again and lay on the bed on our tummies holding our hands out like starfish and I tried to encourage Christine to say mean things about Maureen but she just wouldn't. Eventually it was teatime and I was hungry but also a bit worried about more interrogation from Mrs Bell. I decided to say, 'I don't really know,' to any questions about the B and B. We headed back to the kitchen but this time Christine's brothers, Kevin and Bryan, were there. I tried not to stare at sixteen-year-old Bryan. He was directly opposite me, his school shirt unbuttoned and the same thick black hair as Christine, a healthy mane around his shoulders. I wanted to grab a handful of it. I looked over at Kevin the Younger to stop myself imagining the feel of it in my hand and the heat from that open shirt. Kevin's chin was a dense angry landscape of spots, crusted and scarred. They spread upwards onto his cheeks and nose though there weren't quite so many there. He kept his eyes on his plate. His hair was greasy. Unbrushed. His shoulders hunched. He still had his coat on like he might have somewhere to go.

A large plate of buttered bread was in the middle of the table and a pot of tea and the boys were already reaching over and folding and stuffing the bread into their faces. Mrs Bell brought over large plates with chips, fish fingers and peas for us all but, apparently, she wasn't eating, just serving us. The boys grabbed knives and forks and started eating noisily, whole fishfingers went in at a time, chips were smashed between pieces of bread and gone in two bites, forkfuls of peas were glugged with ketchup and spooned in in rapid succession. I'd barely cut my food and they were pushing their chairs back, slurping the dregs from their cups and grabbing a *Penguin* biscuit as they exited the kitchen. All the while Mrs Bell kept up a singsong monologue over this bad behaviour detailing her day and asking unanswered questions about theirs.

'Sometimes I worry I won't be able to buy enough to feed them,' she said to their receding footsteps. She winced as the volume of the telly was turned up and a loud belch was heard followed by loutish laughter from both boys. She closed the kitchen door and sat, finally, carefully at the table, pouring herself a cup of tea.

'Now, girls, what have you been up to?' she smiled as if the boys were never there.

Christine showed her her nails.

'Jennifer brought nail varnish. It's lovely, isn't it? We did each other's. It's allowed at school as long as it's clear.'

'Oh it's gorgeous. Don't you look grown-up. Oh I can't wait until we can do all sorts of girly things together. My little angel,' and she pressed Christine's tiny white hand to her cheek and I was so jealous. My mother had never expressed the desire to do anything with me. Why was that?

I look at Mrs Bell's hands now, they are dry and old. One is linked through the handle of the mug of coffee, the other lies limp and lifeless on the garish blanket. They look lost. Detached. Her eyes are dull, like something is missing. How can someone have changed so much in such a short time?

'Come on,' Kevin says to me and I follow him down the hall to his bedroom.

It's dark in there, the curtains are closed.

'I keep them shut all the time because of the reporters. We've had them in the garden. Fuckin' nosy twats.'

He busies himself with his record player carefully selecting an LP, wiping it delicately with a cloth before setting it on the turntable. He gently nudges the needle across to the last track and slowly sets it down. A piano starts. Then briefly a man's voice. Then a woman wailing.

' 'S Pink Floyd,' Kevin says smugly, 'Dark Side of the Moon.'

I nod as if I know what he's talking about.

He picks up the black cover and stares at the triangle and rainbow of refracted light coming from it.

The woman is still wailing.

'I bloody love this song,' he murmurs, turning the LP cover over in his hands. ' 'S Bryan's LP. I've borrowed it. He doesn't really like it but I just listen to this song. *The Greatest Gig in the Sky*,' and he smiles sadly like Dad does when he's listening to the French women. Men are so soft.

Finally the record clicks finished but he jumps up and puts it on again.

I fish for my sweets in my pocket.

'*Black Jack*?' I offer.

'Ta,' he takes one.

We chew together. He is a bit slurpy and disgusting. The woman is wailing as if she is a long way away.

'So there's no words,' I say.

'Na. Don't need any,' Kevin says, wetly.

'Oh,' I nod again.

It's the first time I've been in an older boy's bedroom. It's very tidy. Much tidier than mine. Christine's school picture is lying flat on his bedside table. It's been cut out of a newspaper. It's grainy but definitely Christine's frozen and familiar smile.

I want to ask why it's there. Surely he doesn't need reminding what she looks like?

We finish my *Black Jacks*.

We listen to the wailing woman over and over until by the end I think I'll crack the record over Kevin's egg shaped head but I don't. I say I really like it and that *Pink Floyd* are great. I want to ask what a Floyd is but I don't. We haven't got much to say to each other and

Bryan isn't at home so I decide it's time to go.

'You could come back another time if you want,' Kevin says looking at his foot and twisting his mouth.

'Yes okay,' I say politely. He must be asking because he misses Christine, I think.

'Be quiet when you go out in case Mam's asleep,' he's already moving the needle across the record again.

'Will do. Bye Kevin. See you soon,' and I creep down the hall past the pink crocheted mound that is Mrs Bell and slip on my shoes and coat and get out of the terrible heat and misery.

I run home.

On Sunday no one's been out to play all day. There's still talk in the village of it Not Being Safe. Maureen won't come out and Andrea and Timothy Gallagher are too shy. I think they might be a bit more frightened of me than The Murderer. Dad has lit a fire in the sitting room and a log is hissing and spitting. The telly is on and Mum and Judy are cuddled up on one of the old deflated sofas. Dad is on the other, staring bleakly at the feeble flames. I flop down next to him. I think the sofa feels a bit damp under my hands. I try not to think about it.

Songs of Praise is just finishing. I realise the day is almost over and I've hardly spoken at all. 'Why did we move here Dad?' I ask.

'Because I couldn't live with your grandfather,' he sighs.

'David,' Mum says, softly. It's not that she's telling him off for telling me the truth; it's more like she's too tired to have the conversation.

'I see,' I say.

Judy gets up and changes channels. We watch the ads. Currently, I know every single word to every single ad. Judy thinks she does too but she doesn't. The fire is hurling shadows around the room. I don't like it. 'What will we do if no one comes to stay in the bed and breakfast?' I ask

'We'll do something else.' Dad replies, patiently.

'How long before we decide it's time to do something else?'

'I don't know.'

'Are we going to get proper heating?'

'Probably not.'

'Why not?'

'This place is far too big. It's too expensive.'

'But it's really cold.'

'You'll get used to it.'

'I don't want to get used to it.'

'It's good for you.'

'Why?'

'It will toughen you up.'

'I don't want to be tough.'

He smiles a little. 'None of us do, but you have to be.'

'My bedroom is too cold.' I have managed thus far not to sound too whiny as, behaving like a child is a sure-fire way of getting Dad to switch off, and Mum too come to think of it, however, here I realise my tone is changing. The misery of Christine and Mrs Bell and this cold, gloomy village are all filling the raw hole left where the root of my previous life has been ripped out. Where my world fitted snuggly and safely, this grating day has aggravated and irritated, straining and rubbing in all the wrong places. I am, in short, Very Unhappy.

My father says nothing.

'My bedroom is too cold.' I repeat, loudly and with a more petulant tone 'and I don't want to go to school. And I don't want to share a room. And I want to go back to a house with proper heating and no ice on the inside of the windows and a better life where there isn't a murderer.' I am building myself up into a state, my voice is rising, and tears are coming, with luck.

'Stop it Jen.' My mum is calm and detached. 'We are here. It's cold. You're safe. Stop being melodramatic. Now, you and Judy go and brush your teeth and I'll come and say good night.'

I don't even manage a tear. I am too cross. Judy gets up without a peep and skips across the revolting flowery carpet like a little lamb. I thunder out after her, I know Mum's tone and there's no point in trying to get anything from that. Why do I have to suffer because of their stupid ideas?

I catch up to Judy at the top of the stairs and give her a hard shove on her neat little shoulder blades. She falls forward on to her knees. I stop and tower over her, fairly tempted to give her a kick for good measure. She looks up at me, a little frown on her sweet face. 'It'll be alright Jen Jen. Don't worry.' She blinks her fair lashes.

I decide to kick her anyway.

Dad has taken Mum's three sketches off the kitchen wall and into Penrith and had them framed. They sit in ivory card mounts in pale gilt frames and they've been hung in the guest lounge. Despite Mum and Dad's disgust at the assumptions made by the newspapers, they reason that the guests may be interested in them.

The Castle is officially Open For Business and, thanks to Mrs Stoddart and Gillian it looks reasonably presentable. Dad has shifted an old desk and chair into the hall which has now become Reception. There is a bell to ring on it and a large guestbook to sign. Mrs Stoddart has collected a few leaflets for local attractions and these are thinly displayed on the desk, next to a garish vase of daffodils, too bright for the sullen eastern light of The Castle.

Mr Sheen has been liberally applied throughout, but it all still smells a bit like a church. A new, extremely large, fridge has been delivered to the back pantry. Neat fires are laid ready and waiting for the fizz of a match in every bedroom and the beds are made up with plump pillows and old-fashioned cotton bedspreads. Apparently Mum and Dad will be serving Full English Breakfasts to our guests every morning in the dining room. I ask if I'm allowed one too. Absolutely not, is the reply. I wonder how long it will be before Mrs Stoddart is cooking them or, worse still, me.

'Why did you buy The Castle with all the furniture in it?' I ask Mum as she sits and half-heartedly polishes a pile of brass bits and pieces Mrs Stoddart has gathered from around the place. 'Didn't the people who lived here before want it?'

'They moved to the South of France. It was a job lot. They took their favourite things I suppose, and anything that was valuable, and left the rest.'

This explained the various brighter squares of wallpaper in some of the rooms. 'Why did they move?'

'Well, The Castle had been in the family for generations but Mrs

Stoddart said the old man had just had enough. Wanted some sunshine and fun in St Tropez before it was too late. His three boys were off his hands. His wife was livid and so was his eldest son. He was going to inherit it all.'

'So did it cost a lot?'

'Well, it would have if we'd bought all the land but that's been snapped up by the farmers. We've only got The Castle and the gardens. It's taken ages to sell. Been empty a long time. No one wants to live here.'

'Really?' I say, sarcastically.

'I know it's hard to believe, isn't it?'

As she's been talking she's become more animated and is rubbing furiously at an ugly little dog sitting next to a tree stump. It doesn't seem to be making much difference. It's clear why the dog was in the cheap pile.

'How do people know to come here?' My next question is meant to gauge how much longer I will have to put up with this nonsense.

'We've placed an advertisement in *The Cumberland News* and,' she pauses for effect, '*The Lady*.' I have no idea what this means so look at her with, what I hope is, sneering resentment.

'Everyone reads *The Cumberland News* so that should attract anyone passing through and *The Lady* is taking care of advanced bookings.' She's very pleased with herself. She's finished with the dog and is looking at it more closely. It's baring its teeth. I wish I could.

I leave the kitchen.

Christine has been gone for five weeks and there have been a few days where she hasn't been mentioned in school conversation. Viper still offers up dreary prayers (fat lot of use they're proving to be) but we are back to the stultifying boredom that constitutes the daily grind of lessons. Christine's desk remains empty and no one touches her chair. I've given up thinking about asking to move there.

We watch The News all the time still but Christine features less and less. Patty Hearst has joined her kidnappers in robbing a bank so, in some ways, appears to be living some kind of Happily Ever After. I can't believe Christine is.

The clocks go forward and the days are lengthening and our first guests arrive. A serious middle-aged couple with bland faces who finish each other's sentences. They 'are going to'/ 'explore the lakes'; they 'love the' / 'countryside'; they've 'always been keen'/ 'amateur birdwatchers'.

Dad is actually quite impressive. He chats and smiles and carries the lady's suitcase upstairs to the nicest bedroom. After a little while they come down to the Guest Lounge and Dad brings them through tea and Victoria sandwich cake.

The weather is a little better so the room isn't quite so cold but they're both standing by the fire. I have brushed my hair and wander in as if I don't know they're there. They smile sweetly at me.

'Hello,' I say brightly, and I go and stand next to the sketches, where I take a long look at The Lost Child and then sigh heavily.

I see them look at each other.

I go over to their tea tray and the husband edges towards the sketches. 'Would you like me to pour your tea?' I say.

The woman rushes over, 'No, no dear. Please I'll do it. I wouldn't want you to,'

'burn yourself.' The husband concludes, still hovering by The Lost Child.

'I'm very careful,' I reply, 'and capable,' I add.

They both laugh a little but they are preoccupied by the sketch I can tell. They just can't find a way to bring them up. I quite enjoy their discomfort.

'I hope you enjoy the cake,' I say, 'It's very good. It was Christine's favourite,' and then I quickly turn my head away, delighted at my cleverness.

'Oh dear. Do you mean,'

'the little girl?'

'Christine?'

'Was she your friend dear?' They bat the words to and fro like it's *Wimbledon*.

I wait for a moment before I turn back. 'Yes, she was a very dear friend. And I'm very good friends with her brother now, actually.'

'Oh really?' the woman's eyes are getting bigger and she gulps greedily at her tea holding the cup and saucer up to her chin.

'How long,' starts the man, peering down me like a bird eyeing a worm.

'has it been?' his wife finishes. Slurp, slurp.

'Well, nearly five weeks, has it? I can't believe it's been that long. It's just been so terrible.'

'Of course it has, sweetheart,' she soothes and she reaches over and touches me softly on the knee like I'm a statue in the church. What she wants to say is 'Tell me everything. Spare no detail. That's why we're here,' but she can't. It would be rude.

'At first,' I begin, looking at each of them in turn, 'we just expected her to come back but the hours turned into days then the days became weeks and there's been no sign of her.' I had heard a news reporter say this a few days ago and had stored it up for future use.

'And how have,' he starts.

'her parents coped.' she finishes eagerly.

'Mrs Bell is a different woman. She used to be a Model Housewife. They run a B&B too, you know, and it was immaculate. And so was she. Beautifully turned out. Really looked after herself. But now...' I pause sadly.

'Yes.'

'Yes.' Tell us, tell us!

'She just sits all day on the sofa, drinking coffee. And brandy.'

A collective gasp.

'And...' I tantalise them.

'Yes?'

'Yes?' They lean in.

'She can't accept that Christine's been taken. She thinks she's run away. She screams if anyone says any different.'

'Oh Lord,' she says, 'that poor woman.' Her eyes are bright with delight.

'And...' There's more.

'Yes?' He can't believe it.

'Yes?' Neither can she.

'The eldest son Bryan has begun Underage Drinking. To forget. He is Out Of Control.' I shake my head in despair.

'Jennifer!' Dad's voice makes me jump. I have not heard him come in. His face is dark with disapproval. 'I think you should leave Mr and Mrs Cuthbert to enjoy their cake in peace.' He is glaring at me.

'Oh no,' she starts, she scrabbles a little at her collar.

'she's fine,' he finishes, still looking at me.

'We were just chatting about the poor little girl,' she encourages Dad, demurely. 'So awful,' she presses on, hopeful dad will add more juicy morsels to the gossip's bowl.

'Least said about that the better,' he dismisses and rebukes her in one swipe. He looks hard at me, 'Jennifer?'

'Okay,' I say, crossly and stomp out past him, hoping to make a quick exit but he catches me on the stairs.

'Don't you dare go spreading any horrible little stories about the Bells to anyone, young lady, do you hear me?'

'I wasn't saying anything?' I try to sound casual.

'I heard exactly what you were saying and I will not tolerate it.'

'It's only what's in the papers,' I attempt Judy's innocent tone.

'That is not in the papers and you know it. You respect the privacy of that family do you understand or you won't be allowed to go anywhere other than school. You've already done enough with your 'Lost Child' nonsense.' He really is quite angry which is an unusual state of affairs. He is hissing so the Cuthberts can't hear otherwise I think he would be bellowing at me.

'Well, at least that's bringing in a bit of money,' I raise my eyebrows at him. He glares and I think he might hit me, so I turn and run up the stairs.

When it's close to suppertime I walk quietly down the corridor to the kitchen and can hear Mum and Dad talking. The walls are slightly damp from whatever they've been boiling to eat and it's dark. I skulk and listen.

'... all about the Bells,' Dad is saying, 'Heaven knows what else she'd have come up with if I hadn't gone in to check on them.'

'She doesn't know about Pete and Daphne, does she?' Mum's voice is tense. I breathe more quietly.

'No, I don't think so. It's not in the papers. Yet.' Dad confirms.

'It's only a matter of time. Someone is bound to say something. For the right price.' Mum is resigned to the fact.

'He must feel sick about it. Though I don't think Hilda's taken it in from what I've heard. She's in her own world.' Dad sighs.

'Playing around while your daughter is being snatched though. No wonder he's in such a state,' Mum sounds disgusted.

'She's had dark glasses on every time I've seen her since, which hasn't been that often. Richard Robson's got old-fashioned views on keeping his house in order...' There's anger in Dad's voice.

'Probably why she was off shagging Pete Bell.' Mum gives a dry laugh.

'He's mean though, Richard. You can tell. I wouldn't like to meet him in a dark alleyway when he was looking for a fight.' I can hear Dad clattering the plates.

'Probably only batters women. That type usually do.' Mum's voice is tight and sneering.

'This is ready. I'll call the girls.' and suddenly Dad is in front of me. I jump away from the wall and try to look like I've just arrived.

'I'm starving. Is supper ready?' I ask, quickly, 'I've been thinking about my birthday. Am I going to have a party?' and I squeeze past him into the kitchen, hoping he hasn't realised I've eavesdropped the whole conversation.

'What do you think Mum?' I say. She's sitting at the table, flicking through one of Mrs Stoddart's *Woman's Weeklies*. I hear Dad walk away, up the hall to fetch Judy. 'Am I going to have a party for my birthday? It's only three weeks to go if you're going to organise anything.'

At home I had had some lovely affairs, a magician, a fancy dress, a trip up to London to the children's Unicorn Theatre. I had invited most of the girls in my class and some of the boys, and Mum and Dad's friends had come too and hung around chinking iced drinks and crunching salted peanuts whilst we played games and got overexcited and fell out. I'd always had a new dress and a lovely cake made by Granny. I didn't hold out much hope this year.

'I don't think it's a good idea to do anything too grand this year, Jen,' Mum barely looks up from the magazine.

'Why not?'

'Well it's hardly a time for celebrating, is it? What with Christine and everything.'

'But that's not fair. I mean, life goes on, doesn't it?'

She says nothing just keeps reading an article on *Perry Como's Christmas*.

'I'm sure Christine would've wanted me to have a party,' I try.

Mum looks up. 'Did you actually like Christine, Jennifer?' I am surprised by the question. Mum doesn't usually pay attention to anything.

'Of course I did,' I say, pretending to be angry, 'she was my best friend. Why are you saying such a stupid thing? It's just because you can't be bothered to organise a party for me, isn't it? Wait until November, I bet Judy gets one!'

Infuriatingly, she just goes back to the magazine, muttering, 'Set the table,' as she reaches for her box of cigarettes and lighter. She is the laziest person I know.

I crash over to the cutlery drawer and Dad reappears with Judy. I start to slam the knives and forks around the table, pushing Judy out of the way as I go.

'What's wrong with you?' Judy asks quietly.

'I suggested it might not be the best time to have an extravagant birthday party,' Mum drawls.

'Quite right,' Dad is dishing up Spaghetti Bolognese. 'We need spoons not knives, Jennifer.'

I snatch the knives from the table and hurl them back in the drawer whilst picturing them as hedgehog prickles stuck in Mother's back. I slide spoons across viciously in their place. No one comments but they catch them with accomplishment and begin the focused business of spaghetti twirling.

'What presents am I going to have then?' I whine, eventually.

'Something small. It's been very expensive getting everything ready for the guests.'

Well, great. Looks like turning eleven will be highly memorable. It wouldn't have been so expensive if they'd got off their lazy arses and done some work themselves instead of paying Mrs Stoddart and

Gillian. So, no party and a small present. Hurrah!

   We have arrived at the Easter holidays and I have completed a full
term at the horrible little school. This means Tillie Berman will be
home and I realise I've barely given her any thought nor started a
single letter to her. Worryingly, she hasn't written to me either. The
only time I have considered her is on one of my wanders past her
house. Today, the first day of the holidays, I think I'll try and catch up
with her.
   It's only been ten days since the Cuthberts arrived.
   Mum and Dad are going to bed early, sometimes before us.
   We are eating beans on toast for supper every day
   The Castle is now annoyingly alive with activity. Because it is
Easter next week and we are on The Doorstep To The Lakes plus we
have a Child Murder on our hands, nearly all our beds are full for the
next two weeks. At first this was seen as a tremendous success as the
phone rang with each new booking and the GPO arrived to install
another guest amenity – a payphone in reception - but now the reality
has become clear. Breakfasts can be demanded any time from 7 until
9.30 so Dad is constantly quietly cursing over a haze of blue smoke
from the *Rayburn*. Mum is now saying they have to get a dishwasher
as she has had to get out of her pigsty bed and help as Dad can't do it
all himself. Once the breakfasts have been served (with a smile) and
the guests have tottered off for their days out, with or without
requested packed lunches, beds have to be made, laundry done and
the bathrooms cleaned, carpets hoovered and cakes made for
afternoon tea arrivals ('Why did we start giving them cake David?
They don't need cake!'). It's hard work and Mrs Stoddart has had the
school dinners to do so Mum and Dad have had no choice but to Get
On With It. In short, they are both working, every day, for the first
time in their lives.
   They hate it.
   The same was always true when Granny and Grandad went on
their annual holiday. Mum and Dad never coped then. Whilst there
was a lifting of spirits that The Grown-Ups had gone, after a couple of
days everything began to crumble. Washing up piled higgledy-

piggledy in the sink; the cat yowled for food at all hours; milk bottles were left grey and unwashed and not put out clean each night; coffee cups lingered on the occasional tables and our toys steadily encroached across the carpets like a stealth army. The descent into bedlam continued until the day before Granny's return when *Mr Sheen* would be brought out and Dad would finally tackle the washing up, cigarette hanging from the corner of his mouth, one eye squinting against the smoke, a socked toe tapping to the crackling jazz on the record player whilst Mum flew around the house bitterly complaining about the amount of toys we had, threatening they'd all be chucked out unless they were returned to our bedrooms immediately. Then Judy and I would be dragged to Mrs Marne's, the laundry lady's house. This was usually a treat with Granny as we'd ride at the top on the front of the double-decker bus and there'd be cocoa and thin, spicy biscuits in Mrs Marne's kitchen whilst Granny and Mrs Marne chatted as the washing was done. Or we would go to do other shopping or sometimes up to Windsor Castle to see the Changing of the Guard. But Mum was just embarrassed by the whole affair. The kitchen felt colder, drab, chilly with steam. Mrs Marne kept trying to chat but Mum wouldn't really talk to her even though she'd known her since she was a little girl. Then there was the race for the bus and a march back up the hill to get everything put away before their return when we had to pretend the house had run like clockwork and we hadn't had egg and soldiers for supper every night. But Granny would be home and order would be restored and she would put on her hat and coat and go to the butcher's for chops and we'd all be very pleased she was back.

Whilst we've been at school we haven't been able to be roped in so on the first day of the holidays, I get up early and make a swift exit while breakfast is still on the go to make sure I have at least one day of freedom.

I stroll lazily down to Tillie's. It's a bright day, windy and fresh, with birds flying the wrong way. I try not to think about the first day of the last school holidays, my anger over Judy, missing out on going to Maureen's, my red car story being ignored. It seems like a long time ago but nothing has really changed since then. Christine's still gone. Mrs Bell is still mad. The Bermans haven't come back to the house.

I knew who Daphne and Richard Robson were but I didn't understand why Daphne was shagging Mr Bell. She was young and pretty in a Dolly Bird kind of way and Richard drove a sleek car too fast through the village which made some of the women tut. He dressed smartly, much better than the other village men, and worked in Penrith but there was talk about why they didn't have a baby.

Mr Bell was a red faced chap with a belly. He had a sensible car and three children. He was also going bald unlike Mr Robson who had a fine head of reddish blonde hair. How had Mr Bell managed to bed Daphne? I had heard that phrase on *Upstairs Downstairs* too. It sounded like something to do more with animals than people. Poor Mrs Bell though. Despite her delicious coffee, her husband had gone pleasure seeking elsewhere.

I have had no one to tell this latest piece of gossip to. It has burned away inside me, so much so I nearly told Judy and I try never to speak to her. My last chance is Tillie. I really hope they're here today.

As I round the corner to the house I can sense it is occupied but my heart sinks. There is a For Sale sign solidly planted by the gate. The car is there so I go through but with misery and half-heartedly. If they're moving, is there any point? But I have nothing better to do. I knock on the door and wait. The marvellous Gideon Berman answers the door and peers at me.

'Is Tillie in?' I say eventually.

'Yes,' he steps aside and I step in. Obviously we are not going to engage in chitchat.

The house is different.

'She's in the Orangery.' Mr Berman nods along the corridor and drifts off up the stairs. He was far more impressive the last time I saw him. I feel a little nervous as I walk through the comfortable drawing room and then the French doors to Tillie at the back of the house. I expect to find her on the floor playing cards, solitaire or something. She will look up and smile, pleased to see me. Perhaps she will jump to her feet and hug me. But when I push through the doors the room is empty. It's interesting to see the room in daylight but it's strange to be back. The last time I was here it was crowded with dark-suited men and police and all Tillie's sisters and Mr Berman had formally announced that Christine had Failed To Return Home after having tea at Maureen's. My first thought was that I should have been there and it was typical that I wasn't when the only exciting event to occur in the village since my arrival takes place. There had been much gasping and a few sobs and then I had announced I was supposed to have been at Maureen's last night too (a lie). As soon as I said this, the whole room changed from a bleak frozen tableau to a fluster of voices and activity with me at the centre. I had told them she was my Best Friend (also a lie) and burst into tears. The tears were a surprise even to me and Mr Berman had produced a smooth clean handkerchief from his pocket, patting the top of my head, like I was a dumb animal, as he placed it in my hand.

I am smiling at the memory of it all when Mrs Berman appears at the door.

They are packing. Mrs Berman appears with her hair protected with a fresh headscarf, her thick blonde fringe glistening in the morning sun. She looks adorable. I can't believe there's any dust anywhere in this gleaming palace.

'Oh hello Jenny. How are you?' she says this as if I have a terminal illness but doesn't wait for an answer. The packing is the priority. 'Tillie's in her room. Go on up,' and she smiles sweetly.

I knock on Tillie's door then open it. Her room is practically bare; her books and toys spirited away into crates piled in one corner but she is sitting cross-legged on the floor with a small collection of dolls and animals in a circle. A wicker basket is open and they are enjoying a tea party.

The day we found out Christine had disappeared, on the Saturday morning I'd finished the washing early. Having been assigned the job of family washerwoman, I had a weekly wrestle with the twin tub washing machine in the back kitchen. That day, Mum had put jumpers in so I had to use the mangle as I couldn't put them in the spinner. When I used the mangle, I pretended to be the maid in a Victorian drama with Mum as either the evil housekeeper or mistress of the manor. As I squeezed the jumpers through the smooth wooden rollers, I imagined tricking Mum into putting her hand in and all of her turning into Flat Stanley. I could fold her up and post her off to Timbuktu and have Mrs Bell as my mum instead. A proper mum. I kept the Water Heating Button on throughout the washes so, even though by the last wash it was filthy, the water was piping hot and the little back kitchen had warmed up nicely. I slung all the clothes on the dolly that hung from the ceiling over a little stove, and lit this before I left thinking it would be dry by teatime, more or less, and I could fold them and put them away. I was pretty sure no other kids in the village were washing their own clothes. 'Why should I do everyone's washing?' was Mum's response when I pointed this out to her.

'Because that's your job,' I had replied calmly.

She didn't get cross but just smiled. 'Oh Jen, it's 1974, not 1874. I've burned my bra.'

This didn't seem to be true as I was still washing them.

That morning in February I grabbed my coat and nipped out the back door and down through the village before I could be dragged into any more jobs. There was a persistent wind skirting down from the fells that frame the back of The Castle. It sliced through to my skin as I trudged down the frozen mud track despite my many layers.

It really was bleak midwinter. Few lights warmed any windows and the only sign of life was a disgruntled cat huddled on a stone gatepost waiting for the return of its owner. I was familiar with the geography of my friends' houses in this tiny, tiny place. Christine's house was at the bottom at the end opposite the school and Maureen was on the left as the dirt track curves in from the right. Christopher Robert lived in the big farm halfway down the right hand side and Andrea and Timothy in the tiny cottage next door. The pub was bottom left and Viper, our teacher, lived in a smart house next to Mrs Stewart's shop. The church was down the fork to the left at the bottom and I realised I hadn't ventured far down there.

I trudged past the hodgepodge houses as far as the church where the road became proper tarmac, albeit single track, and opened out into fields and space. The road took a turn to the left and I thought how dull the countryside was. The hedges were dark, criss-crossed, bare and unfriendly looking. There was no sign of any interesting birds. I couldn't even hear them singing. I couldn't hear anything except the wind.

I kept walking thinking I would turn back soon when a house

came into view. A very nice house on a little hill, set back from the road. It had a sprawling tree in the garden with a swing attached to it. This was most puzzling. All the children at school lived in the village so who lived here? I quickened my step and soon I was at the open five bar gate at the bottom of the short drive.

There were plenty of lights on in this house. A shining silvery car was parked in front of the garage. I could hear a dog barking excitedly. The front door opened and it made me jump as it was an unexpected and sudden noise. In moments many people had spilled out, all talking at the same time. They were warmly wrapped up against the winter wind in soft coats, bright scarves and bobble hats. They were smiling; I hadn't seen much of this in Cumberland. It was like a *Horlicks* ad. I was staring and continued so to do (we were not allowed to end sentences with prepositions at school; it is habit-forming).

A shaggy golden dog barked around the crowd of, I was counting nine or ten people, of varying sizes; they all seemed to be girls and were moving towards the silver car as the garage doors swung open revealing another dark car inside.

There was a straggler. About my size. She was hovering by the front door and she was looking directly at me, straight mouthed and stern. There was a squiggle of speech from her, coupled with the point in my direction, and she set off towards me. I took a step or two back from the gate. Her stride was determined and I already felt like an intruder. When she reached me I saw her wide set clear blue eyes and almost white blonde hair poking out from under her thick red hat. 'Hello. Who are you?' she said in a direct but not unfriendly tone.

'Jennifer Wentworth,' I managed with a confidence I didn't at that moment possess.

'I'm Tillie,' she replied with a small nod, 'Tillie Berman. I haven't seen you before.' She didn't have the broad accent of the village kids.

'We just moved here a few weeks ago,' I paused, 'I haven't seen you either at school.'

'We don't go to school here,' Ah. 'W'r'at boarding school.'

'Oh. Which one?'

'Harrogate. Harrogate Ladies College.'

'Oh,' I was a bit dejected by this news. 'Is it holidays?'

'No, it's an exeat.'

'I see,' I said but I didn't. I'd never heard the word before, 'I'm just out for a bit of a walk,' I added with a thin smile.

'We're going to buy sweets and comics for a treat.' She peered at me more closely, 'I could stay behind if you like. You could come in and play for a bit.'

'That would be nice. I'm quite cold,' This was working out very well.

We trotted back to the cars and Tillie informed her mother, who looked like a film star in a long, dark, fur-collared coat, we were staying behind. They had a housekeeper, Sarah, who was American, Tillie told me as she squelched off her wellies in the porch, who was at home. The house felt airy, bright, softly carpeted and very warm. I followed Tillie up the stairs to her pristine bedroom, which she clearly did not have to share, where she retrieved a large slab of chocolate from a dresser drawer, plonked herself on her bed and invited me to join her.

'I have five sisters,' she said, breaking off chocolate for me and cracking some between her teeth, 'There are six of us altogether. I am the second to last youngest. Ruthie is my younger sister. She's an elective mute,' I must have looked puzzled which I was, 'Ruthie never speaks.' Tillie said. 'Then my older sisters are Rachel, Hannah, Esther and Miriam. They're all teenagers. Rachel's the eldest, she's seventeen.'

She broke off more chocolate for me and crammed more in her mouth too. 'And we have a beautiful dog called Pasha.'

'Pasha,' I repeated, 'Yes I saw him.'

'He is called Pasha after the king of Persia who was famously surrounded by women just like he is.'

'That's a clever name for a dog. I've only heard of dogs called Fido and Spike and that sort of thing,' I flattered her, wanting her to like me.

'Actually he's not completely surrounded by women, there is my father here too,' and she looked a bit smug and pleased with herself, 'yes, my father is Gideon Berman,' and then she just looked at me with a little smile and I wasn't sure what she wanted me to say.

Tillie repeated, 'Gideon Berman,' and raised her eyebrows encouragingly. 'Haven't you ever heard of my father?!' she demanded, sounding haughty and cross.

'Er, no, no, I don't think so.' I was caught off guard.

'Well that's very surprising. He is a very famous author. You can read, can't you?' She looked at me as if I had just spat in her father's face.

'Yes I can read. I have many read many books including Charles Dickens and Charlotte Brontë.' I didn't tell her I found quite a lot of *Jane Eyre* a bit boring.

'Charles Dickens and Charlotte Brontë aren't *books*, they're authors,' she said, jutting her chin with a clever look on her face. I was worried I was not going to like Tillie.

'I know that,' I snapped back, 'You know what I meant.'

'These are my father's books,' she said, grandly moving towards a bookcase and running her fingers along a row of slim volumes in pastel colours. 'He gives each of us a signed copy every time one is published.'

I looked closely.

'It doesn't look like you've read them,' I said evenly.

'Of course I haven't read them. I'm not old enough. They're grown-up books. I'm not allowed to read them, yet.'

Tillie had a most annoying way of over articulating and emphasising words; she said 'allowed' as if she was a snake dislocating her jaw the better to eat a small mammal. I stared at her.

'If they were mine, I'd read them anyway. *Jane Eyre* isn't a children's book but I read that. There's a mad woman living in the attic. There's bigamy. It was great.' I was challenging Tillie.

She looked at me, frowning.

'Don't you want to know what your dad has written? Maybe he's written about you?' I looked at the titles. *Summer Casts A Shadow. No Time to Deny. David's Star. Little Bo Peep.* 'Look *Little Bo Peep*. That could be all about you.' She looked worried.

There was a gentle tap at the door and we both startled. An older, darker woman pushed open the door. She had a generous tray of milk and biscuits. 'Drinks and cookies for the two girls. Careful of the crumbs. You two play nice, okay?' She set the tray down on a table near the window and made to leave.

'Thank you Sarah,' Tillie said politely.

I waited for the door to close. 'Your housekeeper, I presume. How lovely. I can't believe there's room for anyone else here.' I had the upper hand. I was the bad girl even if Tillie did have a father who was a famous writer. I casually picked up a biscuit and walked slowly around the room making clear I was not going to be careful of the crumbs.

I lingered by a shelf with neatly stacked boardgames. They were arranged precisely and perfectly.

'Do you want to play *Monopoly*?' Tillie asked timidly.

'Yes, why not.' I said, generously. After all, I could hear the wind picking up outside. She wrestled the box out and we cleared a space at the table. We both relaxed a little. I liked the warm room and all her toys and pictures. I would have liked to be her friend and I was regretting being mean. The *Monopoly* game looked like it had never been played with. Our set had dog-eared Property cards and we'd used most of the money for other games. The plastic tray to keep everything tidy had been lost too so all the pieces just forlornly littered the bottom of the box in a muddle. Tillie's set sat neatly stacked and ordered. I watched her carefully count out the money and place the Chance and Community Chest cards on the board.

I was the top hat and she was the dog. We trundled round and round the board trying to collect as many £1 notes as we could. We nibbled at the biscuits and she told me they had been skiing in Switzerland after New Year and why her younger sister Ruthie might be an elective mute (deafness, shyness, badness) and I told her about The Castle and did impressions of Christopher Robert and Maureen which made her giggle.

At some point we heard the cars crunching up the drive, the doors slamming and lots of lively chatter spilling into the house as the rest of the family arrived back from their trip. No one came to check we were alright or to deliver any sweets. Tillie said nothing. We kept playing *Monopoly*.

'Do you like being at boarding school?' I asked.

'It's okay,' she shrugged as she shook the dice for the millionth time, 'I'd rather be at home.'

'My dad and my Auntie May went to boarding school while his mum and dad were in India. He says he liked it but I don't think he did. My Aunt May said he used to cry when he went back.'

'It's quite hard not to.' Her pale eyebrows crinkled. 'Come on. I'll show you round the house. I'm bored of *Monopoly.* '

We left her room and she opened various doors. If they were occupied we went in or we didn't depending on the sister. Ruthie stared at us blankly from her bed where she was completing a sticker book. Hannah and Miriam were doing each other's hair and Esther threw a shoe at Tillie. In Rachel's room, which was empty, she showed me a secret packet of cigarettes and a Zippo lighter. We raised our eyebrows at each other. Her mum and dad had their own bathroom off their bedroom. Tillie showed me a proper first-aid kit in the cupboard under the sink. There was a chunky box of plasters. We chose one each and rolled up our jeans and stuck them on our knees. I love the smell of plasters.

We went downstairs to The Orangery. I had never been in an orangery before or even heard the word and Tillie was obviously very smug about this smart glass room with its cream tiled floor and soft squishy sofas.

'We have our Christmas tree in here, even though we're Jewish,' she said and she showed me a photo on a wooden dresser of a fancy tree with a skirt of presents and all the girls standing next to it. I had never seen a tree like it except in fancy London shops, nor had I ever seen so many presents.

'You're Jewish,' I said.

'Yes, well Dad was born Jewish and Mum converted but we don't really practice.'

My experience and knowledge of Jewish ran to *Fiddler on the Roof, The Sound of Music,* Fagin and *The World at War*. I wondered if it was too early in our friendship to ask about the Holocaust. I decided that it probably was.

There was a clock in the Orangery. It was later than I thought.

'I'd better be getting back Tillie. I've been here ages.' Tillie's face changed.

'Yes, we'll be leaving soon. After tea anyway.' She did look sad.

'It's not because you're Jewish,' I add hastily.

'What? No of course not,' she smiled a little bit, 'Let's go and finish the chocolate first, shall we?' and I nodded.

Back in her room Tillie produced the chocolate and began long stories about different girls at her school and who was friends with who and what Amelia had said to Hannah about Frances and how Frances wasn't going to stand for that and who had caught flu and been in Sick Bay and I just ate the chocolate, which was delicious, and thought it all sounded like *Mallory Towers* but without a proper story.

Finally she asked about me and I did impressions of Christine's brothers eating their tea and Maureen adoring her pets and she laughed in a polite but not uncontrollable way. We hit a bit of a lull and she got up and looked out of the window. I was worried I was not going to be entertaining enough for her. I cast around for something to say. She was now the only girl I wanted to be friends with in the village.

'Tell me more about your sisters?' I came up with and this was perfect as one of the older two had a boyfriend and Tillie began to tell me about it. She was in full animated flow. His name was Joel and Tillie over articulated his name as if he was called Joe Elle, which I found quite annoying, when we heard Mrs Berman calling us both. Her voice did not sound happy. I expected to be in trouble and wondered if the chocolate had been snaffled but Tillie looked merely perplexed and innocent. She clearly was not a naturally deceitful child.

We padded along the hall and made our way downstairs to be told that Christine had disappeared and much, much later that night I briefly thought in bed about that lovely warm home and having a Mum who had the foresight and care to have a whole box of plasters in the house. Lucky, lucky Tillie I thought, and poor, poor me.

Today, despite her marvellous mother and famous father, Tillie appears forlorn. 'We are moving to Holland,' she announces, as she pours tea for a bedraggled bear who has lurched forward onto his empty plate.

'Holland?' I squeeze in between an over-stuffed golliwog and a ringleted doll in maroon velvet.

Tillie formally passes me a tiny cup. I nod acknowledgement.

'Father says we cannot live here a moment longer. Not after all that Business In The Village.' She is practically crying.

'What Business?' I say, delicately sipping my tea. It's very good.

'They thought he was the murderer because he is foreign. They came here, a whole crowd, after the pub shut. The police were called but you could tell some of them believed it too. Mummy was beside herself. We had to leave, there and then. They smashed a window. Threw something through it. It was horrible. The things they shouted.' She shakes her head.

'What sort of things?' I offer my cup for a refill.

'Filthy Jew. Where have you buried her? You must like little girls, you've got a house full of them.'

'Oh Tillie,' I sympathise. It does sound quite scary

'Mummy said she thought they were our friends but Daddy said no one is ever really a friend when something like This happens. So we went to a hotel and then sailed over to Oma's, my granny's, near Utrecht, the next day. We are renting somewhere until Father decides where we are going to live.' She replenishes the toys' cups and passes round tiny paper cakes.

'Will you keep coming to school in England?' I ask.

She shrugs, 'Don't know. Depends on where we end up. I love this house. I don't want to have to learn another language. We're always moving. Always changing schools.'

I don't really know what to say.

'This is a very nice tea set,' I opt for.

'Thank you,' she says politely.

'They really don't know what's happened to Christine,' I say, 'There's been loads of searches and a reconstruction and no one's found anything.'

'I know,' she is bored by this. She sips her cup and looks out of the window, then pats the bear gently on the head.

'I went to see Mrs Bell,' I say lightly.

'Really?' Tillie is interested.

'Yes, Kevin invited me.'

'Really?' Tillie doesn't believe me.

'Yes. I came up here to see if you were around and he was sitting on the gate in the next field and then we got chatting and he said come home and see Mum so I did.'

'And how was she?' Her eyes are wider.

I nibble my cake a little. 'She's gone mad.'

'Really!' She leans over her teacup.

'Yes. Won't believe Christine's been murdered. Sits and boozes all day. No make-up. And Mr Bell was shagging Daphne Robson when Christine got snatched.'

'No!' Tillie drops the tiny teapot.

'Yes. Shagging another man's wife while his daughter is being dragged into a van kicking and screaming. No wonder Mrs Bell's gone mad.'

Tillie is looking a bit disgusted.

'But Mr Bell, he is so blotchy and tubby.'

'I know and Daphne is so little and pretty.'

'How did they manage to...'

'Surprised he didn't squash her with his big jelly belly!' I say and I smile and Tillie giggles, 'she'd be lying squidged like an ant under his great big roly-poly tum. 'Oh Pete get off you're squashing me', I make my voice all squeaky and flutter my eyelashes, then I make my voice all gruff and deep, 'I can't Daphne, hang on, I'm having it off,' and Tillie and I fall about with laughter. We both make Daphne and Peter noises which make us giggle more but I don't think either of us are quite sure what Daphne and Peter were actually doing.

It cheers us up though.

After we've calmed down a bit Tillie says, 'So, what was Kevin like?' and she smiles as if I have a big secret to tell her.

'He had a very tidy bedroom,' I reply honestly.

'You were in his bedroom?' This is apparently big news.

'Yes, we ate sweets and listened to the same song over and over again.'

'Mummy won't let any boys in the bedrooms. She says they're Not To Be Trusted.'

'I don't think anyone cared. Mrs Bell had had some brandy and Mr Bell wasn't there. It was a bit boring really. We didn't really talk.'

'Did he kiss you?' She is coy again.

'No!' I am horrified.

'Did he try?'

'No!' This is all getting a bit annoying. I think this must be the sort of conversation her older sisters have. I think Tillie can tell I'm cross as she goes quiet for a bit and then starts to clear away her tea party.

'Do you worry about the murderer?' she says, eventually.

'Not really,' I say.

'I would,' she says, darkly.

'Why?'

'Well it's been really easy for him to take Christine, hasn't it, so why wouldn't he come back here and take another girl? In a little while, I mean. There's hardly any police around here now, are there? And they're not clever enough to have caught him so he may as well come back for another. Don't you think?'

'No I don't think,' I say crossly, 'Don't you worry about crossing the North Sea in a boat?'

'No,' she says, quietly.

'I would,' I say, 'if it sinks and you end up in the water, you only last ten minutes before you get hypothermia and die. It was on *Tomorrow's World*.'

Her mouth is open.

I stand up. 'Well, good luck wherever you're going to live. It's been nice knowing you,' and I leave.

I run down the stairs and out the front door, crunching down the gravel path and out onto the road as quickly as I can before Mrs Berman can catch up and reprimand me for upsetting Tillie. Stupid tea party. We're nearly old enough for secondary school. We're too old for dolls.

I walk briskly up the road towards the church when I see two figures standing by the lychgate. Now there is the start of buds on the bare branches of the hedges, it's a bit more difficult to make out who it is, but they are grown-ups and they're arguing, and it's a bit of an odd place to be doing it. Why aren't they arguing at home? Aren't they worried about what God will think. As I get closer, both of these questions become irrelevant, as I see the grown-ups are Mr Bell and Daphne Robson. Mr Bell is holding her arm quite tightly, like she's about to skitter away, and she's fidgety and her hair is all messy and her voice is very high-pitched. I really want to hear what they're saying but I'm quite scared of what will happen if they catch me. Mr

Bell is a big, beefy chap and I look at his fat, sausage fingers around her skinny arm and I don't know how I'm going to get past without them seeing me.

'I just need to see you for a bit. Christ, I'm not asking for much,' he's saying into her face.

'I can't Pete. I daren't. You know what Rick's like? You know what he did last time? I need to go.'

'But I miss you, kitten, I need you, I need some warmth,' he sounds like he's going to cry.

Daphne Robson is looking at him now. 'I can't take the chance. It was fine when no one knew but now it's all over the village and what if the papers get hold of it. There's no point pretending Pete. We can't ...' but she turns her head away and the wind surges through them and I can't hear the rest of what she's saying. I hang about for a minute hopping from one foot to the other but it's very cold.

I decide I have to make my presence known. I start to hum, then gradually build up to singing quietly then more confidently and then I begin to walk past, deliberately looking at the opposite side of the road. They startle and rush up the path to the church, her with tiny steps and him stomping along next to her, like a tottering showgirl and a galumphing, trained animal. They disappear around the back of the church.

I decide to call on Kevin. Anything to put off going back to The Castle and getting roped in to the inevitable jobs that are going to be my holiday treat.

I knock confidently on the door and eventually Bryan answers. He has no shirt on. Just jeans. His chest is smooth. His black hair is past his shoulders. It's wet. He must have just got out of the bath. My confidence shrinks a little. 'Is Kevin in?' He looks at me then smirks a bit. He keeps looking, eyes glinting, and shouts for his brother. Then he disappears back up the hall.

Kevin arrives, looking sad.

'Hi,' I say brightly, 'I thought I'd come and see how you are.'

He looks like he's really thinking about the answer to this question. Eventually he says, 'I'm okay.'

'Good,' I say.

There is more silence then he says, 'Do you want to come in?' and he says it like it will be alright so I say 'Okay,' and I follow him into the once lovely kitchen which is now filthy. I gather Mrs Bell is no better, judging by the smell of stale fat and unwashed plates. The men of the house are yet to take matters into their own hands.

'Should I wash up for you Kevin?' I say.

He looks at the sink and seems a bit surprised by my offer.

'Na. Don't bother. Do you want a coffee?'

'Okay.'

I can't think of anything to say as he makes us both a cup so I pretend to be interested in the photos on the wall. I am anxious and excited at the thought that Bryan may reappear at any time. He puts the coffee down on the heavily ringed table. The side of my hand touches it. It is very sticky. No bedroom today then or chat with Mrs Bell.

We sit.

'How's your mum?' I say.

'Same.' He slurps the coffee. His spots look worse. His hair is wet with grease. He smells. Really unpleasant. Not like Bryan.

I sip my coffee. It's awful.

'Any news on Christine?' I ask him in my most sympathetic voice.

'No. The police are useless bastards.' Today is obviously not a good day.

We drink.

'Are you doing anything over the holidays?'

'Like what?' His answer is tetchy.

'I don't know. Going away? Relatives coming to see you?'

'No.' He sounds glum.

I cast my eyes around the room. Nothing to help out here.

We drink.

The front door slams hard and Kevin jolts.

The bulk of his father appears, breathing heavily through his nose, face more florid than usual, eyes bulging.

'Alright Dad?' Kevin says warily. Mr Bell looks at me, closely, frowning.

'What are you doing here? What's she been saying?'

'Nothing,' I say quickly.

'She came for a coffee,' Kevin says, at the same time.

I smile as innocently as I can. Kevin looks both embarrassed and annoyed. Mr Bell stares at both of us.

'I just came to see how Kevin was. I've been to see Tillie Berman this morning. She's moving to Holland so I thought I'd call in on Kevin. That's all. I'm sorry Mr Bell. If it's a bad time I'll go. We haven't really been talking about anything much,' I stand up. I'm very convincing.

Mr Bell looks like he's going to cry. He takes it a gulping breath.

'No, no, no. I'm sorry Jenny. I don't know what's got into me. No, you sit down love. Listen, I'm sure I can find some biscuits here.'

'There aren't any Dad, haven't been any for weeks. I keep tellin' you,' mutters Kevin.

Mr Bell ignores his son and begins to scrabble in the cupboards, opening several tins and scattering them on the cluttered worktop when he finds them empty.

'No biscuits,' he is surprised by this turn of events. He faces us, digging in his pocket. 'Here Kevin,' he says, producing a grubby, softened £1 note, 'you to go to the shop and buy some sweets or biscuits or whatever you like, for you and Jenny. Whatever you like, you hear?'

We stand up, taken aback by the generosity.

He is looking at me and I know he's thinking of Christine. He gulps the air like a drowning fish and dives out of the room, having thrust the money into Kevin's hand.

Kevin grins. 'Come on,' he says.

We march across the green, driving into the wind. I wonder if we're getting 50p each but don't say a word. Kevin is like a dog straining at the end of a lead. He hasn't bothered to put the note in his pocket and I see it flap flimsily against the weather. His knuckles are white though so he has a tight hold.

Mrs Stewart is dragging on the end of the cigarette as we clatter into the shop. She peers at us, suspiciously.

We huddle together; Kevin seems smaller. He inhales noisily.

'Dad wants ten *Embassy Number Six*,' he blurts.

Oh.

'Does he now?' Her slow Scottish drawl has a wheeze underneath it. She takes another drag. 'He usually has *Benson & Hedges*.'

'Does he?' Kevin slaps the money on the counter, 'I don't know.

He just sent me over.'

Mrs Stewart looks at the note. It carries some weight.

'And he said we could get sweets if there's any change?' He is sounding more confident.

Mrs Stewart doesn't move. Kevin sighs.

'Bryan would've come but Mam's not so good,' and then he sniffs. I am very impressed. I put my hand on his shoulder.

Mrs Stewart leans over and spiders the note with her bony fingers, never taking her eyes from Kevin.

'11p each,' she says, and turns to get the cigarettes from the shelf behind her. Kevin gets a box of matches for 3p and a quarter of pear drops and I choose a *Milky Way* and the rest in liquorice shoelaces.

We walk slowly away from the shop not daring to look back.

'Where are we going?' I say.

'Somewhere out of the rain,' Kevin says, looking up at the sulking sky.

'There's stables and sheds at The Castle,' I test.

'Okay,' he replies and walks with more purpose.

We choose one of the old potting sheds. There's a couple of wooden stools and chairs and a bit of thin light from the very dirty window. We're careful not to be seen from the house. It's a bit like being in a kids' drama on telly. I wish Kevin was a bit better looking and more talkative though.

We wipe cobwebs and muck from the seats and sit opposite each other and Kevin gets out the fags. He takes off the cellophane and slowly pulls out the foil wrapper to reveal the neat little rolls snuggly tucked in their bed. He takes one out, then offers the packet to me. I accept, wondering when I should let on I've never attempted smoking before. I am reasoning with myself that just about everyone does it, so how hard can it be. Kevin opens the matches, strikes and lights his, it flares vivid orange and crackles and he expertly blows out the match with the smoke from this first puff. I want to applaud. He takes another drag and then sets the fag down on an upturned flower pot and gets another match out for mine.

Enough is enough.

'I haven't done this before,' I admit.

He looks at me and takes my cigarette. 'It's okay. I'll light it then you can smoke it.' He strikes the match and draws on the fag, then passes it back to me.

'Just suck, then breathe in. It's easy.'

'Okay.' I take it and I can feel the heat of the tip on my skin. I put it between my lips and I'm thrilled with myself. I suck hard and take an enormous breath. It is the most horrible experience of my life thus far. My throat closes with the heat and I choke and cough. The taste is disgusting and I want to be sick. My eyes and my nose run. I stand up, coughing and retching, knocking over my chair, not able to see, my lungs hurt from the brief invasion rudely endured.

Kevin is laughing. A lot.

I try to calm down. Eventually I manage to swallow and wipe the tears from my face.

He offers me the cigarette again.

'This time just take a little puff and a little breath in,' he says, 'You're not trying to swim a length underwater.'

I feel humiliated and want to grind the fag into his spotty face. I take the cigarette and have another go.

More coughing, spluttering, watering eyes. It is horrible. Why do people do this? I feel dizzy and sick.

More laughing from Kevin, between happy puffs on his fag.

'I don't want any more,' I say and offer mine back to him, 'It's horrible.'

'You'll like it next time,' he says cheerfully, 'Dad says it's like that with beer. It's horrible at first but you grow to love it.'

'My throat hurts,' I croak.

Kevin is looking around, 'I like it in here. It smells good.'

Maybe he's lost his mind but he is the most happy I've seen him. He finishes smoking my cigarette, then says, 'Let's light a fire,' and he begins to gather up little bits of sticks and paper and puts them in a plant pot. He pushes open the little window to let the smoke out, then sets a match to it and happily feeds the flames.

I wish we had the wailing woman to listen to because we have nothing to talk about. While I eat my sweets, I watch him smoke all the cigarettes one after the other then quietly vomit into an old metal watering can in the corner. It's a great afternoon.

I am dragged into the hectic but dull world of the Bed and Breakfast. Surprise, surprise Mum has a series of terrible headaches and can't get out of bed most days, so Judy and I are roped in as I knew we would be. 'Let's make it a game like on *Little House in the Prairie*,' Judy gushes 'these can be chores that Pa has given us.' We are washing up. I elbow her hard in the ribs and flick dirty water in her face and her smile dissolves. She is so pleasingly easy to crush. I have been solidly moaning at every opportunity since Dad woke me up at seven o'clock this morning. I'm hoping he'll get sick of me and banish me to the village.

He appears at the door with laundered sheets.

'Jennifer. Bedrooms please. Change the blue room, the pink room and the garden room.'

'Oh for God's sake, I hate changing beds!' I throw the washing up brush into the water, splashing Judy again. Like a dog, she doesn't complain.

'You barely change our sheets. Why do they have to have their beds changed all the time? They're only sleeping in them.'

Dad is saying nothing but waiting patiently. Actually not patiently, just waiting. He looks really fed up. Eyes dark, skin sallow as putty. He looks tired. It's his own fault though for taking on this stupid bloody Castle.

I shove Judy again, in the passing, as well as a chair. 'What's wrong with Mum anyway? Drank too much wine again? This is supposed to be my holiday. I'm not supposed be working. I need a rest. It's not Victorian times you know. This stupid Castle was her idea - she should be making the bloody beds. Lazy bitch.'

Dad put the sheets down, catches my arm and slaps me hard across the face. I hear Judy shriek but I don't make a sound. I'm too surprised. From the look on his face, Dad is too. He's never hit me before. As far as I know, he's never hit anyone.

I look him in the eye.

'Was it you who murdered Christine?' I say as calmly as I can.

Judy begins to sob like a stupid baby.

A terrible look crosses Dad's face that makes my tummy turnover. He really looks at me. Closely. As if he's finally seen me. Like a tiger. Hunting.

I don't like it.

I stare back.

'Make the beds,' he says very quietly and turns and walks out of the kitchen softly, with no fuss or noise as if nothing has happened.

I can't feel any pain in my cheek. I hope I'll have a blackeye. I turn and look at Judy.

'Why did you say that?' she blubbers, her face messy with tears.

'Because he shouldn't have slapped me.' I feel tired. I hate The Castle even more, the cold, damp air inside, the hostility of the place. Dad is changing.

I grab the sheets and thump up the stairs hoping I'll wake up Mum. As I go past her room, I bang into the door viciously. In the first room, as I strip the bed, I imagine her shock if I were to take the solidly neat pile of laundered sheets and place them over her pretty face. I imagine her milky legs thrashing and tangling in her bedsheets as she struggled for air, her freckled arms whipping and reaching, fingers grasping trying to free herself but no, I would be too strong. I will punish her forever for what she's done to me. For what I have become; her scullery maid. I picture myself laughing over her blueish lips and dead glassy eyes, tossing my head back triumphantly. Then I picture Dad at the door, then Judy, then the solemn detective and my dream isn't so much fun anymore. I sit down on the half-made bed and I feel sorry for myself. I look at the stupid guests' belongings scattered around and at the blue sky outside. I am determined I will leave here and my Mother as soon as I can.

We head into the last term of primary school with Christine's chair still empty, an unadorned shrine, an unmarked grave for a lost girl. There is no news, no new leads and it looks like everyone has given up hope. The reporters have dwindled and even Mrs Bell has been glimpsed once, at church, clinging onto Mr Bell's arm. 'Life must go on,' people sigh sadly to each other as they steal a glance at the still drawn curtains of the Bell's bungalow.

We find a dead bat in the girls' toilets at school. After lunch on my first day in January, I told Christine I needed the loo. 'I'll show you,' she had said and I had followed her in confusion outside, around the back of the school and through a latched wooden door.

'The loos are outdoors!' I had almost shouted as I took in with horror three stalls with heavy black seats and long iron pull chains.

'Yes,' Christine had said cheerfully, as if this was perfectly normal.

Consequently it is no real surprise to find visiting wildlife when we go to relieve ourselves. The bat is unusual however. It is inky black and soft as a kiss and so light you hardly know it's in your hands. It is all curled up like Dracula asleep. I'm the first one brave enough to pick it up. Andrea squeals.

It is tiny and perfect.

'Must've flown into the wall,' I say.

'I thought they had sonar radar?' says Maureen

'Maybe it was ill. Or old,' says Andrea.

It's a mystery. We take it out onto the playground for the others to see. They are suitably impressed.

'Let's open it's wu wu wu wings out,' says Timothy Gallagher, eagerly.

I put it down carefully on the tarmac and tenderly take one pointed tip concertinaed over its tiny body. Maureen takes the other wing and I steady it and we gently pull. They stretch out magically diaphanous and intricate and fragile and so enormous in comparison to its tiny body and then we gasp. Clasped to the chest of the bat is a tiny baby. It is a mother. Maureen and I let the wings go and they slowly fold back in.

I feel a bit sick. It's like the wildlife programmes but up too close. I can see the close-cropped velvet fur and the tight shut eyes and now I know there is a little baby bat in there. I don't want to pick it up again. I can feel the texture of its wing, the resistance as I pulled, on my fingers. I want to wash my hands with the horrid green soap and cold water in the loos.

'What shall we do with it? 'Maureen says.

'Flush it down the loo.'

'Put it on display.'

'Look at it under my microscope.'

'Give them a funeral.'

'Yes bury them somewhere.'

I get up. 'I'm going to wash my hands, you can do what you like with it.' I try to sound like I don't care but really, I want to cry and I'm cross that I feel like this. Horrible, hard place with nasty nature always there. What happened to pavements and pets on leads and everything being contained and no horrible surprises?

I leave them to it and as I'm drying my hands on the rough roller towel, I hear the bell ringing. I take my time. Everyone is inside and sitting in silence by the time I get to my place. I don't know what they decided to do. I don't want to know.

Andrea has asked Maureen and I round for tea and, even though she's much younger than me and barely has a word to say for herself, I accept as there's nothing else to do. It's one of the first warm days we've had and we're all feeling a bit giddy as we're let out of school, enjoying the heat of the stronger sun as, for once there's no wind skidding down the village off the fells to cool it.

Unusually, there are quite a few people out and about. Maureen's mum is stabbing at her flowerbeds while a couple of the younger Kirbys push a little pram bumpily up and down the track in front of the house. There's a cluster of older lads stretched out on the grass at the bottom of the green by the bus stop too. I can hear the tinny thread of a portable radio they've got with them. Richard Robson is cleaning his bloomin' sports car. Again. He's got shorts on and there's a couple of women standing on the opposite side of the green watching him and his lion's mane of hair. As we get closer he looks over at them and blows them a kiss. I'm sure he should be at work. He spends most of his time zipping around in that car. Or cleaning it. I wonder what his job actually is.

We trip down the green together with an unexpected sense of freedom. Timothy is buzzing about, bouncing a football on the road and talking to himself as we walk through the long grass. Timothy loves football but sadly has little obvious talent. He is keeping up a rambling stammering commentary as he knocks the ball from toe to toe and is grinning over at us as he trots on zig-zagging so he doesn't get too far ahead. I think he might fancy Maureen.

'And that's a g g g good save by Clemence,' he says, 'and now it's L l l liverpool on the attack as we g g g go into the last minute of this exciting FA c c c cup final.' He puts the ball down and kicks it a bit in front of himself and then runs after it. When he catches up to it he stops and turns around. 'And that's the Liverpool captain Emlyn Hughes to Tommy Smith,' he says and kicks the ball really hard at Maureen. It hits her on the leg and she shrieks and nearly falls over. Timothy looks a bit cross.

Andrea bends down and picks up the ball. 'G g g give it here,' says Timothy, 'p p p pass it over here.' Andrea drops the ball then does a kind of hopping on the spot before she swings her leg as hard as she can at the ball. Her shoe comes off and flies through the air towards Timothy while the ball rolls slowly into the Eternal Puddle, so called because it never ever disappears no matter how hot and dry the summer is.

'Get my shoe,' shouts Andrea and starts to run after it. Timothy has watched the shoe land beside him and is now looking dejectedly at the ball as it settles in the first heavy mud patch under the water. Andrea tries hopping a few times and then loses her balance and puts her sock down in the thick, still damp grass. She hops another couple of times and I can see mud clinging to her sole. Timothy recovers the ball gingerly from the puddle and kicks it ahead of him again. 'And it's Heighway on the w w w wing,' he says. 'He goes past one man, past two men.' He kicks the ball hard in the direction of Andrea's house. 'And he crosses to Toshack,' he shouts and runs as fast as he can after the ball which is heading towards the road.

Andrea retrieves her shoe and the three of us stop walking to watch Timothy as he stumbles over the ball and nearly hits his head on the road. 'And Toshack heads it down to Keegan,' he is very excited now and very loud, 'And Keegan shoots and scores,' screams Timothy as the ball cannons into air.

We watch the ball's inevitable trajectory towards Richard Robson's car. It is a tremendous kick, powerful and confident, quite unlike Timothy who stands forlorn, mouth gaping, as his filthy ball splatters onto the front of the sleek bonnet of Mr Robson's Pride and

Joy, bounces up and catches the windscreen and slithers back down across the corner of the boot. There is a sickening moment of silence when I quite want to shut my eyes before Richard Robson turns his attention from the alarmingly muddy smears on his gleaming car to little Timothy Gallagher who remains rooted to the spot, a tiny terrified scarecrow. Mr Robson strides over, long paces on his gingery hairy legs, strong arms jabbing and pointing and roaring at him, 'What the bloody hell are you doing? You stupid little moron, that's my car! That's my bloody car! Are you blind? You cretin, you stupid fuckin' cretinous little prick! I'm gonna bloody kill you! I'm gonna skelp your arse! Do you hear me?' And his voice is so loud. And his face is terrifying. His eyes are black with rage and he's upon Timothy in seconds and has him by the arm and then has hold of his shirt by the neck and is bellowing in his face and has lifted Timothy practically off the ground so his toes are pointed like a ballet dancers and are just scuffing the grass. Andrea is whimpering and Maureen has hold of my dress and we've all moved over towards Timothy and the raging Mr Robson even though we know we can't do anything to help.

'You bloody kids, you just do whatever you bloody well like. Bloody vermin the lot of you.' Timothy's face is white and slack. He is such a little scrap of nothing. He can't stand up to this monster who is bawling into his face. I really want my dad. I really want this to stop. 'There's the whole fuckin' green, the whole fuckin' green to kick your stupid ball on but you kick it at my car, you bloody idiot. I've been cleanin' that car for a fuckin' hour, a fuckin' hour just for you to kick your shitty fuckin' ball all over it, you little...'

'Put him down!' There's someone behind Mr Robson. I can't see his face. 'Put him down, now. You're hurting him. Leave him alone you fuckin' bully.'

This enrages Mr Robson even further. He drops Timothy on the grass who sprawls where he's landed, lifeless, winded, a rabbit that's been shaken by a dog. 'What business is it of yours?' He turns his fury on Bryan Bell, unchecked he shouts into Bryan's face now but Bryan is as tall as he is, not a little boy. He's only sixteen but he's furious.

'Leave him alone. He didn't do it on purpose. He's just a kid.' Bryan stands his ground and shouts back. He doesn't take his eyes off Mr Robson. He's in his school uniform but he's got his shirt unbuttoned and his sleeves rolled up. He looks strong. Young. Powerful.

Richard Robson drags the back of his hand across his mouth. He is weighing up the situation. He stands staring at Bryan. It's one thing to pick on little Timothy Gallagher but to have a go at Christine Bell's brother is another matter.

And there are half a dozen of Bryan's mates standing by to help if needs be, including Jason Thwaite who's quite a bit older and has been in trouble with the police for fighting. He doesn't live in our village. He's ugly and rough looking, all thick black eyebrows and dirty, crooked, snarling teeth.

'Don't think you can tell me what to do,' Mr Robson says, but more quietly, and he turns to Timothy who's still crumpled on the ground, 'Youse keep away from my car,' he spits out and he walks away. Timothy's football lies in his path. He kicks it viciously as far down the green as he can. Then he disappears inside his house, slamming the door behind him.

One of Bryan's mates jogs off down the green after the ball and Bryan hunkers down next to Timothy and speaks quietly to him. Timothy does a lot of slow head shaking and then some nodding and wiping of his face with his mucky hands. Eventually Bryan helps him up and they head off together towards Andrea's house and we follow them, Andrea snivelling quietly and Maureen grimly silent. I look over to where the women stood who were ogling Richard Robson. They've gone. Maureen's mum has disappeared too. In fact, there's no one to be seen but us kids.

At Andrea's gate Maureen rallies a little, 'Thanks Bryan, he's a nutter, isn't he? I thought he was going to kill Timothy.' Timothy is up the path and at his front door, tears bubbling in his chest. He nods as we look at him again.

Bryan shrugs, 'S'ok. He only picks on women and kids doesn't he? Fuckin' coward,' and he turns away to his mates.

I really want to say something to him too but nothing comes to mind. I watch him as he strolls off back across the green to the bus stop. I wish I was old enough to go and sprawl on the grass with all those boys and drink cider and listen to the radio and look moody rather than have to go into Andrea's and listen to Maureen's wide-eyed version of what just happened relayed over and over to Andrea's bovine mother. But there aren't many choices in the back of beyond when you're nearly eleven.

Maureen tells me they let the grass on the green grow long every year and then there's a haymaking day when it's cut and baled all in one go. It's a day the whole village looks forward to. The kids drag all the bales together and make a castle and two of them are crowned Hay King and Queen. They set up a pig roast on the school playground and The Lamb rolls up kegs of beer and crates of pop. Everyone brings their own chairs and blankets and it's like a big picnic with Mrs Turner playing the accordion and Mr Platt on the guitar and lots of rowdy singing until really late. This year it's set to happen around the end of June though Maureen says it all depends on the weather and no one ever knows quite when it will be. But May has been quite wet so the grass is long and strong and June has been dry which is a good sign for baling too apparently.

I am very much looking forward to this event.

I do not dare to wish to be Hay Queen. Traditionally it is a girl in the final year of primary school which leaves Maureen and I. I know who I would choose. Scrappy little Timothy Gallagher is the only candidate for King. His ears will securely hold the crown at least. Perhaps I don't want to be Queen to his King. The photograph in the paper will be ridiculous.

Mrs Platt makes an announcement in school. 'Our own dear Christine would no doubt have been this year's Hay Queen and, with this in mind, in her honour, and in deference to her family, we are crowning her Hay Queen in absentia. Her photograph will be placed on top of the castle alongside the crown and this year, there will be no Hay King. I'm sure you all agree, this is the only course of action and we will await the return of Christine when she will be able to wear the crown and claim her rightful title.'

Timothy and Maureen both look crestfallen. At break Maureen's cheeks are hot red and her brow is rigidly furrowed. 'Why is there no doubt Christine would be Hay Queen?' she says, 'I've always wanted to be Hay Queen. You get to wear a white dress and daisies in your hair and all the grownups give you sweets. Everyone wants to be Hay Queen. Why is there no doubt? Bloomin' Viper. What does she know? I could have been Hay Queen. I should be Hay Queen! It's not fair.' She clamps her lips together and Andrea takes her hand and pets it a little.

'At least you won't get tooth decay,' I say eventually, 'and there's no girls in Christopher Robert's year so you could be Hay Queen next year.' I am looking at Andrea's scrubbed cherub face and thinking they'll pick her however. It's a change to see Maureen angry about anything to do with Christine though. I decide to test this.

'It's about time everyone just forgot about Christine,' I say, 'It's been ages. She's not coming back.'

Maureen and Andrea recoil as one as if I have suddenly become infected with a deadly disease. 'What do you mean?' Maureen manages, her eyes glassy and blinking, 'Of course she's coming back.' Andrea's head goes down and she begins to smudge her nose with her fist and sniff. Maureen stares at me, mouth open but no words. Just noisy breathing.

I sigh heavily. 'Sorry,' I say. I'm not. 'I was just trying to make you feel better. If she is coming back then the crown should be saved for her after all that she'll have been through. Of course Christine should be Hay Queen. Let's just say no more about it.' And I smile as if the matter is closed and I have said nothing wrong and the pair of them look a bit confused but then Maureen nods her head a little and Christopher Robert kicks a ball at us and Maureen shouts at him and that seems to cheer her up. I hope there'll be no more moaning about her missed moment of glory though I do think it's very selfish of her not to consider my feelings. After all I could just as easily have been Hay Queen. I suit white with my dark hair and eyes and I could have made a lovely speech and I would have spoken very clearly and loudly to any reporters who might happen to be there not like stuttering Timothy or tongue-tied Maureen. I wonder how long all this Christine business is going to keep stealing my limelight.

They start haymaking on the last Saturday in June and it feels like the whole village is out. After the tractor has slowly trundled up and down slicing through the coarse grass spraying fine seed and pollen in its stately wake, everyone begins the business of raking up the grass in the strips in front of their houses ready for the bailer. It is a surprisingly hot day, a clear sky, warm since early on and supposed to stay dry well into next week. There's a lot of sharing of rakes and pitchforks and we children are constantly being yelled at to keep out of the way of the way of the tractor and then the baler which arrives a bit later, or to stop hurling ourselves into the mounds of grass which are blossoming across the green. As the heavy, loose grass is transformed into tight neat bundles, we children start to behave like a pack as the grownups, their work over, converge on the playground to drink greedily from tall glasses of sharp lemonade and cold beer. A site for the castle is chosen and yelled instructions volley up and down as we lug the bales by the coarse twine that binds them and begin to fashion our marvellous new den. It is the teenagers who are in charge. They have had years of haymaking days. They know roughly the right number of bales to form the base and how high to go but there are a few false starts and lots of swearing as the bulky blocks are tugged and kicked into different positions. The boys are bare chested and the girls let their long hair fall as they reach down to drag another bundle up higher and higher. But we all help, even the tiny tots, who push uselessly against the solid wedges beneath their chubby mitts; they want to be part of this adventure. And we all want the hay castle to be perfect.

The best part is the entrance. It's low down, thick and close; designed to fit the kids in and keep the grownups out. It's a squeeze to get in and, oh the thrill as the roof starts to go on and the brilliance of the sky begins to disappear. A couple of thick planks from Christopher Robert's farm have been carried across to provide a frame to support the hay roof. Maureen tells me the same ones have been used for years and years but then later Andrea tells me lots of the dads clambered onto the roof a few years back after a few too many beers and the planks snapped so they may not be as ancient as Maureen claims.

Once it's built everyone wants to be in but that's impossible. It's the older kids who take over and we sit outside, bare shoulders leaning against the prickly walls, waiting for them to get bored or hungry so we can have a turn. We watch the grownups getting ready for the picnic. The pig has been cooking all day and the still air smells heavy with grease and smoke. We are past midsummer so the night will be long and I am breathless to be staying up way beyond bedtime, outdoors. Mum and Dad have packed their basket with a bottle of gin with little berries bobbing in the bottom of the bottle so they won't care what I get up to. I think about Bryan. He's inside the hay castle now. With no shirt on. I think I've seen him more times with his shirt off than on. He must be what Dad calls an Exhibitionist.

Maureen is singing a little song to herself next to me. She's looking decidedly mucky. Good job she's not Hay Queen.

Some people have carried a couple of their dining room chairs over to sit on and they've brought the fold out tables we use for our dinner out of the school house to serve the pig from. Some mums are putting bowls of things out and Maureen's mum and Daphne Robson are buttering a mountain of rolls. I'm quite hungry. It's been a long time since I ate anything. I look at Maureen to suggest we go and see if we can scrounge something but she has her eyes shut now. I look back and Richard Robson is talking to Daphne. I say talking, he is staring at her.

Mr Robson is quite a bit taller than Daphne and he is just glaring at her. His mouth is set at an angle. You can't see his lips. Just his ginger moustache. Sticking out. In a very cross way.

Daphne is trying to ignore him looking at the rolls like it's a tricky job needing all her attention, and so is Maureen's mum. Then Maureen's mum says something to Richard Robson and turns and goes into the school. Daphne does a little shudder and has a little look at her husband. He begins to talk to her but it's too far away to hear what he's saying. He's talking very slowly though and close to her face, like he wants her to pay careful attention.

He looks like the Headmaster at my old school telling off the very naughty boys.

I decide to see if I can hear what they're saying. They won't notice me. I'm just a kid.

I head towards the playground and walk past, skirting the edge as if I'm heading for the girls' loos. I look straight ahead and I've a bit of long grass that I'm fiddling with too so I look very absorbed and not at all interested in them.

Unfortunately he's talking pretty quietly and I catch nothing before I end up in the stall of the loo with no clue as to what is going on. A ladybird is crawling up the wall. I watch her for a while and remember how horrified I was when I discovered there were outdoor toilets here.

Suddenly the door to the toilet yard slams open and Richard Robson's voice says, 'Get in there!' There is a scuffling and scraping outside my stall. I sit on the seat of the loo and draw up my feet. I slap my hand over my mouth.

'What are you doing Rick?' It's Daphne, 'What will people think?'

'I don't care what people think! I want a straight answer. Now.' His Geordie accent sounds very strong, like it did when he got cross with Timothy Gallagher.

'Why can't we go home and talk about this?' Daphne's voice is quiet and whiny.

'I divn't want to go home. It's Haymaking Day. Everybody's out. Nobody's at home are they?' There's a pause. 'Are they?'

'No, Richard'

'Or at least they shouldn't be, should they?'

'No, Rick. Look, let's just ..'

'So, I want a straight answer.'

Another pause. I try not to breathe too loudly. I hear Daphne shift and sigh.

'Where were you this morning? Eh? Because you weren't haymaking, were you?' I can see his foot step closer to hers under the gap below the weathered wood of the stall door. 'At least, you weren't making hay with me, were you?'

I am sure they must be able to hear my heart thumpity thumping.

'Richard, please,' her voice is so quiet. I really need a wee which is ironic as I am sitting on a loo.

I hear the slap and jump as Daphne yelps. The second time it sounds more like a punch, a softer, duller sound and Daphne just grunts. The third is a definite punch. I can hear the momentum in his clothes and the force of it as Daphne buckles over. There is scuffling and little sobs as he pulls her to her feet.

'What do you want me to say?' she manages eventually, her voice tight and angry now.

'Where the fuck were you?' His voice is a whisper.

'I was with him. I was with him. I was with him!' she sounds furious, 'But you know that! Of course I was going to see him today. Christine is being crowned Hay Queen. How is he going to get through that? If you weren't such a ... I only went because I knew Hilda couldn't ... Look nothing happened. Oh what's the point. You've bloodied my face for the whole village to see. Again. Christ Richard.'

'I knew it,' he sounds happy. Triumphant. The winner.

'Then why did you bother asking?' Another slap.

'Clean yourself up. You're a fuckin' disgrace.' The outside door slams. Richard Robson has left.

There's movement and then running water and whispered muttering which I can't quite catch. I stay as still as still while Daphne makes herself presentable and hope that she doesn't need the loo as my stall is the nearest to the sink. I hear her suck in her breath a few times, presumably as the cold water hits her wounds. There's no hot water out here. Sometimes there's been no water at all when it's been biting cold; a matter I have pressed Mrs Platt to take up with the appropriate authorities; she has just glowered at me.

Eventually Daphne decides there's nothing more she can do and I hear her slip out through the outside gate. I let out a sigh of relief and wonder where Maureen is so I can tell her what has gone on. I picture the upset on her face. She doesn't take well to real life drama. Tillie Berman would have enjoyed it far more.

I study the ladybird for a while longer. It has been remarkably calm through all the fuss, no house on fire or missing children. Maureen and Andrea are cross-legged and playing a clapping game where I left them. The teenagers are still in the Hay Castle. We decide to get some food. I see Daphne, obscure and dimly lit, at her bedroom window.

It's cool and damp inside when we finally get a turn. The older kids crawl out, bits of grass in their hair, their feet white and eyes squinting in the sun like animals emerging from winter hibernation. They slope off towards the food, a few of the boys have arms slung heavily across the shoulders of the girls, a couple hold hands. They all look hot and sleepy.

We are joined by Timothy and Christopher Robert and a few of the younger Kirbys who grub around a little but soon decide it's too dark and there's nothing to play with and toddle and scrabble out. I thought I'd like it much more but I can't see the appeal, mainly because of the company.

Christopher Robert sit bolt upright side by side, staring straight ahead, like they're in a prison cell, not saying a word. Timothy Gallagher tries, and fails, to scale the walls, his pigeon toes and knock knees pushing and pulling the wrong way and sending him tumbling down over and over. He gives up eventually and attempts sucking on a long blade of grass like a cowboy instead. He cuts his tongue. Andrea and Maureen huddle together in one corner.

'You're not scared, are you?' I say, not managing to keep the contempt from my voice.

'Well, it is very dark,' says Maureen, and Andrea nods rapidly in agreement.

'It's broad daylight outside and there's about a million adults in shouting distance. What is there to be afraid of?' I am annoyed. I don't know what I was expecting but it wasn't this.

Maureen looks cross. 'There might be ghosts,' she reasons.

'Ghosts,' I snort, 'This thing was only built at lunchtime. No one's had time to die in it.'

'Well maybe other ghosts might come because it's dark,' she persists.

'I thought g-g-g-ghosts were trapped where they d-d-d-died?' Timothy pipes up.

'Exactly,' I say, 'There can't be any ghosts here.' And then I have a funny thought, 'Unless...' I say and I turn purposefully to Maureen and Andrea.

'Do you really think there might be a ghost?' I ask seriously.

'I don't know,' Maureen is a bit suspicious.

'I mean, do you all feel that there could be a supernatural presence here? Does it feel unnaturally cold? It is very, very dark isn't it?' I begin to look around as if I am searching for something.

'I'm cold,' says Andrea, 'I'm freezing and I was lovely and warm outside.'

'I'm thinking…' I pause, 'No, it can't be.'

I have their attention now. All their anxious faces are turned to me. Even Christopher Robert are paying attention.

'What?' says Maureen, 'What are you thinking, Jen?'

'Well,' I turn to each of them, 'What if, by chance, we've accidentally built the Hay Castle where… no, I can't say it.' I put my hands over my face but I peak through my fingers to see their reactions.

'Where what?' says Christopher Robert in their monotone drone. They always were slow to catch on.

Timothy has crawled closer to Andrea. He is frowning and silent. Maureen is casting darting looks around her and clutching Andrea to her.

'Where Christine was …' Maureen whispers with a catch in her voice.

'Murdered!' I add loudly and they all jump. I want to laugh.

'If it is her ghost,' I say, 'we've no need to be afraid, she was our friend. We could ask her some questions?'

'How would she answer?' says Maureen. Her voice is very worried.

'One knock for yes, two knocks for no,' say Christopher Robert.

'I'm sure she'll find a way,' I say, 'Now what shall we ask her?'

We are all silent. Looking from one face to another.

'Why do you think her ghost is here?' says Andrea quietly.

'Maybe some of her blood is soaked into the ground,' I say putting my face close to hers. She starts and huddles closer into Maureen. 'Now come on, let's think of a question,' I say briskly.

'I've g-g-g-got one!' says Timothy, putting his hand in the air like an idiot.

'Very well Timothy, ask away. I'm sure she's listening,' I say solemnly.

'Are you d-d-d-dead?' says Timothy.

'Well of course she's dead she's a ghost,' I snap.

'Oh yes. S- s-s -sorry.' Timothy looks glum.

'Where are you?' says Andrea softly.

'We don't need to ask that. She's in heaven,' says Maureen hotly, 'This is stupid. I don't believe in ghosts. And I don't believe Christine's dead.'

'Have it your own way Maureen,' I say reasonably, 'It was you who said there might be ghosts. It was you who suggested the Hay Castle could be haunted. But I have a question for Christine.'

'Ask her!' blurts out Timothy.

'Who is the murderer Christine? Who killed you?' I say to the air with all of them watching me like I am talking to Christine beyond the grave.

While we have been talking I have been edging my hand behind Andrea and Maureen. I pretend to listen really closely and once they are too, I give Maureen's t-shirt a sharp tug and whip my hand back. She screams and jumps and so does Andrea. We all scrabble to our feet, knocking and bumping into each other in the gloom.

'What is it Maureen?' Andrea is now petrified.

'Something grabbed me,' she says, 'I felt something grab me really hard. I'm not staying in here!' and they all race to get out of the narrow exit and I join in and it is tremendous fun until Maureen becomes hysterical and can't stop crying and has to breathe into a paper bag and her dad has to take her home and I am left with a clingy silent Andrea who will not go near the Hay Castle no matter what.

Much later a bonfire has been lit and it's getting darker. Livid sparks and violet smoke twist free into the sky above the heat of the flames as the villagers sing to Mrs Turner's blurry accordion and Andrea and I huddle on a blanket trying not to fall asleep. Mum and Dad are dancing in a slice of light thrown from the open school door. They are shadowed and dark aside from the glint of Mum's coppery hair or a flash of white from her cheek or chest or leg as she throws her long neck back to laugh or does a flamboyant step to show off. A few of the men are watching her quite closely, leaning against the school wall, fists around the necks of beer bottles and sucking on fags, briefly bright in the twilight.

The teenagers are back in the Hay Castle and I wish I was in there with them. Bryan is in there with a girl from the next village. She has greasy permed hair but very short shorts. Daphne Robson hasn't reappeared and there aren't any lights on in the house. Mr Robson has been out and about though, drinking, joking, talking and laughing too loudly.

In the first few weeks after Christine's disappearance he was a Person of Interest. Once Gideon Berman, the writer, provided a Watertight Alibi (he was the after dinner speaker at a Round Table event in Leyland in Lancashire the night Christine disappeared), everyone's suspicions had to move on. Richard Robson had no children which was suspicious in itself for a married man of his age. 'Not for want of trying,' I overheard Mrs Kirby saying to Mrs Gallagher in the shop one day though I wasn't quite sure what this meant. He also had a very nice sporty car and he didn't work on a farm or have anything to do with a farm. All these seemed reason enough to point the finger. Plus, he couldn't provide a very good alibi.

'Never could keep it in his trousers,' Mr Stoddart said to Dad when they chatted about the alibi and I assumed he had been off spending his money somewhere he shouldn't. He certainly wore very fashionable clothes for the village and some said he blow dried his hair and possibly his luxuriously thick moustache.

Anyway, despite the police apparently investigating Richard Robson with great care, they found nothing incriminating and their attention moved on. Some people still didn't trust him though or they Had Their Doubts. Bryan, for example, was known to loathe him. In fact, quite a few of the men in the village didn't seem too friendly towards him. I thought this was mainly due to his lack of his farming connections.

When Mr and Mrs Bell had appeared earlier this evening, the atmosphere changed. Bryan let go of the curly haired girl's hand and everyone stood up in dribs and drabs as they saw them walking up the green towards the Hay Castle. Mrs Bell has barely been out since February. She clutched a solid frame to her chest and her dead eyes looked right at the Hay Castle. She had make up on but it wasn't the bright cheery colours of before Christine's disappearance, it was just enough to cover the shadows under her eyes and brighten her tired and sun-deprived skin. Her hair looked brittle and wispy thin and perched unnaturally on her head, like it would blow away in the summer wind, leaving her bare scalp, her true self, a hospital patient, an accident victim, an alien from a world no one really understood. Mr Bell had an arm around her waist as they processed together up the empty road with his lost daughter's photograph. He looked at the tarmac, unable to bear the expressions on his neighbours' faces.

Richard Robson got ahead of everyone though. He had muscled his way through the circle so he could stand at the front and face the Bells first. He stood there, feet planted, chest thrusting like a moustached comic book superhero. Did he do that to show he had nothing to be ashamed of? Or because of Daphne and Mr Bell? Either way, it was noticed and there were a few shaking heads, the odd tut as he swaggered to the front.

Bryan pried the photo from his mother's grip, took the straw crown from Christopher Robert's dad and climbed the Hay Castle where he laid them, carefully for a boy, on the top and everyone applauded politely. Mrs Turner and Mr Platt struck up a song and everyone started singing with relief and smiling a little to each other but when they turned to look, Mrs Bell was hurrying back down the green to her bungalow. She'd not said a word to a soul. Kevin broke away from his friends and ran after her. Once he caught up, they just walked together. It didn't look like they were talking.

Now I can see Richard Robson at the edge of the school house talking to someone, a woman. Someone smaller than him. It might be Daphne, she looks the right height. She moves her head and a sweep of hair falls back. It's much longer than Daphne's. Richard is leaning closer down to her face. They look like they might kiss. I stretch back, digging my elbows into the grass to get a better view but I can't make it out.

I stand up and sneak to the corner of the building. Richard and the woman have moved further away, down to the far end past the boys' loos. She's leaning against the wall and he has one hand on the wall above her head and is talking to her. She is looking up at him. I can still only see his face but it definitely isn't Daphne. She rocks away from the wall and they both start to walk away. He puts his hand on her back then slides it down onto her bum and tucks it neatly into the pocket of her jeans. She looks up at him, smiling. It's Gillian Stoddart. He catches her fully around the waist and buries his head in her neck, grabbing her bottom before they continue walking, soon disappearing into the darkness beyond the school.

In January, Richard Robson had zoomed up the road that slices up through the village green in his sports car. It was a surprisingly fair day and he had the top down even though it was freezing. It was lunchtime and we were out playing in front of the school. Gillian was in the car with him, her cheeks flushed, hair wild from being whipped by the wind. He screeched up to us and grinned at Christine, 'Fancy a ride? We've got room for a little 'un,' and she had squashed into the car between Richard and Gillian and he'd raced up and down the green with Christine's black and Gillian's blonde hair whipping and dancing behind them until Mrs Platt had been roused from her desk and come out to chide him. He had charmed her too though and persuaded her into the car for a spin, even patting her ample bottom as she clambered out. Gillian had hopped back in and they'd raced off together; all we saw was a married man and a teenager. He said he'd picked her up at the bus stop and was giving her a lift into Appleby. We never thought anything was going on. I wonder if Mrs Stoddart knows. Perhaps I should tell her.

I have mixed feelings about both Mrs Stoddart and Gillian. Mrs Stoddart is the only other adult I ever see in school. She arrives in a small van, rearranges the porch and serves us all lunch. We eat in silence at the fold out trestle tables while cheery Mrs Stoddart and Viper have truly boring conversations that make the tepid, watery food appear exotic and enticing. Mrs Stoddart is very friendly and nice to everyone. However I do have to hold her and her daughter responsible for getting The Castle habitable for guests. If they had allowed my feckless parents to struggle on unaided, we could very well have been back in Buckinghamshire by now but it was less than a week before they came to the rescue. Judy and I came home from school the second week of enduring Cumberland and there was an altogether different atmosphere in the house. For a start I could hear Marc Bolan singing Get It On loudly in the kitchen. The hall was brighter like the windows were letting in more of the steadily setting low winter sun and everything smelled different. There was a vase of flowers on the dark dresser and two coats I didn't recognise were hanging on the hooks in the hall. Judy and I scuttled down the corridor towards the music. There was laughter too. Unbelievably it sounded like my mother's.

Mrs Stoddart was standing by the range.

A slender young woman in pale jeans and a red polo neck jumper was at the sink. Even though she was washing-up, she was very pretty. She was curvy but skinny with smooth long fair hair and, as she turned to look at us, her eyes were sleepy looking and her mouth wide.

Mum was, unsurprisingly, sitting at the table but she was smiling.

'Hello you two,' said Mrs Stoddart.

'Mrs Stoddart and her daughter, Gillian, have come to give us a hand getting everything sorted out.' Mum was still smiling, and looking with delight at Mrs Stoddart.

Gillian smiled and turned back to the sink. There was a whole pile of boxes flattened against the back door.

'You've unpacked all those?' Judy said, impressed.

'Yes Mrs Stoddart is very efficient – I just don't know how I've been managing without her.'

'Gillian helped too,' Mrs Stoddart chipped in.

Gillian was wiggling her bottom a little bit to Get It On. She was very glamorous for this village.

'Have you been here all day?' I asked.

'Apart from when I came up to school to serve your dinners, yes.'

'I see,' I looked at Mum. She saw the accusation and, understanding, looked away.

'Where's Dad?' I asked.

'He's gone for another walk as it's stopped raining.'

Judy had started dancing too and Mrs Stoddart was laughing. So Mum had been here more or less a week and she'd already found someone to do everything for her. Two people in fact. I was annoyed because if everything worked out, we'd have to stay. Judy had Mrs

Stoddart's hand and was twirling under her arm. Gillian had stopped and was watching them, enjoying the show. The song ended and Judy said, 'You're very good at dancing, Mrs Stoddart, are you a professional?'

Mrs Stoddart answered completely seriously, 'I am Judy love, I'm in *Pan's People*, though it is quite tricky on a Thursday serving the dinners and getting down to London for filming *Top of the Pops*. Somehow I manage it though.' and they all hooted with laughter.

I left the kitchen and walked back through the downstairs' rooms. There was more order. Everywhere had been cleaned, hoovered, polished. The boxes were gone from the sitting room and the dining room was not such a jumble of furniture anymore. In the little room off the hall which Mum called the scullery, our shoes were neatly laid out expectantly ready for our feet. Some of them even look like they'd been cleaned. The guests' living room had had the dustsheets taken off the sofas and the curtains were opened. The dark paintings were no longer askew and though the room was sprawling, it now seemed like someone might live here though the carpet was still horrible. Mrs Stoddart couldn't possibly be here every day to do everything for Mum? Surely?

I came to the door of Dad's study. We had been told this was strictly Out of Bounds but he was out for a walk. I tentatively turned the handle and pushed the door open a little. Dad was sitting at the ugly old desk, his head in one hand, gently sobbing.

I had closed the door as quietly as I could.

And that was the start of Mrs Stoddart and Gillian at The Castle and they have done the work to get it Up And Running. Gillian has painted some of the guest rooms with Mum, and Mrs Stoddart now makes the cakes or scones that the guests eat when they arrive. Gillian arrives early to help with the breakfasts and she sometimes puts a little wrapped up surprise in our coat pockets like a biscuit or a jam tart. Quite often she's drawn a little sketch on the paper she's wrapped the cake in and Judy has taken to sellotaping these on her side of the bedroom. They are quick outlines of a hawthorn spray of blossom or a horse nibbling grass with a fat lip and big teeth or pebbles on the bed of the beck that runs along the bottom of the garden. There's not often colour, just black or blue ink. I have tried to copy them when Judy is round at Sally Turner's but mine just look clumsy and rigid. Even when I trace them. Gillian is going down to London next year to Art College. Mrs Stoddart mops at her eyes whenever it is mentioned. And Gillian makes us breakfast too, unlike Mum on the rare occasions she is out of bed and Gillian, like Mrs Stoddart, is never in a bad mood.

I have also seen Gillian hanging around with Bryan though, and for this, I have to mark her down. I have seen the way Bryan looks at her as they wait at the bus stop together, eager for her to say or do something other than just her usual easy smile or slight shrug. Even from the top of the green, you can see him jittering around her stillness, desperate for some attention. Now I understand she is giving all of her devotion to Richard Robson.

A few weeks after the Hay Making she is in the kitchen when I get home from school. It is a heavy, warm afternoon though it has rained for days before so everything still feels damp and sweaty. The walk up the lane has taken forever with puddles and flies and the heat of the sun and a heavy, dark jumper tied round my waist. Judy has gone straight round to Sally Turner's whose mother has promised to get the sprinkler out. My head feels itchy and hot and I think about taking a cool bath. I know if I complain about the heat my mother will say yesterday I was complaining about the rain. As soon as I slump down onto the kitchen chair Gillian runs me a glass of water and opens the biscuit tin. I see she's been baking.

'Thank you,' I sigh wearily.

She sits down opposite me smiling. 'Nearly time for the holidays and the end of primary school,' she says.

'Yes,' I say through a mouthful of biscuit.

'The time goes so quickly,' she is twirling the end of her long, long hair and looking at the sky out of the little window over the sink.

'Are you looking forward to going to London?' I say politely.

'I suppose,' she says, 'It's a long way away.' She doesn't sound too happy.

'Will you miss your mum and dad?' I say

'Of course I will, silly. I'll really miss them.' She looks a bit sad now.

'Who else will you miss?' I ask innocently.

'Lots of people. All my friends. Your mum. Your dad. Judy. You.' She is smiling now which is better but I still can't help myself.

'Will you miss Mr Robson?' I look at her closely.

'What? I suppose so. Well, not really. I mean. Maybe. Why?' She's gone red. That's what people say but actually it's more of a deep, browny-pink colour and her neck looks a bit blotchy.

'You like him, don't you?' I try to sound matter of fact.

'What do you mean? What have you heard Jen?' She looks worried, startled. Her eyes don't look so sleepy now.

'It's not really what I've heard, more what I've seen,' I say slowly.

'Oh,' she replies quietly and I can see she's trying to think what this might be.

'Do your Mum and Dad know about him?' I say and I look at her with what I hope is a disapproving face.

Then I take a sip of the water she gave me.

'What? No. No, they don't,' Gillian is flustered now.

'I suppose, more importantly, does Daphne Robson know?' I set the glass down firmly on the table and a little condensation drip puddles on the table.

'Daphne. No. I don't think so. I didn't think anyone knew,' she sounds like she is going to cry. I have never seen her unhappy. This is proving to be quite interesting.

'Does he say anything about Daphne?' I ask. It is fun thinking of all these questions. I fear I may be running out of them though. I wish I had had time to write some down in a notebook beforehand, like a policeman.

'About Daphne? No. No. We don't talk about Daphne.' She sounds a bit ashamed. Actually she sounds a lot ashamed.

'Did you know that he hits Daphne?' I ask

'That's just a rumour,' she is a bit more defiant with this one, 'Who told you that?'

'No one told me that, I saw it,' I say but as I say this I get a twist in my tummy like I might have given away too much. I haven't told anyone about Richard and Daphne at the Hay Making Day.

'What do you mean you saw it? Tell me what you saw!' Gillian has become more indignant now. She is glaring at me.

'It was on the Haymaking Day. Daphne had been round to see Mr Bell and Mr Robson wanted to know about it and he hit her to make her tell him about it.' I say, as confidently as I can.

'And how did you see this?' Gillian says after a pause. She says this as if she really doesn't like me.

'I was in the loo. They didn't know I was there. It happened in the loos. At school. I was shut in one of the stalls. No one knew I was there,' I say.

'And how do you know about … me,' she says. Her mouth is tight and her face hard now.

'I saw you too. With him. On the Haymaking Day. At the back of the school.'

'And have you told anyone?'

I nod.

'Who?' she has panic in her eyes.

'You,' I say. She looks furious at my little joke.

'Do you promise?' she says. Her hands are clamped flat to the table, holding her down.

I nod.

'Alright', she says but it's like she's talking to herself. She looks around the room like she's checking everything is still there. Her eyes settle on me. She leans towards me. Her eyes are cold. 'I always thought your mam was exaggerating about you but I can see it now. You say a word about this to anyone and I'll send him up here for you. Do you understand?'

I nod.

She stands up. 'You keep your nose out of my fucking business you snide little bitch. Ok?'

I nod.

She takes my glass, tips away the water, rinses it and upturns it on the draining board. She puts the lid on the biscuit tin and puts it back in the cupboard. She leaves the kitchen. I hear the front door closing quietly.

My head prickles with cold sweat.

Judy shows me with delight Gillian's drawings found in her pockets over the next few weeks – a spring lamb, a detailed rose blooming, a head of lavender, blossoming clouds and raindrops in a glassy puddle. I receive a decomposing rat, its innards exposed and splayed in intricate detail, a terrifying gaping mouth of a tiger with a severed, bloodied hand caught in its throat, a decapitated head at the foot of a guillotine, tongue lolling and eyes aghast at what has happened and a beautifully accurate portrait of myself with my mouth closed with clumsy bleeding stitches.

I still eat the cakes.

I try to avoid Gillian and Mrs Stoddart and Richard Robson at all times. I don't want there to be any misunderstandings.

Maureen, Andrea and I are sitting making daisy chains at the bottom of the green by the bus stop. It's August. Maureen has already been shopping for her uniform for Appleby Grammar and Dad says we'll go for mine next week. Maureen has said we mustn't talk about the grammar school too much in front of Andrea as she probably won't pass the eleven plus exam to get in. Andrea spends a lot of time daydreaming in school and hates reading out loud. Sometimes I don't think she even listens to a word I say. I was looking forward to the bus journey until I realised Bryan left the grammar school after his exams in June. Mr Bell had wanted him to stay on and do A levels but he has other ideas apparently.

Maureen is attaching a flimsy daisy crown to Andrea's head. It feels like it could rain but we'll wait until the last minute before we go indoors.

'There's no police around anymore are there?' Maureen says. We all look up the green. A discarded trike is tipped over near the eternal puddle. The shop gate is knocking feebly in the building wind. A ginger tom is bunched up looking grumpy on a gate post. No one's about. It's a work day.

'Or reporters,' adds Andrea, adjusting with her fingertips.

'Do you still watch The News?' I ask, remembering our family's obsession after Christine's disappearance.

Both girls shake their heads and Maureen lies back on the grass, crossing her ankles.

'I sometimes do. Just in case. But it's mostly Richard Nixon at the moment. Nothing to do with us,' I say.

'I miss the policemen,' says Maureen, 'So does my mam. She liked chatting to them. She bought herself a new winter coat out of the catalogue so she could stand outside and natter with them.'

'They did seem to do quite a lot of standing about,' I say.

'They were keeping us safe,' says Andrea grumpily.

'They were supposed to be finding Christine,' I snap.

'Sometimes I wake up in the morning and I forget that she's gone,' says Maureen. She rolls over onto her tummy. 'I think I must tell Christine about such and such or I wonder if Christine saw *Some Mothers Do 'Ave 'Em* and then I remember. Her mam and my mam went to school together. Lived here all their lives. I thought me and Christine would be the same.' She's beginning to sound teary. I cannot help tutting.

She sits back up in a rather ungainly manner and smiles bravely at me. 'Never mind though. At least I've got you now Jen,' and I have to stop myself from laughing out loud. Fat wet drops of summer rain burst on our bare legs. We scrabble to our feet and head to Andrea's. As we run over the bumpety green, I know I cannot tell Maureen my plan to leave here as soon as I possibly can and to never return. Why would I stay in this nasty little place with mean, scary people when there's a whole world waiting?

1984

'Okay. We're going to start political theatre by taking a personal experience and creating a socio-political thread through it. We're going to take elements of Brechtian theatre on a quite simplistic level and play with storytelling as an introduction to this unit. You're probably all familiar with Brecht's plays, or at least his most popular ones, I want to look at his practice through your work.' Pete smiles with encouragement. His floppy blonde hair matches his flimsy needle cord pants. He is an old hippie desperate to be adored; he has a rich low voice with an edge of creepiness. He stands too close, touches and lingers, breathes heavily, looks closely for a tad too long. He is generally liked but a little pitied. I have written him a couple of essays and gone to him for extra help in his office. He likes that.

We are all in the matt black studio in a circle, slumped on chairs. It is too early for enthusiasm.

'Can we begin with a few memories that could provide us with a possible starting point?' Pete encourages.

Andy clears his throat. People shift in their chairs and some sigh. 'I'm sorry Pete,' his Scouse accent is thick, he wears heavy boots and greasy, turned up jeans, 'but I think a childhood memory and Brecht,' his face cracks open as he enunciates a fully guttural 'Brecht', 'is just ridiculous. We should be considering something far more apposite. For example, the miners' strike is a rich seam to plunder.' More sighs. 'Not the puerile and inconsequential detritus of our own lives.'

Pete smiles patiently. 'Andy, I know you are all too familiar with Brecht's work but this is an introductory session. This is theatre. We are playing. Indulge me. Let's try to see if my idea has legs before we damn it entirely. What do you say?'

Andy folds his arms, clearly in a huff. Thank God we are not going to have another of his improvisations based on the miners' strike. His Arthur Scargill leaves a lot to be desired.

'So, as I was saying,' Pete continues, 'any memories, quite vivid ones if possible, which we could use as a springboard?'

'My brother pissed his pants during assembly once.' Idiot Steve pipes up. Sniggers. He grins, thin lipped and slimy toothed. I suspect it's him that pissed his pants.

'Okay, okay.' Pete nods earnestly, in that 'every idea is a good idea' way. 'Bit tricky to fit that into a socio-political context.' He smiles warmly at Steve, like a wanker, 'Any other ideas?'

'My parents got divorced when I was nine.' It's Kitty. I hate her. She is tiny and pretty and thinks she's great. She sits with her skinny legs coiled around each other and her dove white hands together in mock anguish. Her big, puddle-blue eyes are turned to Pete. She blinks, 'I don't know if that's socio-political though.'

He licks his lips. 'Well, what does everyone else think?' He says loudly, crossing his legs sympathetically, 'Can Kitty's parents' divorce be seen as a wider socio-political issue?'

'Depends,' drones Andy, 'if their divorce was brought about by economic hardship imposed by the vagaries of the capitalist system oppressing the lower socio-economic classes – perhaps?' Kitty went to public school. She is one of the only students to have a car. Andy is taking the piss.

'Yes, yes Andy, good point, good point.' Pete presses on. The rest of the class are becoming restless, twitching. This is going nowhere. The studio is cold and probably no one's eaten enough to make them docile. The smokers want a fag and everyone could do with a coffee. The girl next to me has taken to doodling flowers around her optimistic Brecht title in her notebook having already developed her underlining into a neat box. She jiggles her pen impatiently between her nail-bitten fingers. I begin to pick at the sole of my Doc Marten boot. Bored.

'My best friend was abducted and her body was never recovered. The police stopped looking. The papers lost interest. Her family was ordinary. She didn't matter.' I always love the effect this has. It's like when you rustle a biscuit wrapper near a sleeping dog. It is suddenly alert. Even if it isn't hungry, it wants a morsel, the crumbs, a sniff, anything.

The class becomes quiet. I stay looking at my boot. I am not a drama student for nothing. I time the pause, then look up at the lighting rig and blink several times.

'Jen,' Pete says quietly, clearly shocked, 'that's terrible.'

There is a respectful silence while they all calculate how long before they can ask the questions that have leapt unbidden into their mouths.

'Yes,' I say, allowing my voice to break a little, 'It was.'

Another pause.

'Perhaps this might be too difficult for an improvisation?' Pete considers, 'How old was she?' He can't help himself. My experience has shown people seldom can.

'Eleven,' I swallow, a lovely touch, 'We were in our last year at primary school.'

'And... her name?'

'Christine. Christine Bell.'

I wait as mutters and murmurs and mumbles break out from my fellow students pretending to remember her or dredge up some vague recollections of the spring of 1974.

'So where was this?' Pete asks.

'Cumbria, well it was Cumberland then. A tiny village. There were only sixteen of us in the whole school.'

'Fuck's sake,' Steve responds too loudly then looks shamefaced.

'And you say her... body... was never recovered.'

'Never.'

'Did they have any suspects?'

Now we getting down to the nitty-gritty.

'There was a van spotted in the village that no one recognised but also her dad was having an affair. Some people said it was his lover's husband. Revenge. They couldn't have kids, apparently. I think that was all gossip though.'

'So what do you think happened?'

'I don't know. I was a kid. I just know everything stopped. One minute there were reconstructions and police searching everyone's houses, ours included, and loads of reporters and the next, there's nothing. It was all over too quickly. They should have kept looking. People were still interested.'

The nail biter, Sam, is scribbling in her book. I find this bizarre.

'So this was a little more than a personal memory, this was a national event?' Pete asks.

'I suppose so. It was on the national news. It was the same time as Patty Hearst, you remember her?' I look at my fellow students.

'Yeah! I've heard of her! I've definitely heard of *her*,' Steve again, jumping in, a couple of the girls tut and then smile a little and roll their eyes at me.

'You would remember her because she was rich and American and she joined her kidnappers. There was a story there, I guess. Or people still had something to say,' I was enjoying everyone listening to me, 'Christine was just an ordinary little girl. People were really keen for a while but once no one was caught, the story just fizzled out.'

'Okay,' Pete tries to focus, 'so let's try to bring this back to Brecht.' He gets up and goes to the portable blackboard. He turns sincerely back towards me. 'Jen. Are you happy for us to use this incredibly difficult memory as a starting point for our drama? I really need your permission before we can proceed.'

'Yes Pete,' I breathe, 'it's fine.'

'Okay.' He is alive and picks up a slender piece of chalk with a flourish. He writes 'Christine Bell,' in the centre of the board and encircles it. 'Right. What are the events of this narrative and who are the characters?'

The blackboard is rapidly filled and scribbled on and I am asked question upon question, all necessary to build the drama. Pete suggests a naturalistic interpretation of events first, designed to elicit audience sympathy, as this was the drama Brecht was reacting against, and the whole class is up and organising. Kitty is Christine and another girl, Tamsin, plays me. I take on the role of Christine's mum and Pete, who has become uncharacteristically involved, directs. Sam plays Daphne and Andy is Richard and all the village residents, no matter how old or young, are created by students in their twenties. I feed in some lines and suggestions and a couple of tech boys add blueish lighting and some mawkish music. It is dreadful and bears no resemblance to anything that happened in Long Tarn but at the end Pete is tearful as are Kitty and Tamsin. I want to laugh out loud.

Pete is effusive in his praise, promising that in the next session we will re-examine the event and reframe it in a Brechtian way in order to drive home the socio-political message of the piece, pushing the audience to question rather than emote. He stops me as I'm gathering my things. 'That was so brave Jen.' He plops a heavy, clumsy hand onto my shoulder, 'Thanks so much for sharing. Just so brave.'

'No problem Pete. Just wanted to help,' I smile.

Kitty is waiting at the door. She's never bothered to speak to me outside class before. 'Do you want to go to the Union and get a coffee?' she says. I know she just wants more details, anything she thinks I might not have wanted to share with the class.

'Okay,' I say. I can make up some stuff to please her. It would be handy to have a friend with a car.

We sit at the sticky, solid tables with flimsy plastic cups of sweet coffee. I wanted a scone but I don't feel I can eat in front of Kitty. She lights a fag and drags on it, looking at me speculatively.

'We haven't really had much chance to talk yet, have we?' she muses. Her face is like a cat's, pointed chin and slanted eyes, precise eyelashes, all entirely symmetrical. Kitty cat.

'Not really. You've been too busy ignoring me at every opportunity I suppose,' I smile sweetly; I know I have the upper hand here and I don't really care that much about her car. I know my clothes are too scruffy even though we all get stuff from charity shops. I know I'm a bit too fat. I know I'm just not that interesting or different or anorexic enough to make it worth her while to talk to me. But now I have Christine.

She, to her credit, just raises her eyebrows in agreement at my comment.

'How did it affect you, losing your friend? What happened?' So no social niceties then, straight in, diving for the gory details.

'I don't know. I guess at first we were all afraid. You think it could be someone you know. My mother was a little bit paranoid about us playing out that sort of thing. Then time passed and everyone relaxed and things went back to sort of normal, except no one ever sat in her chair at school.'

'What? Wait. What do you mean?'

'Well, it just stayed empty, like a mundane memorial for a lost girl. The headmistress just wouldn't let anyone sit in it.'

Kitty rummages in her expensive leather bag. She fishes out a beautiful notebook, soft red leather with thick, creamy pages and a slim gold pen. 'You don't mind if I make a few notes? Do you?'

'Sure. Why?'

'Well, I'm always looking for ideas for plays. I've already written a couple. We took one up to Edinburgh last year.'

I look blank.

'You know, The Fringe.'

'You've had a play you wrote, on at The Fringe?'

'Yes. Just one of the tiny venues. Little room above a pub. You know the sort of thing. So, I'm always just jotting down scraps of dialogue or snippets of narrative that I think I might be able to work up into something worthwhile. And your story this morning, I mean Pete's treatment of it, it was so,' she rolls her crystal-clear eyes, 'expected and, well, a bit clichéd, wasn't it?' she smirks, 'I just thought, I could make it more, immediate. I'm really into this kind of Cinéma Vérité style but translating that into theatre. It's very current.'

I have been punctuating her frankly impressive speech with sincere nodding and murmured uh huhs and yeahs. I really hate her.

'Thing is Kitty,' I smile, warmly as I have learnt how to, 'I'm actually writing a play about it myself, which is why I asked about why you wanted to take notes.' I delve into my Army and Navy canvas bag for my empty A4 notepad. I clutch it to me like precious cargo. 'I'd just hate for our work to conflict, you know. I'm so far through it, you know.' I smile apologetically.

Kitty looks surprised then smiles and slowly closes her notebook.

'You know I thought that line about the chair, the 'mundane memorial for the lost girl' was too good for you to have just made it up on the spot. It's from the play isn't it?' She is grinning at her detective work.

I smile conspiratorially.

'You've got me. Absolutely. Just quoting my own work. Didn't think you'd spot it. But I couldn't get that one past you.' I manage a small chuckle. Kitty leans in.

'So tell me. How are you framing it? I mean you've got the plot and the characters but what about the form?'

'Well let's say it's still in a state of flux but I too am leaning towards a more avant-garde approach.' I have no idea what avant-garde really means but heard a boy describing a playwright I didn't understand as this.

'Shit Jen. That's great. Look, as one playwright to another, I'd love to read it once you're ready to share. In fact, it's great that there is someone else on the course who isn't just thinking about acting and getting famous.'

I am, of course, only thinking about acting and getting famous. What else is there?

'I know. Yes I'd love that but it's still quite a long way from finished. It's just such a hard process, especially when you're so close to the event. It's just raw, do you know what I mean?'

'Oh God Jen, I can imagine.' She touches my arm then leans back and tucks her notebook back in her bag. I don't want this to be the end even though I hate her.

'What have your plays been about?' I come up with.

She is modestly gleeful to go into the details. 'Well the one we took up to Edinburgh was about this woman Hannah Cullwick who used to black up for her husband in Victorian times. I performed in it as well. And I took coal and rubbed it all over my body as the climax of the piece. The critics really liked it.'

I bet they did.

'That sounds really challenging,' I say.

Pete uses Challenging all the time; it doesn't seem to really mean anything. Kitty drags on her cigarette and nods sagely as if I've hit the nail on the head.

'So you were acting as well?' I pick up on, adding a hint of admiration to my voice.

'Yes, I just felt I'd written the piece, and I really knew how I wanted it to be played, and the rest of the company thought I'd be right for the part so I just thought why not?' She sucks on her fag some more with her matt red lips before grinding it out. 'I really just want to write though. Give women great parts on stage. There's such a lack, don't you think?'

'Oh yes, yes, totally,' I say, 'It's a strong motivation for my writing too,' I add. I fiddle with a sachet of sugar.

'Were you naked for the blacking up?' I ask as she takes a gold, vintage powder compact out of her bag and checks her face in the mirror. She presumably finds it to be perfect.

'Oh yeah, totally,' she shrugs, 'but I didn't feel it because the coal was like make-up so I wasn't really nude.' She snaps the compact shut and drops it back in her bag.

'Right.' I nod.

I sip my scalding coffee but I'd like to throw it in her perfect face.

As drama students, we are supposed to have no fear, to say yes, to take risks. I see little point in doing any of these things. I want to have my lines and my cues and for everything to be relatively straightforward. The whole nudity/body-is-my-tool thing of the drama student life really gets on my tits. I have been horrified by what people are prepared to do, and want to do, In The Name Of Art. Have they no shame? Mostly I think they're all a bit pretentious and I try to avoid the worst excesses.

When I started in the first year at this crappy little drama school on the edge of London, I thought having a dad who had been an actor would count for something but I quickly realised talking about him wasn't going to get me anywhere; in fact I had to take the piss out of what he'd become. *Diamonds in the Rough* was still being shunted out intermittently so lots of people knew his character on the show but, in acting terms, he'd Sold Out. He hadn't Followed His Dreams or Honed His Craft. He'd taken on a job on the most tritely derivative factory fodder drivel the BBC had produced. It was popular though in its time and so was a constant reminder of his defeat, his failure. The steady trickle of tiny royalties probably kept the B&B going however.

I quickly dropped the fact that David Wentworth was my dad. Besides, as had been the case my whole life, everyone else had a far more impressive story to tell. A dad who was a producer on *Top of the Pops*, an American cousin working on *Cheers*, a friend who lived near the Redgraves, lots had been extras in various films made at Pinewood Studios or Elstree and some had had paid work already. And then there was the knowledge. They'd all seen so much theatre and read so many plays – or said they had. Most had been in fantastic productions that they littered their conversation with. I had nothing. I'd seen an amateur production of *The Taming of the Shrew* with a wobbly set and a Katherine who was in her forties, and Appleby Am-dram's annual Gilbert and Sullivan. I'd been in plays at school but they were modest, or obscure, or both and I wasn't particularly good. I only managed to get into drama school because Dad helped me with the audition pieces.

And I certainly would not consider taking off all my clothes and rubbing coal all over my body in front of an audience. I recognised this might be a disadvantage during a session on Greek theatre, when one of the students, Liv, a mature student indeed, decided to take all her clothes off and persuaded six boys to bear her aloft as the dead Helen of Troy.

'I just think she'd be naked,' she opined as she shrugged off her jumper and unzipped her jeans. She had an alarmingly bushy mons pubis that matched her frizzy auburn hair. It made a lovely botanical crown as they carried her through the space, hands digging into bare buttocks, calves and shoulders. I'm sure I was not the only person enjoying the lighting effect through her pubic hair. Unfortunately, Revealing All became a recurrent theme for Liv. Apparently many scenes called for nudity as far as she was concerned – Lady Macbeth's guilty revelations whilst sleep walking , the game of questions in *Rosencrantz and Guildenstern are Dead* and finally, and most terribly, Minnie Powell's first meeting with Donal in *The Shadow of a Gunman.*

Certainly, the Doctor and the Gentlewoman were most surprised, nay startled, to see Lady Macbeth enter wearing only her birthday suit, and it was hard to concentrate on Tom Stoppard's clever wordplay as Liv cavorted around the stage, boobs and bottom bouncing about, but Simon, our lecturer in naturalistic theatre, took her to task on her creation of Minnie Powell. He had lovingly created a 1920s Dublin tenement room with a fixed box set, a couple of cot beds, an old typewriter and fireplace complete with rosaries and crucifixion on the mantelpiece.

He was thrilled that we were going to be able to work in such detail. We had been split into groups and given different scenes to work on. I was working with a humourless boy, Damon, from Belfast on the scene with Tommy Owens, ardent lover of the republicans. I really didn't understand the situation in Northern Ireland and I was terrified of saying the wrong thing so I just let him rattle on and made a few superficial comments. Simon, our lecturer, had sound effects all organised. 'In the original production, the sound effects of the raid were so realistic the audience thought the theatre was under attack. It was unheard of,' he told us excitedly. Damon glowered during this announcement, obviously feeling it was in poor taste.

However, when Liv opened the working door and stepped into the space, not in the lovely tailored sage wool suit Simon had purloined from the wardrobe department, but naked, he jolted in his seat. She played the scene like a Medusaen temptress with her snaky auburn tendrils and her staring eyes, circling around a rather hapless Donal (a skinny shrimp of a boy called Glenn) who was definitely more Shadow than Gunman.

She leant over him, pressing her bare breasts against his back, as she made him type her name. Glenn was panting and his fingers were shaking over the keys, as she whispered in his ear. I thanked God I had had the good fortune to avoid working with her thus far.

In the theatre you're not supposed to be overtly rude about someone else's performance. You have to phrase it in terms of Helpful Criticism called Notes.

Simon had very few Notes.

He was very cross. He paused for a moment. 'Why the hell are you NAKED?' he said. It was as if she had personally wounded him, 'This is NATURALISM,' he thundered on, 'Do you honestly think a single woman in 1920 would enter the room of an unmarried man at ELEVEN O'CLOCK IN THE MORNING, NAKED?!'

Liv remained on the stage with her impressively hairy fanny still on display. I wondered if she brushed it out to give it more volume. I thought she might crumble but she didn't. She was furious.

'Christ. It's an interpretation Simon. If O'Casey was alive today, this is how he'd want it performed. You're so fucking timid.' She tried to dismiss him.

'Don't give me that crap. That isn't real life today either. That isn't reality.' He turned round to the rest of us, 'Hands up anyone who has met someone for the first time when they were wearing no clothes. An adult. Not a baby.'

No one put their hands up.

He turned back. Liv had her hand up high revealing a sprout of armpit hair and pulling her tits up making her nipples look cheeky. It really was fascinating watching someone just being nude.

'Oh, of course *you* have Liv. Of course, you have.' Simon was getting more cross.

'You're talking to a group of kids – no offence – what do they know?' This resulted in quite a few muttered retorts but from the evidence I'd gathered, there were quite a few with not much experience so Liv had a point.

'I defy you to go out into this school and find me anyone else to whom this would apply. I am not timid. I am a purist. I respect the work. I do not shit all over it.'

'What!' Liv put her hands on her substantial hips. Shrimpy Glenn sat bleakly looking at the typewriter behind her. 'I respect the fucking work too. I just wanted to try something different that's all. No need to get your knickers in a twist.'

Simon shot her a look 'I think you should go and put your knickers back on.' he said quietly. It was interesting how that gave him the upper hand. It was a bit like Eve taking a bite of the apple and becoming suddenly aware of her nudity and the shame flooding in. Liv looked down and then left the stage. The dust settled for a moment then Simon chucked his script on the floor and jumped nimbly onto the stage, following her through the flimsy door.

'Show's over folks,' said Andy in his booming drawl and we all got up and started to shuffle out. There was a good deal of moaning about time wasting and learning lines for no reason at all but no one bothered to hang around as we moved as one to the Union to pick over Liv and Simon's spat. About ten minutes later I realised I'd left my jacket in the auditorium so nipped back to get it. The theatre was barely lit but I could see Liv and Simon entangled and groaning on one of the skeletal cot beds. Perhaps being prepared to strip off at any given point has some advantages. Then I remembered the waxy tufts of hair in Simon's ears. I crept back out.

I am a mature student too – well, not over twenty-one, but not just straight out of school. I start drama school the year I am twenty, having spent two years mucking about. This means I am going into Higher Education at the same time as Judy. She is at Oxford though, having Worked So Hard and Exceeded All Expectations. I am too lazy to have made much of my A-levels and, in a sulk on results day, I tell Mum and Dad I'm going Travelling, as the place I have at Bristol is now not going to happen. This is what I tell my fellow thespians I have been doing but I am deliberately vague and change the subject so no one gets the full story.

In effect, I go back down to Granny and stay with her for three or four months, getting a job in a local pub for pocket money. She is happy with my company at first, now she's on her own, but I sleep in till lunchtime then monopolise the telly and, she says, I'm Not Tidy. I thought she'd be happy to have the chance to look after me but we begin to avoid each other as her face grows hard and she mutters under her breath and sighs heavily around me.

So, after a brief hug, I move on and stay with my Aunt May for a couple of months. She lives in a remote part of Scotland and there is no work. It's worse than Cumbria in some ways. The weather is relentlessly bleak and, whilst she reminds me of Dad in some of her mannerisms, the way she strokes her eyebrow when she's thinking, the purse of her lips as she fries an egg, she is harder than Dad; the older sister, unforgiving and blunt who scolds me for leaving the top off the milk bottle or not properly closing the door, as if I am a child. Aunt May has never had children; she has never married. She is a botanist and an expert on some type of rare wild orchid. Her life is pinched and frugal but she doesn't care. Every penny is hoarded towards her next research trip – they are often years and continents apart. May has seen the world but has few friends, does not value conversation and cherishes her many meticulously catalogued notebooks above all else.

She is up at dawn and walking with her determined Beagle, Pilot, up and down the hills before she shuts herself up in her study, only emerging for a couple of thickly buttered Ryvita and a pint of blackcurrant squash late in the afternoon, then she's off out with the dog again. On her return, she sleeps neatly and deeply on top of her bed for a couple of hours with Pilot draped over her hip, then we eat a late meagre dinner, soup and oatcakes or mackerel and cabbage. Every day she looks slightly astonished I'm still there and Pilot sits and stares at me quizzically for hours at a time while his mistress works. Dad sends me a bit of money and I try baking the odd disappointingly damp sagging cake and go to the pub. It is full of veneered wood, middle-aged men and stale smoke. I am clinging on, trying not to go back to Cumbria but my options are dwindling.

I arrive back at the Castle in March and Judy shrieks in delight – idiot. As I unpack my small case, I am furious to find myself here again, knowing I will have to be up and serving breakfast in the morning as Mother takes hers in bed.

And the time crawls by and races past, like waves rushing in and dawdling out, and before I know it, another year has gone and Judy has secured a place at Oxford and I have to Do Something. And drama school, the life of pretending to be someone else who has more going for them, is all that comes to mind. Dad helps me work up a couple of monologues, though his lack of enthusiasm is a match for mine, but, somehow, I get a place, though the thought of a life in bloody Cumbria lights a fire in me and I am determined on the day. I actually try to appear interested and display some talent. One of the lecturers auditioning knew Dad though; an old mate from the BBC. I know it's a favour to him really.

So I move into halls that are how I imagine Eastern Germany to be; large bare rooms with rows of loos and baths and a big communal kitchen at one end and doors glazed with obscure glass with trapped wire inside it. I put up a Salvador Dali poster and a moody picture of Marlon Brando and some pretty sheets of wrapping paper over the cheap, brown wardrobe and light some patchouli sticks which smell awful; then I stop caring and take to napping and piling up my dirty washing in the bottom of my wardrobe. I read the plays we're supposed to but mostly I miss the point of them. Sometimes I underline lines in pencil but, in class, I see that I've marked different lines to everyone else. I make a few friends but I'm at the edge of them. I don't speak the right language; they say words like 'simplistic' instead of simple and I don't know what the difference is. They've been to the West End and lived a cultured life. I know about livestock.

The only advantage I have is that I know people. I can see a weakness. I can understand a desire. To that end I am very successful with boys. I can say and do what most girls don't and I don't really care about it. The boys are generally easy to manipulate and I have had a series of interesting couplings but nothing serious to date. I don't want a boyfriend. Judy has a boyfriend. She writes to me about him (Jonathan) on a regular basis. They will probably get married as

soon as they finish university as it's Quite Serious. Her letters are full
of Picnics and Walks and Scrabble. If I wrote to her about my
romantic life it will be full of Quick Shags with People I Hardly Know
and Avoiding Eye Contact with the Bloke I Copped Off with When I
Was Drunk The Other Night. There are some men I have pursued. I
have flattered them, feigned an interest, reflected back what they
have wanted to hear, behaved in a covertly, slutty manner and then
been tremendously exciting in bed. They have then pursued me. I
have thus far lost interest. There has always been a flaw; the smell of
their skin, a forced laugh, a point of view, their shoes et cetera et
cetera et cetera. None of them have suited my purposes. Yet.

We are at the zoo. We are supposed to find an animal which
reflects us but also to observe the animals in order to help us with
character building. Both Pete and Simon are here. Though really it's
Simon, king of naturalism's gig, 'We want you to build an acting
vocabulary, a physical language that you can draw upon, and the
animal world is such a rich resource.'
We wander around in groups with notebooks clutched in hands,
aping the apes, peering at the penguins and trying to identify
ourselves in each animal. Pete has told us he's a lion. Course he is. I
watch the lion; easy, laconic, relaxed, graceful, assured, toned and
fucking powerful. And then I look at Pete trying to open a bag of
crisps.
Kitty has decided she's a Vervet monkey. It's a tiny grey little thing
with a black-face. They swarm around us at one point. 'They're just so
inquisitive,' she says, tinkling with laughter. I think she's a tarantula.
They are surprisingly attractive but deadly, and they move so
precisely and carefully. Kitty walks like she is avoiding the cracks on
pavements. Tiny cracks.
'I am a bison,' announces Andy proudly. I love how everyone has
assigned themselves magnificent beasts. No one has said, 'I am a
millipede or an earthworm.' There is no modesty or humility here. I
suppose it's no surprise – we are drama students. I watch as a couple
of zookeepers stand and smoke and snigger as two of the boys mimic
the chimpanzees, preening and playing. They gambol about shrieking

and chattering, cuffing each other with their knuckles, delighted at the accuracy of their work; we all look on ready to applaud. I hear one of the zookeepers mutter, 'Wankers.'

'Going to need that at the RSC,' the other zookeeper answers, smirking.

'Who are you Jen?' Kitty asks me.

I stare at her, 'A chameleon,' I say flatly.

Somehow it is nearing the end of the academic year but my 21st birthday is also looming. Mother has summoned me back to Cumbria for it. This is quite surprising as birthdays, particularly mine, have never been of much interest to her.

I have no exams but we are supposed to be auditioning for shows to take up to Edinburgh. I call The Castle from the payphone in the halls and try to put Mum off but she is tenacious. 'You're not twenty one every year' is the main thrust of her argument combined with, 'Judy is making the effort and she's at Oxford.'

So, I lug two heavy suitcases up and down grimy, grinding escalators and on and off the tube and sit on a greasy seat from Euston to Penrith for ever, where Dad meets me sheepishly and we pass a drizzly journey with sputtering conversation until The Castle looms and I roll my eyes, even though no one can see, and sigh loudly and resuscitate my long-held grudge against my parents for moving here.

Mum is out.

Bloody cheek.

I put on the kettle and Dad lights a fag.

'Where is she?' I can't help asking.

'Um, I'm not really sure.' He looks around the kitchen as if he doesn't live here.

As I slop the milk into the mugs and spill the sugar, I ask, 'How many were in for breakfast?'

'Not too bad today. We've got five rooms taken at the moment so nine this morning. We're full tonight though.'

'I've brought my washing,' I huff.

Dad tastes the tea; it's obviously dreadful.

'I'm going to have a nap before I do it,' I sigh.

'Ah yes. Your room,' he takes another sip, 'your room. Lovely tea.' Another sip. 'It's just that we've had a bit of a change around.'

I stare at him.

'Mum thought your room has a lot of potential for customers you know. So we've had a shift around. Now you're not here all the time.'

'Unbelievable.' I don't take my eyes off him. 'Is this why she's out? She's never out? She's like Norman Bates' mother normally. Can't bloody move her out of bed. But today she's out?'

'Now, come on Jen.'

'So where am I now, eh? The bloody shed at the bottom of the garden?'

'Don't be so dramatic, Jen.' He looks into his tea, 'No, you're in the attic.'

'Fucking hell!' I explode.

'Jennifer!' I don't really swear in front of my parents but I'm really cross.

'Great!' I slam my mug down on the table sending a slick of tea across it and storm out.

I charge upstairs. The servants' quarters had been a pretty much untouched row of little bedrooms tucked into the attic eaves between the square turrets at either end of the house. Most of them were filled with tea chests of unidentifiable rubbish belonging to people long-dead, forlorn, broken furniture and a lot of dust and grime. How the hell have they made one into a bedroom?

It's worse than I think.

They have chosen the second room along; it is marginally bigger than the first. There is a foldout camp bed with a vile, shiny purple sleeping bag on it which is set against a wall that looks like it has a revolting skin condition. Opposite, someone has slung a large tie-dyed wall hanging to cover more of the embarrassing skin complaint. There is a small, urine coloured sheepskin rug on the floor. What the fuck is this? 1967? The biggest insult is a large poster, obviously painted by Mum, in garish colours, which bellows, 'Welcome Home Jen!' and is embellished with a set of drama masks and a few flowers. The whole thing must have taken about twenty minutes.

So Judy gets to keep her room.

Of course she bloody does.

Her super lovely brainy brain must be nourished with fully restorative Sleep in calm, comfort and peaceful surroundings while I can bloody shiver and rot in the attic with the mice and spiders. I go back downstairs. Dad is still in the kitchen.

'I love it,' I say.

'Really?' He sounds so happy.

'No, of course I bloody don't. How can you expect me to sleep up there? It's no better than a squat!' I shout.

'It's not that bad darling, is it?'

'Have you been up there? It's horrible. Why does Judy get to keep her room? I'm the oldest.'

'Look. It's just the way it worked out. Your room was more suited to guests.' Dad is fidgeting with his ear and looking at the door.

'Okay I'll pay you to stay in my room,' I say.

'What?' He looks at me askance.

'I'll pay. I won't sleep a wink up there. So I'll pay you, or,' I pause for effect, 'I'll go and stay at the Bells.'

'But Jen, we're full tonight. I already told you.' He looks horrified.

'Well, that's decided then. I'll go to the Bells. I'll just give them a ring and see if they have a room.'

I march out and down the hall to the phone. Even for me this is daring.

Amazingly, I still know Christine's number.

'Kirby Thore 216.' I start a little at Mrs Bell's voice, older, placid, a little cracked.

'Hello Mrs Bell. It's Jennifer Wentworth here.' I try to sound confident and grown-up.

'Jennifer! Oh Jennifer. Is that really you? Jennifer, pet! How are you, love? It's so long since we've seen you. How are you keeping, pet?' And it is as if her words are pouring down the phone line and wrapping themselves around me like the tendrils of a plant, growing too quickly, hungry for love, all the emotion there for all these years with nowhere to go. I am a little alarmed but the attic is worse.

'I'm fine. In fact I'd like to book a room with you for tonight if that's convenient.' (I am So pleased with how that sounded!)

There is a blank sound for a moment at the other end of the

phone then, 'A room? Yes, of course. Who for Jen?'

'For me, Mrs Bell, if that's okay?'

'Oh I see.' I imagine her mind racing but, all credit to her, she rallies, 'Well, yes Jen, that's no problem. It will be lovely to see you.' There is another brief pause, 'Now, why don't you come and have your tea with us too?'

'Are you sure, Mrs Bell?' This is working out better than expected.

'Of course, pet. Shall we say six o'clock?'

'That would be perfect. I'll see you later.'

I put the phone down and go back to the kitchen. I have done a terrible thing. The Bells are the opposition, the enemy, even though everyone is superficially still friendly, but my parents want me to sleep in the attic so all's fair as far as I'm concerned.

Dad is sitting at the kitchen table, running a finger up and down the grain of the wood.

'I'm going to do my washing,' I announce, kicking one of my suitcases in the general direction of the back pantry, 'then I'm going to the Bells. They've invited me for supper so I'll see you tomorrow for the party.'

Dad nods without looking up. He doesn't say a word.

I have been back to Christine's over the years but not many times. I fill a rucksack with overnight stuff and the sun feels fairly strong on my bare shoulder as I push through the gate and ring the bell on the porch door. I resist the temptation to start toeing off my shoes, remembering I am a guest today not a little girl.

I hear Mrs Bell clearing her throat before I see her. She looks both unchanged and totally different. She still has her beehive but it is thinner and smaller, less substantial somehow. She is fully made up but her face is more lined and, whereas before I thought she looked flawless, today I think she looks cheap; her coral lipstick is too matte and caked, her blue eyeshadow is too bright and crusting into the creases of her eyelids. It's disappointing. Christine would have had a word if she were around. She's still in the house coat with a tidy dress underneath but she is plumper and breathless, solid but more insubstantial at the same time, as if at any moment she will lose attention and drift away like the last threads of a dream.

'Jennifer!' she exclaims, grasping my hand and clawing my arm, 'I can't believe it's you! Come on, come in, pet. But where are your bags?' She looks around my legs and beyond me as if my bags are a disobedient scamp who is giving me the run-around.

'They're up at The Castle, Mrs Bell,' I state.

Hands to her chest, 'Of course, they are,' she shakes her head, 'of course.' A new thought pops in as she clasps my hand again and leads me into the familiar cluttered hallway, 'But why aren't you staying there Jenny love? I mean it's lovely to have you here, of course, it is but why aren't you staying there?'

'There isn't room for me,' I say in a small voice. I am aware of the effect this will have. She stops dead. We have reached the entrance to the kitchen. She practically drags me to the table and we abruptly sit down. I'm pleased we haven't gone to the guests' lounge.

'What?' poor Mrs Bell declares, 'There's no room for you? I don't understand,' and this is from the woman who would give anything to make room for her own daughter for one more precious moment, let alone a night.

'Well,' I say, looking down at the table as if it's almost too hard to talk about, 'I've come home for my birthday,' Mrs Bell winces – no more birthdays for Christine, 'and Mum and Dad have turned my bedroom into a guestroom.'

She gasps.

'And,' I add the insult to the injury, 'they want me to sleep in the attic without a proper bed or anything.'

'Oh you poor, poor girl.' This is more like it.

'I just couldn't face it. And I thought of you. So, that's when I phoned.'

'Say no more.' She pats my hand and stands up. 'I'm going to make you some coffee and I've got some cake and we're going to have a proper chat.' She busies herself filling the kettle and opening and closing the cupboard doors. A golden Victoria sandwich appears from a tin. The kettle whistles.

Then I realise she's crying.

She turns to me and her face is horribly familiar from the early days of Christine's disappearance. 'I just can't believe they'd let a precious girl like you sleep in the attic. I mean it's just not right. They should thank their lucky stars is what they should do. They should treat you like a queen.'

Her voice is getting too loud and her coral fingernails are digging deeply into the soft flesh of her upper arms. I don't like the way this is going.

'Well, at least I'm here now,' I say brightly, 'The cake looks delicious.'

'Yes,' Mrs Bell seems to calm down a little, 'you are here now. Aren't you polite? Better than the lads. They just wolf everything down. Wouldn't give that sponge a second glance, never mind say anything about it. Always been the same. Like feeding time at the zoo.'

'How are Kevin and Bryan?' I ask. She brings over the coffee and sits down, slicing the cake efficiently and flopping a piece neatly onto two plates.

She licks a finger delicately. 'Well, Kevin is working on the Slater's farm so he's bringing in a bit of cash. And Bryan. Well, Bryan,' she sighs, 'he's got all sorts of big ideas.'

'Really?' I say, encouragingly.

I think of his mop of thick black hair and ice blue eyes. I haven't seen him for years. It's annoying. He really did go travelling. Properly. Beyond Interrailing. I think he got as far as Australia.

'His dad says it's time he got a proper job but I don't know what he wants to do. He's written a few things while he's been abroad and had them printed. You know, travel writing.' She speaks as if she's no idea what Abroad is and has never read a newspaper. I can't fathom whether she's proud or annoyed by this career path. She just seems perplexed as if faced by a set of instructions to construct a familiar object but has found they're in a foreign language.

'I've never been overseas myself. Well, neither has Peter, could never afford it when we were younger. A few days over in Yorkshire maybe. And then, with this place, well, you're tied for the summer. I was always happy at home though. Not really keen on foreigners, me. Don't know where Bryan gets it from.'

'So where is he now?' I ask finishing my cake. I'd quite like another piece.

'He's been in Thailand actually,' she says wearily, 'but, surprisingly, he's at home at the moment.'

I sit up a little straighter.

'Yes, just for a few weeks and then he's off to Peru so he tells me.' She sounds resigned to it but very sad. 'I mean why go to Peru? What's there? I've never heard of anything in Peru!'

'Paddington came from Peru,' I quip.

'He's not real,' she snaps.

'So is he actually at home now, as in, in the house?' I ask, trying not to sound too eager.

'Oh no. He's off in Penrith, selling some records or something to raise some money for his trip. He lives hand to mouth that boy. But he'll be back later, I expect.'

'He'll have to come to my birthday party.' What the hell, it's worth a try. 'Up at The Castle tomorrow. And Kevin too.' I say quickly so as not to make it too obvious.

She smiles.

'It's my 21st.' It slips out and I regret it immediately.

Tears puddle in her eyes but don't spill.

'Christine would have been twenty-one this year,' she says, quietly but she looks at me, 'Do you ever think about her?'

'All the time,' I lie, putting my hand on hers. I really want another piece of cake.

'I never know what to do with myself on her birthday, or Christmas for that matter, and no one wants to speak about her, or speak to me. You should see what people will do in the village to avoid me. I've just stopped going out on any of those days. Spares their feelings, you know.'

'But you should be able to talk about her, if you want to,' I say and I find I do, to an extent, believe this. I take a breath in. 'You can always talk to me, Mrs Bell.'

She smiles bravely. 'Why don't you have another piece of cake, pet,' and then she settles back in her chair and starts to talk about Christine and I am bored to tears but I just nod and smile and match her emotions and don't really listen and all the time I am thinking about sleeping under the same roof as Bryan and planning what I might say to him and hoping he'll come to my birthday party. I can't wait to see him.

We sit in the kitchen for hours and then Mrs Bell starts to make tea. I suggest I put my rucksack in my room and she tells me it's the third door on the left down the corridor.

I leave the kitchen but I can't help deviating via Christine's. The door is closed. I tentatively open it and, though I hope it will be different, it is no surprise that it is exactly as it was when she vanished. Everything is immaculately clean so Mrs Bell is a regular visitor in here. The velvet on the stool is a little faded now and the brilliant white has dulled but all the toys are still manically smiling and sitting up straight, waiting for their mistress to return. I slip into the room and open the wardrobe door. I remember Christine standing in front of all her clothes. They seem so tiny now and dead, thinly hanging and emptily useless, shrugged off, pointlessly cleaned and kept, cold and lost.

I shut the door quickly to head back to my room.

Kevin is standing in the corridor.

He's tanned from the farm work, a surprise as his skin was always so pinkly white. His hair is long and unruly. He looks at me with hostility. As far as he is concerned I'm a guest visiting his lost sister's shrine without permission.

'Kevin,' I say, 'Hi.'

He blinks, 'Jen,' he manages.

'Yes,' I look back at Christine's door, 'sorry. I know I shouldn't, it's just, you know...' I trail off hoping my unspoken words will call to mind some kind of need for resolution, or grief, or a homage concealing the reality of plain nosiness.

'Yeah. Sure. Sorry. I thought. You know. It's fine. Sure.' and he charges off in the direction of his bedroom. The door slams and moments later I hear *Dark Side of the Moon* begin. I wonder if this is a message, 'Do you remember when...'

I go into my room.

I eat with the family. Bryan doesn't turn up. Kevin is silent despite his mother trying to engage him with cheery questions. He mostly keeps his eyes down and barely acknowledges I am there. Mr Bell is friendly but drinks several cans of beer with his food. His nose is red and bulbous and his stomach is as taught and full as a healthy pregnancy; he is not a fine figure of a man.

Mrs Bell announces that she and I have had a lovely chat about Christine. Mr Bell sags and fumbles his fork onto the table. Kevin takes a gulp of beer too and says he's off, pushing back his chair.

'You see Jennifer?' she turns to me, 'You see what I mean?' Her voice rises, 'I can't even say her name and they run for the hills.' She yells these last few words towards Kevin's departing figure. It's quite alarming.

'Those sausages were good Hilda, love. Did you get them in the market?' Peter Bell feebly gambles.

'Oh for pity's sake,' and Mrs Bell is up, snatching his half-finished plate from him and smearing the remainder into the bin. He is left, knife and fork in hand, impotent utensils, mouth agog.

He carefully places them on the table. Mrs Bell is gripping the worktop.

I slice into another sausage and try not to chew too loudly. After a moment, she turns to us, face bright as a glassy pond, 'There's *Arctic Roll* for dessert,' she spits out.

'Lovely sweetheart,' Peter says soothingly as if nothing has happened.

We are scraping our bowls and finishing our cups of tea when Kevin pops his head in the door, 'Just going t' The Lamb. Won't be late,' he announces.

'Mind if I come along?' I chance, standing up with my bowl and cup, 'Wouldn't mind seeing who's around.' I put them in the sink.

Kevin is looking at his fingernails. 'Please yourself,' he mumbles.

'Oh,' Mrs Bell starts. I know she wants me to stay so she can go on some more about Christine but enough is enough.

I smile brightly, 'We won't be late,' and push Kevin out the door.

We trudge the few yards up the village to the pub. It is a warmish evening. It's been hot in London and my skin is brown. I am wearing a pale pink T-shirt and jeans. Since I've had to live on a grant I've lost quite a bit of weight so I know I look good, or at least better. I think

Kevin is a bit embarrassed to be with me but I don't care. I'm hoping Bryan will be in there.

It is dark and familiar inside, beery and smoky with the same aging locals, hands clamped around their pints, at the bar. They look up as we come in and look away again. They never were interested in much.

Kevin heads through to the back where the pool table is and I follow him. A few other lads around his age are playing. He goes to the bar, then turns back to me.

'Do you want a drink?' He doesn't really sound like he wants to buy me one.

'Sure,' I say, 'I'll buy the next one,' I say to reassure him this is not a date.

I sip a Bacardi and Coke and we walk to the pool table. Two boys are hunched over assessing a shot with their backs to us. One of them eventually lines up the cue and pots a ball. They stand up and turn. It's Christopher Robert. They are now gangly young men. As I watched them grow up I wondered if they would develop separate identities. Thus far this has not been the case. Their only hope will be to marry identical twin girls. Or maybe even Siamese twins.

They stare at me as usual.

'Hi guys!' I say. They look at me and they show some appreciation of my appearance. It is barely noticeable but there nevertheless.

'Hello Jen,' says one, God knows which.

'How are you?' says the other.

'I'm fine,' I say, 'how are you two? Still working on the farm?'

They begin a dull monotone response that is basically, 'Yes.' I hardly listen. Looks like we're in for a thrilling evening. I'm already bored and my eyes are flitting round the bar looking for a better option.

It's then that I see Maureen serving. She is behind the bar, flushed and bright eyed as always.

''Scuse me boys, I'm just going to say hello to Maureen. See you in a bit,' and I scoot over and lean on the wood, hissing to Maureen who is at the far end, tongue out as she pulls a pint. She peers in my direction, frowns, then recognises me and quickly finishes serving her customer and lumbers down towards me. Maureen has not slimmed down; she's fattened up. She is grabbing at her hair and wetly smiling.

'Jen! When did you get back? I've got the invite. Can't wait for the party!'

'Good! Yes, I got back today. Just catching up with everybody. I didn't know you were working here?'

'Yeah, well. There was nowt else going. Mum says I ought to be training to be a nurse like Andrea but I don't like blood so that's no good. I had that job at the shoe factory but I got made redundant so it's just been bits and pieces since then.'

'Right. I see.'

'Not like you and Judy. Not enough brains for university or enough courage for drama school.'

'I don't know about that.'

'So how's it going? Are you going to be famous and be on the telly?'

'Well I suppose that's the plan.' This seems highly unlikely to me at the moment. I sip my Bacardi in what I hope is a sophisticated manner.

'I'm counting on it. I want to be able to tell everyone about my famous friend Jennifer Wentworth. Or are you going to change your name? You know like Elton John and Cliff Richard did? I'd love to be famous, me, but I can't think what I could be famous for, that's the trouble. You've got to be special haven't you? Do you think you will get famous, Jen?'

'I don't know Maureen, we'll have to wait and see.' This answer is not the one that fits with Maureen's plans however; I can see she was after wholehearted certainty.

'Or maybe Judy will,' Maureen rushes on, mouth shiny, 'I mean she's at Oxford. She's got to do something amazing hasn't she. She's just so clever, isn't she? We've never had anyone in the village get to Oxford.' She wrinkles her nose, 'Actually I'm not sure that's completely true, no one I've heard of, any road.'

I slam the drink down.

'If you say so Maureen,' I say crossly, 'What are you wearing to the party tomorrow?' I know she won't have been able to afford anything much and will feel fat. Her face falls for a moment but then she bounces back.

'Mam's made me a lovely new top. I'm dead chuffed with it.' She grins.

'Oh good. I'm pleased for you.'

She flicks and scrunches her curly perm and licks at her already slickety slack lips. Then she does a little wave over my shoulder and slyly giggles at me. I turn to look but all I see are Christopher Robert standing like dullards by the pool table. 'Who are you waving to?' I ask confused.

'Chris,' she breathes, bursting with excitement.

'Chris?!' I repeat loudly.

'Shh,' she hushes me, 'don't embarrass him.' She giggles again. It's hard to believe we're the same age.

'So are you and he...?' I ask warily.

'Yeah,' she is so proud, 'Been going with each other for about three months now. Oh Jen, he's grand.' Her voice goes all squeaky, 'And,' she can hardly contain herself, 'he's got a massive knob,' and she bends over, hand failing to stop farty giggles bursting from her mouth. I really laugh. It's a real surprise. Who'd have thought it. I will never look at Christopher the same way again. Except I don't know which one Christopher is.

'Why don't you bring him to the party tomorrow?' I suggest with uncharacteristic generosity.

Maureen looks happy. 'Well thanks Jen, that's kind of you, but your mam already invited him, and Rob.' Then she leans closer across the bar, 'I've said to Mam it doesn't matter what job I do because if I play my cards right, I'll marry Chris and I'll end up with half of that farm.' She clearly thinks that will be some achievement, another flick of her hair.

'So you will Maureen,' I say, contemplating whether marriage to Christopher Robert would be worth the biggest farm in the village, even if he does have, as Maureen so eloquently put it, a massive knob.

Mrs Bell has made a full English breakfast replete with black pudding, but after too many Bacardis the night before I can't really face it and have to tell her I'm too nervous about my party to eat. She is thrilled I'm getting ready there and will see me all dressed up. 'It's only a little lunchtime thing,' I try to downplay it but she's having none of it and says the party has been the talk of the whole village for weeks. She's told Pete he's giving me a lift up to The Castle.

I take a long hot bath again hoping that Bryan might put in an appearance. Where the hell is he? The house is quiet as the grave. Kevin is still asleep and I've no idea whether Bryan is in or out.

I dress carefully; I want to make some sort of impression and when I walk into the kitchen Mrs Bell's face is already set in a, 'You look beautiful,' expression which quickly changes when she sees me. 'Oh,' she says, before she can stop herself.

I am wearing a man's dinner suit, which I found in a charity shop, with red stilettos, a slim, red, satin bowtie and red lipstick. I have slicked my hair back flat to my head. I have a low-cut silky, thin, black T-shirt on under my jacket. I think I look great.

'Well, don't you look…' she falters, 'I thought you'd be wearing a dress but you look like something from a magazine,' she finally manages; though I'm not sure this is entirely complimentary, it's not bad either.

'Thank you,' I say, 'is Mr Bell ready?'

'Pete!' she shouts not taking her eyes from me. I notice she has her little Kodak camera out on the worktop. She doesn't mention it.

'He'll bring the car round,' she smiles thinly.

'I'll see you later,' I stride out, feeling powerful. I am going to conquer The Castle.

'Have a lovely time, pet,' she calls after me.

Mr Bell is facing forward in the car and doesn't look at me until I'm in it. He stares at my mouth. 'Christ,' he mutters and the car jerks away.

The party is in the ballroom. I have arrived a bit early in order to get the main bickering with Mother and Judy over with before the guests arrive. I let myself in the front door – it's still bloody heavy - and walk up the hallway, turning right, away from the kitchen and the back of the house, towards the ballroom. This is rarely used as it's so cavernous it's difficult to heat and the windows are draughty. It must have been bearable during actual balls, if you had long thick dresses and were continually dancing to keep yourself warm.

I go through the double doors; there is no one here but tables are set up with glasses and foil wrapped food so there is evidence of some effort. Dad has moved his record player in here. I hope it's not going to be Françoise Hardy and Edith Piaf all afternoon. There are a few balloons hanging limply from the huge fireplace bumping feebly against each other as a modicum of warm air is produced by the roaring fire. The sun is glaring through but it is still chilly. Good job I'm wearing a jacket.

Voices are approaching. High then low. Laughing. High then low. Someone's having fun. Judy and Jonathan scutter through the door; he is carrying two bottles by the neck and a bowl of peanuts and she has a platter. They are both looking at each other; a picture of Young Love.

'Jen!' Judy shouts and hurls the platter onto the table then lurches for me like an exuberant puppy, hugging me and not letting go. 'Happy birthday! Why aren't you staying here? Where have you been? I've got so much to tell you!' She pulls back and looks at me. She is looking nauseatingly fresh and gorgeous. I swear she has Scandinavian blood. It is as if she has just tripped down off a dewy mountainside having drunk a freshly drawn glass of milk and eaten a crisp green juicy apple. She is fucking glowing.

'And I want you to meet Jonathan,' she reaches to tug him forward. He is as wholesome as she is. Clear-eyed, white, even teeth, strong jaw, broad shoulders. I want to projectile vomit on them both.

'So you must be the birthday girl,' he shuffles and smiles bashfully, thinking he's charming. I hate him already.

'Yes,' I say, with a stone cold stare, tight lipped. I watch his smiling fizzle out.

'I love your clothes,' Judy tries, 'so dramatic,' and she looks at Jonathan with a quick I-Told-You-She-Was-Hard-Work look.

'Thanks. Where is Mother?' I am dismissing her before we've even begun. I don't want to hear about Jonathan and bloody Oxford and how perfect her life is.

'In the kitchen.' I start to walk and she trots after me, 'I love your shoes! How do you walk in them?'

'Watch me.' I march down the corridor.

'I don't think I could manage shoes that high. What do you think Jonathan?'

'Oh I don't know. I think you can do anything you want to do, buttercup.'

I roll my eyes.

'Ah thanks, JJ,' she puts on a baby voice to reply. Christ.

Mother is sitting at the kitchen table. Dad is stirring something on the *Rayburn*.

She looks at me. I look at her.

'I didn't know it was fancy dress,' she smiles lazily.

'Hello to you too,' I say. Dad has turned round. He looks sad, as always.

'Happy birthday Jen,' he says and comes and gives me a peck on the cheek. I keep my eyes on my mother.

She says nothing.

I raise an eyebrow.

'Yes, yes,' she waves a pink-nailed hand, 'all that.'

'You can't even be bothered to say the words to me!' I explode, 'You turn me out of my bedroom and put me in the bloody rat infested attic and you can't even say happy fucking birthday?'

'Jen,' Judy says warily, obviously embarrassed for JJ.

'How was it at the Bells?' Mum says, dryly.

'Really bloody nice,' I say, 'a proper hot meal, no offence Dad, some interesting conversation, central heating, enough hot water for a deep bath. It was really bloody nice. A treat!'

'Well good. I'm pleased for you.' She sounds like she doesn't care.

'And she didn't say anything nasty about what I'm wearing. She said I look like something from a magazine.'

Mum snorts.

'And she took my photo.' I lie.

'Only because she hasn't got a daughter of her own to snap,' she spits at me.

'That's enough, Vivian,' Dad says, 'people will be arriving soon. Go and put your face on.'

Mother stands up regally and moves towards me. 'You've no idea how much you've hurt your father's feelings,' she hisses as she passes.

'But not yours,' I shout after her, 'you'd be glad I stayed there. Made all that fuss about me coming home just to make me sleep in an attic. Where are Jonathan and Judy sleeping? In the fucking bridal suite?'

They didn't have a bridal suite but I bet JJ and Buttercup would have had it if there had been one.

I let her footsteps proceed down the hallway before I turn on Dad.

'There seem to be an embarrassment of riches on the present front,' I say archly. So far I've seen nothing. Not even a card.

Dad looks about him and exhales. 'We are throwing the party, Jen,' he manages without conviction.

'Again,' I say, 'not my choice.'

I turn and leave the kitchen and head back towards the ballroom where I snatch a bottle of wine, opened already and Breathing and glug and gulp from it hoping someone will come in and catch me. I put it back once it is half empty, then march to the record player. I flick viciously through Dad's pathetic collection. Ideally, I would hurl each disc out of the sleeve and let them shatter across the pale polished floor. I realise the records are too modern for this to happen however and really that would be the end of our relationship. I give up on them in disgust and go back to the wine; then I hear the doorbell go, not a modern chime but a literal bell, as the front door opens, like a bloody grocer's shop.

And the party begins.

It turns out the party is for the village and not for me. Mother has pulled out all the stops and invited anyone and everyone. I can't work out why she's bothered until she tinkles her glass and the room hushes and she says she has a special announcement. Everyone knows it's my birthday so I wonder if I'm pregnant. Then I realise in horror that Judy and Jonathan might be getting married but no, it's about The Castle.

'We wanted everyone to share our exciting news today. We've

been granted a license and, in a few short weeks, this beautiful ballroom will become The Castle Restaurant to which we hope you will all want to come and share some lovely meals and special moments with us. We have a dear friend coming to create wonderful food and we hope it will bring even more life to this delightful village where you have made us feel so welcome.'

I look at Judy and there are tears in her eyes. She is plumped with pride. Dad stands at Mother's side, Albert to her Victoria, as she holds forth as if she is Lady of the Manor. And the villagers respond with delight. There are oohs and aahs and more food appears and the platters are unwrapped and, shock, horror, the guests are given *warm* plates for their food which is Delicious-Have-You-Tried-The-Salmon-What-A-Treat. My birthday is forgotten. I am the unwitting Trojan horse.

I skulk out and head for the back garden scooping another bottle of wine on the way. At the kitchen door I find Bryan leaning against the solid brick, smoking a roll-up. The golden light of the evening sun is just catching him and he looks like the cover of an album, one foot resting up against the wall, a worn, white shirt loosely buttoned with pale jeans and thin, dark, leather bracelets on his taut wrist; his black ponytailed hair is so glossy and long it reminds me of Christine's. He exudes warmth and calm and I can see the smooth muscles of his chest. I want to lay my hands on them and feel his heartbeat.

'Hi,' I say, but I can't manage to throw off my sulky tone. I flop onto the low damp wall that skirts the patchy kitchen garden by the back door. There is a smell of mint and lavender just starting. Summer is nearly here.

'Hi,' he smiles through the smoke, 'Happy birthday.'

'Thanks.' It is an ungrateful and begrudging response. I kick at the path with the top of my stiletto imagining it's my mother's head.

'You okay?' He doesn't sound that bothered; he's just being polite.

'Not really,' I say, 'I bloody hate my parents.'

'Oh dear,' he smiles and tilts his head as if I am a child to be indulged. This makes me even more annoyed.

'This is supposed to be my birthday party,' I feel obliged to elucidate, 'and I didn't even want to come home and they insisted and so I did and they didn't even get me a present and then Mother bloody invites the whole sodding village so she can announce they're opening a fucking restaurant and it's nothing to do with me or my birthday as per usual and I didn't even get any bloody presents because I got a party which I didn't want and they've employed some poncy chef to cook for them because they're so fucking lazy and useless and no doubt he'll use up all the money they make in the restaurant because they're useless at business because neither of them has any idea about anything and the chef will probably take them to the cleaners or be really crap because they've no idea who is good and who isn't and all Mum wants to do is nothing and all Dad wants to do is listen to Françoise Hardy and they could have got me a fucking present.'

I am quite drunk.

'You're the same age as Christine, aren't you?' he says, mildly.

We have examined subtext at drama school. I take his subtext to mean, 'At least you're not dead.'

'You mean, at least I'm not dead,' I say. As I said, I'm quite drunk. He looks down at his rollie then takes another drag. I realise I've said a horrible thing.

He looks at me, blue eyes glittering. 'Not many people say she's dead.' I don't want to apologise.

'That has to be the assumption. It's been ten years,' I reason a little more quietly.

'Yes,' he swallows, clears his throat lightly, looks at the sky, 'I hope she is dead,' he says.

'Me too,' I say.

We are silent for a while.

Eventually I say, 'I'm surprised you're here. Your mum said you were heading off to Peru. But I suppose it's free food and drink.'

'Change of plans,' He's finished his cigarette and is tucking in his shirt.

'Really?' I'm a bit too drunk to care.

'Yeah,' he smiles at me. He really is very good looking. 'I've got this gig as a chef. Going to take these cretins to the cleaners. Steal their money.'

'Shit,' I say.

He smiles and turns easily back into the kitchen. I am left alone.

'I suppose a shag's out of the question?' I mutter, planting the empty wine bottle up to its shoulders in the pitiful border next to me. I'm feeling horribly sorry for myself.

I set off down the uneven path that runs around the house. I do not want to go in through the kitchen and see Bryan again. I teeter unsteadily on my stilettos but make it round to the ballroom windows where I gaze into the dregs of the party. Dad is on the sofa and Mum is curled at his feet; he has a hand idly thumbing her hair. Judy and Jonathan are slow dancing, stiffly rocking from side to side, both grinning like fools. Maureen and Christopher are frantically snogging up against one of the windows and I can see her mum looking on with shifting embarrassment as she leans heavily on the buffet table. A couple of Maureen's younger siblings are chasing each other, they must be almost leaving the primary school or just in secondary. Their clothes are untucked and dishevelled and their hair wild and frizzy like Maureen's. They are annoying several guests as they scoot past, grabbing a handful of skirt to corner more effectively, or knocking an arm with a drink in it, as they avoid being tagged.

I want to go in there and demand that they notice me. There wasn't even a birthday cake. I realise no one has sung 'Happy Birthday' to me. I bloody hate them all.

I decide to walk back to the Bells.

It takes quite a long time.

I have forgotten how dark it is without street lights.

I have forgotten that cart tracks and stilettos won't work. I take off the stilettos and continue barefoot. It's slow progress. The inky trees and flitting bats have become unfamiliar and I keep thinking I'm being watched. I am jumpy. Scared. I remember what it was like when Christine disappeared.

By the time I reach the village my feet are caked in mud. I realise with dismay I cannot go in Mrs Bell's neat as a pin house in such a mess. Near the shop, there is the deep puddle that never disappears. That's not true, it did in the summer of '76 and some people took pictures of the dry cracked moon crater hole that was left, but apart from that, it's always there. Andrea Gallagher said it was part of an underground spring.

I decide to wash my feet in the Eternal Puddle.

To do this I have to sit down. My trousers feel too tight after all the wine. I decide to undo them. I sit at the edge of the green on the damp grass and put my feet in the muddy brown water. It doesn't seem to help much but the big chunks come off. I rub them against each other. The water is thick and slow. I can't feel the bottom of the puddle.

I am very tired.

I decide to lie back and look at the stars for a little bit.

The stars are boring. I don't know what I'm looking for.

I decide to shut my eyes. Just for a little while.

Someone is shaking me. 'Jen. Jen.'

I want to open my eyes but I was dreaming I was floating in the Dead Sea and it was really solid but wet. I don't know where I am.

'Jen. Are you okay?' I don't recognise the voice but he sounds worried. Then I know who it is. My eyes open and Bryan is kneeling down next to me.

I stay still.

'Yes. I was looking at the stars then I think I must've had a little nap. What time is it is it?' I don't want to sit up. I like that I'm lying down.

'It's four in the morning. Are you sure everything is okay?' I sense there is something else going on here. I think hard trying to scramble out of the grogginess of sleep. I piece things together. I decide to sit up.

I picture the scene from Bryan's point of view. Discarded shoes, filthy feet in the puddle, unbuttoned pants, unconscious girl.

I do up my trousers.

'I was feeling fat. They were too tight.'

'Oh,' he nods.

'And I couldn't walk in my stilettos. In the mud.'

'Right,' he continues, nodding.

'And then my feet were muddy so I thought I'd wash them because your mum's house is so clean.'

'Okay,' he looks at me as if my behaviour is perfectly reasonable.

'It really didn't work.'

He looks at my feet. 'No,' he says.

'And then I was tired so I went to sleep.' My voice has got quieter and quieter as if, if I speak too loudly I might frighten him away.

'Do you want to go home now?' he says.

'Yes,' I really do, 'my bum is wet. I think all my clothes are. Where I was lying.'

'Looking at the stars.'

'Yes. Looking at the stars.'

He stands up and offers me his hand. I draw my feet up and take it. I stand unsteadily.

'I hated that party,' I say.

'I know,' he says.

We begin to walk towards his house.

'There wasn't a cake and no one even sang 'Happy Birthday' to me.'

'That's tough,' he says.

'The food was good though,' I admit.

'Thanks.'

'Where did you learn to cook?'

'All over. That's how I've managed to travel. Just got jobs in different hotels and restaurants. Earned enough to move on and see the next place. Picked up stuff on the way.'

'Why have you come back here?'

'Wherever you go you take your troubles with you. Need to slow down a bit. That's all. For a bit.'

'Your mum said you were going to Peru,'

'Yeah. I told her that. I wasn't sure whether things would work out. Didn't want to get her hopes up. But tonight was okay. For me.'

'Okay.'

We're at the house and Bryan unlocks the front door. I realise I hadn't made any arrangements how to get back in. We creep in and I feel sad that the night is over. We walk down the corridor to the bedrooms, Bryan in front, long ponytail and slim hips, a rock star, and me, a sorry sight. We reach the guest bathroom and he takes my hand and leads me in, softly closing the door behind him.

I stand and watch as he begins to run a bath. He methodically rolls up the sleeves of his white shirt and calmly churns the water as it fills, a look of concentration on his face. He pours in bubble bath and the room smells flowery and fresh and I begin to warm up. I am sleepy though.

He comes over to me and carefully undresses me. He takes each item of filthy clothing and lays it tenderly on the chair. There is only the sound of the running water rumbling as the tub fills. I give myself over to him completely. The last thing he removes is my bow tie, delicately, nimbly. He carries it as if it is a delicate creature to the chair.

He takes my hand and leads me to the bath. He turns off the taps and the water stills. The bubbles are a brilliant, expectant white. I step my filthy foot into the water and the bubbles start to pucker and pop and it is perfect. He holds my hand until I'm standing in the bath. I sit, then lie down.

It is delicious. He leaves the room.

I close my eyes, the water laps and sucks. I drift.

He returns.

I open my eyes.

He has a Bakewell tart with a single birthday candle.

He sings me 'Happy Birthday' so quietly I can hardly hear it. I blow out the candle.

He takes a bar of soap and lathers his hands.

'Your foot,' he says. He soaps my foot, firmly, in between my toes, his thumb on my instep, his hand cupping my heel, both hands smoothing my ankle and calf. My foot is clean. Then he takes my other foot. I want him to keep washing my feet I want to arch my back and cry out but I am silent.

He fetches a large towel. He stands and hold it out. I get up like an obedient child.

I step out of the bath and he wraps me up and I feel his arms around me. He dries me carefully, wraps me in the towel, picks up my clothes and opens the door. I follow him out.

We go to my room. He pulls back the covers on the bed. I drop the towel and lie down for him.

He looks at me. All of me. I look at him.

He picks up the towel, covers me up and leaves.

I bite my knuckle.

A cool, overcast August has arrived,. On the train up to Edinburgh we stop at Penrith station and I'm seized by the urge to jump off and run to Long Tarn and find Bryan and throw my arms around his neck and kiss him passionately. Or I want him to appear on the station. To somehow know I am on the train and see me through the steam, that no longer exists, and demand I alight and abandon my fellow actors and walk calmly away with him into a rose pink sunset.

'You ok Jen?' It's Sam. She has given up biting her nails but took to twisting her hair into multiple tiny knots instead; she decided to shave her head a few days ago to stave this compulsion. With her deep-set dark eyes and sallow skin, she now has the look of an Auschwitz survivor who's had access to excellent manicure facilities. 'You're sitting there smiling to yourself is all,' she says.

'Just daydreaming,' I reply, 'Shall we run our lines?' and we fumble for our scripts and settle down to check we're absolutely off-book for our opening night in two days. I say night, our performances are at all hours, one is even late morning, but I am performing at The Fringe and that is something.

We had all auditioned for every part, even producing the shows, which sounds important but is basically raising enough money to get us up here; one step up from cake sales for the PTA. The summer term finished officially but we have remained, rehearsing and running up costumes, packing up a portable rig and finally we are on our way. There's a small minibus; the drama school owns it. Pete is driving it and some of the students are travelling in that. Sam and I, as well as Damon and a couple of third years, are going up by train. We'll beat them to the flat. They rent the same one every year. It's massive, the third years say, but a couple of us will still be sleeping on the floor.

We're taking up two shows, a devised piece, scripted by Kitty, about the Tay Bridge Disaster and *Exit the King* by Ionesco. I am dreading the Tay Bridge piece. Kitty has called it *Chattering Ties* and thinks it will go down well with the Scottish audience as it is set in Dundee. The chattering ties refer to sections of the railway bridge that weren't checked and gave way in the high winter winds and Kitty says she likes these words but I think it's a bit misleading as to what the play is about. It sounds quite light-hearted, maybe a conversational family spat or two set around a dinner party, rather than a dour piece about fifty seven souls plunging into a freezing river just after Christmas in 1879. My worry is we'll attract an audience expecting some lightweight Alan Ayckbourn middle class comedy and they'll be greeted with our gloomy, booming cantations in frankly poor and inconsistent accents while we lumber around the space in yards and yards of unwieldy woollen cloth for what feels like an eternity with little to lift the spirits. I did suggest the inclusion of a joke or two but Kitty looked as if I had bludgeoned her. 'This is a tragedy Jen!' she whispered in response. My feeling is that it certainly will be for the audience.

Pete has been ineffectually effusive about Kitty and her work. Right from the start he has mooned around after her, laughing at every remark and feigning amazement at every trite Insight she has offered up. He has praised her leaden dialogue, clunking scene transitions, supported her character inconsistencies; he has shuffled to her with coffees (accepted), brown bags of pastries (refused), lit her thin cigarettes in our brief breaks. I am waiting for him to trot along with her to the loo and offer to wipe her arse. It is clear that they are now shagging but trying to hide it. She never lets on but there are tell-tale signs on his part; his little finger minutely stretching to touch hers as their hands rest next to each other as we sit in yet another circle on the rehearsal floor; a sheepish look, sometimes the start of a blush if she throws even a tiny hint, a crumb, of a compliment towards him; a graze of his hand on her thigh as they turn the corner into the studio at the start of the day; the same, to the minute, staggered arrival and departure, clearly indicating they are leaving together; a sly grin starting at the corner of his mouth if there is any reference to sex directed towards Kitty or anyone fancying Kitty or how unattainable Kitty is. Oh, Pete is desperate to tell as Kitty is quite the prize, but she's not having it. I don't think anyone else has noticed but I wish they had as Pete has lost all objectivity and we are about to make utter tits of ourselves because he has not stepped in as the lecturer. He is our teacher after all. He should be teaching us to make

141

decent theatre. Not working out how best to bed the students. I'm pretty sure that's why he's given Kitty such free rein in the first place.

Even when we've been going through final run-throughs, I've squinted into the darkness of the auditorium and all I have seen was Pete's profile entirely focused on Kitty and Kitty leaning forward, tiny chin tilted up with delight, transfixed by the stage. My hopes of 'This is a disaster, let's start again with something completely different,' heading up Notes at the end of each performance have dwindled.

Anyway *Exit the King* looks pretty solid, quite a good pace, everyone fairly confident. I'm playing The Nurse and I am an old woman – most of the characters are old, extremely old. It is a comic character and I like that. I don't like the make-up though. Or the costume. I look like my Granny Wentworth. I'd much rather have been the glamorous, young Queen Marie but Kitty's playing that part. I think this year's trip to the Fringe is very much about Kitty.

Sam and I play cards and she trundles up and down the carriage to smoke out of the window in the corridor between carriages. She only took up smoking when she shaved her head but she's taken to it very well. My head is stuffy and heavy by the time we get to Edinburgh's Waverley station and the slicing wind that greets us as we leave it, is a refreshing relief. There's a lot to carry and Ross, one of the third years, has the directions, written on a scrap of paper. He sets off purposefully without relaying any information to us. We are expected to tag along obediently and keep up.

I've been to Edinburgh before. No summer holidays for us – The Castle was always too busy – so we had the very occasional day trip up to Edinburgh or Glasgow or over to Harrogate or York. These involved a very early start, a lot of bickering to find somewhere to park ('There's a space there David! Well you've missed it now!'), dragging around unfamiliar streets, then indecision over where to eat a disappointing lunch then home via a traffic jam or a missed junction and cursing that it was easier to stay put and that the road system of wherever we'd been was impossible to fathom. Sometimes there was the added bonus of running out of petrol and/or Judy getting car sickness. My mother abhorred all tourist attractions without exception so we never visited Edinburgh Castle, for example, or York Cathedral. We never went to Betty's Tearooms or, heaven forfend, anything to do with Rennie Mackintosh. Instead we would trudge without purpose. If we happened upon an aquarium, a sign for a zoo, a waxworks, a dungeon, anything, in short, which might prove entertaining or pleasurable, my mother would tut and sneer pityingly at any cheery huddle queueing outside and she would press on haughtily as Judy and I looked back longingly, our feet sore and our minds numb. Consequently, when it was announced we were going for A Day Out, we scrabbled to find excuses not to attend as there was little joy or profit in them.

As I follow my fellow actors, it feels very like A Wentworth Day Out. There's no stopping as we head up a bustling Princes Street and cut up behind it towards the smaller roads and the large tenement buildings. At least on this visit I will have some time to please myself. Edinburgh Castle is ragged and purple-black on the skyline and, at the very least, I resolve to make it up there. I am feeling optimistic, though a little out of breath, by the time Ross is pushing open an imposing front door and we are funnelling into a cool stone hallway.

'It's on the fourth floor,' he announces, 'When the bus arrives, we'll come down and help bring all the kit up. We can't leave it in the minibus and we can't get in the space until the morning.' He turns and starts up the curving stairwell. Four floors! I think I'd rather wait at the bottom until they get here but I'm hopeful for a bed so I crack on.

The flat is large, as described. It's in the roof. Sam and I peek into the corner living room. It has small casement windows on both sides with seats and thin cushions and a view onto a small park on one edge and down to the street on the other. There's an old range style fire with iron cheeks for a kettle or bread proving. I wonder if anyone will light it; even though it is high summer, the flat is chilly.

Sam and I put our stuff in one of the bedrooms. We choose the smallest twin, hoping we'll be able to keep it. They are all quite big rooms, five in all plus a sizeable bathroom and an extra loo. But there are twelve of us and only ten beds, three doubles, two twins, so someone is on the couch and floor in the living room. There's also the matter of Simon. He's coming up too. The thinking is he will want a room to himself. So that's only eight beds. I'm hoping Pete and Kitty drop the pretence and just take a double. If they don't, I might just say something. I'm aware Sam and I are bottom of the pecking order as we're first years and girls and have the worst parts in the plays. The only ones below us are the techies but one of them is really pushy and Pete and Ross like him.

We head back to the vast, scruffy kitchen. It has an old-fashioned chipped china sink, the original wooden cupboards and a pale scrubbed pine table that could easily seat twenty. There's a muddle of chairs around it and Sam is making tea as Ross and Damon forage for mugs. We drink the tea at the table, bitter without milk as no one can be bothered with the stairs. Damon rolls a joint and Ross turns the radio up. Ross is from Glasgow and is The Producer. He is very straight for a drama student. For a start he has a neat, thin moustache more suited to a car salesman than the stage, and today he's wearing a salmon pink polo shirt which looks like it's been ironed. His hair is neatly parted. Combed down. He inspected the chair before he sat on it. He has pale grey eyes and speaks with restraint in a thick accent. Ross looks at us. We are a clutch of ragged, backcombed hair, over-sized coats and boots, clanking jewellery, brash slogans on grubby t-shirts, tiny badges clustered on flopping lapels shouting big ideas. We are all far from neat. Ross is in charge though. Tidily poised in his chair, waiting for the set and the costumes and ready to tell the rabble what to do.

Hugh, the other third year, blonde, long-bodied like a reptile, a little obsessed with Noel Coward, drags on the joint. 'I wish we were in Paris,' he blows the smoke away with mannered ennui, 'I've never been.' He taps the ash of the joint into a saucer and the end falls off. Damon takes it to relight it. Hugh twitches his fingertips. He is never still. I think that is why he is so thin. 'I wonder if it is truly gay.'

Ross smiles at Hugh indulgently. Ross likes Hugh a lot. They are sharing a room. Platonically. Ross is not gay. Despite the salmon pink polo shirt. Hugh talks obsessively about being gay, looking gay, who is gay. He is a bit boring on the subject, truth be told. I see him walking round the campus and am fascinated by how fast he walks as his legs are very short compared to his body. I expect him to spring forward onto all fours and grow a tail like a lizard and crawl on his long belly. Maybe scale a wall. His eyes are quite lizard-like, upturned and greenish. I wonder if he would be a gay lizard. I think I might ask him. Then I wonder what it would be like to have a tail. Nice at first I imagine, as a novelty, then a bit of a nuisance, especially on public transport. I don't think tails can be much use really.

'The Pompidou Centre's the best bit. Fuck the Eiffel Tower. That's dead, that is, that's the past,' Damon is holding forth on the delights of Paris; he's been twice, 'I love modern architecture. The bolder the better.'

We all look at him.

'Yes but did anyone want to bum you?' Hugh says. Damon looks like he doesn't understand the question. He frowns, his unruly brows crumpling, mouth setting into a hard line.

'No,' he says.

'No offence,' says Hugh, 'but I'm not taking that as irrefutable proof,' and he saucily pouts his lips at Damon who looks offended but hands the joint back to Hugh.

'God, it was a riot here last year,' he drawls, 'I can hardly remember it. We didn't stop drinking the whole time, though we didn't have such good parts did we Ross?' This year Hugh is multi-roling in *Chattering Ties* but he is particularly fine as a Dundonian fisherman in a *Haircut 100* Aran roll neck jumper with big black wellies. I am concerned about the historical accuracy of this but Hugh loves that jumper and thinks he looks very sexy in it and he's been working on his accent and it is the least terrible of everyone's. He is supposed to be really macho and powerful though but he kept standing with one hip locked or cocking his head or smoothing his hair. Pete had to show him how to be more manly, much to Kitty's delight, as it entailed spontaneously grabbing her and throwing her over his shoulder and strutting around the studio with his arm locked tight around her thighs. They decided we needed a quick break after that little episode. 'Would be good if someone actually came to watch it this year though,' Hugh sighs, rolling his eyes, 'well, not the bridge one maybe' and Ross does a camp mock gasp and Hugh giggles and I feel a little relieved that they think it's a bit crap too.

Damon has produced a pack of cards and is trying to explain the complicated rules of a game called Fillet for the umpteenth time when there's a shout from the hall. The rest of them are here and we rise from the fug of smoke and empty, chilly cups to welcome them into this temporary world.

Sam and I are waiting while one of the techies fiddles with the lanterns. We have to step in and out of the light for them on command. The others have gone to the pub and will be back for the tech rehearsal. The performance space is tiny, freezing and well off the beaten track. I do not hold out much hope for a full house. First thing, Sam and I handed out fliers in our dreary wool drapes up by the ticket office on the Royal Mile but Sam looked even more alarming with her shaven head after a night sleeping on the floor – we were kicked out of the bedroom – and I kept losing track of the fabric and falling over it. I stumbled into a group of Japanese tourists and my costume threatened to completely overwhelm them. I cursed Kitty. Most of the fliers ended up littering the street. They weren't very appealing. Or easy to read. A very cheap print job; Ross won't waste any money.

Our first show is tonight at eleven. I daydream in and out of the warm lanterns in the darkness, my eyes closed against the glare. Perhaps Bryan will have heard I am performing at The Fringe and will get the train. No, drive up in a soft top car through purplish hills in apricot sunshine. No, bare chested on a motorbike would be better, long hair, a curling, tangling mane in the wind. 'We have some unfinished business Jen', he'll say as I step out of the lights to thundering applause and into his manly arms. He'll never find this place however. I'm not sure anyone will.

'Jen!' Sam pushes me gently, 'We've got to get changed, the others will be back soon. Are you sleeping standing up?'

I don't bother to answer as the house lights come on and Hugh bellows drunkenly from the back of the hall, 'Darlings, we're here! Let's get this show on the road!'

'Two of them were asleep,' Sam mutters as she tears another strip of skin from her ragged finger tips. The stress from the performance has sent her back to the nail-biting with renewed vigour.

We have played to a magnificent house of five. There has been much bickering about opening with *Chattering Ties* rather than *Exit the King* which I've quite enjoyed. Kitty has been Wounded By The Treachery of the company as various actors (Hugh) have made several acerbic comments about Her Work. The gist is the *The King* is recognisable and would have attracted a few more people who might have said we were quite good who would then come and see the disaster devised whereas Kitty and her supporters (Pete) argue that the Fringe is all about experimental work and pushing the boundaries and that's what people want to see and that's what sparks a conversation.

'So why the fuck have I bothered to learn all those lines if no one's gives a tinker's cuss about Ionesco?' is Hugh's perfectly enunciated deadpan response.

Pete stammers around about actors always having to put bums on seats, about Ionesco not exactly being mainstream, about choices suiting the drama school ethos, et cetera et cetera et cetera, just like the King of Siam. Throughout this Kitty looks more and more furious as she clearly wants an out and out backing of her stupendous work. She must have been a little downhearted as the audience barely managed a smattering of applause before she'd finished her downstage centre yoga-supple plentiful bowing. The sleeping couple just stood up and left, one of them unashamedly stretching and yawning so luxuriously he revealed a tight, hairy stomach. This amateur venue did not afford us the luxury of not being able to see the audience because of the glare of the stage lights. We could see all the empty chairs and the few plainly stultified faces as we galumphed around the makeshift stage.

We have met for Notes but I'm not sure these are going to happen judging by the mood. It's ten in the morning. Our next performance is in less than an hour. They really do things in a strange way here. Who will come to this?

There's a shaft of sunlight from the open door at the side and dust motes are drifting in and out. I watch them dreamily as the carping continues. Ross had said good weather is a mixed blessing as some of the punters stay out in the sunshine rather than come in to watch the shows. Ideally he's hoping for short sharp showers. Finally there's movement and we shuffle off to get into costume for *The King*. No one comments on how many tickets have or haven't been sold so I gather it's not a full house. Kitty is blotting tears from her chalk white make-up and Pete is fussing ineffectually around her. She bats him away but he keeps coming back. Hugh is watching them steadily, he looks furious.

I wait and wait for my entrance in the make-do wings and realise things are going rather well. There's not many people in the audience but they are enjoying it. There's laughter, quite loud and consistent laughter in all the right places, and Hugh especially is responding to it, as is Kitty. The pace quickens and suddenly everyone is sharp and alert. Maybe our Edinburgh run is not going to be a total disaster. Before I know it, I am on stage and the audience love me. They can't number more than twenty but everything I say gets an audible response. I feel warmth and love from them. It's quite extraordinary. And most unexpected. The world of the play is coming to an end as the techies detonate a modest pyro and ash falls around us. We rush around the stage in choreographed panic in the fog of the smoke machine and finally, there is fulsome applause for the best performance we have given. We gather for our curtain call and it is the first opportunity I have had to scrutinise the audience. As I lean into the bow, I see Judy's beaming face.

'Jen! That was fantastic!' She rugby tackles me before I've made it through the door of the pub, 'Come and meet everyone.'

She has told Sam where they were going to be and for me to meet them there once I was out of costume. I had taken my time, hoping they might have moved on, but alas, no.

Judy guides me to a table of fellow students, including Jonathan. 'Here she is! My brilliant sister!' and they all stand up and start applauding and saying things like, 'That was a great performance', 'Absolutely loved that', 'You were so funny' and then Judy says, 'Here, you take my seat next to Pip. Jonathan can budge up. We want to hear all about it.' I sit down next to a shy-looking, nerdy boy, a bit older than Judy I'd say, who smiles at me and appears very happy that I am sitting next to him. Another boy, Freddie, jumps up and asks me what I want to drink and Judy explains they're her friends from Oxford who've come up to walk in the Lakes and are staying at The Castle and they thought it would be great to come up and surprise me.

'Well it was certainly a surprise,' I say accepting a vodka from Freddie who does a little bow as he hands it to me.

'I can't believe you're brave enough to perform in public. I have so much admiration,' an earnest, blinking girl called Marie says. Several of Judy's friends agree, voicing horror and terror at the very thought.

'It's no big deal if the material is good,' I say and I realise that they all become quiet when I speak, leaning forward the better to hear what I have to say, as if I have anything of note to report to a group of brainboxes from Oxford.

'So, do you have a process?' asks Freddie and he casts a frank look at my breasts.

'Do you mean like Method and Stanislavski? Strasberg and Adler and all that?' I answer.

'I've heard of Method, yes,' says Freddie, 'but the other names mean nothing to me,'

'Oh God, it's very boring,' I say, 'Stanislavski's considered the father of method acting developed by the Americans, Strasburg and Adler and so on, but no, in answer to your question, at present, I do not have a particular process, I just act.'

'Well you're bloody funny,' says Freddie.

'It is a comic role,' I say, 'Great dialogue.'

'Let me get you another drink,' Freddie says, 'I can't believe we're in the company of one of the actors. What a day!' and he lurches off towards the bar.

'Jen!' I turn at the sound of Hugh's voice. Sam must have told them where I was headed. The rest of the company are here.

Hugh dances up. 'So these are our saviours. What a fantastic crowd. Let's all get pissed!' and there is applause and roaring and the boys slam their pint glasses onto the table and I look around and I notice Pete is gazing a little dumbstruck at Judy.

It is much later and we have become a stumbling jumble, walking up a winding road towards Edinburgh Castle. The surprise success of the play has gone to everyone's heads and no one has given a thought to the matinee and late show of *Chattering Ties* which loom tomorrow. Simon, with uncharacteristic optimism, has declared this year's run A Success No Matter What. Our theatre company's friendship with the Oxford contingent has been fused over an afternoon of swallows and swigs, of compliments and accolades and an increasingly loose grip on the reality of our production and the importance of their opinion. The fact that Judy is my sister is long forgotten. They are passers-by, who happened by pure luck onto our gem of a performance much to everyone's delight, and are now Devoted Fans, and rightly so, because We Are Talented.

The afternoon alcohol has long ago worn off and I am now not that drunk but I am beginning to get a little irritated with the constant noise. I don't know why everyone has to shout at each other. It's been a long day and I'm wondering if I can sneak back to the flat and get a bit of sleep. Judy said they were only supposed to come up for the day so it's inevitable someone will come up with the excellent idea of everyone going back to our place and keeping the party going. Hugh is the most likely candidate. He is very interested in Mackenzie, another of Judy's friends, who is as mannered as Hugh is but who seems quite attached to Marie. Perhaps he's not gay, just upper class. It's hard to tell but he is exceptionally handsome so I can see why Hugh is pursuing him.

I am trailing at the back of the group. The air is warm and the wind has finally died down. The city looks grubby and bumpy from up here, sort of packed in. I'd like to sit down and I don't really know where we're going.

'It's beautiful, isn't it?' Pip, the quiet boy is next to me. I realise I've stopped and the others are trudging on up the hill. I look at him.

'You look older than the others,' I say. It's late. I can't be bothered with niceties.

'I am. I'm a post-grad. I know Jonathan. So yes. I'm older.' As soon as I look at him directly he looks away. He's got reddish hair, kind eyes, a bit of puppy fat around his jaw still.

'What subject?' I say. I'm really staring now, trying to get him to look at me.

'Maths basically, a branch of maths. Yes maths,' he says, looking determinedly at the view.

'I was quite good at maths,' I say, 'Despite all this arty nonsense.'

'Really? I was never any good at any arty nonsense. None of it. Not that I think it's nonsense. I really liked the play. Not that I know much about plays. I thought you were amazing. In the play I mean. Not that I don't think you're amazing in real life. I mean. I don't know you so I don't know if you are, one way or another. I wouldn't like to say. I just thought you were very, very good in the play,' he trails off, 'But everyone's said that to you all day. You must be tired of hearing it.'

'It's hard to get tired of hearing you were amazing,' I say, 'I haven't heard it much before today.' I can't decide if I feel sorry for him or if I'm annoyed by him.

We stand and look at the view. It is surprisingly companionable.

'Where are you staying tonight?' I ask. It is so late and my feet are hurting and he's wearing expensive looking shoes.

'We weren't going to stay at all, just come up for the day and get the last train back. My cousin lives here though. I phoned him earlier when it looked like plan A was going down the pan. He's left a key under the mat.' He's finally managed to look at me throughout this little revelation.

'I see,' I say, speculatively. I look up the hill where the group are a torn black smudge on the brow. It's finally getting dark.

I put my hand in his. 'Let's go and find that key then Pip,' I say.

1994

It is the second week of January and already my resolve to go to the gym every day is dissolving like the first real snow we've had this winter. I slop through the slurry of brown ice on the drive, trying not to slip, justifying to myself that I'm far too busy today to spend an hour on the treadmill. It's Friday tomorrow and Pip's got people coming round from work so I need to be ready. My time is better spent organising and strategising rather than sweating in that torture chamber.

I stop at the deli first and order a couple of plates of hors d'oeuvres, then on to *Majestic Wine* for booze. I do a quick circuit of *Waitrose* for the main course, overpriced *filet mignon* but it's easy and impressive so it will do. I can't be bothered with pudding; hopefully everyone will be too pissed to notice.

I'm back home and unpacking in under two hours.

I open the paper at the jobs page. I scour it. If Pip is going to get ahead he needs to move on soon. I flick over to the property pages. We've already finished this house and I want it on the market before Easter. I'm looking for a better area next time, more work and, therefore a bigger profit.

I say we've finished this house. I haven't physically done anything. I've made decisions, bollocked the builders and written the cheques. I am the Commander-in-Chief. All Pip has had to do is go to work. And provide the money.

I put the kettle on.

It is transparent.

I am slightly mesmerised by the water beginning to bubble and boil.

I flick the switch off. I don't want a coffee.

I cruise through the house. My house. Smooth lines, fitted carpets, large leather sofas. I have read magazines, mostly, celebrity magazines. There are no draughty windows here. I would have had the house hermetically sealed if I could.

Pip wanted to spend money travelling. 'We are young,' he said. But you can't see the money you spend on travelling. It's over. Gone. Like a dream. You can see it in the curve of a beautiful French chair, you can hear it in the closing of a German car's door, you can feel it in the thick weft of a handwoven rug under your perfectly manicured feet.

I didn't say this to Pip.

I just persuaded him that we should get settled in our first house, scale back the holidays, 'for the time being,' and, 'enjoy our friends,' here. He hasn't really noticed that I don't have many friends. He doesn't notice much.

Each night, after work, I pour him a drink in a perfectly clear, square tumbler washed clean in our integrated, practically silent, dishwasher and sit at his feet while he tells me about his day. I sit at his feet so he can't see my face. I am like a fifties housewife, except that I am fake. I don't polish and sweep and cook and clean. No. This is the nineties. I employ someone else to do all that while I flick through the TV channels, or paw the useless objects in one of the colour-drained boutiques on the High Street or plot and plan how to build my husband's career so I will never have to worry about money again and never have to go back to my parents.

He was an easy catch. During the few heady hours at his cousin's flat in Edinburgh, he let slip he had a good job lined up the following year with an IT company. There really was no certainty with anyone at drama school so he was the one I set my sights on.

I was determined.

He was inexperienced and, it turned out, easily impressed.

It wasn't a match made in heaven but it was a match.

We swapped addresses in Edinburgh and I sent him a few well-timed saucy postcards during the autumn term of my third year. He sent me expensive flowers, an old edition of *Exit The King* in French and a ridiculous, large, yellow bear. He came up to The Castle after New Year with Jonathan, and Judy started gushing about his brilliant future. As there was absolutely nothing I could foresee in my future, I focussed all my energies on him.

We were together for the last few months of his postgrad and my degree. He wrote me adoring letters that were repetitive and short and I had sex with quite a lot of other people. We met up every few weeks for increasingly tedious weekends.

It was easy to be enthusiastic when he told me what the future held though. He became less shy. I wasn't completely repulsed by his florid skin and his receding hairline. He was very straight though. I would have to do something about the old man trousers and the brogues.

Once he started his job in Richmond things took off. He wanted to Take Care Of Me. 'Be my guest,' I thought. We moved in together. A roomy flat in a converted Victorian building near Battersea Power Station. He got a company car and I began picking out furniture. We talked vaguely about me playwriting or starting my own theatre company and then as the months passed, wistfully, he brought up children. 'I'm sorry but I'm old-fashioned,' I looked down, demurely, 'I'd have to be married but,' I said, looking straight into his bland, blue eyes, 'I'd love children.'

He proposed three days later, awkwardly and with no great aplomb, but the ring was impressive.

The wedding was small and in November. 'Why wait?' I opined. His mother wept bitterly throughout. A tiny, spare woman, academic in her own right, another mathematician. Clearly I was not what she had in mind for her brilliant son.

I gave him a wedding night to remember. He actually looked a little pale at breakfast the next morning. I rubbed the wedding band on my finger and began to calculate the minimum amount of sex I'd have to have with him to keep him happy.

He looked at me adoringly, 'What are you thinking about?' he asked.

'Just how lucky I am,' I answered and bashed in the top of my boiled egg.

We have been married just over two years.

I sit and tap at the computer, updating Pip's CV ready to send it out to a few jobs I've spotted. One of Pip's company directors will be here tomorrow and it will look good if he has some interviews lined up, some Irons In The Fire. The firm he is with is promising and, if they offer him the right promotion, it might be worth him staying and maybe buying shares in it.

I update his letter, print it and sign it and put stamps on it ready to go.

I click on the *Friends Reunited* website. I registered and keep looking for people but it's mostly dullards I can hardly remember. There are a few show-offs from drama school who are doing fairly well who I've Reconnected With – they may be useful in the future. And I'm messaging Maureen who is now married to Chris and Expecting imminently. They are in the farmhouse and I can hear her gushing tone every time I login. First it was the new cot, then colours for the nursery, now, unfortunately she's onto piles and stretchmarks. I keep my responses to a minimum. I don't want to encourage her but every so often I drop in a subtle enquiry about the rest of the village hoping for news of Bryan. She never mentions him and, so far, he has not succumbed to *Friends Reunited*.

I'm at a loose end.

This happens quite a lot and is one of the hazards of having neither a job nor children.

I decide to go for a nap.

Pip is getting ready for the dinner. I sit on the bed and consider the auburn hair growing out of the pale moles on his back as he dries himself and puts on deodorant. I know he is tense. He doesn't like socialising. He doesn't like small talk. I told him he has to get better at it and we've tried to work on it.

He's not interested in many things most men like. He doesn't like cars. Or football. Or any sport. Or even women in an objective way. I took him to a *Maserati* show room to see if I could spark an interest but, as the spunky young salesman chatted to me, his eyes kept sliding away from the magnificent metal beast before us to the view through the sparkling windows. It overlooked a bleak, squashed playpark. A couple of kids were tearing around, abandoned, yelling, while glum, huddled parents looked on. Pip saw me looking too and smiled at me, hopefully. We left. I didn't speak to him for hours. How was having kids going to further his career?

I move across the bed to him and rub his fleshy shoulders. I can't have him in a state for tonight. 'You need to relax,' I begin.

'It's Friday night,' he sounds sulky, 'I just want to veg in front of the telly.'

'I've gone to a lot of trouble Pip. They're your friends.' I am stroking him, like a pet.

'I know. I'm sorry.' He really is very irritating.

'How about I make you feel a little better?' I move down onto the floor and kneel between his legs. His skin is still chilled and clammy from the shower. At least with a blow job I won't have to get in the shower again and I've got to baste the beef.

'I love you Jen Jen,' he says and touches my face. I resist the urge to swat his hand away.

Everyone looks better by candlelight but the group of people at my table are singularly unglamorous. At the head I have placed Tony Charlesworth, financial director of Pip's firm. He is portly and grey-haired in a snug, three-piece pinstriped suit and has come straight from work. Tony is between wives and his conversation is routinely peppered with *double entendres* which makes Pip uncomfortable. Tony holds a lot of shares in the company though so I want him on my side.

'Oh Jennifer darling, top me up would you?' He offers his glass greedily; this is his third refill. He drinks a lot but there is no visible change in him. Years of practice.

On his left are Terry and Alex. Met at work. Married. Still work together. Imagine that. They could be either gender and Terry announced this the first time we met, 'I'm always getting letters for Mr Terry Peterson. I mean, do I look like a man?' She does though. She has a flat chest and a Plain Face as my mother would say. Tonight she's put on bright blue eyeshadow and pink lipstick. The effect is unsettling. She looks like a teenager experimenting with make-up or an adult painted by a child.

Tony Charlesworth loves attractive women. I know if he is sitting next to Terry with her droning voice and tedious stories about pebble dashing the house and being overcharged at the dry cleaners, I'll have his attention.

Alex, her husband, has a bit more to him and they are both at the same level as Pip, but Alex is a yes man. He is ambitious too but won't dare to disagree with Tony about anything. I've invited them so Tony can rule the dynamic Mr and Mrs out of the forthcoming promotion I know is coming up, even if it's only subconsciously.

Terry is already holding forth about a new one-way system. It's thrilling. Tony is sneering at her a little over his wine glass as he chugs it back. Pip is looking young and uncomfortable at the other end of the table but smiling politely as Terry drones on.

To my right I have Guy and Sarah. Guy is Head of IT Development and a pale, nervous man who is very bright but you wouldn't know it. His wife is friendly enough; I think she might be an evangelical Christian but I'm not sure. She can be very earnest but then she laughs loudly if anything is slightly funny. It's hard to tell what will set her off so it's like having a Jack-in-the-Box slowly winding up and then shooting off unexpectedly. Perhaps this accounts for Guy's nerves. After she has been laughing for a while, I imagine pushing her head into a bucket of wet sand. Guy will be involved to an extent in the decision making side of the promotion, so, even though he is far from your dream dinner party guest, he needs to be here.

At the bottom, next to Alex, are Ed and Jackson, part of the team. I find it hard to tell them apart but Pip likes them and insisted they come. He Feels Comfortable around them. Jackson has a bright shiny spot on his chin and Ed has spilt something crusty on his shirt. Nice to see he's made an effort.

Opposite Jackson, to Pip's left, is Trish, a last-minute addition to make up the numbers. She is mousy and frail and won't impress anyone. She's blowing her nose so she's probably starting another cold. Next to her Pip looks hale and hearty. I look around the table and wonder how I have come to be spending my Friday nights with such people; it was bad enough when we were nibbling on the hors d'oeuvres but now we're all seated, what an earth is everyone going to talk about?

The food is a triumph though and everyone tucks in heartily. Tony attacks his bloody beef like a warrior and I can hear the sinews splitting as his teeth grind away determinedly. Sarah drops her fork and is grubbing around under the table for it. She bangs her head, coming back up. I should offer her a clean one but I don't.

'Bloody good Jennifer. Just what we need after the week we've had, eh?' Tony booms.

'And what kind of a week was it?' Alex asks, waiting for Tony's response before he decides which way to go with his facial expression.

'Bloody good!' Tony bellows and they all join in with guffaws apart from Trish who is carefully blowing her nose.

'How so?' I focus on Tony.

'Well Pip here managed to come up with a nifty little fix which is going to save us a tidy sum,' Tony raises his glass to Pip.

'Really?' I say with mock surprise; I know all about it.

Alex leans forward. 'Yes, we really worked well as a team on that. There was a moment there when I didn't think we were going to pull it off.'

'But Pip sorted it out?' I interject, my innocent tone masking my deliberate shutting down of any talk of teamwork.

'Well...' Pip begins and I know he's going to start with his tedious modesty and self-deprecation.

'Yes, he bloody did!' Tony jumps in, ' And I love it when anyone saves us money!' I top up his glass again. Alex grumpily returns to shoving the food around his plate.

'Any plans for a holiday this year, Terry?' Christ, I sound like a bloody hairdresser but I know they love France and so does Tony Charlesworth.

She perks up, 'Yes we booked a gorgeous gite in France.'

Pip becomes more animated as we talk of holidays, as was my plan, that pathetic yearning eager look he has appears. He tells a few charming stories of childhood holidays on the Med; they're nostalgic and funny and Tony belly laughs, wiping a tear away with his silk handkerchief. I top up his glass again and give his doughy hand a little stroke. Pip laps up Terry's details about the hidden delights of the Poitou-Charente, the joy of French cuisine, the French way of life. Everyone agrees two hour lunch breaks are what we are lacking in our lives.

'And the property is so cheap,' Terry drawls, 'we're thinking of investing. Would be so great to have a bolthole.'

Yes, I think, because your life is bloody torture, with your great job, loads of cash and your fixed rate mortgage.

'I agree,' Charlesworth chimes in, 'you can pick up something pretty decent with the change in your pocket. Got a friend who's bought a couple of places there. But she's moving on to Tuscany now.'

'Not like house prices here,' Trish whines nasally, 'I've been thinking of moving but the prices are going up each week. And it all goes so quickly. Mind you, the amount you can borrow is getting better.'

'Where are you looking, Trish?' says Ed. He's picking a bit of steak from his teeth while he's talking, 'If you're getting a bigger place, I am looking to move out. Fancy a roommate? I'd appreciate it muchly.'

Trish flares her nostrils but manages not to say anything too offensive. 'It's early stages Ed. Where are you now?'

'Still at home,' Jackson butts in, laughing and punches Ed on the arm, 'it's a teeny bit pathetic, isn't it?'

'It's not bad. I like Mum's food and there's no cleaning.'

'Not very good on the shagging front though mate,' Jackson laughs at his hilarious quip, then catches Tony's eye, 'Sorry Tony, didn't mean to be crude. Just joshing.' He smiles weakly.

'Nothing wrong with that,' Charlesworth booms, 'we've all got to think of our love lives, eh Jen?' He turns to me and I feel his pudgy hand squeeze my thigh, speculatively, under the table.

'We certainly do,' I say, sloshing the last of the bottle into his glass. I catch the final drip on my finger and lick it, looking straight at him. 'Better get another bottle,' I say and exit into the kitchen.

Pip brings through plates smeared from the bloodied beef. He looks even pinker than usual. He smiles. 'Are you enjoying yourself?' I say, warmly.

'I really am,' he says with surprise in his voice.

'They're such interesting people,' I say as I wrench the cork from another bottle, 'you know, the people you work with.'

We go back through armed with more wine and an extravagant box of chocolates Charlesworth has provided. Trish asks if I have any *Lemsip*. Alex has begun talking at length about his car; Charlesworth is assessing Terry's tits; Ed and Jackson are working out where would be the best place for an arm wrestle.

It's February when we get the invitation to the wedding. I've been expecting it for months but I'm too indifferent to ask for details. Judy and Jonathan have been engaged for a couple of years and this year was earmarked as The Year in their Life Plan.

They're getting married in Cumbria. At the church in the village. The reception is at The Castle.

The invitation is nauseatingly tasteful, plain cream, heavy card with fine navy lettering. I can't even remember if we had invitations or not. If I had I would have wanted these.

The wedding is in June. A lovely time of year I can hear Dad saying. I wonder if I'll have to book a room. I'd better do it now. I haven't been home since my wedding. I am excited. Maybe I'll see Bryan. I think about what I will wear. How impressed everyone will be with me. How I will outshine Judy. Then I picture her as a bride. She will be perfect.

I put the house on the market and start serious house hunting. I've also got a part-time job doing radio ad voice-overs; it passes a few hours. I find myself in a state of constant tension. My attention span is even shorter than usual. I flick through magazines, not taking in a word. I stop bothering to listen to Pip's day and start running a bath as soon as I hear his key in the lock. Once in the bath, I'm desperate to get out and I force myself to sit as the water cools around me. I am tired and fidgety and full of energy and exhausted all at once and I know it's because I'm going back to The Castle. A terrible dread and exhilarating anticipation creep and course through my every moment. My life here is empty, monochrome. I try to spur Pip into argument picking at him if we happen to be in the same space but he slinks away from me bewildered, retreating into the imaginary world of the green light of his computer. The tension between us swells as taut and full as the belly of a greedy kitten. He begins to bring home gifts; flowers that smell of death, old-fashioned sweets that make my jaw ache with the effort of eating them, smooth big-boxed kitchen appliances for which I have neither need nor desire. In his mind, he hopes the gnawing malevolence that I carry as my aura will just dissipate; he hasn't the language to navigate this. He reaches sweatily for me under the sheets and I knock his hand away. He has no idea why he is being punished but I know he thinks he deserves it.

I consider divorcing him when the house sells. We will make a lot of money but I don't want to work properly, I'm not ready for that. I just need to stop, bite back the screams that threaten normality.

I find another house. I put in an offer before Pip views it. It's solid and practical. It needs work and we won't have neighbours on both sides. There is a good school at the bottom of the road which means it will sell quickly once I've finished it. It's early 1930s. Only one previous owner. Remarkable.

The offer is accepted and I walk back through the house, and in my head I pull up the carpets, strip the walls, and pare it back to its original state, stripping all the layers of lovingly chosen paint and paper, eradicating that single family's magical memories, that family's life lead. I will possess this house and make it mine.

The chain is short and we move quickly. I barely pack a thing, insisting we have a removal company to do all the work. Pip has got the promotion. He agrees without hesitation. Anything to try to bring me back. I find this fascinating. How much ill-treatment will he take? I remember my father saying his mother Took To Her Bed for a period when he was a boy. The inference was there was not much physically wrong with her. She just absented herself from his life for a while, and presumably from her own. I toy with doing this myself. I wonder how long Pip would put up with it.

Then Judy phones.

She's coming to London to buy her wedding dress.

With Mum.

And will I be Matron of Honour?

What a horrible phrase. I think of Hattie Jaques as the fun-sapping disapproving matron in the Carry On films.

No, I don't want to be Matron of Honour but I'll come to the dress appointment.

Judy and Jonathan are living in Oxford. They're both still ensconced in the University in some way. I've never visited them. I imagine them in wood-panelled rooms with piles of books and papers, having earnest discussions over cups of cocoa and fruitcake. I imagine them in the 1950s. I have no idea what their life is really like. I have never accepted any invitation to visit because I don't want to know.

I meet my mother and Judy off the train from Oxford at Paddington. It's been a couple of weeks since the move and it's odd to be up, dressed and out. Taking a leaf out of my paternal grandmother's book, I have taken to staying in bed most of the time. We have a portable telly set up in the bedroom. I scuttle down to the melamine kitchen to get toast and tea, then go back to bed and watch soaps and quiz shows and stare out of the window at the sky. I have found no compunction to behave any other way.

Judy looks fucking gorgeous and Mum is wearing a plush, teal blue, velvet coat with an orange scarf. I notice a few people look at them as they laugh their way up the acrid platform towards me.

I hug them begrudgingly and Judy keeps up a monologue of wedding preparation drivel as we wait for a taxi, ride in the taxi, get out of the taxi. Mum just keeps smiling. I try this a bit too but it becomes hard work so I give up.

The wedding dress shop smells wonderful and, for a moment, I am captivated by the calm and order, the femininity of the muted flower arrangements, the romantic pictures, the gently frothing gowns beckoning from the rails. The owner, Sabrine, is quietly excitable and pristine. She and Judy begin gabbling to each other in a language I fail to grasp and Sabrine begins to pull dresses from the rails, fanning them out like the flayed skins of exotic animals stroking the delicate lace and stitching as if they are still alive and may take flight. Judy and Mum 'ooh' and 'aah'. I sit. I say nothing. I wait.

And finally it happens. Judy has tried several dresses. She looks beautiful in them all. But then she steps out of the capacious changing room in a soft, slipper satin ballgown and no one says anything. The dress is the colour of bleached bone and it emphasises her creamy skin; her waist is tiny, her honey hair falls perfectly into the deep V of the back and, as she looks over her shoulder at the tiny covered buttons trickling to the floor and the sweep of the magnificent train, she sighs, 'This is it,' she breathes.

Sabrine reverentially nestles a delicate veil with a simple ribbon edge into her abundant hair and Judy turns into a Hollywood star. I feel my skin will rip apart, split and crack and burst and a roaring, raging, scaled beast will finally spring forth and devour her.

'You look beautiful, Judy,' Mum gulps, wiping her eyes. She never shed a tear on my wedding day. She never told me I was beautiful. But then I'm not.

'You really do,' I manage, 'Jonathan won't know what's hit him.'

Apparently, I am not after all a complete monster. Jonathan, clever, devoted, gorgeous. A real catch. I think of Pip and swallow a howl.

Mum reaches for my hand. I startle and snatch it away. She never touches me. I realise that was not necessarily the right response. I stand up quickly. 'Just need the loo,' I say and cut past Judy and the excessively huge skirt and head up the polished wooden stairs to a tasteful bathroom. I pluck tissues from the box next to the basin as I blub and wonder how many bridesmaids have done the same. Does Sabrine realise women stand in this room consumed with misery at the emptiness and pointlessness of their existence? How dare bloody Sabrine impose such despair with her beautiful gowns and her fairy-tale ideals? I think of Pip's pudgy hands gripping my hips as he fucks me and I look at the diamond on my finger. I look at my blurred face in the mirror and pull myself together. This is not part of my plan. I pee and set my jaw. I'm not going to cry anymore.

Downstairs, Sabrine is flitting around Judy with a cloth tape measure and writing figures in a hefty black notebook. The tilt of her mouth shows how much she approves of the size of the numbers she is recording. Each one is a further delight, greeted with a little cluck or nod or raise of her brow. I'm glad I didn't get my dress here.

Now Judy is changing and she and Sabrine are calling to each other through the changing room door *vis a vis* fittings. Judy will return promptly with shoes ('We're off to buy some now,') and then the dress will need to be taken up and in as she such a little doll, but, 'rest assured it will be perfect for the day.'

Sabrine kisses Judy and my mother as we leave; I get a perfunctory nod. I suppose this befits a spectator. I have barely spoken throughout the appointment. I barely smiled. We bundle into another taxi. We are going to one of my mother's favourite Old Haunts for lunch. I wonder if she's paying for it. She's paid for the dress.

I sit and look glumly look out of the window, trying not to take up too much space. Judy and my mother chat about the perfection of the dress and all the many possibilities *vis a vis* flowers, shoes, jewellery. I consider throwing myself out of the taxi into the path of an oncoming double-decker bus. I doubt they'd notice. I doubt they'd pause for breath.

We arrive at the restaurant. The door is padlocked and the windows are boarded up. I look up and down the street. A skip squats on a greasy pavement two doors down with a weathered collection of litter huddling by its side. There is a homeless guy asleep in the doorway opposite, a pile of brown rags with a grubby boot sticking out of them. A skinny ginger cat is peering at us through the grimy film of an upstairs window.

'Where have you brought us, Mother?' I ask and turn back assertively to the cabbie, 'Hang on a minute.'

Mother looks at the restaurant, 'Oh. It's closed. Oh well,' She looks up and down the street, 'it didn't used to be like this... We'll have to go somewhere else. Back in the cab, girls.' and we clamber back in, Mum and Judy laughing over the rundown area and the shut shop.

'You pick somewhere, Jen. You're the local,' Mum says, 'you must eat up here all the time. Anywhere is fine. Isn't it, Judy?'

'Yes, anywhere's super,' Judy beams into my face, thinking how lovely it is that I'm getting to be part of the day and to make a decision and to feel included.

But the truth is, I don't eat up here all the time. Hardly ever in fact. Why would I? I've no one to eat with. I barely know London at all. When I was at drama school I skulked around campus most of the time, hardly ever going Up West except to see the occasional play if a trip was organised. Now we live here, Pip likes to eat in Richmond if we go out, which is hardly ever. He says there is more of a Village Feel and I don't care because it takes so long to get anywhere and there are so many people. But I'd never admit that to anyone.

So I have no ideas where to go. I can't come up with a little gem of a place off the beaten track to impress these out-of-towners. No. I am going to Fall Short. Lose Face. Have to Admit Defeat. Again.

I take another tack.

'I'm sorry but I'm just getting over the flu and I'm just feeling dreadful. I think I'm going to have to go home,' They look at me aghast, 'The nearest tube station please,' the cab moves off, 'I think it's all the excitement of the dress and hearing all your news. I've barely been out of bed for the last couple of weeks.'

'Really?' Mother is suspicious.

'Yes. Pip's had it too. Had to have time off. Anyway, I'm just not up to lunch. I've just got to get home.'

'You're not... pregnant are you?' Judy is delighted to have leapt to this laughable conclusion.

I imagine my fists pummelling her face repeatedly.

'No,' I say calmly, 'absolutely not.' I see the Underground sign; the cab stops and I open the door. 'Enjoy the rest of the day,' I say from the safety of the pavement, 'See you in June,' and I slam the door and charge down into the artificial brightness of the station.

I've had the kitchen gutted and two new bathrooms fitted by the time the wedding comes round. The army of workmen marching through my front door on a daily basis has, for the most part, kept me out of bed during the day or at least required me to dress. I've given up providing nutritious meals for Pip, resorting to microwave mush and takeaways. So many takeaways that, if I were a different person, one or two of the delivery drivers would be fairly good friends.

Pip has grown fatter. But it's like his skin is thicker, like the thick skin of a pig, pinkish with a hefty strip of solid lard running below it. I think if I pushed hard enough into him, my fingers might leave indentations. I imagine this particularly around his thick bullish neck. How can someone have a fat neck I ponder? But it bulges over his shirt collar. Even his hair seems to be sticking up more as if forced out by the fat forming underneath it.

He's given up bringing me gifts. We are living in virtual silence. He spends hours tap, tap, tapping on his computer keyboard. He's taken over one of the four bedrooms as his study and it is filling up with dark boxes of various sizes with multiple wires. He perfunctorily explains what they are if he forgets to close the door and I pass by and look in but I barely listen to what he says so I never remember. I don't care what he purchases as long as he doesn't stop me buying what I want.

We settle into a routine of him padding up and down the stairs to and from his study like a sulking bear. He rarely sits in the newly decorated living room with its refurbished art deco fireplace and

William Morris wallpaper. He plods up the stairs, changes, then hides in his study, comes down to eat, trudges back up to his study and eventually goes to bed.

It's more like having a teenage son than a husband.

Meantime, I sit warily on the beautifully upholstered, and very uncomfortable, Chesterfield and watch videos, listening, waiting for something to happen, waiting for him to crack, to say, 'We can't live like this any longer!' or, 'I'm sick of you! Why are you such a bitch?' or, 'I'm leaving you! I've met someone else.' But he never does. He just pads up and down those stairs, making as little noise as he can, moving as little air as possible, and quietly closes the door of the study and gets on with his life. His life on his computer.

I wonder what will happen at Judy's wedding.

I have bought him a suit, shirt, a tie, shoes. He dutifully put them all on for me with barely a word, just like a boy with a new school uniform. Then he simply took it all off and went back to his study.

The suit I have bought myself cost nearly as much as Judy's wedding dress. But I deserve it. I have worked hard on the house and I hardly ever go out. And it is my sister's wedding.

The day before the wedding, we travel up on the train. We have been allocated a room at The Castle. 'Of course you're staying here!' my mother is affronted on the phone but I can't be bothered to remind her of having to sleep at Christine's for my 21st.

The last time we visited was November, a bleak, washed-out time of year, cold and raining. As we fly through the countryside, it is fresh, green, bright, an impressionist painting of light and the promise of summer. We have had hot days in London and I have sunbathed in our unruly back garden as much as I can, baking my skin to a decent colour. It won't have been hot in Cumbria yet, maybe an odd day in May. The forecast looks good for the wedding because of course the sun will shine for Judy.

We have hired a car at Penrith. I've arranged all this to avoid sitting alone in the car with Pip for five hours. On the train I can read, wander along to the buffet car, go to the loo. In the car, the silence would become heavy with blame and resentment. We have hardly exchanged a word but he has looked through a few magazines and a programming book and done a bit of paperwork. We have deftly avoided each other whilst maintaining a veneer of concern and civility, exchanging tight smiles and polite 'Thank yous' over cups of coffee and dreary sandwiches before returning to pretending we're strangers.

Pip drives purposefully and we arrive a little after one. I wonder if anyone has taken in when I've said we'll get there. There are significant changes. The drive has been tarmacked to create a dark and impressively smooth sweep up to the front of the house. Along the edge are masses of brilliant purply blue flowers frothing up and spilling onto the matt black of the drive. They make the moss in the grass look vivid and rather beautiful.

Either side of the front door are two handsome displays of flowers, blue and creamy white hydrangeas, clustered with dark green ivy. It's very simple but lovely. They are nearly as tall as Pip.

I push at the front door, expecting to heave it with my shoulder as usual, but it springs open and I trip forward. They have finally had it fixed. I regain my balance. There are more flowers. It smells delightful. It seems brighter. Fresher.

'Hello?' I manage fairly half-heartedly, and we drop our suitcases and head down to the kitchen.

Dad is stirring something in a large aluminium pot. It could be twenty years ago. I expect him to tell me Mum is in bed.

'Hi Dad,' I say.

'Jen.' He drops the spoon in the pot and comes over, giving me a big hug. 'Pip. How lovely to see you. It's been too long.' He is vigorously shaking his hand.

'How are you David? Lovely to see you,' Pip's face opens, relaxes at the simple human contact. He's very pleased to see him too.

The kitchen is completely different. They've knocked the back wall away and gone through into the back kitchen and beyond. There are sleek units and yards of worktop combined with lovely Victorian pitch pine cupboards. There is a new Aga and a stainless steel industrial oven and hob; it manages to be functional yet homely at the same time.

'This is a bit of a change,' I say.

'Oh yes,' Dad scratches his head, 'we had it done last year. We couldn't go on as we were, what with the restaurant as well. Needed somewhere sensible to work. Couldn't make do any longer.'

My eye is drawn to the wall where Mum's sketches were briefly displayed, it has a large abstract canvas on it.

'That's impressive,' I say.

'It's one of your mother's,' Dad says with muted pride, 'She's been painting again, for a while now. She's very successful. Using her maiden name though.' He returns to the pot, fishes out the spoon and starts stirring again with renewed vigour. Pip stares at the art.

'I see. That's interesting. Where is she?' I try to sound normal.

'She is in the marquee with Judy, I think.' He too is trying to sound normal.

'Marquee?' I say, quietly.

'Yes,' He stares intently into the pot.

'The ballroom wasn't big enough then.' I try not to sound too bitter. Actually, I don't try at all.

'Well,' he pauses, 'there are an awful lot of guests. We've set up the ballroom for dancing in the evening but the marquee's for the wedding breakfast. It was Jonathan's parents who were really keen. They've invited half the ruddy country as far as I can tell.'

'I see,' I say. I remember the Discussion I had with my mother about Keeping Numbers Limited at my wedding, not that I had anyone much to invite.

'Well, shall we go and have a look. I presume it's on the back lawn or have they taken over the village green?' I smile sweetly at Dad's hunched back.

I march down the corridor as I had done so many times before in a state of fury.

I hear Pip hop-skipping behind me, 'Jen,' he whines, 'don't make a scene.'

I ignore him.

'It's their wedding. It doesn't matter.' I continue to ignore him and scoot through the ballroom noting that it is also freshly decorated, 'We couldn't have had a marquee in November, it would have been freezing.'

I push open the doors to the garden.

'You just want an excuse for a fight. You always do.' He doesn't say this with any malice. It's just like he's stating a fact. A fact that makes him Very Tired.

I stop for a moment.

The marquee takes up most of the width of the lawn. It is a beautiful day and the tent is a glorious white, fluid and solid as a sail, anchored below the purplish fells far in the distance. I am stabbed through the heart with jealousy, but Pip's words and his close physical presence behind me are a brake on my actions. Perhaps it would just be easier to go home, I think. Retreat. Admit defeat. Not put myself through it.

Then Judy appears, closely followed by my mother. Judy looks like fucking Doris Day, her hair caught up in a blue cotton scarf, a white shirt tied efficiently at the waist, neat cropped blue jeans and whiter-than-white plimsolls. Mother has a flowing green silk shirt, and her copper hair catches the light. She has a bunch of lush greenery in one hand and secateurs in the other. Her throat is white against the jade of the shirt. She sees me and waves the secateurs. Judy races towards me, the eternal pup wanting to please its master.

'Jen! So pleased you're here. There is such a lot to do! Pip!' She shrieks in my ear and leaps to hug Pip who smiles gamely, 'J's ma and pa are here too but we are snowed under.'

I say nothing. I cannot say anything.

'Well just say the word,' Pip pipes up, stepping forward, 'I'm fresh as a daisy. The train journey was a doddle compared to the M6.'

'Wonderful! J is just doing the tables. Perhaps you could go and help shift them? You're so sweet, Pip. Thank you,' and she kisses his cheek with easy affection.

Pip trudges off down the lawn. She turns to me, 'What about you Jen?' Her face is expectant.

'I'm going to just take our stuff up to our room, then I'll be with you,' I say and turn and go. I can picture her nonplussed face as I walk away but hell, she's known me her whole life, I am an absolute dyed in the wool shirker.

At the reception area I see the key rack has been labelled with the wedding guest names on old-fashioned luggage labels. I want to puke. I take our key and my case and leave Pip's in the hall. I go up to the room, push off my shoes and get into bed, fully clothed.

It's after six when Pip wakes me up with an unfriendly shaking of my shoulder. I am dreaming that I am in the Wild West and I'm driving cattle across the prairies. The sun is warm on my skin as I canter easily in the wake of the dust turned up by the obedient beast before me. I feel calm and purposeful. I am annoyed to be woken. The late afternoon sun is on my face, flooding through the window. My cheek is hot.

'You need to get up. There's going to be a dinner in the ballroom at seven,' Pip's voice is tight. He stalks away and rummages in his case then shuts himself in the bathroom. I hear the shower swish on. I roll over and doze and try to will myself back to the rhythm of riding across the new frontier. It doesn't happen.

Ten minutes or so later Pip emerges fully clothed from the bathroom. So, we're not even dressing and undressing in front of each other anymore. I speculate as to whether he's actually shagging someone else. It seems unlikely.

'You've changed,' I say.

'And showered.' I add.

'Yes,' he says, tying his shoes. He doesn't look at me. 'There was a lot to do. We all got pretty hot and sweaty.' It is an accusation.

'Did you get it all done?' My tone is frosty. I dare him to comment on me not helping.

'Yes,' he replies and stands up abruptly, 'I'm going down to see if I can help with dinner.' He leaves.

He can't stand to be in the same room as me.

I get up and start running a bath. As I sink into the water, I resolve not to step into the ballroom until at least five past seven to minimise any accusations. I shut my eyes and hope that Bryan still cooks here.

All the tables are together in one long line, like a big Italian wedding, so there is still room for clusters of people to stand with drinks and chat at the periphery. It's hard to believe that we are in rural Cumbria. The evening is warm, balmy even, and everyone is in good spirits.

A limp boy in a big-necked shirt and tiny bowtie stands at the door with a tray of champagne. I take one as I cross the threshold and look around for Pip. He is talking to a cluster of Jonathan's sisters and their husbands/ boyfriends. Everyone is smartly dressed, and I don't really understand why we're going through all this tonight when we have to do it again tomorrow. I'd have been happy with fish and chips in my room. There are place names at the table which means we are being manipulated into talking to people we don't know, or like, in the hopes that this will change. There will probably be toasts. I think I might just leave now as there really is not a single soul of any interest to me here. The champagne is chilly, and I hover at the door as I can't seem to make the commitment to move into the throng, to become a part, to mingle.

Dad appears in an expensive, dark, tweed jacket. He must be boiling. He looks like a country gentleman. In his Best Actor Voice, he announces, 'Ladies and gentlemen, dinner is served,' and grins broadly as people fluster their way to their places. I am on the end of the table sitting next to Jonathan's only unmarried brother James. I'm pretty sure he's gay after he spends the first five minutes telling me about what he's wearing tomorrow and how talented Ricky Martin is. He talks quickly and at the same time he's managed to motor his way through the fish pâté starter. He is all bony fingers and smacking lips. Opposite is an unmarried sister and a female friend. I'm changing my opinion of James. Maybe he's on speed. He is now recounting the whole plot of *Shallow Grave*, a new film that's set in Edinburgh and involves a lot of digging up of bodies and sawing of hands and feet and someone hiding in an attic and light shooting up into it and a massive amount of paranoia. If he could, I think he'd be up and acting it out. He has been to see it three times because it's so brilliant. Do I want to go and see it with him? I hear in the middle of his mile-a-minute monologue. I don't bother to reply.

I let him natter on and observe the sister, Hannah and her friend, a gorgeous mixed-race girl. I was wrong. They are clearly the gay couple at the table. I see their hands knit, then slip out of view under the table. They lean into each other. Hannah arching her neck the better to hear the whispered offerings from her companion poured into the tiny cup of her ear from her glossy, brick-red lips, so close they all but touch.

They are alone in the room.

They shift and stretch beneath their thin, summer dresses. Everything just for the other one. I don't think I've ever experienced this kind of intimacy. I feel hot with envy.

We are waiting for the main course. Very young and very old people are serving us, none with much confidence. Perhaps they are saving the better staff for tomorrow. James has moved onto *Psycho* now. The Best Film Ever. He doesn't seem to care that I'm not even looking at him. Every so often he has a little pause to examine the tines of his fork or a flower in the table arrangement. This doesn't happen much though.

'And when Mr Arbogast reaches the top of the stairs, which takes forever, and the mother runs out of the bedroom, Jesus Wept, I nearly died. And he falls back down the stairs once she's stabbed him and you see it all from a birds eye view and that's a recurrent motif in the film, see.'

Our chicken arrives but it doesn't stop him talking. In some ways, I'm pleased I've been side-lined, placed at the end of the table, closest to the exit, next to the brother, who is high, opposite the self-absorbed lesbians, far away from my husband who is next to my mother and having a whale of a time with her. I'm sure I'm here so I can't say anything controversial or offend anyone important. Fine by me. James and I are facing the unlit fire, we have our backs to the view. Another negative. They've taken down the aged portrait that used to hang there, a rather cross looking woman in her early thirties in a dark dress sitting by a table with a dove and a bowl of shining purple cherries. As a child, I used to wonder how the dove got into the room, why it sat there long enough to be painted and why it didn't eat the cherries. A much larger more modern painting hangs in its place. It is abstract and colourful with swathes of thick buttery paint generously applied across the canvas. I can see a V at the start of the artist's signature. It must be Mother's.

The chicken is over. I decide to leave James; I don't believe he'll notice and go in search of Mother's studio. How seriously is she taking the painting? Can she really be any good at it?

I start at reception and assess the room keys. By my reckoning every room on the first floor is accounted for and there are more so they've converted some of the servants' rooms in the attic for guests too. I suppose it could be up there. I am feeling restless so I bound up the front stairs two at a time and then cut along the corridor to the attic stairway. It's all been re-plastered and painted and, indeed, there are now a handful of simple little guest rooms up here. 'Cosy' will be how they are marketed. No sign of the studio.

I come back down the kitchen stairs (a misnomer as they are at the back of The Castle by the kitchen, but don't lead directly into it) and head outside through the back pantry. There is no more room for a studio in doors; it must be in one of the outhouses.

I note the garage has also been given a new lease of life, repainted, and cleared out. I walk round to the row of three potting sheds where I spent an afternoon years ago watching Kevin tar his lungs and puke. Work has definitely taken place here. Smart new windows have been painted olive green with a matching door on the first. The doors have been bricked up on the next two and there is a new aluminium chimney poking out of the third. 'Bingo,' I think.

The door is unlocked, and a chunky light switch illuminates whitewashed walls, stacked canvases, open shelves plump with paints and brushes and palette knives and an easel centrally lit by the last of the evening sun. There is no doubt she is working. This isn't like her studio at Granny's where nothing was ever produced; there is definite evidence of graft.

I look at the canvases.

The first group are more or less abstract like the ones in the ballroom and the kitchen. A few are vast. They have the oppression of the fells. The dark greens and greys, a brooding presence. They are not peaceful pictures.

I move onto the next pile. The first one is blank. I rest it against my leg. The next is a group scene. It's on its side. I've had a few glasses of wine, so it takes me a moment. The central figure is however unmistakably, my father. He is dressed, from the waist up, in a garish parody of a jester's costume; he is dancing on a table that is threatening to break, with a group of leering farmers surrounding him. There are no jester's tights or trousers, though this would be bad enough, but a coquettish, flouncy skirt which he is daintily raising to reveal prim, girlish knees for the farmers to admire. A mannish woman is biting hard on a short pipe in the dark background and squeezing a small gleaming accordion. She has the colouring of my mother. Her eyes are full of wickedness.

I set the canvas aside and look at the next. It's a version of *The Death of Marat*. It is beautifully done. The paint is sleek and refined. It must have taken her hours.

It's my father again.

He is draped over the edge of the bath. He's clutching a letter. But on the floor are masses of letters, overlapping, higgledy piggledy. I look closely; they are all rejections for acting parts and they all detail different reasons. 'We couldn't give you the role because of your spineless cowardice,', '... had to go with someone who *could* act their way out of a paper bag,', '... your accent was woefully inadequate,', '... provided us with a good laugh in the pub afterwards at your expense,' '... insulted that you call yourself an actor ,', 'no vocal control', 'wooden physicality', 'little or no stage presence,' It is horrible. I feel an unfamiliar fear crawling into my throat, constricting me. How can she be so cruel? I truly hope my father has not seen this.

I put it aside and reach for the next. He is naked on their bed. Their bedroom is depicted in meticulous detail. Piles of paperbacks on the bedside table crowd the furry-with-dust table lamps. There are several coffee cup rings and crumpled tissues on the floor, an allusion to mother's slatternly ways no doubt. The bed is out of proportion to the room. It dominates and is extravagantly unmade, each deep fold and crease of sheet and blanket and bedspread lovingly rendered with scrupulous accuracy and my father is lying, like a centrefold, on top of it all, reclining, gormless. He's trying to look seductive, but he looks retarded, mouth lolling, eyes vacant. His stomach is paunchy and slack, and his skin is dead, lifeless. Where his genitals should be there is a hungry rat which looks ready to pounce, it's wiry tail coils down his thigh with horrible intimacy. Its eyes are bright and piercing. My heart is beating too fast.

I hear Dad saying that Mum is, 'successful'. Has she shown anyone else these? Has she sold anything like this?

I move it aside trying not to catch the rat's eye.

I am hoping against hope this will be the end of my mother's artistic humiliation of my father but, alas, no.

In the next, my father is dying on the cross. He is being crucified. It is horrible. The nails through his palms are heavy, rusted and brutal and the blood seeping from his feet, rich and viscous. She really is very good. He has a crudely drawn clown maquillage on his face, crusting and peeling. And his expression is bewilderment. There are onlookers. But they are disinterested. We are back in Jerusalem, but no one cares about my father's demise. A group of raggedy kids are crouched, playing some form of marbles with stones. Three women huddle, laughing freely over a shared joke. A man holds up a bucket to let his donkey drink. No one is looking at my father. Life is carrying on. No one has turned up for his execution. His grinning painted mouth strains as the sun sets in a cloudless sky behind it.

There are two more canvases behind this one but I don't know if I can stand to see another. I hear music building. Dancing after dinner no doubt. I am filled with a hollow sadness. I carefully re-stack the canvases and head back to the house. I retreat to my room. No one will miss me.

In bed, I dream of Dad dancing for the farmers. 'Higher, higher!' they demand, both for how high he kicks his legs and how he pulls up his skirt.

Much later Pip is next to me, pushing against me, drunk and desolate, I relent, and he clambers onto me clumsily, all swelling belly and porcine grunting. He cries noisily into my hair after he's finished. 'I'm so sorry,' he says, 'I love you Jen.'

'It's alright,' I say and pat him like the domestic animal he is, 'Let's go to sleep,' and I roll him off me and lie wide-awake with my teeth clenched, disgusted by his snuffling, contented snores.

The church is chilly and uncomfortable.

We had both woken up early to a new embarrassment at the shared intimacy of the night before. Pip showered first and emerged in a towel trying to catch my eye, hoping to talk perhaps, salvage the dying embers of our marriage, fuck me again, inflame my lust, I had no idea. I avoided all of this and escaped into the bathroom. I felt his hurt even through the closed door. When I came out, he'd gone down to breakfast. I have skulked through the morning, spiderlike, retreating into corners, avoiding contact, still, watchful, unobserved. I managed to see neither my mother nor father and avoid the bride. If only I could have sidestepped my husband too.

Now we stare straight ahead, thighs barely touching, awaiting the grand entrance. I am freezing. The thin silk of my jacket is no insulator against this stone-damp chill, despite everyone's bright smiles and bubbling excitement, on this perfect day.

Finally the organ begins, a little unsteadily, and we all stand. Pip turns, expectantly, grinning and oafish. I stare straight ahead. The organist gets a bit of a spurt on, and I hear the momentum of her arrival. The church is packed. This is no ordinary, 'Isn't she lovely?' moment. My parents have produced an outstanding specimen. Perfectly symmetrical, beautiful clearly defined features in a disarmingly transparent face with a body of exquisite proportions for twentieth century taste, combined with a personality unaware or uninterested in her inherent aesthetic sublimity. The congregation cannot help but gasp and sigh and mutter and comment as she glides down the aisle on my father's arm. I steadfastly do not turn but hear the wash of approval building behind me like a wave of the ocean. I stand unsteady in the shallows, knowing it will crash over me; I will feel its full force when I behold her and be left salty mouthed and sea-weed haired for certain. She passes, a fragile sail of cloud-cream satin, and takes her place next to Jonathan.

Unfortunately, I have a perfect view. Sunlight pours through the south window, and she is alight with happiness and beauty and love and contentment. And I don't understand why for her it isn't a lie and for me it is.

Pip's porky fingers grub blindly for mine and my scarlet nails spike into them. 'She looks like a million dollars,' he whispers to me.

Back at The Castle, Maureen galumphs up to me and gives me an ungainly hug. I hug her back. She has even more children attached to her. 'Oh Jen,' she breathes, 'doesn't she look A Mazing. And this place. It's like I'm at a celebrity wedding. Me and Mam love *OK* and *Hello!* Do you? You get to see inside the celebrities' houses and their photos and their weddings and see who's lost weight and who's put it on. It's like they're your friends.' She smiles as she gathers up one of her brood and slings it onto her hip. It stares at me, frowning. I stare back. Maureen rattles on, 'We get every issue and I keep them all. I reckon Judy could be in OK, easy. She is as gorgeous as any of those celebrities, don't you think? That dress is fantastic!' She is gazing over at Judy, looking all dreamy.

'I don't read that trash,' I lie.

Maureen looks perplexed. 'But it's fab. It's really interesting,' She knocks the brat's finger out of its nose, 'You find out what they're really like. Behind-the-scenes. They get paid a fortune too, for the photos like.' She acts as if she is the only one in who is in the know, 'It's a shame you didn't hit the big time, you could be raking it in.'

'How's Christopher?' I say, changing the subject. I don't want to argue, or to stab her.

Maureen rolls her eyes. 'He is doing very well, thank you,' she says smugly, 'he's bred a champion bull and he's getting quite a name for himself in AI.'

I've heard Pip mention this, 'Artificial Intelligence?' I proffer.

'What?' Maureen is again perplexed, 'No, Artificial Insemination. You know, impregnating heifers and that. There is a lot of talk about bull's semen. It's really quite unsavoury but that's the life of the successful farmer's wife.' She bats away another one of her offspring who is trying to wiggle a chubby mitt under her blouse.

Pip arrives with two glasses of champagne, one of which he gallantly offers to Maureen. She giggles as she takes it, 'Ooh, thank you.'

'My pleasure,' he replies.

'Ooh, he sounds like Hugh Grant, doesn't he?' Pip smiles bashfully and heads off for more champagne. Maureen watches him leave. 'So, no babies on the way, Jen?'

'God no,' I dismiss, downing half my glass.

'My eldest is nearly ten now. You want to get cracking.' There is a shift. 'You were ten when you moved up here, weren't you?' I know where this is going, we might as well get it over with. It's to be expected but I thought it would be later when she had a few more drinks.

'Let's go and sit down,' I say.

We move over to a cluster of skeletal chairs under the yew tree at the bottom of the lawn. It's shaded and quieter. Maureen chugs more champagne. 'I think about her such a lot, Jen,' she starts.

I say nothing but I notice Mrs Bell, nicely dressed up, chatting by the ballroom doors. She still has the same backcombed beehive and kitten heels. She is immaculate, but her face has gone to origami wrinkles, deep delicate creases, definitely premature. She looks so much older than Mother but the age difference cannot be that great.

'I just wish I'd walked her home that night.' I hope she's not going to cry; she's made quite an effort with her make-up.

'If you had, you'd have probably gone too. We don't know how many people were involved. You were only a kid yourself. You couldn't have saved her,' Maureen looks forlorn, 'realistically,' I add.

'What do you think happened?' she asks eventually as she always does. Usually I say things like, it was a couple who couldn't have kids who took her and gave her a better life. I'd say it was the opposite of Snow White being left in the forest to die. I'd say they saw her jet-black hair and sapphire-blue eyes and wanted to look after her forever. For years, I'd invent a whole fantasy of her being whisked away to another country, to a new identity and a life of luxury. It often involved drugs to help her forget Cumberland and her family. It all pacified Maureen. We made up names and sometimes we'd be watching James Bond films and Maureen would whisper, 'Looks like where Christine lives,' at some exotic foreign location and I would smile and nod.

We kept this going for years never dealing with why Christine wouldn't have tried to find her way back, wouldn't have found some way to get in touch. After all I could remember my phone number from when I was five, but it was all just to make Maureen or Andrea or Judy or whoever was listening, feel better. It wasn't real or watertight or even plausible.

'Raped and murdered,' I state. Maureen starts and slops champagne on to her dress. 'Either that or held long-term by some group of perverts. Then murdered.'

Maureen is silent for a while. 'Why would you say something so horrible?' she says.

'It would be better if it all happened quickly, I think. Better that he, or they, picked her up and killed her quickly. That that's what they wanted to do. If it was my child, that's what I would want. I would rather they'd been killed quickly than put through stuff they didn't understand or that was vile and painful. Wouldn't you? If it was your child, I mean?'

Maureen has hold of one of her children and she is looking at me as if I might kill it. 'I mean we have to face facts Maureen, don't we? The only thing is whether Christine's murderer is still in the village.' Maureen gasps.

'Who is Christine?' The child says breaking from sucking noisily on its thumb.

'She was a friend of your mum's and mine who disappeared years ago,' I say to it.

'Go and play,' Maureen's voice hardens, she pushes the child away and it obediently totters away towards its siblings. 'How can you say that? Her murderer doesn't live in the village!'

'How do you know?' I am casual, relaxed, 'No one knows. She was never found. It could have all been a terrible accident but there were always rumours, weren't there? Whoever it was got away with it then so, who's to say they haven't got away with it since? Could have travelled all over. Repeating the pattern.'

'Why are you saying all this Jen? Today. Of all days. On this day. Your sister's lovely wedding day.' She splutters the words out. I have clearly upset her.

'We are adults, Maureen. There's no point in pretending anymore. That's all. No point lying to ourselves.'

'I don't understand you, Jennifer. I don't understand you at all. Don't you think I don't have these thoughts? Don't you think, I don't know what happened? I'm well aware I'm an adult. I don't need the likes of you pointing that out. It's just that, when I'm with you, I like to pretend, like we did when we were kids. I like to think she might still be out there, might be happy, like to think she might have had a life. I know it's not real, you stupid cow. I'm not that thick.' Maureen stands up and walks away as purposefully as she can manage in heels over the spongy lawn. The children join her and trail and tumble in her wake. She disappears inside.

Dad's speech is funny and sentimental and Judy and my mother gaze at him adoringly. I try to block out the canvases from the studio and search for clues that my father has seen them, but he is generous and humble in the face of his wife's talent, and she reaches across to kiss his cheek tenderly as he sits down which he accepts gladly. Is this all a front or does he know but doesn't care? Are the pictures old or a product of a bygone problem? Or has she successfully concealed them all from him?

I want the day to be over but there is still dancing to endure and the fresh influx of guests for the evening have added new vigour to the proceedings. I have drunk plenty of champagne, as has Pip, who has become rowdily chummy with a couple of Jonathan's brothers. They really are an obscenely large family.

The alcohol has emboldened me, and I decide to finally go and brave the kitchen in the hopes of finding Bryan.

I skirt round the side of the house, avoiding the heave and swell of the ballroom and cut in through the new back door. It's quieter here. The food is over and I'm pretty sure most of the waiting staff have gone home. I hesitate at the threshold for a moment. What is my plan? I'll say to Bryan, 'You washed my feet ten years ago and, thinking about it, is the only way I can achieve orgasm with my husband.' And how do I expect him to react? He's got a life, probably a wife and kids. He'll be thirty six. He might be bored. I lean against the door jam, annoyed at my indecision. It is still remarkably warm.

'Hello,' he says behind me. I turn and he is carrying a crate of empties collected from the marquee no doubt. There is a glint of the evening sun on his skin. How can he be this tanned so early in the summer in the north-west of England? His hair is still thick and dark. No receding hairline here. The ponytail is neat and trimmed. He looks good. He is smiling.

'Hi,' I manage and rock away from the door to let him pass, 'I wondered if you were still working here?' I am letting him know I am here to find out about him. He passes me and walks into the kitchen. I catch a drift of fresh air and sweat and spice. His shoulders are tense from the weight of the crate. I want to fuck him there and then.

He dumps the crate on the floor and stands, smiling. 'How are you?' He is really looking at me. His hands are resting, relaxed on his hips and I check for a ring. There isn't one.

'I'm seething with jealousy that my perfect sister is the centre of attention, again,' I say.

He laughs a little and gets two beers from the excessively oversized fridge. I take one and follow him back outside to sit on the steps to the kitchen garden. The scent of tobacco plants is sweet and fragrant. It is getting dark.

'Are you exhausted?' I say.

'It's been a long day,' he concedes.

'What time did you start?'

'Up at five.'

'Christ,' I glug my beer. I'd like it to be ice cold water.

'Are you living here still?' I'm hoping this might reveal a bit more information.

'No. Moved out a few years back. Needed to get away from work sometimes.' He is rolling a cigarette.

'Okay,' Another drink, 'Don't they pay you enough to buy a packet?' I say.

'I like these.' He puts the worn, leather pouch in his back pocket and the cigarette crackles as he lights it.

'So. Where are you living?' He exhales then looks at me, squinting against the smoke.

'Do you remember Mrs Potter's place?'

I do indeed. Mrs Potter was a deeply religious old lady who lived in a quaint little building at the back of the school. Maureen and I would sometimes go and visit her and marvel at her house. The living room and kitchen were all one, the kitchen just the stove, a larder cupboard and the sink in the corner and her living room a couple of chairs and a dull rag rug. The walls were bare except for a palm cross and a picture of Jesus preaching. We liked going around mealtimes so we could wonder at how little food she prepared. Two small potatoes and a carrot in a small boiling pot would do her she would say. There was a door frame with a curtain which we thought led to her bedroom and bathroom, but we never saw those. It was like a doll's house, and she was like a tiny old-fashioned doll, a faded, flowery pinny, a thin, grey bun. No family. Just the Lord. That was all she needed she used to say.

'Yes, by the school.'

'She died, nearly a hundred. So, I took it over. Suits me.'

Aha. So, no wife and three kids then.

'Me and Maureen used to visit her,' I say, 'She would read us Bible stories. Sometimes, rarely, gave us money for sweets. She didn't believe in sugar or salt I seem to remember.'

'Probably why she lived to a hundred.' I look at Bryan's profile. He is so fucking gorgeous.

'Have you done much to it?'

'A few things,' He inhales deeply and turns to me, 'you can come down and see it if you like. For old times' sake.'

'I'd like that,' I say, 'For old times' sake.' We look at each other.

'When do you finish?' I say.

'Probably about midnight.'

'Shall I meet you there?' I hold his gaze.

'Sure,' he says, with a slow nod.

'Okay,' I say standing up. 'I'll see you later.' I finish the beer and I go back into the house.

I knock on Mrs Potter's door at a quarter past twelve. I have showered and changed. I know I can't walk to the village in high heels. I catch a glimpse of Pip dancing with drunken abandon with Maureen as I sneak past the window. I don't think anyone sees me leave.

Bryan opens the door wide and I step in. The lighting is soft and it's a little unsettling that he still has Mrs Potter's old chairs. The tiny corner of kitchen has been updated and walls have been painted. The palm cross is still there but Jesus has gone. The floor is sanded and waxed. No sign of the rag rug. It is basic. No sign of any feminine touches lightly bestowed by a girlfriend.

He has a beer for me. I drink it but I brushed my teeth, and it doesn't taste nice. I set it down on the little kitchen counter.

'Did your mum and dad help you sort it out?' I fish.

'No. I did it myself. It was only the kitchen and the floor and the bed.'

'The bed?' I raise my eyebrows, 'Maureen and I never saw Mrs Potter's bedroom but we were curious. Or her bathroom. We wondered if it was all in one like in here was.'

He smiles. He is looking at me. I don't know if he looks at everyone all the time or if this is a thing we have.

'Do you want to see?' he asks, calmly.

'Sure,' I say.

He's put a door where the old curtain used to hang. There is a tiny corridor with two doors off it. Bryan indicates the door to the left, 'The john,' he says. Funny that he uses the Americanism, 'And this is the bedroom,' he opens the door straight ahead.

It's smaller than the living room but lovely. 'Did you do this?' I ask. He nods. The whole of the left wall is filled with a raised built-in bed. I recognise the style as Scandinavian. It has a simple wooden frame with deep drawers incorporated under the mattress. There are soft pale green cotton curtains hanging either side. It is painted a warm cream and there are tiny ferns and leaves and animals running up and along the top, picked out by hand in the same green as the curtains. The pillows are plump, and at the foot of the bed is a tiny window with more curtains.

'It's lovely, Bryan. Really lovely.' I cannot help but touch it, 'and you made it yourself?' I run my hand up and over the smooth wood, pull the soft fabric through my fingers.

'Yep.'

'I'm so impressed.'

'Do you want to try it?'

'I don't have my jimjams,' I reply, 'but I'll lie on it,' I concede.

I climb into it, in as dignified a way as I can, and clamber towards the wall, hoping he'll join me. I lie on my back. It is wonderfully comfortable. I exhale and close my eyes. I feel his warmth as he lies down next to me.

'This is fantastic. It's so comfortable. You should sell these for a living. People would pay a fortune for them in London.'

He laughs indulgently.

'It was a right pain to build though. I don't want to do it again.'

I roll over and face him.

'Oh, don't tell me that. I have a fairy-tale image of you miraculously and miraculously and effortlessly creating this.'

'It was fucking hard. There's lots of botches I had to cover up.' He has drawn the curtains and switched on a discreet overhead light. It is cosy and magical.

'Well, it looks perfect,' I smile up at it. 'What was it like in here before?'

'Just a little cot bed, iron frame, really old and a chair and a chest. She had only had two boxes of belongings in the end, you know. A hundred years and that's all she had. Two boxes. Including her pots and pans.'

I think about all my clothes stuffed into my fitted wardrobes in London. 'She always said she only needed the Lord.'

We are quiet for a bit.

'Why are you here Jennifer?' Bryan says. I know he's looking at me.

'You asked me,' I deflect.

'I did.'

'You washed my feet.' I confess.

'I did.'

'Do you ever think about that?' It's hard to talk and try not to breathe too heavily.

'Yes.'

'What do you think about it'

'You know what I think.'

'No I don't,' I turn my body to him and look at him, 'tell me.'

He rolls over towards me, his hand cupped under his face. We are very close. 'I think about taking off your clothes, I think about the feel of your skin, I think about you lying on the bed, clean and naked.'

'I think about it too,' I look at his mouth, his eyes are too bright.

'Do you?'

'Yes,' I pause, 'I think about it much more than I should.'

'What happens when you think about it?'

'It makes me come.' I know I've crossed the line here. I'm telling him to fuck me. He is up on the bed and slowly pulls off his T-shirt. He is really tanned.

'Why are you so tanned?' I say.

'Went to Greece in March,' he says. His body is lean. His jeans are low-cut and loose, and I can see his hipbones jutting. I imagine them pressing into me.

He lies back down. I kneel up and unbutton my shirt. I've put on my best bra. I lie back down on my back. He places three fingertips on my throat and runs them down to my cleavage.

He leans over and places his lips gently on mine, no tongue forcing its way rudely in. It's an introduction.

'Are you sure you want this?' he says. I place my hand on his chest digging a little with my nails.

'I've wanted this for years. I can't believe it's finally going to happen.' It's quite hard to speak.

This time the kiss has more purpose, and his hands are on me and his body presses against mine and he murmurs and melts into me and I want to be transported into a delirium of desire for his salty lean body that makes me giddy. I want us to twine and intertwine behind the curtains in the little box bed in the tiny house, secretly sating each other for hours and hours, while I give no thought to my dreary husband. That is what I want.

His body is heavier than I expected it would be and his hip presses uncomfortably into my groin. As his kisses become more passionate and I find it more difficult to breathe, I try to pull away and he senses this and moves at the same time. We try to adjust but head-butt each other, his front tooth catching my lip painfully.

'Jesus, sorry, are you okay?' His hand is halfway down the front of my trousers; he leaves it there.

'Yes I'm fine,' I can taste a little bit of blood and the inside of my lip is starting to swell. He kisses my neck instead and we relax again. We fumble our way out of our clothes and I like how hot his skin is. He puts his hand between my legs and things are going well, until he digs a nail sharply into my labia. In the living room there's a guitar, presumably his nails are so long to pluck the strings.

The sharpness of the pain makes me draw my knee up and it collides with his crotch. He shouts and tips away, clutching his balls, and curls up next to me. Things stop going so well.

'Bloody hell, I'm really sorry,' I say, 'it's just, you dug your nail right into me, it really hurt, it was just a reaction. Are you okay?'

'Yeah, yes, I'm fine, just give me a minute. I'm sorry, I didn't mean to hurt you, my nails are really long at the moment.' He is still really wincing. I didn't think I'd kneed him that hard. It's a bit of an over-reaction. Things don't look that promising.

'Okay, well there's no rush,' I say, 'I'll just lie here and twiddle my thumbs until you feel better,' and I relax back onto the pillow, and I feel a little drift of sleep come over me. I begin to dream.

'How's your lip?' His voice jolts me back. He sounds a bit more normal. I don't have much sense of how much time has passed.

I explore it with my tongue. 'It's a bit swollen but it's okay. It doesn't hurt.'

I wish I could say the same for my labia.

'Hey,' Bryan nudges me, I turn and look at him, 'I'm a bit swollen too' I smile politely at his erection, but I do feel the moment has faded a little. Bryan clearly doesn't. He swings across me, edging my legs apart with his knees and, wounded labia or not, he's inside me and thrusting. His hair flops and flays into my face and mouth and there's so much of it. I flick my head to try to get it out of the way, and then he's ejaculating without any thought to my pleasure.

He rolls away, 'God I'm exhausted, that was a great end to a really good day though. You're gorgeous,' and I realise he's drifting off to sleep. In the subdued light he looks like a painting, a medieval knight or a Celtic warrior. I lie and look at him, twitchy with unsatisfied desire, my default setting. If I was married to him I muse, everyone would comment on how gorgeous he was, everyone would be impressed that he was mine. Those long nails would have to go though.

I take a hurried and cramped shower in the tiny bathroom, and leave as the sun is coming up. I plan my alibi as I walk back to The Castle. Part of me fantasises with confessing all and living in the toy house with Bryan forever and ever. I'm clean, I'm changed. Pip will have been very drunk by the time he made it to bed last night. When I open our door, he is fully clothed, minus a sock and shoe, sprawled across the whole bed. This is more or less what I expected. I ease off a pillow and get a spare blanket from the wardrobe. I place them on the chair. Then I shake him awake.

'Pip, Pip. Come on wake up. Look. You've been asleep across the bed all night. I've been sleeping in the chair. I couldn't get in the bed.' Pip raises his head, taking in the evidence.

'Oh God, Jen, I'm so sorry.'

'I'm feeling awful. I'm going for a walk to clear my head then I'll come back to try to get some sleep. Let's get you undressed.' I help Pip out of his suit. I fetch him water and paracetamol. He tucks himself back in on his side of the bed, mortified. I leave the pillow and blanket. 'I didn't know where you were,' he murmurs, 'when I came up to bed.'

'I was in Mum's studio. I'll tell you when you wake up. Sleep now.'

I sit in the chair and wait for him to start snoring again.

I undress and climb into bed.

I sleep. So well.

It is nearly lunchtime and Pip has gone when I wake. I go in search of food. I'm starving.

There is the remains of a buffet laid out in the dining room and judging by the sounds of the voices, people are sitting out in the garden. I pile my plate with lukewarm Cumberland sausage and beans and head outside. Pip is sitting with my mother.

'There you are darling,' he says.

'Finally,' she can't resist.

'Did Pip tell you what sort of a night we had?' I say sharply.

Pip's face falls.

'You're very hungry this morning,' Mother remarks pointedly as I start eating.

'Yes, I bloody am,' I take a huge bite out of the sausage sandwich I have made. 'You would be too if you had had no sleep,' I look sharply at Pip. He looks away miserably.

'Who's still here?' I say through my mouthful of sausage.

'Most of Jonathan's family left this morning. Judy and Jonathan are still around though. They're going shortly. She'll be pleased you're up to say goodbye.'

She sips her coffee and eyes me coldly. I ignore this.

'I had a look in your studio,' my tone is confident.

She says nothing. Just holds my gaze.

'Your new work is unusual,' I say.

She allows a smirk to play around her lips. Pip shifts next to her and adds more sugar to his tea. He recognises this game.

'Has Dad seen them?' Irritatingly, I can hear my voice tighten.

'Of course,' she replies, smoothly. She inhales patiently as she did when I was seven and I was testing her with unreasonable demands.

'All of them?' I persist.

'What do you want to say, Jen?' she sounds bored.

'What do I want to say?' I pretend to mull it over, 'Oh I don't know? Do you hate my father? Are you getting a divorce? Do you get a thrill from the public humiliation of your nearest and dearest?' I start off matching her calm tone but the words sputter out faster, louder, tighter.

'Jen!' Pip tries to shush me. He has no idea what's going on but his careful hand placed over my mother's, reveals his allegiance.

She reassures him with a soft smile. Then hardens her face, just for me. 'Jen. It's art. It's not real,' she talks to me as if I am a retard, 'Of course we are not getting a divorce. Christ. Why are you always so dramatic?'

'They're horrible, Mum. They are vile. He's pathetic in them. What was I supposed to think? And how is he going to feel if you put them on a wall for everyone to see? Behold. This is how my wife perceives me?' I am clutching my knife. I may run it into the milky white of her eye.

'Look. He's just a face. It's portraiture. There's not that many models around, you know. And I know his face better than anybody's. It's not him. It's a facade. You always were so bloody literal.'

'So, you are going to exhibit them?'

She is rooting around for a cigarette, 'I don't know. Maybe.'

'And what will people think?' I slam down the knife.

The cigarette hangs from her lip and she removes it slowly. 'I don't care what they think Jennifer. About me that is. Or my marriage. It's art. Its expression. It's bigger than David and I or you or Judy. It's about what I have to say or what the work says to the spectator. It's not personal. Your father understands that. Perhaps you would be happier if you stopped caring so much about what people think.'

'For God's sake,' I am on my feet, 'please don't patronise me with your half-baked notions of what constitutes art or pretend to know what would make me happier or indeed pretend to care about my happiness. Whatever Dad says, he will hate those paintings. Anyone would in his position.'

'Jen, please,' Pip whimpers.

Mum appears unaffected. She pauses for a moment. 'Where were you last night?' she says.

'What?' I say.

'Where were you?'

I look at her; I challenge her.

'She was in your studio, Vivian. That's why I couldn't find her.' Pip's voice is small; he is the child at the table.

'Really?' she says, holding my gaze.

I say nothing. I am waiting. Waiting for it. I know it's coming.

'But you weren't in there when I checked it after the party. When I unlocked it. I had locked it, you know, before the wedding, and if you broke in there, you must have taken a very long way round because I saw you leaving here, changed, off down to the village just after midnight.'

I smile as pityingly and widely as I can and turn and leave, without looking at Pip.

He follows me, dog-like, to the room. 'Where did you go? Where were you? When you woke me up, was that you coming back?' I am hurtling furiously round the room, throwing clothes into my suitcase. I fucking hate her. I will never come back here. Never.

'Jen. Answer me,' Pip stands, portly maypole to my pinball fury, plaintive cries begging, 'Where were you? Were you with someone? Oh God. What's going on? I don't understand.'

I ricochet to a stop in front of him, 'She is evil. I want to leave. Now. Can't you see what she's doing? I criticise her paintings, with good reason I might add, and she treats me like this. I fucking hate her.'

Pip winces like an affronted Dowager, 'Jen. She is your mother,' he blusters.

'I don't care. I want to go. Now. Start packing or I'm leaving without you.'

He remains at the foot of the bed all teddy bear tummy and

shining forehead. 'Jen,' he says quietly, 'I want to know where you were.'

'Do you?' I say as I screw up the silk suit and cram it into my case.

'Yes. Please tell me. Now.'

'Or what?' I say and cast him as sneering look, 'Start packing. I'm leaving in ten minutes.' My face is burning, and it feels like a sharpened comb has scraped down my throat and my chest and my gut. I am raw with anger.

'You left on your own, Vivian said. So, were you going to meet someone? But everyone was at the wedding. God why did I drink so much? I can't even remember who you were talking to. So stupid. Why do I always get into these situations?'

'Are you talking to me?' I shout, 'I am leaving in ten minutes. With or without you.'

He sags and begins to lumber around the room gathering his sorry belongings.

Three weeks later, I get a pack of photos in the post and a card from Judy. These are the Best Photos taken by one of Jonathan's brothers and she thought I'd Love copies. So sorry they didn't see us on the morning... Wasn't it The Most... Perfect... Best Start... Couldn't Have Happened... Blah Blah Blah.

I don't look at the photos.

Pip and I have barely spoken since we got back. He has a business trip planned. The first of many he tells me. His firm has been bought out by a big tech company in the States. He is going out to their headquarters in Houston. I can go too. He'd love me to.

I decline.

There is a sleek new company car. More money in the bank. We can move again if I want to.

I turn away from him trying to decide if I want to stay married. Perhaps I'll wait and see what else turns up

2004

Pip has put his foot down.

When Judy invited us to Finn's birthday party. He Put His Foot Down.

'He is my godson and we're going.' It was surprisingly macho. Who knew it would be this that has finally tipped the balance? 'I'm putting my foot down,' he said.

'I want to go to Greece this year.' No.

'I like the blue sofas.' Wrong.

'What about a gas-fired barbecue?' Veto.

'How about camping?' No way.

'I prefer silver.' So what.

'I love pork.' Who cares?

'Mum's invited us for Christmas.' Over my dead body.

But on the attendance of the birthday party, the Foot Is Down. I suppose I could make him attend on his own but, even for me, that is churlish. Besides, Judy and Jonathan have moved and I want to see the house. I will allow this concession. Just this once.

Often, I wake up and I don't know how I am forty. I have no children. I have no real friends. I have people who drift in and out of my life mainly through Pip's work. I have little to no contact with my family. All that there is, is initiated by Pip or them, never me. I do not know how we have remained married. He has his work. I trot out this mantra in my head and to the blank faced strangers who dance through the edge of my life and it is true. It is everything to him. It has had to be. Or is that the case with most men? I see him look at dads and kids fondly, jealously, from time to time but he gave up trying to convince me procreation was a good idea years ago. And, when I look around me, it's mostly the women doing the work. In fact, now, it's mostly the women with a job and doing all the crappy kids' stuff as well. The dads slot in and out but when I eavesdrop on other women, it's not a shared responsibility; it's not equality. Pip wanted kids but he wanted me to do the grit while he concentrated on his job. I don't really know why people have kids. All they do is complain about it, hark back to life before, or look forward to when Things Will Be Better. Anyway, I said no. He didn't put his foot down on that one.

Jonathan and Judy didn't waste much time though. Hamish arrived the year after the wedding. And then Emily a couple of years on and then Finn sometime later. They're all bloody gorgeous of course. Eager, tawny-cheeked, sparkle-eyed, fruits of her abundant womb. She has evolved into an energetic but quirkily haphazard and adorable mother.

The new house is outside Oxford. Jonathan is now a professor at UCL but their Roots Are Here, Their Life is here. It's Village Life They Love. Doesn't seem like much of a village to me. There are several chic boutiques, a deli, a chemist, two pubs cosily ensconced in ancient half- timbered buildings as well as a large picture postcard school and church. Even the Spar has tasteful galvanised buckets of tight-budded tulips and green daffodils outside.

It's a cold February morning. Judy has asked us to get there early so we can have a family lunch before everyone else descends. I am silent in the car, the better to let Pip appreciate my displeasure. He whistles tunelessly to every song on the radio. He is in A Good Mood. He will see his friends from Oxford, from whom I keep him. He will be able to make a fuss of his angelic godson. He will be able to spend at least one Sunday without wearily drifting between his study and the kitchen and the sitting room hoping for a morsel of interaction with his prickly wife.

Eventually Pip pulls into the sweeping drive which already has several cars generously parked with plenty of room for more. The house is in beautiful condition; it has been lovingly cared for by generations. It is a double fronted, Georgian detached of gently weathered, pale grey stone. It knows its worth. It is solid, dependable. I set my mouth. I hope it's a tip inside; with three kids it's bound to be.

Pip rings the bell and steps back politely. I purposely have my back to the door when Judy opens it. I flinch as she leaps out, squeaking, to hug Pip. She's wearing a cornflower blue cashmere jumper and dove grey cords with rich, soft, dark grey, leather knee-high boots. Her eyes are sparkling gems and her hair thick, glossy and gold; it would take a lot to tug a handful out by the roots, I imagine. Her youngest is not even at school. How can she look so flawless?

We step into the palatial hallway after soft fragrant kisses. I take in the high ornate coving, the original fanlight casting Parma Violet winter light on to the flat matt of the painted walls. There are studio portraits of the children in black-and-white above a handsome marble fireplace. I cast my eye around for a hammer.

Jonathan is clutching Pip's hand and shoulder as they express manfully how it has been Too Long. I catch Jonathan's sidelong look at me. The Wicked Witch.

Finn starts to rip open his gift, eagerly received from Pip. 'No, presents after lunch, Finn,' Judy explains with the exaggerated enunciation and volume of every middle-class mother I have witnessed. Are all their children hard of hearing? No wonder the kids are loud. They are taught you must pipe up, not pipe down.

We are ushered into the Day Room, 'It's our informal living room,' Jonathan explains as we are obviously morons, 'a more relaxed space where we can all just veg.' I fucking hate that word. Veg. I picture a pan or pot of stinking cauliflower or a sack of sprouting potatoes. I do not want to Veg.

Hamish and Emily arrive and hobbyhorse around 'Uncle Pip' until he scoops them up and roars them clumsily around the room, their skinny limbs splayed around his solid, tightly be-sweatered body, heads thrown back, throats soft and white, a knitted whirligig. I stand like a stranger primly pinching my bag. He dumps them in a higgledy heap on one of the saggy sofas and stands up flushed and sweat-slicked, grinning. He looks at me then dives back down to tickle them.

'Is there a loo?' I turn to Judy.

Mum and Dad are in the day room when I get back. I have not been told they were going to be here. Joy.

Jonathan has opened champagne, and everyone is involved in the business of pouring and passing round glasses. Hamish and Finn are sitting on the floor with a ruin of Lego bricks but their serious conversation, led by Finn, suggests a plan. Emily is on my mother's lap showing her the details of a particularly ugly doll. It has freakish exaggerated lips and drowsy lashy eyes. My mother is paying rapt attention. To my horror, I realise Emily is speaking in Spanish.

Judy sidles up to me. 'It's Dora the Explorer.' I look at her.

'The Spanish,' she explains, 'They all love her so we thought, what the heck, let's go bilingual.'

'What?' I manage.

'It's a kids' show. With Spanish. So we all speak Spanish, all the time. It's amazingly easy to pick up. Especially for the children. Their language acquisition skills are incredible.'

I look back at Emily who continues to babble on. As far as I know my mother speaks no Spanish so shall have no idea what she's saying.

'At Hamish's Montessori school, they do Spanish, French, Mandarin, and Japanese. He loves it.' She gazes adoringly around her perfect room at her perfect family.

'A bit difficult for you to help with the homework though,' I say wryly.

'Oh Jen. There's no homework. That's a very old-fashioned idea. If they can't learn everything they need to know in school time, something is far wrong. No. Home is for enrichment, not schoolwork. That's where we can do the really fun stuff. You know, science experiments, art projects, cultural trips. No homework. Not even when they're doing their exams.'

I'm going to have to endure a whole day of their parenting. I'm considering a quick nosy round the house then feigning illness and making Pip take me home. Lunch does smell good though.

Jonathan is charging everyone's glasses.

He stands a little taller and clears his throat.

'I'd just like to say, it's lovely to have all of Judy's family here for Finn's birthday,' Finn lets out a little yelp, 'yes, you're such a grown-up boy,' Jonathan indulges before turning back to us, 'especially as Judy and I want you all to be the first to know that we are expecting another baby!' He raises his glass to Judy and slurps.

Mum slides Emily onto the sofa and jumps up to hug Judy as does Dad. I step back and watch Pip shake Jonathan's hand ferociously.

Bloody hell. Four kids. What a nightmare. The other three don't seem that bothered. They smile vaguely at the adults, not me of course. I am always treated in a similar vein to an unpredictable teacher or the classroom bully. They know they have to be nice to me, but they'd rather not spend any time in my company, especially not alone. I don't mind. What would we say to each other? 'I never really liked your mum and your dad seems like a bit of a dick?' It's not much of a basis for a meaningful relationship. It was difficult enough

196

getting along with children when I was one myself; I don't want to have to do it now. I wish I had some news to top theirs but what can I report? Bugger all.

I see my mother exchange a look with Dad. 'We have a little announcement of our own,' she says. The smirk is there. Next to Judy, they could be sisters. Why isn't she aging? 'You tell them David.' She is very excited.

'No, go on Viv. You do it. I'm a bit embarrassed.' Dad shuffles a bit, gets out a hanky and has a pat at his mouth.

'Your clever daddy is having a book published!' She links his arm and grins up at him.

'What!' brims Judy. Oh, her cup overflow'eth.

'Yes. He's written a novel. And it's terrific. And it's coming out later in the year. Isn't he a clever old thing?'

'It's no great work of art. Not like your serious intellectual work,' Dad nods to Judy and Jonathan, 'but, yes, I've actually got a deal so,' he lifts his glass, 'Bottoms Up!'

'A bloody good deal too!' Mother then raises her eyebrows for swearing in front of the angels and looks apologetically at Judy.

Judy is hugging Dad. 'How have you kept this a secret? Why didn't you tell me?' I'd have loved to proofread it or, you know, helped in any way you wanted.'

Pip claps him on the back. 'Tremendous effort. I can barely finish an email so writing a whole book is brilliant. Just brilliant.'

'Emails. Yes. I don't like those. My agent says I need to use them more. What's wrong with a letter and a stamp?'

'How have you found the time?' I cut across all the abundant laughter at his non-joke, 'How have you found the time to write a whole novel whilst running The Castle? I thought it was more than a full-time job for the two of you.'

'Well it more or less runs itself now, doesn't it Vivien? We've been at this game a long time now, haven't we? We're not spring chickens I know but I wanted to try my hand at something new, to keep the old cogs oiled.'

'I see,' I say carefully. I wonder if his book extends to more than listing clichés. 'So, is it a literary novel?' I ask.

'Yes,' Mum answers defiantly, 'and it's very good. Very good indeed.'

'Do we have to wait for publication to read it? Do we need to place an order with *Waterstones*?' I can't help myself.

It is quiet. Behind us Finn makes a strangled straining noise. We turn to look, and he is squatting over a potty, trousers and pants in a coiled ring around one leg. He strains a little more and we all watch a shiny turd slip and curl into the bowl. I start when Judy and Jonathan, Hamish and Emily applaud. Finn grins.

The smell arrives. It's beanie and sweet.

'I'll just get wipes,' Jonathan disappears.

'Good boy Finn. What a clever boy,' Judy bellows.

'Why is this boy crapping in here?' I ask. Apparently, this is unreasonable.

'We have potties everywhere, Jen. It's natural to evacuate wherever and whenever you need to go. That's the best way to train without trauma.'

'But it stinks,' I say flatly. Finn's face falls.

'Rubbish,' says my mother, 'it's only natural.'

Jonathan reappears and sets to on Finn's backside, 'I think the meat's done, darling,' he says, smiling and scooping a smear of shit for us all to see.

'Yummy,' says Hamish.

Pip gets a call from work during the actual party. By this time, I have a genuine headache. There are about four thousand children and their parents in the house and none of them can communicate in a civilised register. The dining room holds the least appeal to them, so I am skulking in there with a tepid glass of white wine when Pip appears.

'There you are!' Sweat has stamped translucent grey patches under the arms on his new white Italian shirt. No matter what fabric I buy for him, he still soaks through it. It's repulsive. He has his mobile in his paw. He waves it feebly like a mute adult rattle.

'Mihir's been on.' I continue to look at him, 'I'm sorry, but we're going to have to make a move. They've booked me on a flight to Houston tomorrow. It's an early one,' he hovers.

'Fine,' I snap. I may as well seize an advantage if there's one to be had, 'Have you told Jonathan?'

'Yes, yes, they gathered something was up. I mean, I took the call in the garden, bloody freezing, but still, Sunday afternoon and all.'

Shame it hasn't dried the sweat.

'Why are you so desperately needed?' Pip's firm, of which he is now almost in charge but not quite, is the UK division of a big American company. There has been lots of Hopping Across the Pond over the last decade. I know Big Changes are afoot and Pip is going out to the headquarters for several months to be part of the shakeup. He has asked me to go too. Often. He has a luxurious, glossy, white apartment out there with a sparkling turquoise pool; over the years there has been talk of trips to other places in America we could visit, just a Short Hop Away, New York, Las Vegas, LA. I have declined. I am always thrilled that I will have weeks or months on my own without having to shop to fill his stomach, or listen to the dull events of his day, or look at his hair in the shower drain or his face on the pillow next to me. Besides, he gets a fat bonus for any extended trip and all his expenses are paid over there so I enjoy using the credit card and pleasing myself.

'It's just a hiccup. Nothing for you to worry about,' he tries to smile warmly at me but we both know I don't worry about anything very much to do with him now. Perhaps he'll meet someone out there who will be better for him I think, as he turns and lumbers out the door. Maybe he already has.

It is a brisk farewell on the doorstep; the party is in full swing. There are pie crust promises made about seeing more of each other and everyone lies about how lovely it was to see me. The children are indoors thankfully so there is no embarrassment as we refuse to hug and kiss each other. Pip has already sought them out and he hugs Judy close, telling her how special they all are and how he can't wait to meet Number Four. Perhaps he would have been a good father.

In the morning I take him to Heathrow, and we stand a little awkwardly as travellers rush past us and we are lost for the right words to say. We both know that in a moment we will turn from each other and breathe into different spaces with the ease and relief and even expectation allowed by our mutual absence. And we both feel a little regret for this. We manage a meagre farewell. We turn. We walk away

Less than a week has passed when the phone rings and I hear that Pip has slipped in the street, fallen into the path of traffic and is dead.

'I'm so sorry for your loss, ma'am.' This is the fourth or fifth time this particular officer has said this. I realise I'm not saying much and he needs to fill the silence. He has a cute baby face, soft fleshy cheeks, large, old penny brown eyes and dark, dark skin. Officer Fleming. A shiny badge. A tiny stars and stripes on it. I've seen so many American flags since I arrived. At the morgue, I half expected Pip's body to be draped in one, but no, just a blue-grey sheet. A very cold, blue-grey sheet.

We are looking at the photos of the accident. I wanted to do this before Pip's parents arrived. I know they will disapprove. I think Officer Fleming does a little.

'I just need to know everything, to get it all straight in my head,' I say, 'You don't know what it's like for all of this to happen thousands of miles away.'

To an extent, this is true. When I replaced the phone, Pip had already been dead several hours. I was mindlessly drinking coffee in the little café round the corner from the house while the British wind blew and blew, and in a foreign land Pip's heart had stopped, his lungs had sagged, the blood was pooling and settling, his skin was mottling. He was gone and I couldn't even remember the last words I had spoken to him or those that he spoke to me. And as I packed and picked up my ticket and sat and sat on the long flight, he was moving further from me. Dwindling. Fading. There was no immediacy. No vigour to the event. I was running towards it but I was as still as still can be and he had already exited. I was too late. It had happened. His death. The event. It was over. And I had missed it.

So I sit and look at the pictures, as I would a set of holiday snaps, trying to put together the puzzle that has made me A Widow. I was drinking coffee. I finished it. I went home. The phone rang. Pip was dead. Everything is different. Everything is the same.

He was walking to the office. Very British, says the officer. It was a beautiful morning. Pip will have liked the weather; not too hot yet that he would burn but so much warmer than home. He bought a paper from the news stand. I picture how pleased he would have been to do that. So American. I hoped he had bought coffee too. In a takeout cup. To drink on the street. Also, very American. But no, just the paper. He must have been looking at it, glancing down at the pages. Eager to catch up on the news. There was a hot dog. A discarded hot dog. He stepped on it and slipped. He was on the edge of the sidewalk. He pitched into the traffic. He fell in front of a truck. It carried him thirty yards. When it stopped sharply, he fell off the front fender, onto the road. He was already dead. A stopped heart. Breathless. A bag of bones.

I look at the photos.

There is a spray of blood, dark, like a scatter of loose change. His arm is grotesquely twisted, a string puppet dropped by a careless child. There is mustard on his shoe. The shoe is very shiny. What a waste of a new shoe. His face is covered by someone else's coat.

It took a while for the ambulance to arrive. The traffic was heavy. It was rush-hour.

In the morgue, there is a lot of bruising. His fleshy, porky body (they only showed me the shoulders up, like they do in the films – if it's a man) is grey-blue, purple, violet, no pink like normal. All the warmth has gone. His face is broken. Battered. Misshapen. Swollen. Too bad for him to live.

'You bloody idiot,' I say to him softly. I cannot touch him. 'A hot dog. You never look where you're going.' I don't think the sheet is doing him any favours, or the stark lighting. I sigh heavily. So, he's dead. And that is that. It's a shame.

His mother and father arrive later that day. They have been enjoying Winter Sun in Marrakesh now that they're retired. I am drinking a delicious cocktail in the hotel lobby when they charge in, full of energy. I don't know why. They can't resurrect their son. I go over quietly; they are even smaller than the last time I saw them. How did they produce such a bear of a boy?

His mother collapses into noisy tears at the sight of me, tiny fists pummel against her husband's totally redundant raincoat. Perhaps he's worn it for her tears. We wait. Eventually she turns, face full of fury to me, 'He wasted his life with you,' she spits out, 'I wish you were dead. My boy, my beautiful boy.'

'And it's lovely to see you too, Frances,' I think.

'I bet you're happy now. You didn't even love him,' she carries on. The plastic girl behind the check-in desk misplaces her toothy, welcoming smile.

'I'll wait over there. Until you've calmed down. I really don't need to be spoken to like this.' I calmly walk away.

I hear soothing murmurs from the girl and eventually they come over to where I am patiently seated on a firm, leather sofa. They huddle together like war-torn refugees who have lost everything.

'Go on Frances,' his father coaxes. I raise my eyebrow.

'I'm sorry, Jennifer. It's the shock. I don't know what came over me. We've barely slept.' She can't bear to look at me.

I summon the waiter and we order whisky.

'I've managed the formal identification and the paperwork for repatriation myself. We're flying home the day after tomorrow. The CEO at the company has made everything happen with incredible efficiency. It's miraculous. I just have to pack a few things in the apartment,' I pause, 'You really didn't need to come.'

'But somebody had to, didn't they Leonard? He is our son. We wanted to be here.' Her husband nods gravely.

'Do you want to see him?' I say. The whisky arrives and they both gulp theirs down like medicine. 'You don't have to, you can wait until we get back home and things are a bit more... civilised. The morgue's not that great.'

Frances starts crying again, leaning into Leonard, 'Oh Pip, my Pip. Why? Why?' It's a little bit embarrassing.

I am nonplussed by the effusive response I get at Pip's office. The firm sends a car in the morning so I can call in to pick up spare keys for the company apartment. I have arranged to meet an efficient chap called Brad who will pack and ship Pip's effects but I have to meet him there. The drive over is lovely; wide highways, glinting cars, a cloudless sky and then we push smoothly into immaculate suburbia and, finally, the gated apartment complex. In my head, I go over all the expressions of sorrow for me, of love for Pip, of wonder at what he achieved. I see all the anguished faces, tight mouths, downcast eyes, shed tears. I feel their hands on my arms, my shoulders, on my hands, even one or two delicate kisses politely proffered. And it all seems absolutely genuine. Pip is loved in Houston. There are only one or two looks cast that belie the curiosity of why it is his death that has finally made me grace their warm and welcoming world.

The apartment is another surprise. It is wholly contemporary, light, spare and extremely tasteful. A magnificent abstract canvas dominates one wall in the frankly excessive living space. There are generous slashes of scarlet and cobalt paint, chaotic but somehow cohesive. The crevices of the brushstrokes are occasionally picked out with delicate, slithering rivers of liquid silver. It is beautiful. And perfect for the room. I look more closely.

It's one of my mother's.

He must have had it shipped out.

'You devious…' I mutter into the sweet air. The apartment buzzes. It is an intercom. I work out how to let Brad in at the gate. I have allowed a little more than half an hour, then Frances and Leonard are coming over to see if there's anything they want to take.

I cruise quickly through the rooms, a lovely master bedroom and en-suite three times the size of our bathroom at home.

Pip has enjoyed a dressing room too, lots of lightweight suits and golf shoes plus a full set of gleaming clubs.

Then I open the door to his study.

There is a wall of framed photographs.

And it is the whole family over the years, out here, you can tell by the weather, with him, and without me. And they all look so goddamn happy.

Judy and Jonathan and a tiny Hamish outside Cape Canaveral.

Then Mum and Dad, Judy and Jonathan plus Hamish and Emily at Disneyland. Dad has a Mickey Mouse hat on which Emily, a babe in arms, is trying to drag off by the ears.

A grainy photo on a log flume with him in the middle and Hamish and Emily either side, fantastic wings of water framing them. All their mouths are open, caught shrieking with delight, forever.

Him, in long shorts, with Jonathan and Judy and Mum and Dad by Niagara Falls, all in cheap cagoules. All damply misted. All clutching each other against the roar of the water behind them.

Mum, Dad, Jonathan, Judy all dressed in black tie at a casino, looks like Las Vegas but I don't know for sure because I've never been.

And there are more of his own family, his brothers and wives and sisters and husbands, his niece and nephew. All over America. All with him. All without me.

I search frantically for a suitcase. There is a smart *Louis Vuitton* one I bought him for his birthday in the dressing room.

The doorbell rings.

I open the door. Brad offers his hand with the appropriately sad eyes of a dog who has just chewed up your favourite slippers. I cut him off.

'Just start costing it. All the personal stuff. And the art. The furniture is rented. I'll be back in a bit.'

I head back to the study and snatch the photos off the wall and hurl them into the suitcase. I will not give Frances any reason to slate me further. It was bad enough last night, having to suffer all her references to my pursuit of money over academia. How Pip could have had the most brilliant career, if I hadn't pushed him into the commercial world. I had asked her if she really regretted that as she sat fingering the emerald and diamond ring Pip had bought her for her seventieth birthday. Or how she was enjoying their much longed for little holiday home on the Norfolk Broads which he had also financed.

I stuff in their smug smiling faces. I hear some of the glass cracking as I push down hard to zip up the case. I drag it back through and squash it into the dressing room closet. I am hot and furious.

I go back to the living room.

'Now Brad,' I say as calmly as I can, 'where were we?'

I leave Frances and Leonard to weep their way around the place whilst Brad and I clipboard Pip's belongings into numbers of cartons and timeframes for arrival. They are a remarkably accommodating company. Out of earshot of the grieving parents, I explain I want the contents of the suitcase on the plane with me tomorrow. Nothing is a problem to Brad. Brad will even arrange a deep clean of the apartment post packing. I suggest he takes the liquor back to his office for the next shindig. He politely declines. 'Tip it down the sink then,' I say.

I gather Pip's spare watches and his house keys for home and Frances takes a pair of his grandfather's cufflinks. I've suggested all the suits go to Goodwill; no point in shipping them across the ocean for me to send them to Oxfam. Frances has her face buried in a particularly nice, pale grey, double-breasted pinstripe as Brad and I tick off this task. She lets out more sobs.

'You take whatever you need to now, ma'am,' says Brad. I cannot help rolling my eyes.

'I want the computer as well,' I remind Brad.

It hasn't taken long. I herd everyone out and snap the door shut behind me. My husband has spent days and weeks and months in this alien space, living another life, and I have been here under an hour. I can't wait to get outside. Frances is still sniffling in the lift; all this crying is really going to age her.

The flight is late afternoon the following day and I'm tired by the time the flawless flight attendant hands me my first drink. Pip is safely stowed in the hold. Frances and Leonard are on a different plane; I'm pretty sure that's deliberate. This is a bonus of Pip being dead. After the funeral, I will never have to see his mother again.

I have been treated with the utmost care thus far. Not only am I a widow, I am a youngish widow and I am travelling with my husband's body, alone. I am brave. So brave. Strong. So strong. Oh the pity that has been heaped on me. So, so much pity. And I lap at it like a coy kitten.

I am a little concerned about Pip. Mainly, I'm concerned about him not making our connection in Washington. In life, he was an efficient and unflappable traveller, but in death, he will have to rely on the competency of others. Will he be the Unclaimed Item in the Baggage

Area? His sturdy casket precariously cornering the conveyor belt over and over again, cuckoo-clocking round and round, waiting to be corralled onto the next flight. I know this is ridiculous and there must be stringent procedures in place of the transit of cadavers. Nevertheless, it would be most embarrassing to misplace him.

Whilst I am mulling these hitherto unforeseen difficulties, the seat next to me is taken by a stylish blonde woman around my age. She smiles briskly and settles herself, extracting papers and several books from an expensive briefcase. She pops reading glasses on top of her head and relaxes back purposefully, loosely gripping the sheath of documents and her pen. Nice to have a task in hand, I think. She begins to efficiently whip through the papers as we listen to the first officer's updates and are offered more drinks and snacks. I think of Pip, cold and still in the hold. He'll never read another word. He'll never utter another syllable. Another positive.

I realise I'm staring at my neighbour's papers and she's staring at me.

I look up at her and smile. She smiles back.

'I'm sorry,' I say, 'I was miles away. I didn't mean to be rude.'

'That's okay,' she sounds friendly, 'Where are you heading?' She breathes out and leans back against her chair.

'London,' I say, 'Home,' I add.

'Oh! Me too!' she is enthusiastic, 'I mean, London. It's obviously not my home with this accent. Are you connecting in Washington?'

'Yes, we are,' I confirm.

She looks surprised. 'We? Are you travelling with someone?'

'Yes,' I say, 'my husband.'

'Don't tell me, he's in coach,' she smiles.

'No,' I smile too, 'he's in the hold.'

She laughs. 'Boy he must've been really bad!'

'Not really,' I smile, 'he's dead!'

She stops smiling. 'What?'

'Yes,' I say, 'he died. We're going home. For his funeral.'

'Oh jeez. I'm so sorry. I'm so sorry for your loss. Are you okay?' It's a direct and unembarrassed question. I quite like her.

'Yes. I think I am. Thank you.'

'What happened?'

'A stupid accident.'

'Oh God.' She shakes her head as if these are the worst.

'Yes. He slipped. He fell off the sidewalk into traffic. He died instantly.' I omit the hotdog.

'Well honey, that's a blessing.'

'Yes. So I'm told.'

'Except, I suppose you never got to say goodbye,' she muses.

'No,' I say, 'I can't even remember the last things we said to each other.'

'Now that is difficult.'

'It is.'

She turns a little further round towards me, looking at me properly, 'When did it all happen?'

'Three days ago.' As I say it, the fact is fantastic to me.

'Three days? Are you on vacation?' Her questioning is somehow practical, not intrusive, like a doctor ascertaining precise symptoms.

'No. My husband was over on business. I wasn't here at all.'

'Oh hell. That's hard. Real hard.' She is friendly, 'Do you have any family with you? This is all kinda tough to do on your own.'

'No. I haven't got anyone else. It was just the two of us.' It's my version of the truth.

'That's even worse,' she exclaims, 'you poor, poor girl.'

It's a long time since anyone has called me a girl. It feels intimate.

'I'm Naomi,' she smiles.

'Jen,' I answer.

We are quiet then for a minute or two but Naomi doesn't want to go back to her papers. I sense she wants to keep talking but doesn't know where to go next.

'It looks like you've got a lot to do,' I help her out.

She looks at the papers. 'Yes, yes. I always mean to do so much on planes. Full of good intentions. But mostly I daydream or nap.'

'Why are you going to London?'

'I'm visiting friends. I can't wait. It's been too long. I was in grad school at the LSE.'

'Oh,' I say.

'I'm catching up with one of my old professors and a few of my peers too.'

'That sounds lovely.'

'It will be.'

I look out of the window; hard to believe the temperature is -40° out there. If I was sucked out, how quickly would I freeze to death? I think of cold, cold Pip.

I turn back to Naomi.

'What do you do?'

'I'm a writer. Well, a historian first. Civil War's my period.'

'Gosh.'

'This is the last chapter of my book. Should be coming out later in the year, if I meet the deadline.' She is obviously very proud as she smooths her hand over the top page protectively.

'I don't know anything about the Civil War' I say, regretting the way this is going. I fear I may be in for a lengthy discourse on the Battle of Gettysburg. I am after all a captive audience and we have hours ahead of us.

'Why should you?' she replies easily, 'My book is quite specific anyway. Not many people will read it. Don't think it will make The Times Bestsellers.'

I feel I have to say, 'What is it about?' but I add a fake stifled yawn to encourage her not to go on.

'It's about a letter,' her eyes are bright with enthusiasm.

This sounds more strategic than violent, more like Jane Austen.

'Really?' I say.

'Yes, a beautiful, beautiful letter written during the war,' then, she stops herself as if she has remembered something.

'Go on,' I say.

'It doesn't matter,' she says and knocks her glasses on to her nose, 'like I say, it's specific, niche.' She begins to look at her papers.

'A whole book on one letter. It must be good. Did it change the course of the war?' I persist. I want to know what's changed.

She sighs and looks straight at me. 'Look, it's a really sad letter. I forgot that. We probably shouldn't talk about it.' I don't understand why not; then I remember I am A Widow.

'Who wrote it?' I ask.

'A soldier, a major.'

'What was his name?'

'Sullivan Ballou.'

'That's a great name.'

'Yes it is,' she smiles.

'Who did he write it to?'

'His wife.'

'Why is it sad?'

She pauses for quite a long time. I wait. I want to know.

'It's the letter a soldier sends if he dies in combat. He died the week after it was written.'

'Ah,' I say, 'I see.'

I look out of the window again at the fierce blue sky.

'I'm sorry,' she says, 'I shouldn't have brought it up. It was thoughtless.'

I turn back. 'Don't worry,' I say, genuinely, 'my husband wrote me some letters when he was at university. He was no great correspondent though. I don't even think I kept them. He was a computer person. I'm struggling to even picture his handwriting beyond his signature. How odd.'

Naomi looks crestfallen, almost ashamed.

'Do you have a copy with you' I ask.

'Sorry?' she says.

'Of Sullivan Ballou's letter. I'd like to read it.'

'What? Really? Are you sure?' I nod.

'It must be worth it, if you've written a book about it.' She begins shuffling through the papers and then reluctantly produces a photocopy of a tiny penned meticulously neat letter. There are faint pencil markings in the margins which I cannot decipher. Some phrases and words are underlined. I look closely and begin to read.

Headquarters, Camp Clark
Washington, D.C., July 14, 1861

My Very Dear Wife:

Indications are very strong that we shall move in a few days, perhaps to-morrow. Lest I should not be able to write you again, I feel impelled to write a few lines, that may fall under your eye when I shall be no more.

Our movement may be one of a few days duration and full of pleasure and it may be one of severe conflict and death to me. Not my will, but thine, O God be done. If it is necessary that I should fall on the battle-field for any country, I am ready. I have no misgivings about, or lack of confidence in, the cause in which I am engaged, and my courage does not halt or falter. I know how strongly American civilization now leans upon the triumph of government, and how great a debt we owe to those who went before us through the blood and suffering of the Revolution, and I am willing, perfectly willing to lay down all my joys in this life to help maintain this government, and to pay that debt.

But, my dear wife, when I know, that with my own joys, I lay down nearly all of yours, and replace them in this life with care and sorrows, when, after having eaten for long years the bitter fruit of orphanage myself, I must offer it, as their only sustenance, to my dear little children, is it weak or dishonorable, while the banner of my purpose floats calmly and proudly in the breeze, that my unbounded love for you, my darling wife and children, should struggle in fierce, though useless, contest with my love of country.

I cannot describe to you my feelings on this calm summer night, when two thousand men are sleeping around me, many of them enjoying the last, perhaps, before that of death, and I, suspicious that Death is creeping behind me with his fatal dart, am communing with God, my country and thee.

I have sought most closely and diligently, and often in my breast, for a wrong motive in this hazarding the happiness of those I loved, and I could not find one. A pure love of my country, and of the principles I have often advocated before the people, and 'the name of honor, that I love more than I fear death,' have called upon me, and I have obeyed.

Sarah, my love for you is deathless. It seems to bind me with mighty cables, that nothing but Omnipotence can break; and yet, my love of country comes over me like a strong wind, and bears me irresistibly on with all those chains, to the battlefield. The memories of all the blissful moments I have spent with you come crowding over me, and I feel most deeply grateful to God and you, that I have enjoyed them so long. And how hard it is for me to give them up, and burn to ashes the hopes of future years, when, God willing, we might still have lived and loved together, and seen our boys grow up to honorable manhood around us.

I know I have but few claims upon Divine Providence, but something whispers to me, perhaps it is the wafted prayer of my little Edgar, that I shall return to my loved ones unharmed. If I do not, my dear Sarah, never forget how much I love you, nor that, when my last breath escapes me on the battle-field, it will whisper your name.

Forgive my many faults, and the many pains I have caused you. How thoughtless, how foolish I have oftentimes been! How gladly would I wash out with my tears, every little spot upon your happiness, and struggle with all the misfortune of this world, to shield you and my children from harm. But I cannot, I must watch you from the spirit land and hover near you, while you buffet the storms with your precious little freight, and wait with sad patience till we meet to part no more.

But, O Sarah, if the dead can come back to this earth, and flit unseen around those they loved, I shall always be near you in the garish day, and the darkest night amidst your happiest scenes and gloomiest hours always, always, and, if the soft breeze fans your cheek, it shall be my breath; or the cool air cools your throbbing temples, it shall be my spirit passing by. Sarah, do not mourn me dear; think I am gone, and wait for me, for we shall meet again.

As for my little boys, they will grow as I have done, and never know a father's love and care. Little Willie is too young to remember me long, and my blue-eyed Edgar will keep my frolics with him among the dimmest memories of his childhood. Sarah, I have unlimited confidence in your maternal care, and your development of their characters. Tell my two mothers, I call God's blessing upon them. O Sarah, I wait for you there! Come to me, and lead thither my children.

- Sullivan

I begin to clutch and wrench the heavy buckle of my lap belt. The cabin has become tight and small, and I feel the over-breathed air is too warm to sustain my beating heart. I want the cold of the hold where my husband lies. If I can just get to him, perhaps everything will be different. I will become Sarah and he will be Sullivan. There will be a beautifully written missive for me, a declaration of devotion to pin to my heart. There is a clamber, a buzz of distant voices around me, an invasive hand on my shoulder. Someone is rudely shouting, loudly shouting, with all their might. Was Pip's last word my name? My name formed with his final breath? I need to ask him. I have overlooked that essential task. How stupid of me. If I can just get down to the hold, lift the lid of the casket, he can turn his popcorn head to me and tell me, 'Yes my last word, my final thought, my only thoughts were of you, they were always of you.'

The terrible shouting is louder and there are now three hazy faces with livid, lipstick mouths close to mine. I feel water against my lips. It is shockingly cold, like the air my lungs need, but as it tips into my mouth, the shouting stops and I know I am the source of the brouhaha. A cool palm cradles my cheek and the words, *'my love for you is deathless,'* reaches across the decades and thrusts a wretched hand down my throat, gripping viciously around my heart until my body slackens and I finally give in to what has happened to me. I cannot remember the last time I cried but, in the arms of a bird-boned stewardess, I cannot stop up the pity I have for myself.

I huddle into the edge of my seat, the thin, airline-colours blanket tucked up neatly over me. I am parcelled. I have been covered. Tamped down. Medicated, quieted, calmed. I have caused a scene and my shouts about the need to get into the hold have been received with alarm by my fellow travellers. Naomi has been moved, whether at her request or not I am not sure. I know we are nearly at Washington, and I have no way of fathoming how I will possibly manage to get my weary bones all the way back to Heathrow. These decisions, however, are no longer yours when you are in the sky. An ambulance is waiting for me on the tarmac, and I am carefully disembarked and deposited into the clean and complete safety of the neat little unit where I am to be Checked Out. It takes a long time and I feel simultaneously distant and far too close to the paramedics. Eventually I am declared fit for my onward journey but alas, too late. Pip makes our connection, but I do not. I cannot speak so allow all the arrangements to be made for me. It doesn't matter what I say or do. Eventually I won't be standing here listening to Jillian-with-a-J tell me about available flights. At some point in the future, I will walk through my front door. Until that happens, I don't trust myself to make a sound.

At Heathrow, it is confirmed that the funeral directors have indeed collected Pip. I have sat motionless, grainy eyed and with a hollow of terror in my chest for the whole flight. I am somehow in a taxi. None of my luggage is with me. I cling onto my handbag as if it anchors me to my seat. I need to be home. The words so carefully shaped for Sarah Ballou are sifting through and through me. 'How gladly would I wash out with my tears every little spot upon your happiness,' and I think about her unhappiness as she had read that letter in 1861. She read that letter, like hundreds and thousands of women whose husband died heroically and inevitably, 'my love of country comes over me like a strong wind and bears me irresistibly on with all those chains to the battlefield'. It told her of her husband's death; a death of which she could be proud. An honourable death. Lucky Sarah.

My key turns, and I step into the chill of my cheerless house. Only a few days empty but it is freezing. It's not only that that is different; it is changed. There is an absence. I walk through the rooms, and it feels like I'm alone in a school corridor in the dead of night. There is none of the necessary life and energy to give it purpose, the reason that makes it complete. I was here in my house on my own four long days ago but then I was a wife kicking off my shoes, licking my lips and luxuriating in my temporary isolation. Now I live here alone. I am a widow. There will always be just me. Only my dead skin to make the dust, only the dirt I track in from the paths I choose, only the crumbs that fall from the food I take. We were not two peas in a pod, we were not two halves that made a whole, we were not each other's destiny, but I feel a lack of him, the absence of him like a rushing roar of air, sucked from every atom in the house; a full force that rocks and tilts and threatens to topple everything for a single second and then leave it all shuddering to a deafening silence. Every possession is here but there is nothing left. I am alone.

Later the following afternoon the first crate arrives. The pictures. There is still no sign of my luggage, but I've had a syrupy sweet phone call, fat with apology, assuring me it is en route and not lost.

The crate is beautifully packed with paper, soft as silk, and fragrant wood shavings. I take out the photos one by one. They are spotless and perfect. Brad must have had the glass replaced before shipping them out. What a service.

I am not dressed. I have not left my bed. I have not answered the phone. I only answered the door because the delivery guy took to shouting through the letterbox.

Now the pictures are out and stacked against the sofa, I go and make coffee. It is vile. I pour myself wine from the half-drunk bottle. It doesn't seem to make much difference either.

I listen to the answerphone. The undertakers want me to go tomorrow to make arrangements. Judy has left several near hysterical wandering monologues. Dad says they're on their way down in a matter-of-fact way but there is a terrible sadness in his voice. There are a couple of calls from Pip's office: condolences, so sorry, anything they can do et cetera et cetera. Finally, a clipped request from Pip's solicitor to get in touch at my earliest convenience. I didn't even know he had a solicitor, not one of his own anyway. I refill my glass and leave the kitchen, which is still chilly, even though the heating has been on permanently since my return.

I slouch down in one of the chairs and stare at the photo of Pip and the children on the log flume. It's nearly six o'clock. Christ. I realise that's when Dad said they hoped to get here. I think it's a bit unreasonable foisting yourselves on a woman who has just been completely traumatised but what do I know about the etiquette of gruesome accidental death. I begin to repack the pictures and drag the crate back out to the hall. I stuff it into the understairs cupboard. I do all this one-handed whilst slurping my wine. I think perhaps it must be making a difference as, when the doorbell rings, I don't really mind too much that it's my mother, Dad and Judy.

They have picked Judy up on the way and I sense they want to fall on me and have us all wail together, but I step back and just walk into the sitting room. Anyway, Judy is carrying a casserole dish so hugging would have been difficult. She rushes to put it into the oven and my mother busies herself with removing hats, scarves, and gloves as well as plush overcoats, draping them over the banisters, whilst asking politely about my flight.

'It was appalling. I missed my connection,' I say without enthusiasm, 'Judy, there's some wine in there. Bring it through, would you?'

'Perhaps put the kettle on,' adds my mother.

'I've only had one glass! Christ, Mother,' I snarl.

'For us, Jen. For us,' she says lightly, looking at Dad.

I want to say, 'Why are you here? I didn't ask you to come.' They seem to be filling my fairly capacious living room with their too bright voices and sombre clothes. Instead, I say, 'Why don't you sit down?'

They do, obedient as guilty schoolboys.

They wait.

I finish my wine and look into the empty glass.

Eventually my mother says, 'How are you, Jen?'

'I'm okay. Considering.'

'How are all the ... arrangements,' Dad skirts around the elephant in the room.

215

'Do you mean the funeral or shipping the body?' my voice is flat. Judy comes in with a tray of tea and her face crumples, tears spilling. It's obvious she's already been crying in the car. No make-up, pinkish nose. She always was a cry-baby.

She carries on with the tea, blubbing as she pours it out. She knows it's my place to be crying not hers. Eventually she sits and wipes the snot and tears away with a cotton hanky, gulping a little as she does so.

I steadfastly say nothing. They all look at me.

Dad cracks first.

'Bloody good chap, Pip,' and Judy wails.

'Oh poor Pip, poor dear Pip,' she cries. Mum gets up and goes to comfort her.

I look out of the window and sip my tea. It really is very good. I think she must have used the lapsang souchong.

Judy seems to be getting louder and Dad is blowing his nose.

'I think I'll go and have a bath before supper,' I say and step gingerly past their intertwined ankles.

When I come back down, the table is set in the dining room. We've barely eaten a dozen meals in here, even though it's a charming room. I am planning how to get rid of them. I can't have them hanging around here until the funeral; that could be days.

The food is hot and good; I can't remember my last proper meal. Judy and Mum pick at theirs but I clean my plate and fork the choicest pieces from their leftovers as they talk earnestly, largely about me, as if I am not there or am retarded.

'The best thing would be for Jen to move up to near us, wouldn't it?' Judy offers, 'The kids would love it.' I doubt that very much.

'Or back home. Where we can keep an eye on her,' Mother proposes.

'She's a grown woman,' Dad interjects, though he probably had enough of me growing up and doesn't relish the idea of a rerun of the teenage years. 'She doesn't necessarily *need* to have an eye kept on her.'

'But what will she do with herself here? I mean without, you know, Pip's work. I just don't want her to drift or, feel abandoned.' Judy implores as if I am a lost little dog.

'Well, she could buy an absolute pile in Cumbria with what this place must be worth and have money left over,' Mother argues. I can't believe she wants me up there either.

'Perhaps this is an opportunity for Jennifer just take some time and really think about what *she* wants to do. Anyway, I thought you weren't meant to make any major decisions in the first six months or year or something after ... you know.' Dad continues.

They've been going round and round the same points, the whole meal. I have said nothing.

'I have to go to the funeral directors tomorrow,' I pipe up. They all look at me, thrilled that I have at last spoken. I clear my throat because my voice sounds a bit odd to me. 'I also have to go to Pip's solicitor. Mum, Judy,' I turn to them, 'I'd like you to organise all the flowers for me. I don't care what you do. I can't think about it. There's a florist on the High Street. He's Dutch. He'll be fine. Dad,' he sits up, 'I'd like you to come to the undertakers and the solicitors with me.'

They all sit quietly, not a peep.

'Is that acceptable to everyone?'

They clamour to consent to my requests.

'Good. Now I'm going to bed. Will you phone the solicitor first thing Dad and make arrangements? She's left a message on the answerphone.'

'Of course, of course. I'll go and listen to it now.' We all stand together as if this is a board meeting not a family dinner. I leave the room and they hover at their places a little bewildered.

I linger outside the door for a moment and hear my mother say, 'I don't see why I couldn't have come to the solicitors too. I am her mother after all.'

I smile and head up to bed.

Why the bloody hell are they all still here? I want to be on my own. I want to cavort around singing and shouting at the top of my voice, 'Yippee! Hurrah!' as things have worked out better than I could have ever planned, but I also want to go into his study and smash a load of stuff to smithereens. I have the freedom to do neither as I am more closely observed than a soon to be confined royal princess.

Okay, there are some advantages. Judy and my mother have informed every living soul of the time and place of the funeral. My mother has spent hours on the phone soothing Frances. My father has placed a notice in *The Times* and has spoken at length to the caterers. We have had a steady footfall of visitors; Pip's brothers and sisters, some work friends, friends of Judy's, old friends of Mum and Dad's; Jonathan has appeared a couple of times with the children too plus various strangers organising official things.

I stand unseen in the shadows at the top of the stairs as Dad or Judy or Mother answer the door yet again and low voices go back and forth and the kettle boils and cups clink and I scuttle back to my bed so when someone runs up to check, I am sadly Not In Any Fit State to see anyone today. I listen to my clock radio quietly and nap and count down the days to the funeral.

It is to be held at Mortlake Crematorium, an impressive Art Deco building. Twelve o'clock sharp. The cars will pick us up just after 11.30. The service shouldn't be too long then the wake will be at a tasteful hotel on the river. Shame he didn't die in the summer, they've got a lovely terrace. I wonder why it's called a wake when the most important person is very far from that. Maybe it's because it's going to be so dull; we will struggle not to slip into unconsciousness.

The trip to the solicitors was eventful. We went there before the funeral directors. I make Dad solemnly promise not to tell anyone anything we find out before we go in. The office was intimidating and in the city. Pip never mentioned anything about engaging his own solicitor. I wonder what other secrets may be revealed. Another wife? A love child?

The solicitor, Roopa, is warm and striking. She explains that she was at Oxford with Pip, and she is so, so sorry. Then, she is all business. They can't have been close; I would have heard her name, surely. I scan the tremendous view across the Thames from her excessive office window and remember Pip's wall of photos and the whole host of other secrets he kept from me. Dad clears his throat, 'Jen?' he says.

I have been asked a question.

'Shall we go through the details of the will?' Roopa repeats.

'He had a will? How organised,' I say. Obviously another thing he didn't think worth discussing with me.

He'd drawn it up about a year ago. The upshot is, I am a woman of substance. There is a substantial death in service sum I will receive and a generous pension. He also had a platinum life insurance policy, so the house is paid off and there is a handsome lump-sum with that too. He has stocks in the company, which he suggests I hold onto, and an impressive portfolio. Pip also owns a complete row of terraced houses in Camberley which are let through a management agency for a considerable annual income. And he is on the board, and has shares in, several businesses, of which I've never heard.

He leaves the houses to Hamish, Emily, and Finn and any future children of Jonathan and Judy; they are not to be sold but to provide a steady income stream for them throughout their lives. In the event of their deaths, the property passes to the siblings' children or, if they have none, their cousins. Good old Pip, always looking out for those kids. They will not forget their uncle every time they get that tidy little sum; way to achieve immortality. There is a substantial cash amount for each of his brothers' children, only two so far but it's a bit of a surprise this; Judy's kids aren't even his blood relatives.

Roopa keeps reading. Dad wipes a tear with his handkerchief and shifts in his seat.

He wants his ashes spread in Cumbria.

Of course he bloody does.

On the fell behind The Castle where he has so many happy memories. I think people overwrite their lives in their minds to make them more agreeable or they deliberately misremember. So many happy memories?

There is paperwork to sign and then we leave.

In the taxi I try to work out how he could have bought all those houses and not breathed a single word. How did he afford them? Why did he buy them and not tell me? He had more than a full-time job and he had to be a property tycoon as well?

At the funeral directors, I choose the most expensive coffin, the most excessive fittings, and linings. I draw the line at a horse-drawn carriage but only because I'm a bit scared of horses. Everything else is going to be top of the range, even though it will be burnt to dust and a total waste of money. Dad thinks I am showing my love for Pip, but I am spiting him. He would be furious. He has made all these prudent arrangements to ensure everyone's future is secure and I am blowing an exorbitant sum on a box that will be on view for an hour at best. I am furious with him, furious that he has had all these plans and secrets without me. It's up to me now. I can do anything I want to.

We are all gathered, like a tetchy murder of crows in the sitting room, when the cars arrive bang on time. There is so much black, it really is rather depressing. I have new boots which are a bit tight.

'They're here,' Jonathan announces unnecessarily; we all have a perfect view out of the window.

Dad is standing next to me and cups my elbow, 'Okay Jen,' he says tenderly, 'nearly there now.'

And we walk out.

A few of the neighbours are forlornly looking on. I recognise them but don't know their names. Our car is at the gate. The hearse is in front. The coffin looks magnificent. Mum and Julie have chosen a luxurious head to toe spray of large, gloriously golden, yellow roses and creamy lilies intertwined with rich, glossy, green ivy. They are flowers worthy of a film star. It is most impressive.

We get in the car in silence. Leonard and Frances and some of the brothers are in the car behind us. There are many cars with people in dark suits and black ties behind them. We set off so smoothly it is barely noticeable; we are not to be upset. I look out of the window.

It's a fascinating journey. As we process towards the crematorium, people react in different ways. Older gents take off their hats or tip them; a child points and her mother knocks her hand down and scurries her away; two elderly ladies, no strangers to funerals, admire the flowers with bent gnarled fingers and pursed smiles of approval; a young guy throws the butt of his fag in the path of our car then looks stricken, I smile at him. But mostly people turn away, divert eyes, don't want to look. If they pretend death doesn't happen maybe they can ward it off or cheat it. Judy sniffles the whole way there.

I knew I would be watched so I have a hat with a veil. It is very glamorous and bespoke. I had a milliner from a trendy shop in Whitcomb Street come to the house with a selection and we had a diverting afternoon choosing shapes and weights of tulle behind a closed door whilst my mother and Judy tried unsuccessfully to weigh in. The cost was exorbitant. I dab at my eyes underneath it but there is no need; my eyes are dry.

I am indeed watched, but Judy's grief is a sight to behold. She always did look fabulous in black; it makes her hair looks like butter softened in the sun. Objectively, I regret not having a camera. It's a shame she's not playing my part.

It is a service which reflects his life. Two of his brothers speak, taking it in turns to recount childhood tales that paint Pip as the tagger on, the accident prone, who as a child was the one who fell into the river, fell off his bike, skinned his knees, broke his collarbone, trying to do what his older brothers managed easily, who determinedly struggled with his shorter legs to catch them in running races, rounders games, tag, who never had the skill or coordination with a cricket bat or golf club that they did but doggedly joined in with relentless good grace. He did, however, have the brains and here he outstripped them, modestly and effortlessly cruising through school and university and into his glittering career. They tell of his love for his nieces and nephews and his generosity, acknowledging many of the precisely perfect surprise presents he has bestowed on the family over the years. How, even though he is nearly the youngest, he became the one they all turned to for help, advice and guidance. At the end they cling to each other and weep.

I am not acknowledged by name. The only reference is, 'his wife's sister, Judy'

Jonathan then talks of university life and how it was Pip who introduced him to Judy. It's a carefully constructed speech – if I didn't know about all their illicit holidays together, I wouldn't get the references – but they're there. 'So many cherished memories,' and 'wonderful times spent together over the years.' Had I not seen the photos, I would just have passed this off as sentimental exaggeration whereas, in reality, they really did have a whole heap of fun.

I wondered how much duplicitous discussion has gone on to keep the lie intact. For they are all in on it. In some way.

We sing. A vicar speaks more blandly. There are prayers. His coffin disappears behind a curtain.

We are ushered out into the weak, winter light to thank everyone for coming and to admire the vast number of floral tributes.

I am flanked by Dad and Judy. It's like being sandwiched between two celebrities. Okay, I'm the widow but Dad's show is enjoying a revival on *Gold* and Judy is fucking beautiful. I'm the gap in Musical Chairs; no one wants to linger with me and, to be fair, no one really knows me.

I am considering boycotting the wake, but I can't.

I insist on going in first. I turn on them all, 'Can I just have a minute to myself, please. That was all a bit harrowing.'

They all cluck and soothe and I go into the banqueting suite, beautifully prepared for the greedy mourners, closing the doors behind me.

It is perfect.

I have had the photos discreetly collected and couriered over. I must say the hotel have done a beautiful job. They are tastefully displayed around a half decent photo of Pip. They have all been excessively enlarged, the better to see everyone's delight and hypocrisy. The brilliant blue of the holiday skies shines out over and over, stamped against this terrible grey February day.

The doors open, and they come in meekly at first. I am standing next to my display. The children have arrived and, as they are not schooled in the social niceties of funerals, they charge across the room and begin to chatter at the pictures, remembering the lovely holidays with Uncle Pip and laughing at how little they are.

Judy and Jonathan falter once they realise what they're witnessing and Mother and Dad behind them come to a stop. Jonathan looks furious, and Mother's chin juts out.

'Oh Jen,' Judy starts, taking a step towards me, then she begins to cry.

I lift my veil.

'Aren't they lovely?' I say as coldly and calmly as I can.

The other guests, who have no idea what is happening are taking champagne and admiring the photos.

'Yes, they really are,' says some old woman I've never seen before, 'what a happy life he had.'

'I don't know what to say,' blubs Judy.

'Neither do I,' I say.

And I leave them to it. I imagine they will manage to make acceptable excuses for me, if anyone bothers to ask, but I see little point in staying at a celebration of the life of someone I hardly knew.

It's much later when the key turns in the front door. I've changed into a bright pink hoodie that has a garish, sequinned logo glittering across the chest. I wonder what they've decided to say.

There is murmuring in the hall and hurried regrouping in response to the light in the sitting room; they were hoping I'd be asleep.

Dad comes in first, black-tie slack at his neck, cheeks flushed and eyes bloodshot. My mother skulks behind him. I can hear Judy and Jonathan talking over each other in the hall.

'How are you feeling Jen?' Dad tries. He sits down gingerly on the sofa opposite me.

'Put the kettle on Judy,' my mother shouts out unnecessarily as Judy can only be a few feet away.

Feet clip-clop to the kitchen.

I say nothing.

'Look … about the photos,' Dad starts, 'we never meant for you to find out like this.'

'Yes, it wasn't any kind of plot,' Mother jumps in; she already has the tone that I am being ridiculous.

'No, it just sort of happened.'

'It was Pip's idea. He said you didn't want to go over and he was there such a lot, with that fantastic apartment,' she sounds wistful, sad that she'll never be there again.

'He was a bit lonely I think.' Dad turns his palms up, appealing to my better nature, but also criticising me as a wife, 'We didn't mean it to be … an issue.'

'It just became a way of keeping in touch,' Mother justifies briskly.

Jonathan has appeared at the door. 'Yes, and he was our friend before you got your claws into him,' he snarls, 'we never saw him unless we did it behind your back.' Judy's hand is on his shoulder.

'Jonathan!' Dad rebukes.

'Oh for God's sake, David, she's impossible! All those ignored invitations, those pathetic excuses. It would have been easier if you just said you couldn't stand us.'

'Jonathan!' My mother joins in.

'And you never liked Pip. Not really.' He is gathering pace here, 'We buried a good man today and you had no idea what you had. You shackled him. You kept him from us. We were his friends. He loved us. You had no right.' He is starting to cry, 'No right.'

There is silence. Dad looks aghast.

'May I retort?' I cannot help myself, 'Did I really keep you from him? Those photos tell a different story. I think you all sought very hard over a lot of years to exclude me. You all think I'm difficult. None of *you* like *me* so you come up with this fiction that I kept him from you and your only course of action was to have fantastic secret holidays together without me. I don't recall any discussion about family holidays. I don't recall any consultation over whether or not I'd like to come. You *all* decided for me. It's one thing to find out your dead husband has been having an affair, or even that he has another wife but to find out he's been carrying on behind your back with your *family*, for years, well that's frankly preposterous and a bit pathetic.' I shake my head, 'He had loads of brothers, and a mum and dad who adored him. Why did he have to have mine too?'

I stare at them. They do, for a moment, look gratifyingly ashamed, especially Judy.

'No,' says Jonathan, 'it wasn't like that. You're not doing that. Not this time. You excluded him. It's only because he was so bloody decent that he didn't divorce you and find someone else who could love him properly.'

'Really?' I say calmly, 'Was he so decent? I find this all very weird personally. Him creeping around with all of you. And you do know he's left a load of property to all your kids, don't you? He's set them up beautifully with barely a penny to his own flesh and blood. Now why is that, Jonathan? Why would he give your children so much and his own brothers' children so little?'

'What are you talking about? He was just a really generous

person,' Judy stammers.

'Was he?' I thunder on, 'Was he really? Are you sure they're all your kids Jonathan?'

'Jennifer!' Dad stands up, ' That's enough! You will apologise now to your sister. That's a terrible thing to say. A terrible thought to even think.'

'Why? Why do I have to apologise? It was my husband's funeral today and he,' I point viciously at Jonathan, 'comes into my house and accuses me of being cold, distant, keeping Pip from everyone. Telling me Pip should have divorced me. Yet I'm the one who must apologise. I want you all out of my fucking house now.'

My voice has risen to a roar, and where I was calm at the start, I am now beside myself.

'But Jennifer,' my mother starts. I turn on her in a flash.

'I said get out, get out now. I'll be sending back your bloody painting too, that's if I don't decide to burn it first. I'm sick of all of you. You're all two-faced, mealy-mouthed hypocrites. Get out of my house.' And I am shooing them out as they try to protest.

I run upstairs to where Mum and Dad have been sleeping. I hurl their empty suitcases down the stairs. One gratifyingly catches Jonathan on the side of the head. I grab handfuls of their clothes and toss them over the banisters. They flutter down, draping and puddling around the four of them. I chuck their toothbrushes and paperback books like missiles and hear Mum's make-up satisfyingly crack and spray against the hall tiles. All four are grasping and grabbing, trying to salvage what they can whilst dodging Dad's heavy brogues and Mum's sharp stilettoes.

At last I am finished. The room is empty.

I stand at the top of the stairs.

'Now get the fuck out, you fucking traitors,' I bellow and they rush and fumble for the door and tumble out. It swings open, revealing a sepia night. Cold air blasts in, races up the stairs and lifts the roots of my hair.

2014

I am sitting with my second chai latte listening to Madge argue with Connie. ÉgaliThé is the only place I venture out to these days. I treat myself once a week, depending on the weather. It's a small café, just round the corner really. I don't have to navigate any busy roads; there is a pelican crossing. I wouldn't risk jaywalking.

Madge has been going as long as I have. It's the pavement access. She's on a mobility scooter. She has long straggly grey hair, a bulging balloon of a neck that wobbles as she talks and pale, watery eyes behind thick glasses. I don't think she is much older than me, but she looks it. We never speak, only scrutinize each other suspiciously. I try to work out how many layers of clothes she has on. They are all variants of grey and beige and most have tiny holes through which another tone is visible. She is apple-bodied with stick thin legs and long, bony feet. If she stood, I think she'd be tall.

Madge will not speak directly to anyone; she will only communicate through Connie. Connie is as threadbare as Madge is. Connie wears a small fez. Connie is a camel and a glove puppet. Madge and Connie sit in the corner of ÉgaliThé and 'share' a pot of tea and a round of fruit toast and bicker.

At the moment they are playing Hangman, working their way through a tatty little spiral-bound notebook. Connie is winning. Madge is becoming more and more infuriated as Connie draws another arm on the torso hanging from the gib.

'I think you've made this one up, Connie. Or you've made a mistake. This is impossible.'

'It's not impossible,' replies Connie, in her nasal, and, for some reason, Australian accent, 'You're just very stupid,' and she pitches her head back and silently laughs, her mouth wide, revealing a broad red cloth tongue. Madge looks hurt.

The other customers are either fascinated or irritated depending on how often they frequent ÉgaliThé. Those who are fascinated try to position themselves so they can look but without it appearing too obvious. Those who are irritated know that soon Connie and Madge will descend into a full-blown argument and all chance of normal interaction will be gone. Malik, behind the counter, will have no choice but to step in when they get violent with each other. Connie is a vicious hair puller and a ferocious biter whilst Madge favours straightforward bludgeoning.

I don't mind too much. I have brought my laptop and can zone in and out of their shenanigans fairly easily.

I spend most of my life online now. I like it that way.

I check *Facebook* first, though obviously not for the first time that day. There are many accounts I follow so my feed is usually mixed. Judy posts Blissful Family Life stuff regularly and The Castle has its own page. Mrs Stoddart's daughter Gillian oversees their social media. Occasionally, there are pictures of Bryan. I'm *Facebook* friends with Kevin too but he's in Australia now. His skin is a lot better with all that sunshine.

Then there is Maureen. She is very active. She's developed the AI side of the farm. Chris hardly seems to get a look in. She's an expert and does a lot of lucrative consultancy work all over the country. I'm friends with all her children too. None of them are still in the village.

I pour over the photos, enlarge them, judge them, examine the dates. I never comment.

Hamish and Emily have their own profiles now. Hamish is at Oxford. Judy posts photos of the two of them, 'So proud!!' I wonder what it's like to have a son. Emily is bookish and earnest. She's a venture scout and has travelled to build schools in South America and wells in Gaza. She doesn't wear make-up or straighten her hair. In all the group photos she posts, just about everyone is looking at her.

I keep up with all Pip's brothers. His father died. I didn't go to the funeral; I don't go anywhere. Pip would have been upset about it but it looks like he had a good send off. One of them has got very fat and just about all the boys are bald now.

Dad has his own David Wentworth Fan Page. He's written a little run of books. I have received each one in the post. No note. The first one came out the year Pip died. It was sort of a detective story, but the detective is a failed actor married to a narcissistic artist who creates all these massive sculptures. Considering Dad was always so depressed, it is surprisingly funny. The wife bears more than just a likeness to my mother, and she is a monster. She manically creates excessively enormous and ridiculous garden gnomes and believes them to be great works of art. She endlessly thwarts the ploddingly charming detective with her latest hair-brained ideas or outlandish purchases or improper friends. I think his representation of her is completely reasonable after her horrible paintings of him.

The year Pip died I watched an episode of *Diamonds in the Rough*. Dad's character, Cedric, featured very heavily. He is the director of the local amdram group and is organising the annual summer production. Tricia Diamond wants to audition, and Cedric ends up in a compromising position with her so Bobby Diamond thumps him.

The play they perform is *A Midsummer Night's Dream* and Cedric is Bottom the Weaver who, as director, tries to show everyone how to perform their role. There is a wonderful scene where, during the rehearsal, Cedric manhandles Flute off the stage and performs both parts of the Pyramus and Thisbe death scene. I watch this in my bed with my newfound widowhood settling around my shoulders. Dad's performance is both touching and comic; it is physically agile, tender and all the more foolish because of the blackeye he sports from the inevitable mix up with Tricia. While I watch it I smile and I'm surprised. I feel the same as when I read his book; I understand when his status as a minor cult figure begins to develop momentum. He's been on the radio a couple of times, speaking shyly, hesitantly, about his modest success. There is talk of a TV adaptation. 'Ooh yes please!' the *Facebook* comments cheer.

Then there is *Twitter* to follow. Jonathan is on there. A raving environmental voice researching and reviewing the latest technologies to Save The Planet and railing against the decadence and disposability of Western Culture. He is vegan now. He has dug up their beautifully landscaped garden and turned it all over to fruit, vegetables, and chickens. They are part of the composting process apparently. All the water is recycled, and he's posted a video of him flushing the loo with a bucket of water caught from his shower. He doesn't like to wash too much; we all wash too much he says. He sits at their kitchen table, wet shaving with the water that boiled the children's breakfast eggs. He won't drive anywhere and rants about over-population endlessly. All fine for him with his four kids safely tucked up in bed.

If you put Judy and Jonathan's social media next to each other, you'd have no idea they existed in the same world. This is a constant source of delight for me.

I check in with my chat rooms and virtual groups. I have various Internet Personas and I have to be a bit careful not to muddle them up. I never really liked my own, so I have experimented with making some up. No one can check after all. I pick up a chat I'm having with a woman in her thirties in the States. At the moment I'm encouraging her to leave her husband. She thinks I'm a man who lives relatively nearby. I've enjoyed mimicking the American idiom. When I get bored, I'll just disappear. She is already whining to meet up with me. We've exchanged photos. Lots of photos. Mine are from the internet; hers are explicit. She probably doesn't think what she's doing is infidelity, she can probably tell herself nothing has happened, but I bet she thinks about 'Kelvin' a lot.

After that I move onto Reg. He is in the UK and a Silver Surfer. He's very good with the computer and on his own. I'm working on him changing his will to exclude his children who never bother to visit him. We've been talking for months, maybe years. He is a slow-typer though so he doesn't take up much time. I've told him we can't meet up as I'm housebound in a wheelchair; my computer is my only access to the world. He thinks I'm seventy-six.

I'm also Friends with Judy's youngest, Meg. She is nine, coming up to ten. I really think Judy should be more careful about her Internet access. I could be anyone. I've adopted the role of a Spanish girl a year older than Meg, who wants to practice her English. I try to sow the seeds of discord between her and her mother, but it appears that Meg has Judy's sweet nature, and it is hard to get her to say anything negative about anyone. I will have to keep trying. Meg is a keen correspondent, and I am surprised to say that I find her missives disarmingly charming.

As I leave ÉgaliThé, Madge has taken a heavy book from her basket and is beating Connie with hefty whacks; Malik is protesting and trying to grab it from her.

It is getting more difficult to get into my front door, but I squeeze through and edge past the neatly ordered piles of boxes and cartons. At the end I turn and take a photo of them. I like to keep a record. I notice an envelope on the floor.

Post.

I squeeze back to retrieve it.

As I go to the kitchen, I see it is personal, not a bill or junk mail. This is unusual.

It is an invitation.

It's my mother's seventy-fifth birthday in April and there is to be a party at The Castle. I am invited. There is a note from Judy on the back.

Dear, dear Jen,

I know it has been a long time, perhaps too long, but it would mean so much to all of us if you could be there. We love you and we miss you.

Hope to see you then,

Judy xxx

I look around my kitchen. I sometimes struggle to remember how I have arrived at this point. Many would say I am mentally ill, but I don't think that's true. Everything I do is extremely logical. Rational. Besides, it's all Pip's fault.

He thought he'd left me with plenty of money but, not long after he had died, I started ruminating over whether it was going to be enough. I didn't want to get a job. I didn't know what I could do as I'd never really done anything very much. So, the money would have to last. A long time. Granny had lived into her late nineties. My mother is as fit as a young girl. I couldn't risk it running out.

The bank invited me in to Discuss My Options. With such a substantial sum in my account, had I thought about long-term investments? The appointment was with a sharp-faced woman whose gaze kept sliding from mine. I didn't trust her. I had read about people losing all their money from dodgy advice from so-called experts. The bank itself didn't even seem that dependable. We were in a room with flimsy partition walls covered in cheap carpet. 'Why is my money here at all?' I thought.

I began to withdraw it bit by bit on a daily basis. I was careful. I went to different cashpoints at different times of the day. At home, I began to squirrel it away in a suitcase under the bed.

Then that seemed obvious as time went on and, somehow, the need to hide my burgeoning pile of cash, combined with the deep-seated fear that, one day, I might not be able to afford a basic necessity. Consequently, it seemed foolhardy to throw away good reusable items in case I should require them in the future once money was tight. After all, I had no one to rely on but myself now.

I file the invitation back in its envelope. The doorbell goes. I lay the envelope on the table and struggle back to the door. I open it a crack to my fortnightly online shop. A muscly, Eastern European is already unloading the bags onto the doorstep. 'Just hang on, the shopping's here. You'll have to wait for your protein shake,' I yell back into the empty house. This ruse is part of my ritual to convince the delivery people I do not live alone and deter them from trying to take advantage of me. I hook the bags with a walking stick and drag them into the porch. From there I sidle through like a milkmaid to the kitchen where I begin the slow process of unpacking the scant purchases into my bloated cupboards.

I save all my packaging, even from the ready meals I eat and, thank goodness I do; I have used many of the cardboard cases to pack a creaking spongy hole in the corner of the dining room where the floorboard has rotted. The bath leaks steadily down the wall now; the wallpaper, which cost a fortune, has blackened, and brazenly peeled away leaving mouldy plaster on show. No one goes in there though and it houses my collection of bottles and jars; there is a narrow path through so I can occasionally inspect the progression of the damp.

I very cleverly came up with the idea of hiding my money in my collections. I don't think any thief will bother to rifle through empty packets of *Uncle Ben's Rice* or all my washed-out milk cartons. And everything has its place. Everything is very, very clean when it's stored, and I keep regular records via photographs which I download onto my laptop. It's ingenious really; I only need enough money in the bank, from Pip's pension, to cover the bills (negligible – I barely heat the place, just wear a lot of jumpers, hats and socks) and my online shopping. I have the car regularly serviced though I barely drive it nowadays. My only luxury is my latte at ÉgaliThé and I do send extravagant presents to Judy's children. This year, a Solomon snowboard for Hamish, a Sealife underwater camera for Emily, a remote-control helicopter for Finn and a Salini harp for Meg as she is Very Musical. These I meticulously research and I always receive a short, handwritten note in response.

All these letters are stored and catalogued in date order in the original envelopes. It is interesting how their handwriting has developed over the years.

So with this invitation I have the chance to see them again, in person. I only send the presents to annoy Jonathan – he is At War With Consumerism, – and to remind them that I am their Actual Aunt even though they will all have stories of Pip. It is hard to be nasty about someone who, on the face of it, is astonishingly generous. Sometimes, I get a photo with the note. But not often. Everything is digital now and no one bothers to print anything out.

The party is only a few weeks away. I will have to go to the hairdressers; I have chopped at my own hair for years. I will have to find something to wear. I have bought nothing for myself since 2005. I resolve to drive up; I cannot bear to sit on the train with other people. I will also have to decide who I am going to be once I get there.

The journey is both familiar and completely different. I have never driven so far alone; indeed, I have barely driven anywhere over the last five years. Getting out onto the M40 is horrific. I am perpetually in the wrong lane, the traffic moves briskly, flicking and weaving in and around me. I am dazed and disorientated by changed buildings, additional lanes, new flyovers. I grip the steering wheel of the car, an extravagant impulse purchase the month after Pip slipped like a fool; it now feels ancient and lumpen amongst the sleek, glinting metal and glass which whips effortlessly past me.

Finally, the traffic begins to lengthen and thin as I get further north towards Birmingham. I huddle in the inside lane, letting lorries thunder by. I wish I was on a train.

On the toll road, I realise I need to pee. I'm not going to stop at a service station. I haven't been in a public loo since 2004; I'm not going in one today. I pull over and clamber up and over the high embankment and squat amid some bushes.

My slow progress is advantageous for my petrol consumption, and I get most of the way there before I have to refill. I have brought disposable gloves with me for the job. I manage the exchange in the kiosk without too much difficulty, but I think I should have taken my gloves off before I went in.

I have confirmed to none of them that I will be attending the party. Until I left my house this morning, I wasn't a hundred per cent sure I would be. The trip to the hairdressers two days ago was such an ordeal, I thought I would never leave my house again. But here I am driving through the village, which is remarkably unchanged since my last visit. Some of the houses have been spruced up with a coat of paint; some are looking a little more tumble down. The school is determinedly the same. I begin humming the skipping rhymes Christine, Maureen and I used to sing in the playground.

There is now a large, weathered wooden sign announcing The Castle swinging at the entrance; it's very classy. The gardens look lovely, fulsome and lush, and there is a second sign indicating a car park developed from some land they bought back in yet another expansion. I'd seen this on the *Facebook* page: champagne bottle popping GIF and then time-lapse videos of the progress of the tarmacking.

Ignoring the sign, I drive right up to the house and park my car in front of it. I'm exhausted.

A sprightly older chap springs out of the front door, all tweed waistcoat and polished shoes. 'Good afternoon,' he is pleasant, welcoming, 'Are you here for the party?'

I just look at him.

'You've had a long drive, have you? Doesn't look like a local number plate. Shall I get your luggage?'

'Yes please,' I pop open the boot which is a bit reluctant. This was a big deal in 2004. We both watch the somewhat coy progress.

'Where is everyone?' I say to fill in the time.

'David and Vivian have just had tea in the library. They might still be in there.'

The library. Fancy. I wonder where that is? I suppose Dad is a writer so it is the fitting that he has a library.

'I'm Tomas, by the way,' he smiles as he takes out my bags.

'Jennifer,' I reply.

'Jennifer?' he says, 'Jen?'

'Yes.'

He doesn't quite know what to do with his face.

'Well, it's very nice to meet you. Do you want to lead the way or follow me?'

Tomas is very professional. He discreetly rings a bell at the desk in the hall and chats easily about the arrangements for the next day, whilst keeping an eye out for reinforcements. None arrive.

'Why don't I just take you to your mam and dad?' he says, 'We can get you settled in later.'

I don't care.

'I'd love a cup of tea,' I say as I follow him down the corridor.

'Of course, coming right up,' he says, easily.

He pushes open the door to the old guest sitting room, which is now clearly the library. There is a large sun room built onto the back. The library has one wall lined floor-to-ceiling with books. It is painted a bright navy and is very grand. Dark, leather club chairs squat closely together and there is a roaring fire; it has the feel of a gentleman's club though the old sepia globe takes it a step too close to a theatre set in my opinion.

My mother and Dad are sitting by the fire, a finished tea tray on the table in front of them, a fanned newspaper on the floor. Tomas scoops up the tray.

'I have a very special guest for you,' he says brightly, 'I'll leave you to it,' then walks out briskly.

They both peer at me. It is quite gloomy so I step a bit closer. Still nothing.

'Oh for goodness' sake,' I say, 'it's me! Jen!' I am already exasperated.

They peer through their glasses, bloody idiots, and lever themselves up.

'Jen!' Dad comes over, 'We didn't know if you'd make it, well, well, well,' and he hugs me quite formally as if his initial enthusiasm at my appearance has run out in the few paces it has taken to get to me.

Mum stands back. 'Jen. How are you?' and I don't know what she wants me to say. I never know how to answer this question. I never have.

'I'm shattered. It's a long way.' I sit down so they can.

They look at me, hopefully, expectantly.

'So Tomas tells me everything is ready for tomorrow,' and that is enough of a conversational lifebelt for them to pull themselves ashore. They rabbit on, overlapping each other with circuitous tales of ordered hams and far-flung guests peppered with shared laughter and happy sighs. It is almost like normality. They have both aged a lot. Especially their crisscrossed hands; these are bigger, exaggerated, or their bodies are smaller. In fact, all the proportions have changed, their eyes have faded and disappeared under folds and wrinkles and their noses are larger, fleshier, meatier. As they talk, they use their noses more, or they're more important; they wipe and blot them with hankies, they thrust them into the air, on Dad's part displaying broad and coarse-haired nostrils. I can't stop looking at them. Mother's nose is quite mannish now too and this, coupled with her cropped bobbed hair, gives her a not unattractive androgyny. I wonder if she's finally stopped flirting. They don't ask me anything but just rattle on until Tomas brings in tea and I drink it and eat a delicious scone, and then a second, and I wonder if Bryan made them.

Eventually I say, 'Are Judy and the children here yet?'

'Oh yes, yes. They're on a long walk. Couldn't wait to get up onto the fells. They should be back soon.'

'Okay,' I am deliberately neutral and pour myself another cup, the dregs of the pot.

'Do you have room for me here?' I ask. I realise this sounds hostile, 'I mean, I didn't give you any warning.'

'Of course,' says Dad, 'Tomas is sorting it out now.'

'We've expanded quite a bit since you were last here. We put in a couple of glamping pods, and we bought a couple of cottages in the village so there's plenty of room,' Mother adds.

'Quite an empire,' I say. I know all of this from *Facebook* and *Instagram*, but I don't let on. 'What happens to the cottages in the low season?' I ask, 'Don't the locals object to them being empty?'

Mother's face hardens.

'It's been difficult up here,' Dad is serious, 'Lots of people moving away. Quite a few holiday homes. The cottages we bought were practically derelict. We saved them really, like we did this place. We try to get a longer let over the winter, advertise as a writer's retreat or something like that, so they're not sitting empty for months.' He sounds smug.

'They must be grateful,' I say, 'the locals.'

'We are the locals, Jen!' Mum says, 'We've been here forty years. We love the place.'

'Yes, of course,' I say.

We sit quietly for a while and Dad throws another log on the already aggressively roaring fire.

'I think I'll go and unpack,' I say.

'Of course,' Dad gets out an *iPhone* and moments later Tomas appears.

'We're having dinner at eight in the ballroom,' my mother calls as I follow Sam out. I lift my hand in acknowledgement.

I'm in one of the front bedrooms. I've never slept in these. They have all been refitted too, boutique style I think it's called, with a country twist. There is a luxurious en suite bathroom, all porcelain tile with far too many towels. There is an excessive bed. I dread to think what has happened on it and in it. There is a deep, upholstered chair in the bay window; I think I may sleep in that.

My bags have been neatly stacked by the door.

One of Mother's hellish abstract works is over the dressing table.

There is an expensive bottle of water and a single, shining glass on a slender tray.

I perch on the chair and bite the tip of my nail.

I don't think I have room in my bag to take the empty water bottle home. I decide not to open it.

I am horribly nervous before the meal. I haven't taken in how many people will actually be there. I sit in my room fretting over whether to go down and say I'll just have a sandwich in my room, or just pack up and go home. It's been years since I've been in a room with anyone with whom I have to engage. My weekly trips to ÉgaliThé are just a handful of necessary words exchanged with Malik or Lena over the counter. I never speak to anyone else.

At first, the time seems to be passing tediously slowly but now it is draining away like a meagre handful of sand through my fingers. The clock is marching in double quick time, and I can't even make a decision about when to leave the room. I am changed. I am ready. But I am rooted here. I have no idea how I am going to leave.

A little before eight, there is a rap on the door. I manage not to yelp with fright. I've been sitting in stone cold silence, apart from the tyranny of the to and fro in my head, for nearly two hours.

I open the door to Meg, clean, neat and a little smaller than I had pictured her.

'Hello Auntie Jen. My name is Meg. We haven't met yet. Mummy thought you might like to walk with me down to dinner,' and she smiles cheerfully and leans against the wall. She has Judy's blonde hair and Jonathan's wiry frame. She is totally at ease in her compact little body.

'Well, hello Meg. Yes. That would be fine. I'll just get my key.' I reply and moments later we are miraculously walking slowly down the corridor.

Meg is telling me about her walk. It has been a great success. She has seen frogspawn and wanted to collect some, but her father wouldn't let her. 'He has strict rules about Preserving Ecosystems,' she tells me seriously. She has however flung herself backwards onto beds of springy heather. 'Not quite as good as in the summer but still fun,' she concedes. She has identified a field of pregnant sheep and some with lambs and is hoping to see a birth while she is here. She did last year. Ideally, she'd like to see a foal born but, she acknowledges that that is more tricky as there are not so many horses around as there are sheep and fewer foals are delivered each year.

'Do you ride?' I enquire politely.

'No,' she says, 'I just like the look of them. Plus I'd like to be a vet so I want to get as much experience as I can of as many different animals.'

'Good grief. You know what you want to be and you're only nine. That's a little bewildering,' I say.

'Not really. At my school we are encouraged to explore different post-education pathways from a young age. Quite a lot of my friends have made their choices.'

'Really?'

'Yes. What do you do?' she asks. We are making our way down the main staircase now.

'Haven't you been told?' I buy myself a little time.

'No. Only that you are a window since Uncle Pip died. Did they call you that because you see the world differently if you have a dead husband?'

'No, they call you that because everyone looks straight through you to the other side. You're not important anymore.'

'Really? That seems a bit mean.'

'It is. I am see-through. Practically invisible.'

She looks at me for a minute, 'What is your job?' she asks.

'I don't have one,' I say, 'I sit at home all day, washing my rubbish.' Meg chuckles as if I am just being silly. She might like me.

We are at the ballroom. Judging by the noise there aren't too many people. It's not a rerun of Judy's wedding where all the guests were assembled and tortured the night before. I hesitate at the door, my little courage leaking away but Meg puts her slight hand in mine and leads me in. It is the first skin to skin contact I've had for years.

Judy gushes at my arrival, of course, and Jonathan glowers. The older children are polite and restrained. I try not to be too abrupt. Finn is sitting at his place absorbed on some electronic device or another. One of Jonathan's brothers comes over with his son and the focus turns from me and I can take in the rest of the room. My parents are chatting animatedly to old friends. There are a lot of candles, and, in the softer light, they look younger. My mother is telling another involved tale to her rapt audience and Dad is looking at her with absolute wonder. Generous bowls of rich, velvety roses break up the smooth plane of the long table. It reminds me of a Renaissance painting, the pools of waxy light and the dark edges of the grand room. I want to retreat to the shadows.

We sit down and begin to eat. It's watercress soup. Meg is next to me, and I am at the end of the table again. She chirrups along and I hear about her friends Khadijah, and Georgie P. I hear about the trouble she's had with a boy called Myles Carter who thought he was cleverer than her and Amrit, and that just wasn't the case and everyone knew it. I hear about her understanding of, and genuine excitement for, the Hadron Collider. She is very annoyed that the whole family had travelled to the site in Cern at some point, but she was too young to remember. They didn't see too much; they were just in the vicinity, but it obviously galls her that her siblings have had that experience and she hasn't. I barely have to say a word except murmur agreement or acknowledge surprise or disgust in the right places. It's one of the easiest conversations I've ever had.

We finish the soup. The flavour was both salty and sweet and I want to ask for seconds. I've forgotten what real food tastes like. I realise with a little jolt that I am enjoying myself.

'Tomorrow we're having a buffet,' Meg informs me, 'I like those the best.' She is dragging the meat off a perky lamb shank bone. 'I like the fact I can get lots of what I really want and not bother with what's good for me. Mmmm, yum yum.' She chews the meat, 'We don't eat meat very much. It has too high a carbon footprint Daddy says. Shame because I like it. A. Lot.' She crams in another forkful.

'How did you get to Cern?' I ask.

'I don't remember. Probably on a plane. We're not allowed on those anymore either. We're just going to have holidays here.' She sounds a bit glum about this, 'It's a bit annoying because all my friends have been to Disneyland and I've never been and now I don't suppose I ever will.'

'It's probably not as much fun as everyone says it is,' I console her. I look over at Jonathan. He is talking earnestly to Dad. Dad looks a bit confused, as if he can't hear him properly. Poor Meg. They've all been to Disneyland without her. Easy to have principles once you've lived your life, seen everything you want to see, done everything you want to do, bought everything you want to buy.

'Finn and I are sharing a room,' Meg is telling me, 'But he hardly talks so it's quite boring. I wanted to share with Emily, but she says I'm a Distraction and she has to study. I mean that's a bit rude. I'm not that bad. It's the same at home. I'm *never* allowed in her room. She is always working. Really, it's like I haven't got any brothers and sisters at all. I wish I'd been a twin. I think that would've been great.

Ideally identical, rather than fraternal, then we could've played lots of tricks on people which would be fun. Plus, added bonus, you'd have someone your age, to play with, all the time, plus, you'd have someone who thought like you so you wouldn't argue. It would be really cool. I wish I was a twin. That would be like having a proper sister.'

'Don't you talk to your mum?' I've noticed she hasn't really mentioned Judy much.

'Hmmm,' she gives this some thought as she stuffs in more food, 'not that much. She is quite busy with her job now, she's on her phone quite a lot too. And I have a lot of homework.'

'I see,' I say neutrally.

'Do you have any children?' she asks politely.

'No,' I say as if this is a silly idea.

'Why not?' she says.

'I never really liked them,' I see no reason not to be honest with her.

'Oh,' she looks a bit perplexed but not particularly offended, 'I know what you mean,' she says, 'they are a lot of work.'

After we've had coffee and chocolates, I tell Meg I'm quite tired, 'Shall I walk you back to your room?' she offers. I wonder if Judy is paying her to be nice to me.

'Yes, okay. I've had a very long drive. And it will be a busy day tomorrow.'

'Okay, let's go,' she nods, and we disappear without a word to anyone else.

I unlock my room.

'Do you want a quick game of *Top Trumps*?' asks Meg. I really don't.

'It's *Lovable Dogs*,' she smiles winningly, clearly thinking this will clinch the deal.

'Okay. Just one,' I concede.

She rearranges the furniture, so we have a table to share whilst chatting over the rules with me. She has the pack in her back pocket, 'For emergencies,' but it's very hard to persuade anyone to play a proper game these days she laments.

There are four categories – size, rarity, good temper, and

cuteness as well as an overall *Top Trumps* rating. Meg is very soft; she favours the underdog, the stray dog, the ugly dogs, the grumpy dogs. She wants to see the best in all of them. Essentially, she fundamentally rejects the *Top Trumps* scoring system. 'How can the pug only have a cuteness of twenty seven? It's not his fault he's been overbred, and he's got a funny shaped skull because of it.'

'How has the boxer only got five for good temper? Dogs are as happy as their owners make them. All dogs want to be happy all the time.'

It's a terrible game for her. She loves all the dogs.

'Do you have a dog? I ask.

'No. We're not allowed.'

'Why not?'

'They're not environmentally sustainable.'

Aha. Hence the *Top Trumps Lovable Dogs*.

She's also not in the least competitive. She apologises every time she wins and is thrilled if I pick a better category and take her card, 'Way to go Auntie Jen,' she grins. She ekes out the game as long as she can but eventually, she is the Top Trumper. She packs the cards neatly away with a sigh.

'I'll see you at breakfast,' I say, 'I've had a really lovely evening,' I add.

'Me too,' she says, 'I think they must've been talking about a different Auntie Jen all those times because you're really nice,' and she comes over and plants a big uncomplicated kiss on my cheek.

'See you in the morning,' she calls as she trots out.

The day is full of promise as I sip my milky coffee and watch Meg carefully butter her toast. It's still only early April but the sun is strong and uplifting as it floods through the windows in the dining room. The fells aren't the dingy green of my childhood. I am seized by the desire to fling open the French doors and to stand tall and take in lungfuls of the fresh clean Cumbrian air.

'I love these little butter parcels,' Meg tells me, 'I wish we had these all the time.' She is carefully folding open her third of the morning, 'I think they're made by pixies. Butter Pixies,' and she smiles at me. I smile back.

'It's okay, Auntie Jen. I know pixies aren't real,' she says happily, carefully taking half the butter with her knife and spreading it neatly on the second half of her toast.

We are the only two at breakfast thus far. Meg knocked quietly a little after seven thirty. I had been up for hours. Though magnificent as a chair, it was not triumph as a bed, and I had barely slept. She was thrilled I was awake.

'I think everyone else had a bit of a late night,' she told me as we made our way downstairs, 'Mummy said she thought there would be dancing.'

Tomas is on breakfast duty and there are coils of Cumberland sausage, poached eggs and peppery mushrooms. It is hard for me not to groan as I eat each lovely morsel. Meg tucks in heartily too, keeping up yet more chat about what she is reading at the moment (*Oliver Twist*) and who her favourite teacher is (Mrs Okinawa - extra maths, strict, funny, a bit rude) and who her least favourite teacher is (Mr Baxter – PE, strict, not funny, head like cereal packet, bad-tempered).

'I thought you only had one teacher at primary school?' I say.

'Yes we mainly do, but they do swap about a bit.'

'How do you like your harp?' I ask.

She puts down her toast. 'Oh, I *love* it. Thank you so much. It is wonderful. I've learnt to play quite a few tunes from YouTube but even if you play the strings all together it sounds beautiful, like something magical is about to happen. When I go to high school the year after next, I'm starting lessons. I can. Not. Wait.' She shakes her head a little, 'I meant to say thank you last night. I forgot. Sorry.'

'And I meant to ask you about it, but I forgot too. Doesn't matter.' I look out of the window again, 'Shall we go for a little walk after breakfast? I think we'll have time before we have to get ready for the party.'

'Sure' she says, reaching for another pat of butter.

We decide not to bother with a coat as the morning is unusually still and clear. We follow the sheep track up away from The Castle, a slight climb at first gently curling and twisting higher up into what I have always considered a bleak, desolate and essentially dull landscape. With Meg it feels a little different. She scampers ahead, a fount of knowledge and optimism. She points out some Moss Campion and tells me the ferns I plaited obsessively as a child, are called Oblong Woodsias. She pushes aside last year's papery, tattered leaves to reveal a knuckle of fresh lime green fronds tightly coiled, waiting to unfurl. She spies a kestrel, hovering and dipping, searching patiently for his breakfast and spots rabbit holes and rock types in a way that is a little disconcerting. She is quite keen to take me back down the fell to the pond to show me the frogspawn but that is a long walk. As we get nearer the top, the green peters out and more rock faces appear cowpatted in the grass or protruding from the fellside. I realise we are heading up towards Dead Man's Drop, a favourite place for Cowboys and Indians or pirates when we were kids. It's a sheer face of sandstone etched into the hill, dramatic and impressive and surrounded by smaller boulders, lips and ledges making it a perfect place for conquering stories, stake-outs, tags, endless ups and downs. At the top there is an unmistakably dangerous drop, perhaps the height of a two-storey house, you had to be careful not to get too close. We didn't actually know anyone who had fallen off it, though there were jumbled stories of accidents and suicides of distant cousins or uncles, none confirmed by grown-ups.

The view at the top is remarkably good though I can't recall ever taking it in properly as a child. Meg sits down on the top of the rockface and dangles her feet over the edge. 'Let's have a rest,' she says, 'your face is quite pink.' She pats the stony ground next to her. I sit and carefully swing my legs over the edge too, leaning over to take in the fall below. It doesn't seem as high as it did when I was a kid but it's still a fair way.

Meg has picked up a scatter of grit and pebbles and is casting them over the edge. Some of them bounce against the jutting sharper edges lower down. Some are tiny so it's hard to see where they land. I lean back on my hands and shut my eyes, tilting my head towards the sun. It's wonderfully warm. I hear Meg scrabbling for more stones. She nudges against my hand. At least she's not talking for a change. Children are never still or quiet unless they're asleep. Or dead.

In that instant I think how easy it would be to just put my hand in the small of her back and give her one hard shove. It would all be over very quickly. I picture Pip lying broken on the pavement and think Meg would probably be pretty similar, if she bounced off the rocks a couple of times. No one would see. I could easily get away with it. It would just be a Terrible Accident.

'She went too near the edge I called to her, but it was too late.' I picture myself being comforted by everyone after I appear in a state of near hysteria back at The Castle.

'There was nothing you could do Jen. You mustn't blame yourself,' they would say.

I toy with whether I would carry her little body back but decide against that; we've come quite a long way and blood is the very devil to get out and these are the first new clothes I've bought in nine years. Realistically, I don't think I'm strong enough to carry her all the way back – if she was a baby, maybe.

'Auntie Jen,' she interrupts my little daydream.

I open my eyes, squinting against the sun.

'Look at this lovely stone,' she is holding a pearly-white pebble in her palm, 'Feel it,' she says, 'it's really smooth.' She drops it into my hand. It is indeed very smooth and warm from her examinations.

'I don't think it comes from here,' she pronounces, 'I think someone brought it here. It looks to me like it would be more at home on a beach rather than a Cumbrian fell.'

I turn it over and over. It is so very smooth.

'I think you're right,' I say, 'it's a very pretty stone.'

'You keep it Auntie Jen. To remember our lovely walk,' and she jumps up and offers me her hand to help hoist myself up.

I could still push her off no bother, we are right at the edge, but I have the little drop of stone, warm and solid in my hand, a little present. No one has given me a keepsake for years.

Judy calls her in from the gardens as we near The Castle. We've been a bit longer than either of us anticipated and Meg has to get ready. There's not a lot for me to do so I have a wander around to the back to see what's what with the glamping pods.

As I walk past the kitchen door Bryan steps out, mug in hand, an apron tied low across his hips. He sees me and smiles. I imagine I look pretty windswept, but I don't really care.

'So the Prodigal daughter returns,' he smiles.

'Hardly!' I say, 'More like the black sheep.' I walk towards him, 'How are you, Bryan?'

'I'm fine, Jen,' he walks towards me, 'They weren't expecting you.'

'No. I had to move some things around. It was last minute,' I sound like an idiot. He probably knows everything about me. A recluse. A hoarder. Should be sectioned. 'I'm on my way to see the glamping. Where are they?'

'I'll show you,' he says.

'Aren't you busy?'

'No, there is an army in there. I said I was going to have a break anyway. Come on, it's this way.'

We tramp off in silence past my mother's studio and over towards the new car park.

'So, how are you?' he starts, 'I was sorry about Pip. Nice bloke.'

'Thanks. Yes, I'm okay. I suppose. How about you? Still in Mrs Potter's house?'

'No, no, God, moved out of there eight year ago. No, we've got the house up by the church now. That big one on the brow before you come into the village.'

'The Bermans' old house?'

'Aye, that's the one. Nice bit of land wi'it. For the kids like.'

'So you're married?'

'Partners. Yes.'

'How many kids?'

'Three girls.'

'Wow.'

'She comes from a big family. Wanted lots of kids. I know I've come to it later in life but what the hell.'

'So it's all worked out for you Bryan, hasn't it?' My voice sounds mean and tight. I can see the pods. I speed up. Bryan plants his mug on a fence post and pursues me.

'Look, sorry Jen, I wasn't meaning to brag, like. It is what it is.'

'No, it's fine Bryan. Everyone's life has moved on. It's only mine that's gone backwards.'

We reach the pods. They are like the little wooden hobbit houses, three in a row, fairy tale homes for woodland creatures. I push open the door of the first one. He follows me in.

'So are you happy?' I turn and face him. There's not much room in here. A bed, a stove, a couple of chairs, a rustic hanging rail.

He doesn't know how to answer, 'I love my kids,' he says.

'I suppose that's a start,' I say. I plonk myself down on the bed. I look up at him. He is still very attractive, lined, weathered but he was always going to age well.

'What about your partner?' I say, 'Do you love her?'

He shrugs, 'I guess so. We have the kids. We're together.' A pause. 'It's her house.'

'So it's convenient,' I say.

'It's a bit more than that.' He is getting cross.

'Good. I suppose that's something.' My irritation is showing too. 'Why did you come with me just now?' I say looking at him.

'I like you. I wanted to talk to you.' He's trying to salvage the situation.

I continue to look at him.

'Have you been faithful to your wife, sorry, partner Bryan?'

He looks up at the ceiling, then at me.

'No,' he says.

'How many times?'

'Once.'

'Who with?'

'You.'

'You were with her then?'

'Yep.'

'You didn't say anything.'

'No.' He looks away.

I am silent.

'I still think about that night,' he says more softly and sits down next to me.

'Do you?' I say, my modicum of patience has disappeared, 'Bryan, it was twenty years ago.'

'I know. That doesn't matter.' He moves a little closer to me. I can smell him.

'Hold on,' I say, 'Do you think we're going to have sex now?'

'Maybe?' he growls.

'You're on a tea break!'

'Well it won't take long,' he tentatively lays his hand on my upper thigh.

'No, from what I remember it won't,' I stand up. Bryan looks deflated, saggy, old.

'I'm going to get changed,' I say.

'Will I maybe see you later?' I hear him call as I leave.

I sit at my window and watch the guests troop up to the house. It's quite the parade. I recognise a whole collection of villagers. Maureen arrives with her mum in the back of a smart, boxy Range Rover. She is driving. She talks to Christopher the whole way. He is painfully thin, coat hanger frame in a dark suit. He stares straight ahead, unseeing. There is no flicker of a response to Maureen's urgent words. He is a living ghost.

Mr and Mrs Bell arrive. They both look chirpy at the promise of a day out. Mrs Bell is immaculate as always and now has a pretty stick. Her progress is slow, but she disguises it by stopping every so often to remark on the flowers or the view. Mr Bell hovers at her elbow, attentive, ruddy faced as ever, resigned as to how long it will take them to reach their destination. They are trying to be optimistic, but their faces habitually settle back to a well-worn sadness. At least there are grandchildren now, more little girls to distract them; I hope they take after their auntie.

I can hear my mother greeting everyone as they arrive; how much she adores them correlates to the pitch of her greeting. There are already small children in pale dresses cartwheeling on the front lawn and I hear glasses clinking as everyone takes a welcome drink. I spot Meg leading a chubby toddler onto the grass. I cannot deny that I am wounded to have been discarded, especially for something so dull. I must therefore make my own way down and navigate the choppy waters of small talk and nostalgia.

I go straight to the ballroom which is full of milling folk on their best behaviour. There are, I know, quite a number of people I've never met. Never mind. I am fifty years old. I will cope.

Jonathan is holding forth to a small group, mainly his family. Why are they always here, I think? Don't they have their own lives?

'We are thinking of making it is as carbon neutral as possible. It's the only way to go and that way you can attract a whole new type of clientele.'

There are murmurs of agreement.

'I mean, don't get me wrong,' he forges on, 'they've done a terrific job, but you've got to find a new way in 2014, it's only right. I mean, we're building something for our children.'

'So what are you thinking?' chimes in one of the brothers eagerly.

'Well firstly, there is a fantastic resource here, the wind. So, I'm putting in planning for a wind turbine and solar panels obviously, that's a given.'

'Of course,' another brother pipes up.

'Then we've got to rethink the whole dynamic here. I mean look at this room. It's massive. But all this glass and the insulation implications... I really want to look at the numbers and see how cost-effective the restaurant side really is.'

I walk over, 'Excuse me,' I say, 'What are you talking about?'

Jonathan looks a bit shifty. 'Oh Jen. Er, we were just talking about some plans for, you know, upgrading things here, you know, environmentally.'

'Yes, I got that,' I say sharply, 'I'm not a moron. But you're talking as if you're in charge. What's going on here?'

'Judy! Judy!' Jonathan calls over to Judy who is chatting to the Vicar and her husband, 'Look I, er, I suppose I shouldn't have been... Look, Judy! Judy!' he shouts again. I continue to stare straight at him.

Judy arrives. I say nothing.

'I was just talking about the, um, the plans and Jen overheard,' he stumbles out.

'The plans?' I say, 'What plans?'

'Oh Jen,' Judy says, head tilting, ready to soothe and salve my bitter temperament. Christ, I think, I've heard her say those two words with that simpering tone so many times I want to ram my champagne flute down her throat.

'What plans?' I repeat.

'We were going to tell you later,' she stalls.

'Were you?' I say, 'Tell me now.'

'Look Jen. Don't cause a scene,' Jonathan is next to me. His voice is low and in my ear.

'If The Plans are fair and reasonable, they'll be no need to, will there?' I turn and dismiss him with the roar of contempt that washes through me. I turn back to my sister.

'So?' I say, feigning control and patience.

Judy swallows, 'Mum and Dad are properly retiring, not before time, and we're taking over here,' she says quickly, then braces herself.

'I see,' I say quietly.

We all wait.

'Are they giving it to you?' I ask.

Jonathan and Judy exchange a look.

'More or less. Yes.' Judy smiles weakly, begging me to sanction the agreement.

I nod slowly and take a sip of my champagne. The whole group is looking just at me.

'It's only that they didn't think you needed it with your house paid off and the pension and everything,' Judy starts.

I nod again.

'And we've been wanting to make a move up here. We're *stifled* where we are. We want to slow things down, enjoy the children a bit more, life's so hectic with us both working full-time.' She thinks she is making a strong case. Yes, how are they existing in their five bed, three bath, and one and half acres? Totally claustrophobic.

'It must be difficult,' I concur.

'And if we're here, we can look after Mum and Dad, not that they need anything now, they'll probably outlive the lot of us,' she tries to laugh like she used to when she knew I was on my way to punch her, 'and we can keep the business in the family.'

'Your family,' I say.

'Oh Jen, it's just, you've never really liked it up here, you couldn't wait to get away, we thought you wouldn't be interested, we thought you'd run a mile.' Another failed attempt at a laugh. How ludicrous that I would want part of my inheritance?

I look up and along the beautiful, coved ceiling, my eyes glide down to the elegant fireplace and out to the expansive gardens. I hope they can all read my exceptionally good non-verbal signals. I breathe in deeply. I look at Jonathan first, then Judy.

'But no one thought to ask me. Again,' I say. She says nothing. 'You just decided for me,' I nod, 'Like you did with all those holidays with Pip.' I arch my eyebrow, 'I do realise it is very hard to contact someone when they live in London.' I wonder if she's going to cry. The suspense is tremendous.

I let out a shout of a laugh. Judy jumps. 'I'm joking,' I smile brightly, 'Of course this is what should happen,' and I squeeze her arm, a little too tightly. She grins with relief and disbelief, looks at Jonathan.

'Really?' she says.

'Really,' I say heartily, as if she is a silly goose, 'It's fine; we get what we deserve,' and I turn and walk away.

'I think that went rather well,' I hear Jonathan guffaw as I leave the ballroom.

Meg is playing on the lawn with some other kids. She smiles as I approach her. I crouch down close to her so they can't hear me speak.

'I've just been talking to my friend Christopher. He's a farmer. One of his mares is in labour. Shall we go and watch a foal being born?'

'Oh Auntie Jen! Yes please.' She is thrilled.

'Now everyone will want to come if we let on so I promised Christopher, I would only tell you. Can you keep a secret?'

'Of course I can.'

'Okay. I'll meet you at my car in ten minutes in the car park.'

'Okay. Ooh, I'm so excited.'

'Me too!' And I tap her on the nose.

Meg is waiting by the car as agreed. My bags were already packed. No one has seen me leave. We head off down the lane after she has carefully strapped herself in.

It will be hours before anyone notices she is missing. Or that I have gone too. And who knows where I will be by then? Or what I'll have done.

I have a suitcase of money; I brought a lot, most of it, as much as I could stuff in, in case of emergencies and because I didn't want to leave it all in London. I look in my rear-view mirror and The Castle is receding, a dark silhouette against the fells and I know with the next turn of the track, it will be gone forever and we will have our whole lives ahead of us.

So, it is all a matter of chance after all. I ponder where we will go. With the money we could head to the coast. I could buy a boat. We could sail to another country. Or pay someone to take us there. I could concoct an elaborate story about escaping a violent husband. We could start a new life where Meg would have all my attention all of the time and she would stop me from rescuing my rubbish and fretting over my future. I feel full of energy; like never before. All because I have this child with me.

And I wonder if this is what happened to Christine. She was there. A chance. She was an opportunity and whoever took her just realised he could. There was no one to see and she was easily persuaded into the van; a trusting innocent. And maybe his motives weren't that dark in the beginning. Maybe he couldn't believe his luck at the outset, to have that pretty little scrap, full of promise, in the seat next to him. Maybe he entertained the idea of a different future together as she told him about her life, her mam, her brothers. Maybe he liked her the more they chatted, like I like Meg. His intention was not to rip apart all those worlds. I conjure up Mrs Bell's terrible grief, her hollow despair. And then I cast it onto Judy. She will be beautiful for the press conferences. She will be centre stage. The public will not be able to get enough of her. They will clamour for more, more, more.

We are through the village and beyond. Meg has been whistling a tune from *Mary Poppins*. 'Is it much further?' she asks in a matter-of-fact voice.

'Not far,' I lie and it's then I realise there is a fatal flaw in my plan. Meg will not comply. Meg will realise sooner rather than later that there is no foal. The jig will be up. And what then? Can I convince her to run away with me? Will she share my dream?

I think about the boat again. I think about sailing out, into deep water. Cold, deep water. I think about crushing her skull and sinking the boat and moving on to a different life. Maxim De Winter did that and no one thought any the worse of him for it, apart from Mrs Danvers. Meg's whistling is beginning to grate after all.

'We've gone an awfully long way Auntie Jen,' she's looking out of the window for clues, 'Are you lost?'

'I think perhaps I am,' I concede.

I pull the car over.

She looks at me, expectantly.

You never get over losing a child.

That's what everyone says.

They should have paid more attention. They should have thought about their actions. Why should I always be the only one who suffers? Let's see how they like it.

'Have you got a map, Auntie Jen?' Meg has opened the glove compartment and is rummaging in there, 'Or we should we try and find someone to ask?'

I stare unseeing through the windscreen.

'I don't really need to see a foal, you know. It's really nice of you to try and sort it out for me though.' She's fiddling with the edge of the ribbon belt of her dress, 'You're not at all like my other aunties and uncles.'

This is interesting.

I turn to her. 'How so?' I ask.

'I don't know. You said you were invisible but that's how I feel. When I'm in the room with Daddy and all his brothers and sisters and all their husbands and wives, they ask a few questions like, 'How's school?' or 'What do you like watching on TV?' but sometimes they don't even listen to the answer and then it's like I've disappeared, or they don't know what else to say to me. No one has ever talked to me and listened to me like you did last night and on our walk. It was special Auntie Jen. You're special. And you even remembered I wanted to see a foal and now you're trying to find a farm for me. You are such a kind person. I don't know, I'm just really sad I haven't known you before. Does that make sense?'

During her little speech she has been frowning. Her words have not come out quickly and confidently as usual but slowly and hesitantly, as if she's struggling to express herself for the first time. I am taken aback.

She looks at with me with solemn, much older than nine years old eyes. 'I think we should go back to the party now. There's going to be fireworks later.'

I turn the key in the ignition and check my mirrors with a heavy sigh.

2024

I am standing quietly at my father's grave, staring into the dusky colours of the velvety lichen that have crept across it. Tomorrow, or maybe later today, they will dig down ready to plant my mother with him and, later, her name will be painstakingly added to his on the stone. The ground is still warm and soft, and we are in the trough of the virus so there will be enough mourners to please Judy. Rumour has it an internationally acclaimed artist is attending and arriving by helicopter. The village is whistling with anticipation.

It is very early. Soon I will walk back up to my house. There may be eggs from Maureen's hens on the doorstep or, more likely, a partial corpse left by the cat. I will pick up or step over depending and make breakfast for two in my warm kitchen. A proper breakfast with fresh coffee and homemade bread and marmalade and maybe a scrambled egg or two.

It is five years since Meg persuaded me to make the move back up here. Five years since she and Finn came and cleared out my London house, laughing and chattering as they wheelbarrowed all my treasures into the kerbside skip as I stood back stunned by Meg's capability at fifteen. We were firm friends by then. A friendship she had nurtured with honesty and grit.

I had resisted her first visiting me in London. We skyped, texted, phoned, wrote letters back and forth. I suffered many long weekends with Judy just to enjoy Meg's company. We tramped through bogs in search of toads, smashed tiles to recreate Roman mosaics, pummelled dough and rolled out gingerbread as we explored her latest enthusiasm, uninterrupted by the rest of family who I felt gazed from afar, bemused by our odd little relationship. At every opportunity Meg asked to come and stay; I just said no.

The shrill ring of the doorbell was a surprise as there were no deliveries scheduled but I squeezed my way down the hallway and sagged in despair at the sight of Meg on my threshold.

I couldn't turn her away, so I shrank and shuddered as we walked through the house to the kitchen and I saw it all through her eyes.

'You can't live like this, Auntie Jen. You're not this person. I do not accept that you want to live like this,' were her first words on that strange day. Life is straightforward for Meg. She is a practical problem-solver. She determined to change my situation and I was enfeebled against her. She has all of Judy's light and warmth and, I discovered, it is luxurious to bathe in it. It was true I did not want to live like that, but I couldn't find a way out. She made tea, efficiently, and we sat at my kitchen table. She produced a notebook.

'We're going to make a list together of all the reasons for you to stay here in London and all the reasons to leave,' she announced. It was a long list of reasons to leave but really, I could have just written her name, over and over, because on that afternoon I discovered I will do anything I can to please her.

We finished the list and the pot of tea, and she went out to buy food for supper. She returned with a fat roll of black bags and chatted to me as she stripped off bag after bag and cleared the work surfaces, the floor, the dresser and draining board of the piles of mess that had accumulated for so many years. She behaved as if it was all completely normal and, a little touch that made my heart ache for her, she did it all without those horrible rubber gloves. I thought I would care as each bag was tied and hurled out of the back door, but I felt more and more elated. In fact, it all seemed a very simple process that I could have been doing for years; I just needed someone to show me the way.

'I think you'd be happier back in the village,' she announced as she waited for a handful of spaghetti to soften into a pan, I'd forgotten I owned. 'I want you closer to me. London smells horrible. And Veenie Platt's old house is up for sale. You should live there. It's a fine house. Not as nice as this one but it's big. It's one of the best ones in the village. And I can have my own room,' she smiled smugly at the thought and stirred the spaghetti, 'I'm coming back next weekend with Finn. We'll get this house ready to put on the market.'

I didn't argue. I let her take charge. I had let her into my world in its entirety and she, with her precocious wisdom, saw only solutions and a future.

We collected the keys for Mrs Platt's house from the estate agents in Appleby, a few weeks before the first lockdown. Meg was following the virus closely and announced to Judy that she would be moving in with me if Covid-19 began to cause real problems. Judy, however, was too preoccupied to listen, but my heart leapt and sang and jumped for joy.

I listened to the news bulletins desperate for confirmation of confinement to barracks.

Of course, there have been several lock downs since as the world has changed, and Meg has been my constant companion. She is here much more than she is not, and I noticed that she used my address, not her mothers', for her student loan applications. We walk and talk together, cook and eat side by side, sleep and wake at roughly the same time. It is a constant source of amazement to me that I am so very rarely irritated by her, and I find myself weeping at the thought of her finding a boy or girl who will take her away from me. She is nineteen now; this is bound to happen sooner or later.

For Meg is the love of my life. My second chance at happiness. My only chance at happiness. The daughter, the mother, the sister, the friend I never managed to find. She is a miracle. A joy.

Out of habit I feel for the small, smooth pebble she gave me at Dead Man's Drop all those years ago, tucked away in my pocket. Just a few moments in my palm and it is as warm as it was when she handed it to me. I carry it with me always. It is a touchstone, a reminder of a different ending, a near miss, a close shave.

I look up as a crow flies slowly across the vivid ribbon of lilac sky slashed below a bank of clouds. I feel a hand slip into mine.

'I thought I'd find you here,' says Meg, 'You're cold. Let's go home.'

Acknowledgements

Major Sullivan Ballou (1829-1861) is known primarily as the author of one of the most stirring letters written during the Civil War. The letter, dated July 14, 1861, was written to his wife Sarah, shortly before his death from wounds received at the Battle of Bull Run. It was featured prominently in Ken Burns's 1990 PBS television series *The Civil War*. It is held by The Rhode Island Historical Society Manuscripts Division.

Thank you to Graeme for listening to me and encouraging me, for reading and re-reading drafts, and for always offering such creative inspiration. You are my love.

Thank you to Pat and Amy for reading early drafts too; your guidance was invaluable. Thanks also to my mum Sue and my brother Rory for your sterling work proof-reading and editing. Thank you to Emma for your terrific suggestions and enthusiasm.

Special thanks to Laurie, a much loved friend, who read this and rang me full of excitement and joy just when I needed a boost. So, so sorry you are not here to hold a copy in your hands, my lovely Laurie.

Printed in Great Britain
by Amazon

20413811R00149